Secrets & Submission

W WINTERS &
AMELIA WILDE

kiss me

I was born into luxury and used to getting what I wanted.
What I desired most, with my life in disarray, was the man who sat
across from me.
He was tall, dark and handsome. Most notably, he was forbidden.

It made every accidental touch more sinful and every court-mandated
session more addictive.

So much tragedy had happened and he was supposed to fix me.
I shouldn't have wondered how it would feel to be trapped under his
broad shoulders.
I shouldn't have focused on the way he licked his bottom lip every time
his gaze dropped from mine and roamed my curves.
I shouldn't have dreamed about him breaking the rules to comfort me
the way I desperately needed.

I did, though, and I was the first one to submit.

He was my protector and my confidant, and then he became my lover.
I teased him, tempted the two of us and now there's no
way to take it back.
With everything I've been through, I didn't expect to fall for him.
There's only so much heartache I can take.

No one can know, not a single soul, but secrets in the life I lead never
last for long.

playlist

"Sweet but Psycho"—Ava Max

"Turn Down for What"—DJ Snake and Lil Jon

"River"—Bishop Briggs

"Unsteady"—X Ambassadors

"Overwhelmed"—Royal & the Serpent

"Are You with Me"—nilu

"Sit Still, Look Pretty"—Daya

"Scars To Your Beautiful"—Alessia Cara

"Issues"—Julia Michaels

prologue

My mother used to say, "If you can't stop thinking about someone, it's because they can't stop thinking about you either." It bears noting, though, that my mother was a fucking lunatic. She stalked a man and killed his wife because she was in love with him. Having no idea, he married her and shortly she became pregnant with me. It wasn't until years later that he discovered the truth.

I was only seven years old when the trial was broadcast.

Cameras rolled and my sadness was caught on film. With interview after interview, journalists said the nation was entranced. As my fairy-tale life fell apart, what was left of me went viral. Every household knew my name, and the public begged for more. More of my twisted life; born into wealth and power, yet the daughter of a murderer. More of who I was.

My first kiss was photographed and the images sold to every major tabloid.

The first time I had sex, the world knew immediately after.

I talked about it with everyone.

I didn't know any better.

It's simply the way it was after my life imploded. I lived for sharing everything about my life with my followers, and they loved me for it.

I made my own happily ever after, and then it was ripped away.
In a single moment, my life changed forever.

I broke. There was nothing left after I'd loved and lost.
And then he came into my life in a way no one else ever had.

He was my protector, my therapy; he became my everything.
It's a dangerous situation for so many reasons.

I'm starting to believe the things my mother used to say … which scares me because I know I've already broken down and lost everything once.

But when he looks at me like that …
When he tells me it's going to be all right …
I believe the things my mother used to say. *If you can't stop thinking about someone, it's because they can't stop thinking about you either.*

chapter 1

Zander

The Firm is an elite, full-service private security company for high-profile clients and those who require the utmost discretion. Please inquire directly for assistance with booking. All sensitive matters will be handled with complete confidentiality.

THERE ARE TWO THINGS I CAN'T STAND FOR ANYONE TO BE when they enter a courtroom: late or rattled.

Being late never looks good, but people get lax about it. They tend to brush it off. What's a few minutes in the grand scheme of things? Could be nothing.

Could be everything.

As for being rattled—there's no place for emotion in a courtroom, not from my position. Calm, logical … even ruthlessly cold is far preferred over rattled. Being focused is a personal rule of mine no matter what a judge says or what some lawyer pulls out of his back pocket. Not coincidentally, steady focus is also the number one rule in my profession. When we're with clients this directive is absolute.

I don't slip up when it comes to this charge. There are other areas of my life that require strict focus. The last time I slipped up, there were consequences.

I was late. I was rattled.

Today, hurrying up the wide stone steps at the county courthouse, I'm both late and rattled, which only serves to piss me off even more. The bitter autumn wind bites against the exposed skin on my neck as I grind my teeth and pull open the heavy floor-to-ceiling door after rushing up the marble stairs. I hustle as quickly as I can to make up for lost time, while still keeping my pace and gait professional.

The entire time I scold myself, adding anger on top of annoyance.

And it gets worse. The hearing today is an important one for The Firm. It's the most important hearing we've ever attended, according to my brother Cade.

I rush through the metal detector and snatch back my phone on the other side. The brightened screen's full of messages from my older brother. Cade owns the company; among other businesses, he created The Firm. He took on the responsibility of having the final say in which clients we take on, which is a hell of a lot harder than leaving it up to the group. He wants to know where the hell I am. With a steadying exhale I shake off everything from earlier this morning; namely, the hell of the phone call that lasted far too long. Rounding the corner and making my way to the elevator, I ignore the buzzing of my phone in my suit jacket pocket.

One last pause outside the courtroom doors to correct myself. I'm not taking the news from the phone call, and the memories that come with it, into work with me. I can't. That cursed entity needs to go back in the locked box where it lives most of the time. Calm focus. Eyes on the client. *Don't fuck it up.*

The door to the courtroom opens beneath my hand with a muffled squeak. Although adrenaline courses through my veins at knowing I'm surely disturbing the ongoing hearing, I keep my outward appearance unperturbed. It's one of the smaller courtrooms, which makes it even more obvious that I'm late. Nothing I can do about it now except stride in and take my place.

Damon's the only one to turn his head and watch me walk up the center aisle, even though the rest of the team's scattered along the last two benches too. Cade has a front-row seat to the proceedings. He's angled forward in his chair, breathing down the neck of the client's lawyer. Silas sits next to him, dark eyes trained on the judge, silent as usual. Dane's on his other side, with Damon behind him. Just as Damon and I make up a pair when it comes to relying on someone from the team, Silas and Dane have each other.

As silently as possible, I tuck in my tie and take the seat next to Damon, arguably my closest friend after the shit we've been through. He doesn't waste any time to lean over, pitching his voice low. "What did they say?"

My voice is deathly quiet when I respond, "I don't want to talk about it." My blood chills at the recollection and the back of my throat dries up. I don't want to think about a damn thing that involves that call. Sure as hell not right now.

Damon knew the call was this morning. I'll tell him the details later. For now, I need all my attention on the back-and-forth between the judge and the lawyer. This conversation is why we all need to be here. Our presence is proof we can handle this particular case and client. It's a deal that will set this company down a path my brother has been after for years.

I scan the judge's face. He's familiar and I know him by name. The wrinkles around Judge Martel's eyes and his thinning, combed-over white hair are proof of his experience on the bench. Ever self-possessed, with his lips pressed in a thin line, it's impossible to decipher which way he's leaning. My gaze quickly moves to the back of our lawyer's head, and then—

A pair of dark eyes.

Peeking at me from up front.

Instantly my body heats. The depths of their darkness stir something inside of me. The stunning stare is both intoxicating and pinning. As if I've been caught. But not by a predator, by prey.

It's only a moment that our eyes meet and lock, but something thumps through my chest like a heavy book falling to the floor. Then she faces the judge again.

The client. She's the client. Eleanor Bordeu. Born into wealth and a high-profile individual, but I hadn't even seen a photo of her. The simple white blouse that drapes along her curves is obviously expensive, yet it doesn't compare in the least to the woman who wears it. "Strikingly beautiful" would be putting it mildly. Her elegance is in the details; from the way she holds my gaze, to the manner in which she breaks it just as easily, squaring her shoulders to retake her place before I interrupted.

The moment is gone as quickly as it came and I surreptitiously clear my throat, adjusting in my seat.

Bringing me back to the present, Damon presses a thick folder into my hands. "Maybe you should read the file this time. The rest of the paperwork came in this morning."

I accept the folder but keep it closed and lay it on the bench beside me. "You know I'm not going to do that." I speak just above a murmur, as does he. Both of us are careful not to disrupt the hearing.

He noticeably shrugs. "I know. Cade wants you to have it anyway."

My gaze instinctively moves back to the client and I rub a knuckle into my chest to try and dispel the lingering shock from ... whatever the hell that was. A strange anomaly. Not something that ever happens with clients. Not something that ever will again. I drag my focus back to the hearing at hand.

"—client is only being held because of a temporary lapse of judgment. We believe this is an appropriate transition out of institutionalized care."

The judge turns over a sheet of paper, the mundane sound carrying through the quiet room. "There's mutual agreement between the parties, yes?"

"That's correct," answers the representative for the Rockford Center. His name is Aiden and from what our lawyer tells us, he's more than happy to comply. He stands a few inches shorter than the lawyer, his thick head of hair at odds with the crew cut the lawyer wears. I've met our lawyer a few times now. He's a good guy, which is rare to find in that profession; at least it seems to be that way since we've come to New York. We've been working with him on this transition for at least a year now. In our line of work, it's beneficial to have a lawyer on retainer. In our case, it's a whole team of hotshot lawyers, given the profile of the clients we take on. Cade is well versed in the law and has kept up with his license to practice, even though he graduated with his JD and passed the bar ages ago. Still, we rely on the best to represent us and Cade is more than willing to admit the legal team we have is better at what we need than he'll ever be.

"The Rockford Center is prepared to relinquish custody to The Firm." My spine stiffens and I sit straighter as the judge scans us in turn.

I'm certain the judge is aware this is a first for us. The Firm started as a high-end protection service. Given the team's background and expertise, we've pivoted recently in our niche. It's not something I agreed with, and this situation … this isn't what I signed up to do years ago. But here I am.

From my experience, some judges have piss-poor poker faces, but not this one. I can never tell what he's thinking. That uncertainty is only reinforced as Judge Martel scans the documents in front of him. "The Firm has representatives present, I see."

"We do, Your Honor," answers Cade as he half rises. His tone is professional but his deep baritone still gets the attention of the judge as if he's caught off guard. My brother, and boss, continues, "We are more than happy to answer any questions or address any concerns you may have in order to help make your decision."

"Mr. Thompson, the Rockford Center is prepared to relinquish custody. Have you been made aware of the requirements for this transition?"

"Yes, we have, Your Honor."

"Are you prepared to present your plan for the client's home modifications?"

"Absolutely, Your Honor." Cade stands fully and passes a stapled stack of papers to our lawyer. He takes them up to the judge, but the client—Eleanor—doesn't move. She's so still, her chest barely rising and falling with each breath. I search for subtle movements in the curve of her neck, in her shoulders. Her hair is twisted into a prim bun at the nape of her neck. She appears quite polished, but also as if she's scared for any bit of her presentation to go astray. That's exactly what it is, a presentation. If I had to guess, she's been in this position before. Maybe not in front of a judge, but in some other way.

This is why I don't read client files before I meet them. What you see on paper doesn't tell you what they need. Half the time it clouds your assessment. The black letters on white paper don't do justice to the grays of morality. Every shade matters because they all come with a story. A reason. A thread that makes up the fabric of who they really are when no one else is looking.

I trace a path down the loose, white shirt she wears to her slim-fitting black dress pants. The shirt has a keyhole detail at the very top on the back of her blouse, a few inches below the dark twist of her hair.

Before I can stop myself, before I can swing my attention back to the judge where it belongs, I think of touching her there. My fingertips on soft skin. Would she shiver? Would she lean back into it?

As if she can hear my thoughts, she turns her head and her somber gaze meets mine.

Oh, shit.

I yank my eyes away from her. Back to the judge. Outwardly, I'm wearing a professionally neutral face. Inwardly, I feel the hum of an electric shock. That phone call shook me up more than I thought it did. It's not the client. Not Eleanor. My reaction has nothing to do with her.

The judge finishes reading Cade's plan, detailing what's already been done to accommodate the guidelines, and the mood in the room shifts. "Mr. Thompson, do you have adequate personnel to ensure two individuals are on hand around the clock?"

"We do, Your Honor."

"And you're equipped to provide appropriate security?"

"Yes, Your Honor."

"The Rockford Center has signed off on the proposed plan of care?" The judge's eyes flick to Aiden. The man's navy blue suit hangs well on him. With his slicked back hair, it's hard not to notice he took great effort in his appearance for today.

"We've met extensively on the proposal. The Rockford Center has full faith in The Firm to provide care."

The judge taps the papers with his knuckle. "I'd say we've moved beyond providing care and into full guardianship. I've never signed off on a transfer of custody this extensive. Your company will not only be responsible for providing personal care. The level of mental health services needs to be comparable to, or exceed that of the Rockford Center."

"Your Honor, we are equipped to provide those services." Anyone else would think Cade was sticking to the rules of engagement—calm focus. But I'm his brother. I see the tension in the side of his jaw. He wants this to go well. We all do. And not just for the company.

I've made it a point not to know all the details of Eleanor's past. She deserves a clean slate with me, just like any other client. But the situation itself is different. The judge isn't exaggerating when he says he's never done this before. There's never been a custody transfer from the Rockford Center, or anywhere like it in the state, to a private company. Eleanor's case will be the first.

"If it's a matter of documentation, Your Honor—"

The judge waves Cade off. "This is a matter of character." He looks Cade in the eye. "You assume all of the responsibility for this patient's care. You also assume all of the risk. The state will intervene if there's cause to believe you're not meeting your obligations."

"Understood, Your Honor."

The judge shuffles his papers again; for once, the gentleman is showing his nerves. "Does the Rockford Center have any additional input?"

"Only that we've vetted the plans by The Firm and have full confidence in Ms. Bordeu's care. The staff at the Rockford Center all agree that the institutional setting has served her to its natural endpoint. It's time for Ms. Bordeu to return to her home. Under appropriate supervision, of course, and getting all the care she needs."

With a simmering strain, the courtroom awaits the judge's verdict with bated breath. I hold mine, keeping with it the pent-up tension from the call this morning, the guilt I feel over being late, and my burning, driving curiosity about Eleanor Bordeu.

There's a small movement at the front of the room that grabs my attention.

Eleanor's eyes, flicking toward mine.

This is the third time she's looked at me. The third time those dark eyes have pinned mine. It's as if we've met before, but we haven't. I would remember a woman who looked at me the way this woman does now.

Only one other woman has looked at me that way.

The memory of her tiptoes across the back of my mind. She had blue eyes, not brown, but the curiosity was the same.

Eleanor drops her gaze to the floor, and I remember to breathe.

The judge considers each of us in turn. "What you've requested today is unusual. So unusual, in fact, that I've considered denying the request to change custody simply to avoid setting a dangerous precedent. But you've impressed me today, Mr. Thompson. You and your team." An exhale leaves me as he waves the papers in front of him, held in a loose fist. "I'll grant your request to transfer custody and care of Ms. Bordeu from the Rockford Center to The Firm, with the full understanding that a life is at stake. Perhaps many lives."

A shiver moves over my spine. Judge Martel referring to future cases with future patients makes me uneasy. If he opens the door to Eleanor's custody transfer, then it's open for more people after her. He and other judges will have to preside over cases like this one, but there will be precedent—us. I know that's what he's talking about. But the words "a life is at stake," combined with the phone call, feel like ice at the center of my gut.

The conversation continues but dims and seems to blur into nothing as I stare ahead absently. My attention is on my own pulse. Steadying myself and refusing to allow any unwanted emotion to surface. I can't meet the rest of this day with a knot in my stomach.

I can't meet the rest of this day with the delicate curve of Eleanor's neck on my mind. Or the way her sleeves flutter near her wrist in a simple, classic detail that makes me want to trace her bare skin there all the way around.

I can't, and I won't. I will not think of her that way. Not ever again. She is beautiful and tempting, but she is not mine to have.

With the pen held tightly in his hand, the judge signs a paper in front of him and taps his gavel in a perfunctory way that seems anticlimactic for all the work we've put in. As soon as his decision is finalized, there's a flurry of motion. Aiden leaves his place at the front first. "Quick call," he says on his way past. "Then I'll be available." The lawyer nods, and with a thin smile his hand lands on our client's shoulder, gaining her attention. A heat rises up my chest, but it's quickly displaced. Cade leans over the partition to talk to the lawyer. Silas and Dane get to their feet next to him. Then Damon. I'm quick to follow, taking great care not to give much thought to how slowly the lawyer's hand drops back to his side.

Eleanor bends to lift her periwinkle wool coat from where it sat folded over her chair and pulls it on over slim shoulders. My palms ache in the strangest way. Like I should be helping her into that garment.

She doesn't look at me as she dutifully follows her lawyer out of the courtroom.

Damon's hand comes down on my shoulder, giving me a short squeeze. "You ready?"

chapter 2

Ella

THERE'S AN EMPTINESS THAT'S UNSETTLING. I'VE STOOD IN THIS exact spot more than a dozen times, taking in the sight of this home. One of several I've lived in over the years, and truthfully, it was once my preferred home although with everything that's happened, it was never an option for it to be more than a refuge.

I don't believe that places can be haunted. Haunted houses and such … I've never given much credence to the notion. Do I believe in ghosts? I do … ever since I was a little girl. That sense of wonder and shiver of fear never left me. I think we all do to some extent; it's simply a matter of what has happened to each of us that leads us to believe.

But I've never thought that ghosts can haunt a physical place. My aunt, who I haven't seen in nearly a decade now, once told me that spirits don't haunt locations; they haunt people. She told me there was no such thing as a haunted house.

She said lost spirits follow people who they miss, the ones they have unfinished business with, or a long-lost soul they wish would remember them. So I've never been scared of ghost stories. After all, my mother and father didn't want a damn thing to do with me when air still filled their lungs; surely they didn't give a shit about me once they were buried six feet under.

Never once have I felt the presence of any being … But as I stand in the foyer, I can't help questioning my beliefs. Every corner of this house seems to hold a memory that's desperate to come back to life. Even with my eyes closed, the laughter from events long gone echoes in my mind as if it's all so close. As if I could reach out and my hand wouldn't meet cold air and proof this home has been vacant for nearly two years now. If only it was so easy.

No. My aunt wasn't right about spirits and ghosts.

There are no haunted houses; there are no ghosts at all. There are only haunted people.

"When was the last time you were here?" The deep timbre brings me back to the present and the voices go silent. There's only a creak of the floor as my memories slip away back to the corners of my sorrowful mind. I wish they would stay. I wish I could go back to them more than anything.

With a shaky breath blown out from between my slightly parted lips, I bring my eyes up to a kind gaze, although behind it is intention.

"I'm sorry," I respond respectfully, taking in the fact that I am not at all alone, although it certainly felt like I was for a moment. For a very long moment, if I'm honest; too long of a moment. "What was that?"

The gentleman named Cade is the owner of a company my manager holds more confidence in than I do. I focus on his rather large hands as he forms a loose fist to clear his throat again. He's nervous and for the life of me, I can't understand why Kamden put his faith in him. Once he's done clearing his throat, he repeats his question. "When was the last time you were here?"

Letting out an exhale that's far from easy, but for his comfort, I allow it to be seemingly casual, I respond, "Over a year." He tucks in his tie, although his deep green eyes never leave mine. There's kindness there. He's professional but kind. I add, "Maybe two by now." My voice turns raspy at the last two words. I'm still recovering and I've barely spoken for the last few months as it is.

There's been no one to talk to. No one I've wanted to hold a conversation with either. For a moment the memories of laughter and happier times threaten to come back and instead I hold the poor man hostage in a trivial conversation.

Gesturing to the nearly empty space, I tell him, "Last time I was here we furnished the foyer with the rug and bench, and I intended to finish the space …" my voice trails off and I don't bother finishing. With my chest feeling hollow, I remind myself that I don't owe them anything. Not an explanation, not an answer.

"We can work on that, if you'd like," he offers and it takes me a moment too long to understand that he's referring to picking out furniture for this far too large house.

Nodding, I take a half step back, my cobalt wool coat providing the only warmth I feel as it's draped over both my arms that are crossed in front of me. "We could start by turning on the heat?" I joke, keeping my cadence as smooth as I can and my voice gentle, to make up for my tardiness in comprehension. As if on command, there's a click of the furnace that's undeniable, and rather unsettling.

The white macael porcelain flooring is elegant and fresh, but is at odds with the vintage, pale and distressed medallion rug I chose years ago. The entirety of this home consists of shades of creams and dark blues. Modern furniture with retro accents and polished copper details only add to the iciness of the mountain setting when we came here to ski for the winter. It's a careful mix of hard and soft, but I never realized until now just how cold it all is.

My initial instinct is to start fresh and redesign everything; I used to love doing that. Donating what's here and bringing in new pieces, playing with color and all things from the newest collections. My teeth bite down on the tip of my tongue at the thought. A moment flashes before my eyes as I stare at the thick rug, and I know then I'll never replace a thing that graces this home.

"Is there anything you'd like before we start?" he questions me. I have to lift my chin to look up at him. I'm rather tall, all legs so I've been told, but this man with his broad shoulders is even taller. He resembles the other man in the courtroom, the one whose dark gaze pinned me more than once. A chill runs down my spine at the thought, although the rest of me seems to heat with anxiousness.

"I think I'm fine for now," I offer with a tight smile I'm all too aware doesn't reach my eyes.

Silently, Cade nods.

One breath in, and he offers to take my coat for me. One breath out and he leaves my side. It feels like all the warmth in the room leaves with him although he's only a few short feet away.

The din of chatter drifts toward us and muddled within is the familiar, confident pitch of my manager. Giving orders as he always does.

"Shall we?" Cade asks and again, I question everyone's decision. His. Kam's. Even the judge.

I'm not certain he knows what he's getting into, especially after the court hearing. I don't know what he knows about me or what research he's done. I imagine all he's been presented with is the file Kam gave the Rockford Center. Which is as barren as this empty foyer.

Lord knows there's plenty on the internet for him to find, but none of it is what truly matters.

My heels click as he leads me through my own home to the sitting room across from the open kitchen. I wonder if he judges me as I judge him. I wonder what he thinks, the wheels turning as he interacts with me. Am I what he expected? I used to be able to tell from the first time I met someone what they knew about me. The men were the easiest.

A smirk was almost a given if he'd happened to stumble upon some of my younger days online. The corners of my lips lift slightly at the knowledge.

I know there are still a few … risqué videos … still lingering on the web. It's possible he's watched those, but if he has, he doesn't let on. Perhaps, though, what's happened most recently far outweighs the past.

I have to consciously stop my racing thoughts before the spiral begins and it's then that I notice how the chatter has stopped.

"Ella." Kam's voice is the first I hear as I take in the group of men. He's already taken off his suit jacket. It's hanging over the back of a mahogany stool with navy blue tufted upholstery at the kitchen island. The kitchen is a stark white with the same porcelain tiles as the foyer to my right, but the dark navy of the stools is echoed to the left, covering the walls including the wainscoting and coffered ceiling.

"Finally." He announces the word with his hands up, arms outstretched. His charming smile greets me just before he embraces me. Kamden's never been a large man and he's always had a smaller frame, but like me, it appears he's lost weight. His jawline shows it the most.

I vaguely wonder how else he's been affected. I know his boyfriend left him when I was first committed. He wasn't well then either, but in the months I've been away, I haven't heard from him apart from his plans to get me home.

In my heels, I'm eye level with him.

"Finally," I repeat, echoing his upbeat and relieved tone. It does wonders for my mood. To see him, to hold his hands and know I'm safe. To feel truly protected. This man would move mountains for me. He has before.

"How are you feeling?" Before I can answer, he lifts a brow and comments as he moves to the sitting room with me trailing behind him, "It was fucking freezing when I first got here. How the hell do we turn this fireplace on?" If his tone is anything to go by, today is any other day and the last year didn't happen.

Oh, how I wish. All the wishes don't add up to anything I can hold on to, though.

The silence is uncomfortable as all the men in the room watch me, all six of them, and the only thing that can be heard are my heels muted by the rug as I slip across the room to flick the switch to the gas fireplace. It ticks steadily until it lights, and then blue flames rage from the crystals.

"Ah," Kam says, then claps and makes his way to stand beside me. "What would I do without you?"

His calming and comforting voice only eases the brokenness slightly. His genuine smile produces fine lines around his eyes that I never noticed before.

"It's been a cold year," I tell him and my throat turns tight.

"It'll warm up soon, babe," he replies and quickly turns, no doubt in an attempt to hide any true emotion that brought the glossiness to his gaze. If he thinks I didn't see it, he's mistaken.

One breath in, one breath out.

"I'm sorry it took this long." His apology grabs my attention and I catch his gaze skipping from my collarbone back up to meet mine when he asks, "Have you eaten?"

Self-consciously, I reach up to pull the blouse back in place.

Cade cuts in before I can answer that I don't think I've eaten since this morning. "Should we discuss the menu that was suggested—"

"Absolutely not, she can have whatever it is that she wants to eat. There's no reason that she can't," Kam cuts him off, responding with a strictness that he's always had. Ever since I was a teenager, when my dad died and Kam took me in to keep me from going to the state, I've never wanted for anything a second longer than it took for me to tell Kamden what it was I'd set my sights on.

Whether it be food, drugs … a man. He's the brother of my long-time friend Trish, although I haven't seen her in forever. He's a good friend, a father figure in some ways, but in all things, my rock. If I'm honest, I felt most comfortable with him more than anyone else simply knowing his preference for men. I could tell him anything, show him anything, and he would never use me as other men had tried. Hiring him as my manager was unquestionably the easiest decision I've ever made with my estate. Recently, he's also become my conservator.

"Everything was a misunderstanding and that place did more harm than good," Kam says, meeting my eyes rather than Cade's or the other men in the room I've yet to be introduced to.

A misunderstanding. The very word steals my breath.

"What'll it be?" Kam asks, ready to take any order I give him and, in my periphery, Cade watches the two of us. I don't miss the skepticism. Kam's gotten me out of trouble for years. Never anything like this, though.

"I think I'd like to go over the necessities and meet these … gentlemen first?" I state, turning slightly so I'm facing the room. With the fire blazing just beside me, my back is to the corner. As the sun sets beyond the paned windows, the fire casts a shadow along the man standing the closest to me at the end of the long white couch.

The roaring flames seem to dance a little hotter as I take him in. His white collared shirt is tight over his broad shoulders. I'm not certain if it's the lighting or something else that makes him appear even more intimidating in my home than he did in the courtroom. There's a tension that crackles, an undeniable feeling that's nearly suffocating as I force myself to meet his stare and not to back down. His eyes are gorgeous, a concoction of shades of emerald and ambers, his jaw chiseled as he remains where he is across from me.

After a moment he nods, acknowledging me for the first time.

I dare to speak, barely breathing. Interrupting whatever is brewing between Kam and Mr. Thompson, I comment, "Let's get on with it," and with that I break this man's gaze to turn to the room again. "Shall we?"

chapter 3

Zander

All partners of The Firm have extensive backgrounds in high-profile security and personal client care. We are equipped to respond swiftly and appropriately to any need or crisis.

Ms. Bordeu stands through Cade's introductions the way she stood through the hearing— still. Her delicate hands folded in front of her. Next to the fireplace in the sitting room where we've gathered, with her manager, Kamden Richards, close by her side.

Maybe I imagine that she glances at me a moment longer than the others.

Maybe I don't.

Unlike in the courtroom, it's my job to watch her now. I'm required to do it. Required to observe her reaction to everything. So why does it feel so damn forbidden?

There's a tension I can't shake, no matter how much I ignore it and focus on Cade. The gentle ticking of the clock seemingly intensifies as every second passes, as does the need to loosen my tie. Clasping my hands together, I ignore the heat that threatens to suffocate me.

I can't ignore her, though. Every small sway of her body, every nod at Kam's interruptions, every time her eyes glance down and then land back on me. Holding me there, daring to look away. I'm never the first to break our shared gaze. She's always the one who closes her eyes and, once they're open, directs them on someone or something else.

It doesn't feel like a job right now. It feels like a peep show. As if studying her face for every tiny reaction is something forbidden and off-limits, not the thing I'm being paid to do as part of The Firm.

Cade doesn't allow silence after the introductions are made, and summarizing the mundane details from the hearing goes on too long. "Now we'll need to go over protocol, Ms. Bordeu. Would you like to take a seat?"

It's a smooth transition, meant to put everyone at ease and direct the client's attention. But when Eleanor's eyes slide to mine, ease is the last thing I feel. Calm focus has gone to hell and brought the heat back with it. Tension tugs at the air between us. It's written in the set of her slightly parted, pouty lips. My thoughts tussle with lewd desires that shouldn't be anywhere on my mind. This situation is never a comfortable one, the introduction of a client and reviewing their specific needs from us. It makes sense that she's uncomfortable. Especially given her mental health, which is why we've been called in. It's not protection from a stalker or a former coworker or lover … It's protection from herself, from what I can gather.

It makes sense that she may feel on edge. Skeptical, perhaps. Saddened or embarrassed by the entire ordeal given the excuse her manager continues to state: just a misunderstanding.

But … that is not at all what I gather from her reticence.

It's my eyes she looks into, far too often, with wariness a dull flare. It makes my palms itch to touch her. To comfort her in a way no professional should ever do. Once again our gaze is broken, but this time it's due to my brother walking the length of the room as he closes the folder of paperwork, satisfied there were no issues with the general outline of our arrangement.

This woman is in our care as she resides in her private domicile. We will see to it that she receives the same level of care as she was before, including twenty-four-hour surveillance. The evaluation of her treatment will occur at regular monthly intervals by Mr. Aiden Miller the representative of the Rockford Center, along with an approved concierge doctor. Which means we will be here with her for a month, at minimum.

Cade claims a seat by the fireplace and gestures for Eleanor to take the one across from him, then Dane and Silas sink into two free chairs. Damon positions himself behind Cade's chair, leaning against the wall by the fireplace. Kamden hovers in the open archway between the sitting room and great room, positioning himself to observe although I have no doubts that he'll be the one speaking on her behalf. He's already taken that initiative.

Across from all of them, and farthest away from our client, I lean against the wide, black windowsill. This way, I see her in profile. This way, I'm not staring into her eyes.

Professionalism is required and I am a damn professional.

Eleanor lowers herself into her seat and I twist the top off my water bottle. My mouth has gone bone dry, heat prickling at the back of my neck. This woman, in this room—it does something to me.

In this light, I see more of her, more details she's hidden. Her haunted eyes and too-slim wrists are on display. In the first moment, as everyone gets comfortable, she reaches for her throat, only to brush her fingertips over it and then put her hand back in her lap.

It's as if she's out of place in her own home. A home that reeks of luxury and wealth. Old money she was obviously born into.

Her gaze flicks to various places in the room, no doubt noting the changes we've made. Even though the room is clearly kept spare and clean, there are pieces missing. Items we took out. No bottles of alcohol wait in the gleaming bar stand in the corner. The picture frames have had the glass removed, which was one of the many recommendations we received from the center.

As I lean back, feeling the cold windowpane against my back and grateful for the chill, I remember how opposed to this I was. I fought Cade and questioned his decision. There wasn't a single desire in me to babysit an affluent woman who didn't want to receive her care in a private institution.

The Firm has a background in law and psychiatry, but we're known for our military experience. We're more than just professional bodyguards, although that's what I'd prefer we stick to. Cade's vision for transitioning this company isn't why I signed up to be on his team. I wanted an adrenaline rush and as little interaction with the clients as possible. He wants to move into a more high-end, private and potentially gray market.

There wasn't a dollar amount that made me lean in favor of his decision.

Now that we're here, I understand the intrigue and the desire for a more complicated situation.

Cade lays the folder in his lap and shakes out his arms.

"If you don't mind, I'd like to roll up my sleeves and get comfortable with the particulars," my brother says, directing his statement toward Eleanor. She merely gives him a thin smile and nod in return.

"We should be through this quickly, starting with the schedule." He launches into the shift rotations and designated meeting times, followed by how any items coming or going, including any shopping, will be handled.

That, and more, until Eleanor interrupts him. Her soft voice cuts right into an explanation of the around-the-clock care services we'll be providing.

"I'm expected to talk to you?"

"To talk to us?" Tilting my head slightly, I wait to hear Eleanor's response to my brother.

Her hand goes to her throat as if she needs the physical support to get the words out. My eyes narrow as she swallows thickly. It hurts her to speak. I'm sure of it. That knowledge makes the hairs on the back of my neck stand up. "You want to conduct therapy sessions in addition to the mandated monthly sessions from the center?"

"That's correct," Cade answers. With his hands folded, he leans forward and looks her in the eye. That's my brother. He doesn't flinch, doesn't shy away from other people's discomfort. "It's essential that we're involved in your care. We cannot help you or protect you if we aren't included in each aspect that's questionable when it comes to your safety."

"I think you'll be rather disappointed." Eleanor's voice is low and strained, like it's been brushed with steel wool. "I haven't much to say." There's a note of melancholy that's tangled in her nearly dismissive response.

"As part of our agreement, we need to offer on-demand access to emotional support."

Eleanor's manager, Kamden, pipes up from the archway, his tone hopeful. "Therapists will be coming and going. You'll meet with them as well."

She glances incredulously toward him, the corners of her mouth tugging down. But then her dark eyes come back to Cade, back to his attention. Eleanor nods without speaking, seemingly accepting the terms against her will. More questions are asked, this time from Cade. Her responses are short. Occasionally she follows the lead of her manager, searching him out before answering.

It's like she's conserving her words. What makes her choose one moment over another to use them? I give the manager a once-over as Cade moves through his agenda. I don't know what to think of him. He prefers to go by Kam, and that's the sum total of facts I have on hand. Obviously, he makes his money off Eleanor. I have questions. Like what happened to her that she ended up like this—withdrawn and wary and broken—and he appears to be just fine and speaking for her more than she speaks for herself.

The fourth time Eleanor's fingertips grace the dip of her throat, Kam interrupts to offer her tea. She nods and I anticipate that being the only response, but she adds "please," just above a murmur.

Their relationship is … unique. Something about him doesn't sit right with me. I file my skepticism away for later.

Damon takes a half step forward from where he stands to the left of the fireplace as Kam turns on his heel to head to the kitchen, and my brother's focus follows him. Leaning forward, he meets Eleanor's eye level. She observes him with both curiosity and hesitation.

He softens his expression to question, "Everything all right so far?"

Her nod of acknowledgment comes with the faint sounds of Kam's efforts to make the tea just behind us in the kitchen. "Damon, right?"

He mimics her response with a nod in affirmation, offering her an asymmetric smile as well. "That would be me." Damon's dark skin is complemented by his cobalt blue suit that nearly matches the walls, and his smile is as white as the shirt he wears under the slim-cut jacket.

Giving him a simper she relaxes slightly, although there's still the tension that would be expected given the situation.

"I want to put your mind at ease," Damon continues. "Each of us has received training in emotional support, and I am a board-certified physician." A psychiatrist, to be exact.

Her smile wanes and the light in her eyes dims. For a moment, I think she's not going to respond, but then she explains, "What if I don't want to talk at all?"

Again, a nervous prick travels down my spine as Damon jokes with her that he's comfortable in silence. It puts her at ease at least. That or the tea Kam offers her.

"Are we good to continue?" Cade asks just as Kamden gives Eleanor's shoulder a light squeeze and returns to his position.

Taking a brief swig from my water bottle, I get the attention of Dane and Silas who have yet to speak, but luckily it doesn't distract anyone else.

"I think it might be helpful for you to record your thoughts to share with the therapists at the Rockford Center. Either by writing them down or recording yourself. That way, you could maintain a connection with them, even if it's through videos."

Eleanor's shake of her head is firm, although her eyes are luminous with anguish. "I don't want to talk to a lens." Every word out of her mouth feels carefully weighed. As if she's balanced them all against the pain it'll cause her to use her voice. "I've done that enough."

"Ella," Kam's tone is pleading. He takes three long strides into the room at the same time that I speak.

"I like to talk." I ignore the burning look I'm aware Cade is giving me. "I've got stories to share if you want to listen. Maybe share some with me?" There's a note in my offer I wish wasn't there. A smoothness in my tone, casual and inviting, that I don't use with clients. One I hope the rest of the men don't pick up on.

Clearing my throat and standing up straighter, I cover my tracks, motioning toward Damon as I add, "It can be easier to share in group settings."

They all stare, even Eleanor. I'm aware of every inch of my body. Of my too-casual lean against the windowsill. Of the water bottle that's seconds away from being crushed in my hands. I loosen my grip on it and meet her eyes. A semblance of a smile lifts the corners of her mouth. My lungs feel tight from holding my breath. I don't let it out. Don't even move. If she smiles right now, if that hint becomes something real, it'll be an accomplishment.

Eleanor's lips part, her brow arching as she eyes me, and—

"This will all be recorded?" Kam's voice takes the weak start to an inquisitive smile off her face and draws her eyes back to him. He's taken a step into the room to hover over her.

His comment is a rock through glass. Eleanor holds my gaze for another beat, and then it's back on my brother. Cade nods at Kam but then quickly returns his attention to Eleanor. "Of course. You don't have to stare into a lens. Cameras are already placed in each room."

The details continue without me as if I hadn't spoken at all, which is best. It takes great effort to ignore Damon's stare that burns into the side of my face.

It doesn't take much for her to agree. It's a battle she seems not to want to fight.

He carries on with the daily schedule, the rest of us shifting in our spots, listening along with Eleanor. My heart beats too fast for what this is. A status meeting, essentially. A way to get the lay of the land. Time set aside for all of us to be in the same room before we're on rotating shifts, in and out of the house, devoted to her care.

By the time Cade gets to the end of his list, shadows have fallen over Eleanor's face. The sunset is on its last gasp. It'll be pitch black soon. I peel myself away from the windowsill and reach for a lamp in the corner. With a gentle click, it bathes the room in a warm glow. Eleanor tips her face toward it like it's the sun and all I can see are the dark circles under her eyes. *What is it that keeps her awake at night?* At first glance, she was striking, although slender. Too slender. After spending the last two hours watching her, it's more than obvious she's not well. Kamden Richards is full of shit. It's not a misunderstanding.

"With that settled," Cade announces, "I believe that's the end of my agenda. That's all the information we have to give you right now. Was there anything you wanted to discuss before we call it a night?"

Eleanor shakes her head. There's plenty I want to discuss and unravel. Too much. I'm too curious, and I know it.

She's already standing when Cade offers to show her upstairs. She clears her throat with a hint of amusement. "I think I can find the way."

Cade gets to his feet, the rest of us hanging back although we're all standing now. I don't know what this woman's been through, but I'm certain she has no idea what to expect from us. Even after hours of going over details.

"This arrangement included minor changes to each room I'd like to go over with you." His tone is gentle, but not patronizing. Eleanor hasn't been through the whole house yet. She should be aware of the cameras and intercoms.

She seems to hear Cade's words a few seconds late. I see the moment they land. Her eyebrows go up, eyes widening, and her shoulders tense. If I hadn't been staring at her all this time, I might not have caught it. She begins to lift her hand but catches herself. "Not the west hall, though?"

Kam speaks up, his tone calm, "Everything in the west hall is untouched. Every room up there is just how you left it, Eleanor." Although his outward appearance is at ease, his grip tightens on the back of the stool. So tight, I can see the whitening of his knuckles from here. Kam's glance flickers to Cade when he adds, "I gave explicit instructions."

Heat trickles down my shoulders. Cade confirms nothing has been touched in that wing. We don't have access to it and neither will Eleanor.

Relief is exhaled along with her response. "Good." She mouths the word more than she says it. Eleanor crosses both arms loosely over her belly. She's still not comfortable—who would be?—but the fearful shine that flashed in her eyes is gone. Easing the tension out of my shoulders, I note that I'm left with more questions than anything after this meeting. So many that I consider reading the file. The idea lingers in the back of my mind.

"Let me walk with you upstairs?" Damon offers with an easy smile. He's muscular, as we all are, and the kind of guy you want to have in an emergency. I would know. He's helped me before.

Eleanor doesn't quite smile back, but she looks like she might simply to be polite. When Damon steps to her side she moves along with him, the two of them striding past her manager, who trails a few steps behind.

He'll take her through the great room and into the foyer, and then they'll climb the herringbone steps.

Besides my brother, I'm closest to Damon. He's the one friend I could count on without fail in the last four years. Damon's a good conversationalist but given her sore throat, he's also comfortable with silence. There won't be a second of awkwardness between them.

Friendship doesn't do a damn thing to ease the possessive knot that coils my muscles as I watch him lead her away. Gritting my teeth, I force myself to look anywhere else.

This isn't like me. I'm not jealous, and I never have been. Let alone the unethical thoughts that have run rampant since I first laid eyes on her. Excuses come to mind and pile up, the most obvious being the call I took first thing this morning and how much that fucked me up.

Dane and Silas call me over to where they're standing, more than likely discussing the schedule and their thoughts of our new client. Holding up a finger and then the empty water bottle, I silently motion to the kitchen as if I need to throw away the trash before talking to them.

In the bright light of the kitchen, I steady my thoughts and my breathing.

It must be because Eleanor is not well. It makes her seem delicate. In need of protection.

Or in need of someone to take control.

All damned good explanations for why I feel like sprinting up the stairs after them, and for the same reasons I stay where I am, my mind shuddering away from the possibility.

I shake it off and come back to the task at hand. Cade has joined the other two men in front of the fireplace. I don't think any of them have noticed how scattered my thoughts have been. Or how the majority have been focused on Eleanor in a way they shouldn't. They'll notice if I keep this up, which I don't intend to do.

"Have you had a chance to read through the file?" Cade asks me as I join their circle.

"No. I'll get to it."

Cade doesn't push me on the lie. It wouldn't matter if he did. I want to hear her side of things. I want her to tell me what the hell happened to her.

chapter 4

Ella

The Firm will provide for all necessary modifications pertaining to the security and comfort of each client. These may include, but are not limited to, home renovations and the installation of complete monitoring systems. Modifications are subject to change as the service progresses.

MY EYES BURN AS IF I DIDN'T SLEEP AT ALL. WHICH DOESN'T make much sense given that last night I slept the most I have in months. It was off and on and took hours before sleep came for me, but still. I slept. A dreamless sleep, thankfully.

I'm busy rubbing my eyes when I hear heavy footsteps walk into the kitchen. I'm grateful my back is to whomever it is so they don't see the exasperation in my expression.

I'm grateful to be out of the center, grateful for my own bed and an ounce more privacy, but I'd like a moment from under the shadow of these strangers.

Gripping the cardboard box, I tilt it and the clink of cereal hitting the bowl is all that can be heard. The second the box is placed on the counter, whoever has joined me pulls out a stool from the island, the legs dragging on the porcelain floor.

If I didn't feel as exhausted as I do, if I wasn't grateful to be out of there and safe in a familiar place, I'd have contempt for all of them. Them telling me what to do, making changes to my home without my consent … it's never sat well with me for a man to take control of my life. Other than one man.

"Morning." A deep baritone interrupts my thoughts, soothing them and giving me a much-wanted distraction.

Taking my time, I peer over my shoulder, ignoring the warmth the sight gives me. His broad shoulders pull the collared shirt tight as he leans down to reposition the stool once again and then takes his seat. He opted for a burgundy shirt and black jeans today. The dark tones bring out the flecks of gold in his hazel eyes.

Zander is a handsome man in a traditional sense. Although he's clean-shaven today, I most certainly prefer the stubble he came with yesterday. His hair is short on the sides, but there's plenty to grip on top. His tanned skin is a stark contrast to how pale I've become. I'd guess from his appearance he worked a blue-collar job, not this.

His last name is the same as Cade's—Thompson—and I wonder if he's related and that's the only reason he's here.

"Good morning," I offer him and ignore the raw pain at the back of my throat. The doctor said I needed to practice speaking again to lessen the vocal strain. After the surgery, I could barely speak for weeks. But then again, I could barely do anything for weeks.

"I didn't expect you to be up this early," Zander tells me. His name and his promise to tell me his stories kept me company as I lay in bed last night. I believe I remember each of the men's names, but Zander's is by far the easiest.

"I never met a Zander before," I comment rather than offer up my dry humor with the accusation of how he could possibly know what to expect from me. After all, I haven't known him for twenty-four hours yet; I probably shouldn't risk offending him.

"Well, I'm glad to be your first." The corners of my lips tilt up at his drollness. Perhaps he would have liked my joke after all. He adds quickly, as if second-guessing his choice of words, "How are you this morning?"

"My throat hurts," I whisper but it goes unheard as I pour the milk into the cereal.

"I'm sorry, I didn't hear you," he says.

After putting the milk back in the fridge, I move the ceramic bowl to the island across from him and answer politely, "I'm all right." I mean to ask him how he's doing too, but my throat burns; the cold milk is too tempting not to drink some of it first.

In my silence, Zander says, "I'll try not to be obvious."

"Hmm?"

"I'll give you space while I'm here."

"Oh," I say and the word falls flat from my lips. Loneliness creeps between us.

"Unless you'd like the company," he offers. It's kind of him, and obvious that he only offered because of my despondency.

"I thought you had stories," I murmur, peeking up at him from beneath my lashes. There's a quick spark, one that frightens some side of me I'm not yet ready to confront. It's too early for such things.

A tall disposable coffee cup hits the counter and I stare at it, rather than the prying gaze that fuels the heat rising into my cheeks.

"We could share stories," he states lowly. A prick travels along my skin as the tips of my fingers numb. The sugary puffs that float in the bowl come with memories. They dare me to tell Zander why, for two years, I made sure this cereal was always stocked.

At that recollection, I push the bowl away from me. The porcelain protests as it drags against the stone.

"Do you want something else to eat?" I meet his gaze as he adds, "I'm no chef, but—"

"No," I say and then clear my throat, hating that the simple act makes it hurt that much more. "I'm fine." What a lie that is. A lie I'm sure this man can read as easily as the written words on the back of the cereal box. I debate pulling the bowl back and eventually give in, my hunger winning out. It's the smallest things that bring me to the edge. Something as simple as a brand of cereal.

"You all right, Eleanor?"

"Call me Ella … please."

"Ella," he echoes, seemingly testing out my name, his deep voice caressing each syllable. It stirs something inside of me, something that buries my previous thoughts, making me grateful for him repeating my name.

There's a quiet moment before he picks up the conversation again.

"What kind of music do you like?"

With a smirk I think the topic is one step above asking my opinion of the weather. Although given how kind he is, and how pleasant he is simply to look at, I'd talk about whatever he'd like.

"All kinds," I tell him and finding my own answer lacking, I elaborate before he can respond. "I have two favorites I used to listen to: "Heart Attack" by Demi Lovato and "Sit Still, Look Pretty" by … I forget who sings it."

I peek over the counter at where he's seated to find an amused expression.

"Daya, I think."

I soothe each of the burning words with a spoonful of milk. My gaze drops to the streaks of gray that marble the pristine counter rather than holding his any longer. I haven't the energy to keep up with the pretense of yesterday. Regardless of my pride, he's practically my prison warden.

"You know them?"

"Not a clue," he answers and a bubble of laughter warms my chest.

He starts to say something, getting my attention but waves it off. "What?" I push him but he taps the empty coffee cup on the counter instead of answering.

"I have a coffee maker," I say, picking up the spoon and point with it, "if you'd like to make a cup."

"I'm fine with this. Thank you, though."

"You're a coffee drinker then?" I ask him. Yet another topic that's one step above the weather. Just doing my part in this ice breaking, I suppose.

"I am."

"Let me guess how you drink it." He grins slowly, taken aback by my tone. Even I'm surprised by the eagerness in my voice.

"Black with sugar. No milk?"

"Why do you think no milk?" he questions, not telling me if I'm right or wrong.

I shrug and he shakes his head. "Milk, no sugar."

"Oh," I say with mock dismay, "so close." I can't hide the semblance of a smile.

"Let me guess how you drink yours?" he asks and I nod, biting down slightly on my lower lip. "Lots of sugar and no milk."

"You just took my guess," I say accusingly.

"You didn't say 'lots.'"

"Well, you're wrong anyway," I say between more spoonfuls of milk.

"So how do you like it?" he asks and my body reacts to his words as if the way he posed the query wasn't innocent. As if he was asking how I like something else entirely.

A mundane conversation with this man feels just as dangerous as playing with fire. Whispering, and not feeling any pain at all, I confess, "I don't drink coffee. I drink tea."

His eyes spark and it's in tune with a thump in my chest. Then I'm met with a rough huff of humor. "I knew that," he comments.

Even with the quietness surrounding us, I simmer. There's something about him that pulls me in, but there's also something that warns me to stay the hell away from him.

I've never been good at obeying warnings, though.

"Did you already eat?" I dare ask, interrupting the quiet moment.

"We bring our own food."

"That doesn't answer my question."

He gives me an asymmetric grin as my spoon clinks against the bowl and I finish the last of my breakfast.

"Not yet. I'm waiting on Damon, you met him yesterday." When I nod he continues, "Once he's in, I'll be on my way."

There's no explanation for the reason I suddenly feel loss. I ask, "So you stayed last night?" and he nods. "What did you even do? Watch me sleep?"

The sexy smirk he gives me is utterly sinful. It's wrong that it sparks what it does inside of me. He nods and attempts a swig from his coffee cup but finds it empty.

I have to bite my tongue to keep from telling him that's what he gets. It's in this moment that I'm acutely aware of the attraction between us and how very wrong it feels. It's in the way he looks at me. How his stare seems to sink through me, anchoring me to him and holding me steady. He doesn't flinch, he doesn't hesitate, and there's a knowing challenge in his gaze. One that feels familiar although the man himself is very much a stranger who has piqued my curiosity.

My dry humor slips out in a deadpan mutter. "That's not creepy at all." I anticipate him laughing but he doesn't. I wish he would, I want to know what it sounds like from his lips.

I change the subject as quickly as I can, gesturing to his empty cup. "You sure you don't want to make another cup?"

Peering down at the nondescript cardboard cup, he hesitates.

"I don't mind giving to the needy."

He questions with humor, "Now I'm charity?"

I give in to the small laughter that comes with it and shrug. "Your words, not mine."

Instead of answering, he asks, "Cade said last night that you do charity work?"

The mention of Cade and the fact they were talking about me last night makes my throat go dry.

Nodding, I answer, "Kam says it's good for my image and I love it, so …" With a familiar hollow sensation filling my chest, I take the bowl to the sink and pretend I'm all right. It's back to real life and no longer getting lost in the handsome stranger seated so close I can inhale his masculine scent. It's something woodsy yet fresh. Like a forest that rises above the coldest depths of the ocean.

The thoughts leave me without conscious consent as I say, "It's incredible the things people do. All they ask for is a platform, a chance. I'm grateful I can give them that."

"So you do charity? That's your … thing?" I don't miss how his gaze sweeps over the expansive kitchen and past that to the sitting room.

"I don't make money from it, if that's what you're thinking." My brow knits and I question, "You haven't read the file."

"You know what's in there?"

I answer without hesitation, "Of course I do. Kam makes sure I approve it all."

Shock lights his hazel eyes, brightening them but he doesn't say a word.

Curiosity eats away at me until I ask him, "What do you know about me?" The suspense heats every inch of my body as I wait for an answer.

"Only what I've seen in the courtroom and at the briefing yesterday," he admits.

"And what Cade told you last night," I point out. I don't know why I feel so at ease knowing he doesn't know. I shouldn't feel relief, but I do.

"Yes, and that."

Something compels me to tease him as I make my way to the hot water spout, in desperate need of morning tea. "So you don't read the file and instead flirt with me in my kitchen in the early hours before anyone else is awake ... None of this sounds like conflict of interest at all to me."

The very moment I begin to second-guess myself, I feel his dominating presence behind me and when I turn to face him, I'm disappointed he wasn't there caging me in. Instead he stands two feet too far from me, tossing away his trash. A sharp tension snaps between us as the implications of what I've said hit me. The front door creaks open, alerting us to someone else's presence and Zander ends the conversation succinctly by saying, "So many interests. So many conflicts."

chapter 5

Zander

Twenty-four-hour care is the standard for each client contracted with The Firm. A partner will be on the premises at all times, with additional detail on standby within a thirty-minute radius of the property. If at any time more security is required, it will be addressed immediately and without hesitation.

THE DOOR OF THE RENTED ROOM STICKS ON MY WAY IN. ITS resistance in the new autumn sunlight, slanting down the motel wall, echoes what I felt leaving Ella's house twenty minutes ago. There's a magnetic pull to her I can't fathom. She's a beautiful distraction who's mesmerized me. I could've listened to her talk all day, or even longer, about virtually nothing. It was as if a door had cracked open, letting in a little light. Her eyes hadn't seemed so haunted. Guarded, yes. Cautious— especially when Cade was mentioned.

This may be a different kind of case, but her reaction isn't unlike other clients. My reaction, though … is certainly unusual. It's typical for our clients to react that way—relaxing a bit, once the initial awkwardness dissipates. Although I hardly interact with the clients. That's Cade's job. It's rare that I'm required to be social, and more than likely for the best. I'm a bodyguard, plain and simple. What makes our company, and our talents above the competition, is the attention to detail. The monitoring, the research. Knowing who the threat is and more importantly why. What motivated the need to call us. Emotions don't factor into it nearly as much as simply knowing people.

When it comes to Ella, though … The first day has certainly been different from all the others.

My gaze drops as I toss the keys down on the barren dresser that doubles as a TV stand. It must've been a bit of a relief, sleeping in her own house with us to watch out for her.

I wouldn't know much about that. I've been alone for a long time now.

Inside the room, I close the door and lock the dead bolt. Cade secured a row of rooms in a mom-and-pop motel on the edge of the city. It's cheap but homey. Well cared for. You can tell the owners take pride in the place. My room has a queen-size bed with stark white, fresh bedding. A table and two chairs sit by the front window, the table decorated with a few stems of some pink flower in a vase. Fresh flowers, not fake. It's a nice touch, but the feminine flair is lost on me. They've repainted recently, because the new paint smell still lingers. I fall into one of those chairs and kick my shoes off, one at a time.

Alone.

Part of me relaxes at knowing there's nobody watching me. All night at Ella's, I felt eyes on my back. Maybe I was anticipating the moment she'd come down the stairs and say my name into all that quiet.

Maybe I was hoping she would do just that.

But Ella slept all night, and then this morning she lifted that spoon to her lips like it wasn't the most delicate, graceful thing I'd ever seen and told me about those songs she liked. I've already got them downloaded on my phone. They're already taking up space there, waiting for me.

Old guilt crashes in at the thought.

I let it hit. The waves bring exhaustion with it.

I can keep it shut out for the most part. I've had two years to learn to live with it. And I do live with it. There's no other choice. I'm alive, and I live with this hole, a wound, where someone else used to be. It feels like a deep gouge, but I know better. I've been to doctors about physical pain.

This is something else. Something I'll have for always. Even the psychiatrist said so. Two little blue pills may help me sleep, but when I'm awake and conscious, that pain will never leave.

It's the pain of hesitation. Of the loss of strict focus. Once upon a time, I fucked up. I wasn't honest about what I wanted because I was afraid of the outcome.

Now, even thinking about exposing that truth—to anyone—feels like acid in open wounds.

Those wounds are best kept hidden. Tucked away like the words inside a closed book. Though I don't know how long that will work, either. Cade's been making noises for six months about how much time I spend on my own. I keep telling him that's how I like it. No demands on my free time, except for when I spend the weekend with Damon. We'll grab a beer every now and again. We'll work on some project or another. Go to the shooting range or gym to have company. He knows loss as well as I do.

Even Damon's made a few comments. I don't know what they want from me. I work for The Firm as much as I can, and in my downtime, I try not to think about the shit that almost destroyed me.

It might still destroy me. The heat kicks on as I unzip my duffle bag. Two suits are already hung in the three-foot-wide closet. I go through the motions of this part of the job without much mental effort, just as I have for the past few years. The job keeps me moving. The requirements are all-consuming. So I take them all. Falling into place and performing as needed. This one, though …

It's more complicated, what with the news I got about the trial.

Stripping off my shirt, I drop to the floor and do a set of twenty push-ups. Then another. Followed by four-count breaths. Twenty more push-ups and the burn seeps into my muscles, stiffening my shoulders. I hold the position and do twenty more, faster, letting the heat break along my skin. Holding the upright position and then I break in another four. After eight sets the crush of guilt around my lungs eases up, and I head into the tiny bathroom for a shower. My chest rises and falls deeper, needing to steady, but my mind still races.

Turning the metal knob, the squeak of the old piping is followed by a spray of ice-cold water. By the time I've stripped down, steam has started pouring into the stall.

This, at least, is standard for missions. An affordable motel. A series of night shifts. I'm used to places like these, and schedules like these. I know how my brother prefers to put money into family businesses, local places that are less well traveled. I also know that he prefers contracts with clear end dates.

We don't have one this time. That's yet another difference with this mission. We're here as long as she needs me.

Needs us.

I work shampoo through my hair and try to ignore a tension in my back. *You're in the wrong place*, it says as I stare blankly at bland white tile and let the hot spray batter against my chest. The fuck is wrong with me? My eyes close and I do what I can to shake the thoughts of her away. She doesn't fucking need me. She's only a distraction, although … It seems as if she may need a distraction as well. Someone to listen to. Someone to talk to. Someone to tell her it's all right to feel whatever it is she's feeling. That thought is what breaks the dam. I can't stop picturing her sitting at the island in her kitchen, her bedhead swept back from her face and her eyes looking more alive for the first time, with a spark of mischief and the dare on her lips that there's no conflict of interest.

Tilting my face, I let the water splash there, condemning the disgraceful images that flick through my mind. I could so very easily get her to talk. One night with her and she would spill whatever it is that I wanted to know.

I can't stop picturing how she looked when she slept, one hand tucked under the pillow, her expression open and dreamy. I can't stop remembering the silence of her house. The expansive, open-concept space. All the room we'd have away from the outside world to—

To do nothing. We are not going to do anything. She's my client, and I am in charge of her care. I won't cross those lines with her.

But damn it, I want to.

I lean my head against the wall of the shower and sit with this urge the way I sit with my guilt. I feel it. I feel all of it. My palms burn from not touching her. My arms ache from not folding her into them. Glancing down at my cock, I let out a huff of incredulity.

This situation is unbelievably fucked up.

Forbidden.

The kind of shit that could tank a career like mine.

Lathering soap across my body, the scent fills the room and I breathe it in, ignoring the baser instincts. I can handle this case and this woman, *Ella*. That's the only option, handle it like I've been trained. I ignore the ache below my waist, turn off the shower, and towel off. Washing the two pills down with water, I prepare to pass the fuck out and fall into a much-needed deep sleep.

Back in the small bedroom my phone stares at me from its spot on the table. What I need to do, more than anything, is sleep. I have to be fresh for the night shift. No dozing off when this case is still developing and all her secrets are still there, ripe for the picking. No slipping up because my mind is clouded with equal parts of emotion and want.

I snap the curtains shut over the windows and take my phone off the table. I'm not going to avoid the damn thing just because Ella's songs are on it. Other than a thin sunbeam slipping through the curtains, the screen is the only light in the room.

Stretching out on the bed brings a moment of relief. I sink into the mattress and let my head fall back. Scrolling through the phone, I can't help that it feels loaded.

I know that downloading a couple of songs doesn't erase the past. It doesn't mean I owe less. It doesn't mean I'm moving on and betraying anyone's memory.

It doesn't.

And neither does the attraction I feel for Ella. Because I am attracted to her. Damn it, I am. I take in a long breath and blow it out to the ceiling. Unread emails stare at me from the small screen. Maybe I'm attracted to her because I'm looking for an escape now that the date for the hearing has been set.

The hearing has hauled the weight of the past two years right up to the present and parked it on my chest. This could be my mind's way of finding a way out from under it. Or at least a way to hold some of it up so I don't suffocate.

I shove the phone under my pillow, where I can't see it. It's dangerous to be having these thoughts. Dangerous to be having any kind of feelings for Ella. The whole damn thing feels risky in a way it didn't before I stepped inside that courtroom and those eyes met mine.

A harsh exhale brings me back to reality. She's nothing but a fantasy. Running my hand down my face, I remind myself that it's merely a lust-filled diversion and I imagine whatever pull she felt to me is the same.

Even entertaining the idea of more than a quick fuck with a woman makes my chest ache with that same scarred-over guilt. I hesitated before. Pushed back on the idea, and there were consequences to that hesitation. There are always consequences. It's twice as true now. If I can't get rid of these feelings for Ella, it won't just affect me. It'll affect the entire team, and especially Cade, who's trusting all of us with this.

I sling an arm over my eyes and swallow those feelings down. Wrestle them into something I can carry. Through sheer force of will I make the intensity fade, at least for a moment. At least for now. If it comes back …

I tried. And I'll keep trying, because this can't happen with Ella. It simply can't. I'm not going to put us in that position. Me. Ella. The Firm. I won't do it.

"The first days with a client can be like this," I say out loud, to no one but myself. I justify these thoughts, and why they won't turn into anything more than a delusion. There's an adjustment period. We're in that adjustment period, and it's more intense than usual because we've never taken on this kind of job before. We've never had a client with these needs.

I feel foolish, attempting to convince myself, but it's better than allowing this to get any further. Taking my phone back out, I stare at the two new songs, but scroll past them, deciding on a familiar melody.

I don't know what the hell I was thinking. Today was a mistake. That's exactly what Eleanor Bordeu is. A mistake.

chapter 6

Ella

Partners of The Firm will document client interactions and provide status updates to their team members at each shift change. Client records will be maintained by each partner and supervised by Cade Thompson, owner.

I HAVEN'T SPOKEN A SINGLE WORD ALL DAY TODAY. MY THROAT hurts, but that's not why I've been silent and avoiding the other men from The Firm. Not overtly avoiding them.

I'm not trying to make it obvious, or draw attention to my mood.

It's because I want to save my voice for him. On the days my throat hurts, I save my voice for what matters most. And what matters most right now is talking to Zander. It's not something I can explain. It feels dangerous to talk to him. So risky that I know I shouldn't be doing it. And yet the sound of him—just the pure sound of his voice, the rumble of it over my skin—it made me crave more.

I've been craving him all day.

No, not him. Just talking to him. Just his presence. I don't crave Zander the man. That's not why he's here. He and the rest of the men from The Firm are here to protect me. To … care for me.

I'm certain that's why I feel this need. He's obligated to care for me and he reminds me so much of the life I had before.

It scares the hell out of me, honestly. It's good to be home but it's terrifying in these ways I didn't expect. When I was at the Rockford Center, I knew things were bad. How could I not know? You don't go to a place like that unless the situation is dire. The rules there tell you exactly how bad things have gotten. Exactly how far you've fallen. People who are still holding it together don't need escorts to the bathroom or constant monitoring to make sure you're still breathing every night.

I woke last night, twice, when they came in to check on me. The creak of the door ripped my eyes wide open and just as I have for months, I woke with my heart racing. Thankfully, I don't remember what I dreamed, but I can imagine what it was. It doesn't take a shrink to point out the obvious.

They're still checking, the guys from The Firm. I know they are. But there are no harsh lights, and no nurses shaking me awake in the morning, and it's my house. Which means I have something to lose. A height to fall from. I don't want to go back. I can't. All I can do in that place is remember. The white walls are painted with memories. The empty chairs are filled with ghostly visitors.

I won't go back. I'll be good. I'll listen. So long as they're here, I promise to behave.

Zander feels like a risk because he is. The warmth that moves through me when he looks at me, when he talks to me—it's dangerous with what it could do to me. He makes me forget it all. It occurred to me last night that it's because he doesn't know. I don't want him to know. If I'm only given the chance for a single line to speak today, it'll be a plea for him not to read the file. For him to keep looking at me as if he doesn't know I'm so unwell and damaged.

That's what my breath is saved for. It's why I'm still awake, fighting the pull of the medication I was given at dinner. It didn't go unnoticed that my pills are different here. Kamden told me what was changed, but I don't remember. Either way, I'm so damn tired. Too restless. And wanting.

I'm not sure what my emotions are capable of. That's why I was in the Rockford Center in the first place. I used to wonder what was so wrong with being emotional ... now I know.

The sun sinks below the horizon early, an autumn fireburst in the trees outside my windows. Dying light paints the blue sky gold and I drift between the windows, watching. The old restlessness from the Rockford Center creeps through my veins. It used to happen every night there. The sky would get darker, and my heart would beat faster, as if the night were something to be afraid of. I don't know why that happened. There were always lights on in that place.

Maybe I knew it was because that marked the point when I couldn't resist sleep for much longer. My worst fear was dreaming, remembering, and waking up screaming.

But this … this is different.

My quickening heartbeat is the same. The urge to walk around, to pace, is the same. Only it's not anxiousness I feel.

It's anticipation.

For Zander to get here. I want him to arrive, to start his shift. I want to sense the danger in the air. I want to put myself near the risk of him. It's safe, although it seems the antithesis. I know it is. Maybe that's why I feel so brave, and so reckless. He has to protect me. He's obligated to.

With the warmth of the ceramic mug pressed against my palm, my gaze shifts from the handmade lantern seated near the covered porch to the stone driveaway. My heart races, although I don't show it. Damon's eyes are still on me, so I merely sip the tea and return to the blank notebook in my lap. Blank with the exception of the sketch of the lantern. It was a gift from my girlfriend, Kelly, on her last trip to Alaska—she thought it would suit my home perfectly, and she was right. The light is brilliant at night, peeking through the varying sized holes of the glazed pottery. It creates a constellation against the dark wood roof. It's one of the things I dream of that doesn't bring the past to haunt me. Staring at the stars, imagining the northern lights I still have yet to see.

His car trundles down the street in front of my house at five minutes to nine. I take the interruption of the quiet night as my cue to stand, gathering my teacup to take to the kitchen. I allow myself a single glance before opening the large glass porch door. I can't see him, except for the outline of his shadow and his hands on the wheel, but every inch of my body tightens. Air flowing through my house caresses every inch of exposed skin.

There's not much, what with my cashmere burgundy sweater and leggings. Headlights illuminate glimpses of the picket fence and the planters outside as he makes his way to the back of the house.

Where am I supposed to be?

My room? The sitting room? He'll come through the kitchen, through the door in the back entrance, and I have the urge to present him with a pretty picture. A relaxed woman, waiting on him. Exactly how he'd like me to be. The heat of my skin only adds to the untamed gallops in my chest.

But I'm not that woman. This is not a normal evening, and Zander's not coming home to me. He's coming to do his job.

I want him to do that job. Call me a sinner, or whatever name suits me best; I can't help what I want.

Striding through to the kitchen, I offer Damon a tight smile when he peeks up at me, checking as he's done all day. When I flip on the recessed lights over the stove, I'm certain Zander will know I'm in here, and I wait in front of it. The tap to the heated water begs me to fill my cup and I do, then add in a fresh sachet. Inhaling the comforting aromas of peppermint and chamomile, I do what I can to calm myself.

My heart pounds with the silence of the day and with Damon's prying eyes.

Damon steps into the kitchen as Zander's headlights cut off. "Is there anything I can help you with?" he asks softly. He's almost casual about it, the way he might be if he were a guest in my house and not one of my bodyguards. *Or prison wardens,* as my internal voice sarcastically jokes.

I swallow hard and summon up a sentence for him. Better to get warmed up now, before Zander comes in. "It's just a cup of tea, so I can manage, thank you." It didn't hurt much at all. If I keep my voice low, the vibrations limited, I find it doesn't pain me like it used to.

"You were fairly quiet today. I hope you know you can come to me whenever you want to talk."

"I do. Thank you."

"And the notebook? Is there anything you'd like to share?" he questions and my smile is genuine in response.

"I've done a poor drawing I wouldn't want to bother you with." My shoulders relax and with the rough laughter from the man across from me, I smile into the cup of tea. A cup that needs to sit longer so the tea can steep.

Damon's got an easy smile. He's not like Zander. Zander has a seriousness that follows him like a thundercloud. Like a dark suit, though he doesn't wear one when he's here. He wore a suit for court, but that's not what he wears on the night shifts. Dark jeans, and a long-sleeved shirt. Clothes he can be comfortable in. It was my request. I remember staring Cade straight in the eye when I told him I didn't want to be outdressed and they were putting too much pressure on me. It was a joke, but the poor man took it seriously until I apologized for my dry humor. I'm grateful he allowed the change in dress code. They still read as professionals, and it does put me at ease, a little more than before.

Cade is the most serious and the least inviting; luckily, he's also rarely with me. Damon's casual outfit of a plum button-down shirt and jeans puts me at ease. As does his warmth. He's kind, although I'm more than certain he's capable of brutality. They all are. Yet another reason for them to wear anything but the harsh professionalism of suits.

The comfortable silence is broken with the click of the back door opening.

Zander greets us on a breeze that carries the scent of night air and crisp leaves. The amber in his hazel eyes flares low in the dim light from above the stove, deep like whiskey in a glass, and those eyes burn into mine for a beat too long. "Evening, Ella."

"Hi, Zander."

Damon crosses the kitchen to meet him, and the two men confer for a moment in low voices while I busy myself pretending to stir something nonexistent in my tea. I'm used to this. When they change shifts, they update each other on how the hours have gone. I imagine it's a boring conversation. Three days of this have passed and the most I've done is slept long hours, sketched in a notebook and stared at the sky from the lounge chair in the back.

Even through their lowered voices, I catch glimpses of their conversation. I'm welcome to add my own notes, but I haven't yet. My pulse races through the short update. I read in the sitting room, and I spent time in various areas of the house. Thinking and waiting. Waiting and thinking.

Passing the long day. I know I'm supposed to begin therapy sessions with Damon. Or else the professionals will be called in, which I'd rather didn't happen.

But I *want* to talk to Zander. I'm curious what it would be like to hear his secrets. I'll show him mine, if he'll show me his. The wicked thought curls up my lips and my moment of perversion is cut short by the fare-wells between the men.

Zander reaches out and claps Damon on the shoulder, a warm, famil-iar gesture, and then Damon leaves with a wave directed at me. The way he glances between the two of us when Zander isn't looking is knowing, and it pricks my nerves. Not so much, though, as it does when Zander's gaze reaches me.

The door closes behind him and I breathe in a new magnetism. With that boundary between Zander and me and the outside world, it feels like anything could happen. Electricity runs rampant in my veins but I don't react to it, except to say what I've been waiting to tell him since I woke up this morning. "I'd like a session."

He blinks before narrowing his gaze, hazel eyes deepening in the shad-ows near the door. An almost imperceptible tightening around his mouth tells me he's surprised, but otherwise he doesn't let on. Zander stands straight and tall in his hard body, his hands at his pockets, his posture alert but not rigid. "Where would you like to talk?"

"The sitting room."

It's nearly a dance. That's what it feels like to me. A give and a take. Each judging the other with every small step. Maybe I give myself too much credit, maybe I'm carried away by it all, but it gives me a reason to want, and I'm unwilling to give that up.

Zander gestures for me to lead the way, then falls into step next to me. My heart climbs up into my throat inch by inch until it flutters there like a trapped bird. He's the one to enter the sitting room first, flipping the switch to turn on the fireplace and then moving to a lamp in the corner. It's not very bright. The perfect complement to the fire burning brightly in its grate. He sits in a chair facing away from it and gestures to the one across from him.

I take it.

This—this is uncomfortable. The moment I'm sitting I don't know what to do with myself, or with my hands, but old habits kick in and I fold them neatly in my lap. Zander takes this in. His hazel eyes see everything.

"Kamden says this should be filmed," I say, though we've been over this. We've all been over this. "This will be recorded, right?"

"Everything is being recorded." He nods and adds, "Always."

His confirmation sets something off in me. Something deep, and old. A desire I thought was long gone. A very specific desire, tied to a very specific memory. A warm bar. Fingertips on my jaw, on my throat, on the neckline of my dress. Heat glides up the back of my neck and wraps around to meet the warmth in my cheeks. "Not for the professionals." I offer a huff of a laugh. "Just if I want it."

Zander cocks his head to the side. "For you?"

"To share with people." I already feel exposed to him. I already feel like I'm telling him deep secrets, and I'm just saying what I want into the space between us. "I haven't seen them in a long time."

"I'm not sure exactly what—"

Zander's calm, even tone is interrupted by the sound of the kitchen door banging open. Kam moves through the house with heavy footfalls. He knows I'm still awake. We were texting not too long ago. But I don't understand why he's here. I didn't ask for help.

He makes it to the archway of the sitting room before Zander holds up a hand. "We've just begun a session." I don't miss how his grip tightens on the edge of the chair.

Kamden's blue eyes dart between the two of us and I don't miss how his left brow rises slightly. The man knows me well. Gently he asks, completely ignoring Zander, "Do you have a moment for me, Ella?"

He crosses the room and crouches down in front of me. "You sounded off. In your texts."

"I'm fine." It hurts to say things in irritation, so I try to pull it back, but it's right there. I can feel it. Waiting to spill out. "You could have texted if you were concerned."

"Or checked in with The Firm," Zander comments and it takes great effort to keep my smirk hidden.

"I wanted to check on you … myself."

A tingle travels up the back of my neck. It's from a combination of guilt and unease. Kamden doesn't trust me. Not only that, but I'm certain the memories that haunt me have taken over a piece of him as well.

"I'm all right."

"You're sure?" he presses and the frustration is too great to keep my voice anything but tight.

"I have people here all the time." Like the man sitting behind him, waiting to have a session with me. "If something were really wrong, they would know about it."

Still Kamden stays where he is, between the two of us, unmoving and not believing me.

"I promise—" I run frustrated hands over my hair. "I'm trying to do what I'm supposed to do, Kam, can you please leave?"

Kam's jaw sets. "I won't leave. You don't seem well right now, and I'm not going to walk away until I'm sure you're all right."

Anger fuels an uncomfortable heat that forces my body to move. Not only that, but pain. Am I to be punished and not trusted forever now? He didn't come to see me nearly as much as I would have liked at the center, and now he comes unbidden?

This is so ridiculous. So over the top. I get up out of my chair so fast that Kam has to scramble for balance. "Then I'll be going to bed. We'll talk another night, Zander."

I push past where Kam stands still with disbelief. All day. I've waited all damn day for this, and Kam has to rush in like he knows everything. He doesn't know everything. None of them do. Kam might know the most, but that doesn't make this okay.

"Ella," Kam pleads with me in a tone that brings about a renewed sense of guilt.

I don't stop. "Wait. Ella." I don't turn around, even though it's Zander's voice behind me and not Kam's.

I get one foot on the bottom step and turn my head back to look at him. "Don't follow me," I snap, not realizing how close Zander is to me. So close my breath is stolen.

Zander's a foot away, maybe two. About to catch up with me. At my words his whole face changes into a commanding countenance. A hard one. A no-bullshit, no-nonsense expression that shakes me to the core. "Don't say that to me," he orders. "Ever."

Dominating. That's what he is.

And I like it. I like this about him. I crave that power radiating from him. It's as much need as it is desire.

I'm only vaguely aware that Kamden isn't in sight.

"Fine," I answer back. "Please, I want to be alone," I add and then turn on my heel and rush upstairs.

chapter 7

Zander

As part of its protective detail, partners with The Firm may conduct research on clients using record requests or background checks with or without their consent so long as information is attained in good faith and kept strictly confidential.

THE LARGE HOUSE IS QUIET EXCEPT FOR THE WIND BATTERING the sitting room windows. That, and my thundering pulse.

I listen for her. Of course I do. I strain to hear soft footsteps on the stairs or even the creak of the floor above me, but there's nothing. I check the security cameras from my phone. No sign of movement, either in the house or outside. Silent and still. If only my heart would settle.

Not much chance of that.

The only cameras to watch are focused on her sleeping form. Even with the darkness, her luscious curves tempt me.

My exhale is uneasy as I lean forward, my gaze moving from the laptop to my phone. I occupy one of the modern white chairs in the room, while my phone sits on the one beside me. Those two fucking songs burn holes in it. As if they'll whisper more of Ella's secrets.

Snatching it off the chair, I put in a pair of headphones, and lean back in the chair. The laptop sits on the small coffee table surrounded by the four chairs. The screen is still very much lit and the cameras prove to show nothing of use. I blame boredom most of all.

So—the songs. I hit play on the first one.

It nearly blows out my eardrums. Cursing under my breath, I stab at the volume buttons on my phone until it's less skull shattering. I'm grateful at least there wasn't a soul present to witness that stunt. Readjusting in my seat, I take a gulp of water, wishing it were whiskey, and set back to listen to the first of the two titles Ella said were her favorites.

My brow lifts as the first one plays.

The song turns out to be … cute. Even if it is about a love so strong it causes a heart attack. I prefer alternative to pop, but I can't say that I'm not surprised. It's the kind of song I wouldn't mind hearing on the radio, but not one I would turn to myself. Same with the second one.

Cute. They're cute, and maybe they used to reflect on her. Maybe these songs are an echo of the woman Ella used to be before the Rockford Center, and before we came on the scene. Before her "misunderstanding."

My eyelids get heavy with the beat. Not a usual response to pop music, I guess, but it's been a long night. My gaze finds Ella's sleeping form again. The prim and proper presentation she first put on are at odds with this melody.

She's not the kind of woman who listens to music like that anymore. Whatever happened to her has weighed her down. So much, in fact, that I can't imagine her dancing to this music. I can't imagine her with an infectious, broad smile on her face and a lightness to her step.

I could, though …

My eyes widen as the thought strikes me. The information on Ella is out there, as evidenced by plenty of social media posts. Maybe even videos on YouTube or in the depths of Google. If I wanted to spend five minutes searching for it or reading her file, I'm sure I could find plenty of information regarding Ella's former life.

At this point, I'd have to go with a broad internet search. I lean toward that over the paperwork Cade gave me. If the file has been heavily curated by her manager, which Ella hinted at before, then they'll have left out any unsavory matters. Let alone instances in which "Heart Attack" and "Sit

Still, Look Pretty" would rear their jubilant heads. It won't be the whole story. Nothing will be the whole story—not without Ella telling parts of it. But I could get hints. Glimpses of what she was like before.

It would mean going against my own personal code for clients. It would mean crossing another line, even if Ella never knows. A hundred justifications fill my mind, but the one that shouts the loudest is the one that's desperate to know a side of her that may be lost forever.

Tossing my phone down, I bring the laptop back in front of me and my thumb taps softly on the space bar. I don't dare press it. I don't do anything but flick through the cameras once again. Hating that there's nothing to watch but her. A woman who already occupies too much of my mind.

I take my time with a few more checks to confirm that everything is under control—and that Ella isn't coming back down—and I finally settle on scratching that itch and sating my curiosity, opening up a tab to search her name. There's relative privacy in here to conduct my "research."

It's not unusual to investigate the pasts of our clients when necessary. Most notably if their story doesn't add up. It used to amaze me how many lies we'd be told that only added to the threat. As if they'd rather die in a lie than live in the truth. This, though … this type of search is unwarranted. My entire body knows this search is different, from the hairs rising on the back of my neck to the uneven beat of my heart. Excitement and adrenaline and trepidation. I don't feel a thirst for knowledge like this with other clients. I never have. But I knew Ella was different from the moment I first laid eyes on her.

Four-count breaths. Four times. Then my mind is clear enough to type in her name. My thumb hovers over the enter key for only a split second.

It's easy.

Too easy.

This is no back-alley hunt through the dark web with exchanges of cryptocurrencies and code words. Every tap of the keys echoes under the sound of the wind against glass. Scroll. Click. Scroll. There are numerous videos to choose from. So many with small thumbnail images of Ella's face. One of her giving the camera the middle finger forces the corners of my lips up. None of them seem too current. All dating from two years ago and further. A tick in the back of my mind notes that it seems some things have been cleared. I'll have to dig deeper for those if there were takedown notices issued.

She has the typical social media platforms. Although I don't dig through those just yet.

Refining the search, and clicking away, I scroll past more photos.

They're all so different from the Ella I know now. The version of a younger, stronger woman in all these thumbnail pictures doesn't have dark smudges under her eyes. Even in the photos, she doesn't appear still and quiet and wounded. I couldn't picture this past-life version of her before, and now that it's in front of me, the change in her is stark and jarring.

A few videos appear in the search, the name of the site flicking on a switch of alarm. Several clicks and my gaze drifts back to her sleeping form, before I go against my better judgment, and follow the link.

More than the pictures, more than the videos themselves, I'm drawn to the comments.

Given that the site has subheadings that include "hardcore," "girl on girl," and "amateur," I'm prepared for some type of deviant evidence to appear. Searching her name, more than twenty videos appear. Each of them displaying her face. Her head is thrown back with pleasure written in her expression. One of her leaning forward in the middle of a bar, her legs spread on the sofa, her attitude playful, yet seductive, and both of her hands wrapped around a champagne bottle, the bubbly spilling down the side. She's clothed in the stills, but I'd be surprised if she remained that way once I clicked on them.

Slipping the headphones into place, I do another check of the monitors, before returning to the site. I have … specific tastes so I'm not unfamiliar with websites that cater to a certain clientele.

Each video post has hundreds of comments underneath. These are the digital footprints of people who have sat where I'm sitting. They watched these videos in the glow of a hundred different screens, in different sitting rooms and bedrooms and basements.

My body hums with the recognition that this is technically research, but still … jealousy and possessiveness threaten to piss me off. My skin pebbles with goosebumps and my breathing comes fast and shallow and my hands—

My hands are clenched into fists so tight that my knuckles are white above the keyboards.

It's all because of these fucking comments. Men and women who watched her and discussed it freely. With anxiousness, I shift in my seat, noting each of the videos falls under the category labeled "Exhibitionist."

There's an enormous variety in the types of comments made. Some are completely irrelevant, a simple thumbs-up or emoji. Then there are other, more detailed comments and conversations. Feminist opinions. Misogynistic ones.

And summaries of what happens within the clips.

Summaries—and reactions.

I can't help lingering on those. The first few comments are written in all caps. Ten, twenty exclamation points. They urge the viewers to keep watching. *It gets hotter*, the comments read.

It only takes ten minutes to start recognizing names of the users. Some have returned to the videos again and again, the comments providing that evidence with the dates beside the comments. I recognize two usernames in particular—two men in conversation across multiple videos.

One conversation in particular gives me insight I didn't imagine I'd ever find on a site like this. Dated four years ago.

Where's the one with her on her knees?
Deleted. :(
Fuck me. That was one of my favorites. This one's close, but not the real deal.
It went down with the others when they got engaged. He decides what stays and what goes.
Selfish bastard.

Engaged. Ella was engaged before. A concoction of emotion stronger than whiskey hits me all at once. She was engaged, and from the looks of it, the two of them had a shared proclivity to be watched.

The Dominant side of me shifts in my seat from the uncertainty of their relationship. My preference has always been for discretion when I indulge. The level of discretion displayed in these videos is obviously a different boundary than I have ever committed to.

I almost close the laptop, my mind reeling with more questions than answers, but I stop myself short, one thumbnail calling out to me more than all the others.

The thumbnail is a still of Ella, like the rest, but in this one she wears a bright, innocent smile. When I click through it has the most comments of any of the videos I've searched for in the last half hour.

I can barely focus on them. The first line I read several times, and still the words don't register. I'm not a fool; I know what I'm going to see when I click the play button. Still, I know I shouldn't. And yet, I know I will.

Ella's simper reaches right through the screen to me. Her teeth are sunk into her bottom lips, painted a cherry red as she sits on a man's lap. The man's hand wrapped around her waist splays across her hip. It's a loose hold on her, not at all possessive. The black man smiles, his focus elsewhere as she stares at the camera, a beer held in his right hand. It's not hard to tell that they're at a bar. In public. The mischievousness that glinted in her eyes yesterday morning is there in this photo. Begging me to play.

I have to click play. That's part of the research. Witnessing this is my job. A barely audible voice whispers that it's not my job. That watching these videos—labeled as pornographic in no uncertain terms—could be avoided. No, *should* be avoided.

I don't want to avoid it, though. I'm damn sure of that.

The comments under this particular video are about how it's the beginning. The commenters say it over and over. This is the beginning. This is how it started. How the incident began and to keep watching.

From one of the familiar names, I read the comment, *It's her foreplay.*

I hover my cursor over the video, and it plays a few seconds in a loop. She's not alone in this three-second clip. Far from alone. I know the place— it's a Hard Rock in Vegas. The background is crowded with patrons coming and going. There's no possibility that anything salacious could happen within this public venue. But whatever did happen, it's clear the other woman in the video was involved.

Because she has her fingertips on Ella's jaw. I'm caught for a long minute watching the three-second clip of her tracing her pale pink painted nails down Ella's jaw, down her neck, and even lower, to where her black-sequined dress barely covers her. The hemline skimming her thighs makes my mouth dry up. Clearing my throat, I check the empty room again. Comforted by silence, I return to the two women.

A hard swallow, watching them, in what I would guess is their midtwenties. The second woman's caramel skin is a few shades darker than Ella's. Her black hair is loosely curled and as Ella leans into her touch, she plays with her friend, or lover's, curls.

The video begins with the other woman, dressed in black leather leggings and a burgundy crop top that shows a sliver of her olive-brown skin, tracing her fingertips over Ella's skin. Over her neck, where I want to touch her. And lower, to where my entire body wishes to be. The two women are standing close to a high-top table, their backs to the crowd. And the way they're looking at each other, the way they're touching—

I scroll back down to the comments. Someone identifies the woman as Maggie, her friend. The name suits her, with her girl-next-door smile and expressive eyes. The comments are also right that the scene is hot, but it's not just hot.

There's something … suspenseful about it. The man she was with in the thumbnail watches in the background, his gaze mostly focused on Maggie, but it shifts to Ella as the two women clink cocktail glasses filled with a pink liquid. Over the pounding music, you can barely make out their laughter.

Though they're standing in the bar, it doesn't seem sleazy or even staged, the way most porn on the internet appears. Two women, flirting innocently with each other. Every so often, their eyes go to people outside the frame. I keep the volume down low, really low, but when they speak and I miss what was said, I have to turn it up a notch and then another.

There's not an ounce of shame. And from what I gather on the site, this isn't professional and nothing Ella would be paid for. This isn't her job, it's her life, her wants and desires.

I wonder if she knew it was being filmed. There's no doubt when she stares at the camera, not more than a handful of seconds later, blushing and leaning closer to Maggie to whisper in her ear, all the while keeping her eyes on the camera, that she knows.

A genuine enjoyment shines in her eyes. It sparks in Maggie's too.

"More drinks!" she shouts out of nowhere, downing the beverage in her hand through the thin black straw. The video continues with the two of them dancing, drinking, and Ella finding herself between two men. The front of one whose face is never shown, and the tall, cleanly shaven black man who towers over her. I wonder if he was her fiancé. Although I don't have to wonder for long. Maggie joins them and doesn't hesitate to kiss the man. She calls him Noah. There's a possessiveness but then she holds Ella's gaze, bumping her shoulder into her and the two of them share a sinful look.

And Ella responds to Maggie's touch. Little shivers. Little glances. And those raised eyebrows at someone else behind the camera. The dancing continues and eventually it's the two women again, partying and laughing. For a moment it seems like it was all in good fun and there wasn't a damn thing sordid between any of them. Until they're at the bar and a conversation takes place.

I'm desperate to know what they're saying. A little more volume, and—

"—all play," Ella's saying, to whoever is holding the camera—a phone, I'm assuming. Judging by how the video is in short snippets, and even then, the camera pans and shakes as one would if it were a phone.

I back it up a few seconds.

"We could all play." Ella's grin is a sultry, sparkling thing. "You know I don't mind playing."

A male voice answers her from behind the camera. "Be careful now, kitten." My blood heats at the nickname. *Kitten.*

Maggie's squeal of delight comes with her toppling forward into the frame, a coiled muscular arm wrapping around her waist to keep her steady. "Noah!"

"You better get your girl," jokes a male voice I haven't heard yet. A deep one. If I had to guess, it would be the man from earlier. Answering my guess, he comes into the screen. Noah, Maggie and Ella … but who's the fourth? I pause, rubbing my eyes and then flicking back through the security cameras.

Is he her fiancé? There's no ring on her finger. My mind races with dates and information I gathered from comments. This must be a video from before. I wonder if Ella isn't the one who uploaded these. I wonder if she doesn't want them available any longer. I wonder, for a moment and then another, if she thinks it was a mistake. But there's no doubt in my mind that if a woman with her wealth didn't want these available, they'd vanish. Just like all media of Ella from the last two years seems to have vanished.

At this point, lines haven't been crossed. I could stop while I'm ahead and read the damn file.

My better judgment tells me not to continue. For my own damn good. With the click of my thumb, I refuse the warning, and watch the scene continue.

Ella pouts subtly, the expression so cute on her lips that it crushes some hidden part of my chest. She shrugs and says, "I'm just having fun."

Maggie's thick curls falling down her front, she rests her head on Ella's shoulder to whisper, "I'm into your kind of fun," and this time, it's Maggie's eyes that find the camera. Biting down on her lower lip, she angles away from the camera, burying her head into Ella's neck.

The scene at the bar continues in short clips. More drinks, more dancing and accidental bumps into one another. The alcohol flows heavily. That's one thing I note the most. They're all drinking, laughing, having a good time.

It's only when the women glance at the camera that anything at all seems provocative.

This video is made up of multiple segments, most of them of Maggie and Ella. Whoever is holding the camera wants their faces and nothing else.

My body temperature rises, and I strip off the long-sleeved shirt I wore tonight. I'd take off the T-shirt underneath if it wouldn't be so obviously unprofessional.

Glancing down at the time, it's only two minutes in when the camera moves to an elevator. Swallowing thickly, I brace myself for what's coming next.

It's inevitable. The four of them together, the girls laughing and teasing the camera. Swingers, maybe? Fuck buddies? I anticipate them kissing in the closed space.

That's what's logically next and surprisingly, I don't want to stop it.

She wants this.

At least in the moment she did. Her dark chestnut gaze is filled with lust as the man behind the camera steps in beside her and the sound of the doors closing accompanies giddy, feminine laughter from Maggie.

It's undeniable that I'm just as worked up in this moment as each of them.

Damn, I want her. I want to reach through the screen and put my hands on her hips. I want to run my thumbs over her jaw and feel that flirtatious smirk. I want to corner her in, a hand on each side of the steel wall behind her and feel the vibrations of her voice when she laughs, which she does often. Again and again in these videos. It's sexy as hell, and taunting—a subtle game they're playing.

It's sexy as fuck. Portraying the act of seduction. If I were there, confined in that space, I'd punish her for it, for allowing everyone to see. I want it all for me.

She'd have to beg me for even considering letting anyone else see that look in her eye, if she were my submissive. I'm rock hard imagining it and contemplating if I would allow it.

With an undertone of something else, something familiar, Ella gets this look in her eyes when she looks at the camera the second the doors close. "James?" She says his name then, almost as if asking permission, or maybe to make sure everything is all right. There's no doubt he's her partner in this. He replies easily and with a tone of approval, "Good girl, kitten."

The phrase brings a glint to her dark eyes, sparking a fire in their depths.

It makes my pulse race. It makes my skin tense. I don't let myself dwell on it for long.

Not that I'm given a chance. The next scene cuts to explicit pornography without any easing into it.

Maggie's slender legs are wrapped around James's waist on the right side of the screen as he thrusts into her. Her eyes are closed in ecstasy and she moans in short staccato cadence in time with the pounding of his hips meeting hers. On the left side of the same bed, Ella is on her knees, her fingers digging into the sheets and Maggie's hand grips hers. Behind Ella, Noah fucks her mercilessly. It's zoomed out, so details are obscure, but not so much that the full picture isn't painted.

"Fuck," Ella breathes into the pillow before biting down on it. Her face is flushed and her full breasts sway with each punishing thrust. Noah's fingers dig into her hips, keeping her exactly where he wants her. A thin lather of sweat glistens from his shoulders. The men's backs are to the camera, leaving the women exposed to the viewer. As Ella's head is thrown back, her gaze meets the lens, and in that moment, she screams out her orgasm.

As much as I want to focus on her, I don't miss how James's concentration moves to Ella in that moment. His gaze stays on her as she calls out her release, balling up the sheets and bringing them closer to her chest. With her head buried in the blankets, Noah races for his own pleasure, fucking her harder and faster.

James takes it as his cue to reposition Maggie, bringing her calves to his shoulder and climbing up higher on the bed until her knees are at her shoulders and her dark eyes go wide. The cords in her neck tighten and she no longer reaches to Ella to hold her hand. Instead, her nails dig into James's back as he eases into her, slowly at first and then deeper, faster, taking Maggie closer to a dangerous edge.

"Yes, yes," Maggie chants between clenched teeth, her pitch getting higher as she fuels James on and he picks up his pace, fucking her relentlessly.

Ella claws across the bed, barely holding on as she writhes under Noah, who slams inside of her, finding his own release.

My cock aches with need at the sight of her drowning in pleasure.

With all of them breathing heavily, lips meet the curves of the women's necks and then their panting slows and small pecks turn deeper. Ella and Maggie got what they wanted. All four of them in one hotel room.

Swapping partners, and once again, they each seek out the camera.

It's porn, what I'm looking at. Homemade porn. No one would call it anything else. I anticipate that being the end but as James stands, it becomes apparent he isn't finished. I size up the man and find him not lacking in both stature and frame. He's classically handsome, dark hair, a clean shave like Noah, preppy even. Toned but not overly muscular. The video captures him pulling off the condom as Noah and Maggie help each other dress. The profile of the two of them kissing blocks my view of Ella, but from the bits that can be seen, she's thrown the covers over herself.

As James's condom falls to a trash can tucked under a desk on the other side of the room, Noah lets out a rough huff of a laugh.

"You cheated," Noah comments from across the room and he's met with a smirk from James. Fully clothed, he nods at a naked James. "You definitely took a V."

James only huffs a laugh before reaching for the phone. Again I expect the video to end, but it doesn't.

"Night, love," James says and the sound of a single kiss is heard. The camera faces a blank wall as they all bid their farewells.

I'm hard as a rock.

Watching her. Watching them. One moment brings my thoughts to a screeching halt. Her ex is leaning over her on the bed. His hand goes to her throat, and Ella takes a breath. One breath. One arch of her back. And I know. I know it for a fact, what she likes, what she wants.

What I could give to her.

And what I can never give to her.

Fuck.

The rustling of the sheets is heard and the camera is positioned face up on a pillow, so all that can be seen is the ceiling.

"Spread your legs for me," James whispers and the camera rocks as James continues to fuck Ella, her sweet moans heard in between sounds of them kissing. It's all audio for the last minute when it finally ends with the camera falling off the bed and hitting the floor.

I watch them again and again. This video. The one from the bar. Every other video in the set. They span a seven-year period with nearly half of them from the first two years. Then only a video a year, some with two. The bar scene is the last one. Not all of them feature her ex, but he's there in some capacity for most of them. The night turns to a deep black, black as my soul must be from watching this and confirming my suspicions. The autumn fire of dawn catches in slow increments as I watch and watch and watch.

Once it's over, I click back to the cameras, flicking through the videos of nothing. Not a damn thing has changed, yet it feels like everything has.

"Hey."

Damon's voice scares the living shit out of me, but I control it. I control the startle reflex and the wild hum of my pulse and nod at his silhouette from across the room in the morning light. Rubbing my hands over my face, I play it off as exhaustion. I close the laptop gently as if I've been doing the kind of research that involves files and records and interviews. "Hey." If I were a better man, I'd feel any sort of shame, but at the moment, I don't.

"She still sleeping?" he asks.

"I haven't heard any movement."

He nods. "You're good to go."

I don't wait a second to get the hell out of that room. I want to stay too badly to wait. More than anything, I want to take the steps up to Ella's bedroom two at a time and show her I understand, at least a little more. I understand the part of her who could use attention that I could give her. At least for a little while. Not forever, because nobody wants a fucked-up prick like me forever. But I could satisfy a part of her that shares reciprocal needs and give us both a much-needed distraction.

chapter 8

Ella

A partner of The Firm will immediately respond to a client's distress signals by providing one-on-one support. This may include a counseling session, medical attention, or an otherwise agreed-upon mediation.

TODAY IS NOT A GOOD DAY. THERE ARE GOOD DAYS AND THERE are bad days. "Bad" isn't a strong enough word for how fucking awful they are, but I suppose it's the appropriate counter to good. The moment I woke up, I knew every minute was going to be harder than the last. The moment my eyes opened and I forgot, then remembered … that was my warning. It's an emptiness that takes over initially. It seeps slowly within me throughout the day, making the tips of my fingers cold at first and then it spreads. My mouth turns dry, my stomach empty but I don't wish to fill it. I don't want to be warm, I don't want my thirst quenched. The only desire is to sit in it, to feel that desolation so as to ensure I won't forget again. Because how could I have possibly forgotten? How could I not wake up every day and feel that loss?

Tears prick at the back of my already tired eyes and like always, I ignore them. I don't allow anything to fall. I've never been a fan of crying. Not since I was a little girl and the videos of me mourning my mother being taken from me, her subsequent suicide, and my father's treatment toward me … it all led to useless tears and each video I'd made was played back until I realized how much I truly hated the act of crying. So if I can, I withhold it; I acknowledge the urge, but I don't like to see the tears fall.

Instead, I blow across the steam of the fifth cup of tea I've made today. I thought Damon may have been able to smell the whiskey remnants in the last cup. I thought when he left after he offered to pick up for me and refill it, that he would go check the surveillance feed and discover I'd spiked the drink.

I've never held my breath over the judgment of a man I'm not sleeping with, but I'd be damned if I said I didn't then. All day, he's given me space, allowed me to simply lie here, the television screen on, yet with only a logo blinking across it since I haven't pressed play for hours.

Kam slipped me an apology package a couple days ago after our blowup, six little glass bottles of amber warmth. It's an expensive variety and they fit neatly in the small pocket of my robe. I've gone through three so far today. Well, two and a half. The rest of the previous bottle is tucked away beneath the throw pillow under my arm. I hid it there just in case Damon came back with accusations rather than a fresh cup.

Luckily for me, Damon doesn't suspect anything. If he does, he allows me to have it without mentioning it. Every day, I trust him more. I told him so just yesterday and before he left, he told me every day he trusted me more too. It would be horrid of me to break that trust the very next day.

The thought hovers at the back of my mind as I blow across the tea, feeling the billow of steam tickle the tip of my nose.

I don't sip; it's far too hot as it is. The ceramic clinks as I set it down on the mahogany coffee table and lay back into the tan tweed sofa. The walls of the rec room are an off-white hue and if I truly wished to drift off to sleep, I know I would have emptied that little glass bottle just like Alice did on her way to Wonderland. I also would have chosen the much darker sitting room, or the guest bedroom with its thick velvet curtains.

Choosing the rec room, choosing to prop my head up on the pillow rather than bury my face into the cushion, choosing to turn on the television, although I have amazingly failed at such a simple task of watching a mundane home improvement show that I would have devoured years ago—all of that—proves I'm fighting sleep. The steam drifts from the teacup and I watch it dissipate in the dim light from the sconce on the far wall.

There's a soft creak of the floorboards behind the entryway and I nearly give in to the instinct to look, but I refuse it. If I make eye contact with Damon or someone else, they'll ask me questions.

"Do you need anything?" "What is it you want?" "Can I do something to help?"

Every question adds a weight to my chest. I don't have answers for myself, let alone anyone else. Especially right now, when I'm having trouble fighting back my demons.

Let me be. Let them swallow me whole. Why should they concern themselves with the devil of a hell only I'm invited to?

"There you are." The rough timbre from behind me is soothing as it caresses every inch of me. I hear him, I feel him; his presence overwhelms me before I even open my eyes.

I don't want him now, though. Not like this. Not when I'm barely holding on.

My eyes are barely open as I watch him, remaining completely still where I am sprawled across the sofa. I'm aware my robe is open slightly, the delicate silk so easily parted. Beneath it is what I wore to bed last night, a simple chiffon chemise.

I anticipate the questions. At the very least, some variation of, "How are you today?" And when they don't come, some insecurity I'm not at all comfortable with wonders if he'll chastise me for my attire. Of all the things in the world, that sneaks to the surface. My father's scolds reverberate in the back of my skull, springing up from the depths I'd pushed them to decades ago.

My gaze shifts from the hem of my nightgown, where apparently shame resides, to a dark gray fleece blanket that's gently placed over my body.

With my lips parted in protest, I meet Zander's gaze and I'm silenced by it. The intensity. The ownership.

It steals everything from me.

"You'll be cold without it," is the only explanation he offers me. As he steps away from the sofa, I wish I had the courage to tell him I'm cold with it as well, but I'm silent.

He's donned a faded pair of jeans he wears often, I absently wonder if they're his favorite, and a white, long-sleeved polo. Simple yet still seemingly refined on a rugged man like him. Especially when paired with his five o'clock shadow.

The moment I prepare to ask for privacy, already feeling the disappointment growing in my chest, Zander stands, leaving the long chair on the side of the room and instead taking a seat at the end of the sofa I'm occupying. The sofa groans, the sound swallowing the protest that's caught at the back of my throat. He's so very close, I nearly have to bend my legs even further so my feet won't be in the way. As it is, I don't have to, nor do I dare move at all.

Although I do have the urge to stretch out my legs and place my feet in his lap. I resist it successfully, though, waiting instead for Zander to speak.

I haven't wanted to see anyone else, let alone talk all morning and evening, but right now the only thing screaming to be heard from my lips is *speak*.

I want an explanation. The men typically stay several feet away, but Zander seems to have forgotten that. He stretches out casually, although his stiffness tells me he's anything but.

Leaning back, he exhales in an exaggerated huff and then peers down at me.

I don't have the willpower for silence any longer, so I ask the first thing that comes to mind, "Did you give in to curiosity and read my file?"

"Almost …" he admits and my stomach churns. I used to pride myself on how few fucks I gave over anyone's opinion. Right now, though, it's as if we're surrounded by these fucks like wildflowers in a field. Flowers that could be easily plucked if only he wanted.

"Can you promise me something?" I question and then clear my throat, taking a moment to sip the now lukewarm tea.

"Depends on what it is."

"Don't read it." I speak without daring to look at him.

"Don't read the file, or don't look into your past?"

"Both?" I say, with more hope in my tone than I'd like.

"What if I already know some things?"

I fret under his scrutiny, and place the teacup back down on the table rather than answering.

"I promise I won't read the file, and I'll come to you if I have questions about … well, you."

"No FBI digging?"

"Does the FBI have a file too?"

"Not that I'm aware of." Although my comment is dry, Zander laughs. It's that genuine, rough laugh that's deep and soothing in ways it shouldn't be.

I chew on the inside of my cheek to keep from asking him what he knows. Shifting under the blanket, I realize how cold I was before. It's already warmer, already promising me sleep.

After a moment of only silence, Zander says, "I could read, or I could talk … Or I could listen."

"I'd rather not talk today."

"Mmm," he hums in a deep rumble, "and of course today was the day I chose to bombard you with questions."

I give him a small laugh, part of it genuine.

"You have questions, don't you? Questions for me?" he asks and the opening he's given me grabs my attention.

"You and Cade are brothers?"

"That's an easy one. And yes, we are."

"You look alike but your last name is what gave it away."

"That'll do it," he comments.

"Have you always been close?"

His brow pinches and he quickly exhales. "No. Not at all."

I don't have to pry further. He freely offers me his story, which includes another brother I didn't know about—William.

"He was six years older than me and from that alone you'd think he'd have been the responsible one. There was him, then Cade and then three years later, me, the baby brother."

It's hard to imagine a man like Zander as the baby.

"Our mom passed away while I was a freshman in college. Our dad had cancer and Cade and William were arguing over a few things."

"I'm so sorry," I tell him and his hand falls onto my calf where he gives me a gentle squeeze. The blanket separates us, but still, his touch ignites me. It doesn't seem to bother him in the least. As if touching me were the natural thing to do.

His swallow is audible and when he doesn't continue, instead staring ahead at the same logo flitting across the television that's kept me company for hours, I nearly push for more, but I don't have to. He leans forward with a huff, grabbing the remote and turning the TV off altogether while telling me the rest of it.

"William wanted my father to live with him during chemo treatments. Cade refused to let it happen. William owed him money and had a gambling addiction. He accused William of trying to take our father's income."

Shock widens my eyes. "That ... couldn't have gone over well."

Shaking his head, Zander agrees. "They were fighting on the front porch, screaming at each other. I jumped in the middle of it to tell them both off. The three of us were yelling like crazy and that's when my father got pissed off and told us all to go home." Zander licks his lower lip, then offers me a sad smile. "He died later that night."

The tears prick again, but I can't hold them back this time. "I'm so sorry," I tell him and wipe under my eyes.

"It happened eight years ago now. But I didn't speak to either of my brothers for years after, other than the occasional text on holidays and birthdays. We were close. Then one day ... we weren't."

"What changed?"

"I went through some things two years ago and Cade was there."

"What about William?"

"I was never close with William. He and Cade have their history, but it's the same with William as it's always been. I hear from him when he needs something."

"I'm sorry to hear that."

"You're awfully sorry for me tonight," Zander says as if it's a joke. "Want to know the dirt on Cade from when we were in high school?" he offers with a smirk. "You can't tell him I told you, though."

"You're awful," I say and gently brush my foot against his thigh as if it's an admonishment, although a smile is clearly seen on my face. "And of course I do. Spill it."

The next stories are far more entertaining, although I find myself comparing his childhood experiences to mine. His are … so much more innocent than my own. Even with things like sneaking out at night and replacing his father's bourbon with colored water being his examples of why they were bad children, they weren't at all compared to the horrific shit I got into. My father was long gone by then, though. If Kam hadn't been there for me, I'd have gone off the deep end ages ago.

I don't tell Zander that. I simply listen to his tales as if they were sweet lullabies. The soothing cadence of his deep voice distracts me from my previous plans.

Time slips by much faster than it did before.

My eyes are heavy as my head sinks deeply into the soft down feather pillow. As I shrug my shoulder in an attempt to pull the soft fleece higher, Zander aids me, tugging the blanket up and tucking it under my chin.

With a simper gracing my lips, I peek up at him and he offers me the kind of smile that threatens to break me. A kind one. Sincere and hopeful.

My own vanishes and I close my eyes tighter, feigning exhaustion as I rub my eyes and destroy his efforts to keep the blanket tucked over me securely. I nearly ask him to go, but I don't. As the tears come, I pull the blanket up higher, hiding and wanting to bury myself in it. Maybe I'll regret it, but right now, I'd regret not leaning into him more than anything if I don't do it this second.

I crawl closer to him, turning around so I'm able to push my body into his. His left arm raises, giving me room and I put the pillow on his thigh. At least I give him that to separate us. My breathing struggles as I bury my head there, pretending the dams haven't broken. His arm lays easily against my body, the weight of it hugging my curves. His warmth is instant. He doesn't shush me, but he does hum lightly; it's a soothing rumble.

The overwhelming sadness came from nothing and it feels like everything. I swear I was okay. I was.

With heat rising to my face as tears pool under my eyes, I focus on his strong hand splayed over my hip, his thumb rubbing soothing motions.

The sobs take over; I can't control them. I wish I could hide my face better, but Zander refuses to let me, brushing the hair out of my face. In an attempt to swat away his hand so I can hide beneath my dark locks, I lift my arm, but his grip is faster. Catching my wrist in his hand.

Inhaling deeply, I peer up at him through my thick lashes, tainted with beads of tears. My vision is still blurry when the rough pad of his thumb runs under my eyes. One at a time, ever so gently, and at odds with the calluses he's earned over the years.

The distraction pulls me from my outburst and a moment passes and then another before my breathing has steadied again, and I'm able to fully recollect what happened.

Neither of us speaks for a long moment as I calm myself, taking in long inhales and blowing out even longer exhales.

He's the first to speak and although I dread it, I'm grateful he takes the lead in the conversation.

"Do you know what brought it on?" he questions me just as I'm re-playing the scene in my mind. Shaking my head I whisper no and consider moving, but he's still running those soothing circles through the thin fabric of my nightgown. More importantly, the pillow shifted at some point behind me, and now my cheek rests firmly against his thigh. The jeans aren't nearly as comfortable pressed against my skin, but they smell like him.

And he's so damn warm. Everything about him is comforting. Almost familiar in some strange way.

"I don't know," I add and note that my throat feels like it's on fire. I barely even spoke today. Just as I'm reaching up to my throat, Zander reaches across me, one hand holding me in place, the other picking up the cup and handing it to me.

"Drink and tell me if you need it warm," he commands. I obey, the peppermint soothing even though the tea is now cold.

"Sometimes it'll come from nowhere," he says as if justifying my outburst but then he adds, "Are you familiar with the 'ball in a box' analogy?"

I shake my head, never having heard of it. He explains, "The ball is large, filling the box when grief first appears. There's a small button on one side of the box but the ball is so big it constantly bumps against it, triggering the emotional response. As time goes on, the ball shrinks in size, moving and colliding into the walls and occasionally, the button. There's no stopping it and no matter how small the ball gets, there's always a chance it will hit the button. There's no preventing it."

"I think my ball might be very big," is all I can comment.

Zander nods and says, "There's nothing wrong with that."

A long moment passes of comfortable silence before Zander seems to take note of our proximity.

"You're tired—"

Before he's even said it, I know he's going to tell me I need to go to bed. So I cut him off and say, "I don't want to sleep."

A moment passes, with the click of the heater coming on ensuring we're both aware of just how silent it is between us. For the second time tonight, I feel insecure wondering what his response will be. Whether he'll respect my desire to stay up or not. Or if he'll push me to go to bed. "Please don't make me," I plead with him in a whisper. It's a foolish request.

"I won't ever make you do anything you don't want to. Unless it's for your own good."

I raise a brow in question, unable to help myself from saying, "And sleeping in bed?"

Staring at me, he takes a moment longer before ignoring my question altogether and asking me, "I just remembered another time Cade got in trouble and blamed it on me. Do you want to hear it?"

There's a pull at the corners of my lips and I nod before lying back down where I was, pulling the gray fleece up and setting the pillow back down. I'm more than aware of how inappropriate it is, and how little I care.

And this is how I drift off to sleep. Listening to stories told in the soothing cadence of a man I consider confessing all my stories to.

chapter 9

Zander

*Partners of The Firm will maintain appropriate professional
conduct with clients at all times.*

ELLA DRIFTS TO SLEEP ON MY LAP.

But I've never been more awake in my life. I couldn't sleep if I wanted to. I keep talking long after she's out, until my throat goes so dry I can't say another word. Every heartbeat feels like an electric shock. What we're doing is *technically* within the bounds of her contract with The Firm. That's what I tell myself, at least. Professional conduct can include physical touch. It's impossible to avoid sometimes when you're providing security for a client. You take their arm and shield them from prying eyes as they exit a vehicle, or a building. You tuck them into your side when moving through an unruly crowd.

My hands have been on both male and female clients before. Not once has it been an issue. Not once has it been … like *this*.

There are provisions for physical touch in Ella's contract too. I know there are. I know because we had a team meeting about it when Cade pitched the case to the rest of us. There was no way around it. We're here twenty-four hours a day and we are required, *required*, to provide emotional support.

But this …

Does not feel like providing emotional support.

It feels like knocking down brick walls with a sledgehammer, for the both of us. Her walls are obvious and where my attention should be, yet I can't help but to notice my own. The one I've kept in place for years now. It feels like giving something to myself just as much as it feels like giving something to her.

There aren't any provisions for that in the contract. I don't get anything out of this but a salary. That's the rule, and them's the breaks.

Too fucking bad.

I stretch out my free arm—the one not running softly up and down the bare skin exposed by the sleeve of Ella's robe riding up slightly. My hand splays out under the throw pillow on the sofa in my effort to stretch.

And meets glass.

A tiny glass bottle.

I pull it out and examine it in the light. It's one of those miniature bottles of alcohol.

Are you fucking kidding me? The disbelief is as palpable as the discontent.

No wonder she looked like she was going to pass out. She'd been drinking. Not much, given the size of the bottle, and it shouldn't react badly with the meds she's on. Assuming she only had one.

But she shouldn't be drinking at all. We were supposed to clear the house of all alcohol before she moved in. I thought we'd gotten rid of it all. *How the hell did this get past Damon?*

Irritation wars with concern inside of me. This could have gone so very wrong.

Ella's shoulders rise and fall with a whimper, almost as if she can feel my disappointment with her. And there's that wall again, destroyed and leaving me wanting nothing more than to refuse any backsteps after the moment I had with her tonight.

My thumbnail taps against the glass and I know it's something to look into, but not something I can do a damn thing about right now.

It's a problem for later. After deciding what to do about the matter, I tuck the bottle back under the pillow.

"Ella."

She doesn't wake. Doesn't so much as stir. Her breathing has gone slow and even. I imagine she needs a deep sleep, but even so I monitor her breathing and when she stirs, fighting the urge to wake up, I let her fall back under, rather than rousing her to consciousness.

She can't sleep here. I'm quiet as I stand, preparing to take her upstairs and put her in her bed. The idea of putting her to bed is met with thoughts that shouldn't be anywhere on my mind. Specifically: reddening her ass with my itching palm for hiding alcohol.

Even that small thought has my cock hardening.

Fuck.

Calm focus. Four-count breaths. Four times over. There are eyes everywhere in this house. Cameras. Every move I make needs to be carefully considered, because even if I alter some of the footage, there can be nothing suspicious about the rest, nothing to indicate that my heart is beating out of my chest and I want to kiss her awake. Run roughshod over her boundaries. And punish her ass so she won't sneak alcohol again.

So damn badly.

More than I've wanted anything since Quincy.

But I don't kiss her. I'm a goddamn professional, and I don't kiss her. I maneuver Ella into my arms in a chaste carry, her warm body curled against my chest. Her head rests easily against my shoulder. She's so deeply asleep I have to cradle her tighter than I otherwise would. Far tighter than would be considered professional.

The herringbone stairs leading up to the second floor are dark, but I trust them to be empty in this barren, spotless house. They are. A nightlight in the upstairs hall casts enough of a glow for me to see that Ella's bedroom door is ajar. I nudge it open the rest of the way with my shoulder and carry her to the bed.

This part takes more planning. I don't think she'll stand, so I keep her in my arms and nudge the covers down as best I can, then lower her to the sheets.

Ella's almost there when she startles, a tiny jerk of her body against mine. Her arms come up and around my neck and holy shit, she can hold tight. Her grip is solid and strong and her forehead presses into the side of my neck, her breath warm on my skin. I feel that all the way down to my erection. It only takes a moment for her to loosen her grasp, falling back into a deep sleep.

I take a ragged breath and force myself to it again. She is sleeping. She's not aware of what she's doing, let alone what she does to me. I move to lower her the rest of the way, but even when Ella's body makes contact with the mattress, she doesn't let go completely.

"Sleep with me," she murmurs, her voice tactile on my skin. "Zander. Stay."

My name. Her lips. That voice.

Fuck.

It takes more strength than I would have thought to untwist her arms from my neck. "It's time for you to sleep." I use my professional voice now, firm but not cold. Ella won't remember that I've also used a touch of my Dominant side. She shivers beneath me.

Maybe she will remember.

She turns over and slips one wrist under her pillow. I feel like a monster standing over her like this. Wanting her like this. Wanting, with every last bit of my soul, to crawl into bed next to her and sleep and sleep and sleep.

Then wake to do other things.

It's torture to stay and wait for her breathing to even out.

Ella rolls over again, her eyes catching the faint light. "Please?" The word is a breath on her lips that must contain witchery. It's potent enough to cast spells.

I put a hand out and stroke her hair. This is allowed. This is a professional touch between a client and a member of The Firm. This is to provide her with the emotional support she's desperate for. Calmly I give her the command, "Sleep."

"Sleepless dreams," she murmurs and closes her eyes.

Dreamless sleep. That's what she means. I have dreamless nights now, thanks to the little blue pills, but I know what happens when I go off them. I know what I'll see when I close my eyes for the night. Memories rush in and try to fill the room. I push them away one by one. We're not doing this tonight. I am on the clock.

A few minutes of soft breathing, and Ella rolls over onto her back.

It takes everything I have, every ounce of self-control, to do what I have to do next.

I flip up her nightgown. Not so far that it uncovers the soft flesh of her belly—just far enough to access the belt to the robe. I can't leave her to sleep tangled in the silk garment. I've watched her in bed before. I know exactly how she sleeps, although stripping her down entirely is out of the question.

Touching her as little as possible, I maneuver the robe from her shoulders, sliding it down without disturbing her. Ella is so warm. So soft. Everything I want to do to her strikes me as I focus on simply removing the robe. My hands ache with the urge to touch her and feel exactly how soft she is. I want to skim my hands up under her nightgown to her tits. I want to drag a fingertip around each nipple until it pebbles for me.

I want to put my hand around her throat. Not to constrict her breathing, just enough for her to feel it. No. I only want to hold her in my grip. It would be good for her. Maybe that's the assessment of a broken man who is searching for excuses, but I think it would. Here in the dark, in her bedroom, I think it would be good for her. It would give her a sense of safety. If she can't be in control, then I'll be in control for her.

I bow my head instead of shaking it and ease the robe over her hips, down her thighs, all the way to her ankles.

And then I pull it off.

I watch her a moment longer, ignoring every sordid thought I have, and then I leave, closing the door behind me. I leave her in her bedroom, with all its pristine shelves and empty surfaces. There's practically nothing in there. Sparse as a hotel room. Ella is the room's most interesting feature.

My heart beats hard with new adrenaline. My shift isn't over, and my to-do list isn't finished. In the rec room I sit down on the couch and slide my hand under the pillow. The little bottle of alcohol is half-empty. This can't have been the only one, can it? She didn't smuggle in a single-serving shot.

There were probably more.

If I want to find out, I'm going to have to ask Damon. We work two days on, two days off. Silas and Dane take the days in between. Damon works the day shift on our days and there's no doubt in my mind that she drank at least half this bottle today while he was here.

For a split second, I wonder if I should inform him at all. Partly to protect her from his future precautions, but also because I'd much rather punish her myself. Without prying eyes and paperwork.

The glass bottle stares back at me.

Do I throw this thing out or leave it where it is?

I think of Ella's pale face. The way she crawled toward me. The hundred other small things she did that beg for protection. That beg for a second chance. I'm not going to fuck this up for her. A powerful urge makes me stand up from the couch. I need to protect her.

I picture her here, facing off with Cade as he questions her about the bottle and how she got it and if she has more alcohol. He'd insist on a session with her and the Rockford Center professionals. Her cheeks would flush, and her eyes would dart to mine, and I wouldn't be able to stop myself. I wouldn't be able to deny her an escape, even if this is what I'm being paid to do.

Fuck. Fuck.

Taking long, deliberate strides, I go into the kitchen and throw it out. Bury it deep in the trash can. We've cleared the house, so no one is checking the garbage. And no one will check this time. The deceit burrows into my chest and throbs there like a kind of infection, but what the hell else am I supposed to do?

My options are to call for backup, document this transgression, or take care of it myself.

I'm choosing door number three.

Four-count breaths. Four of them. If the situation worsens, I will follow protocol. But tonight I'm going to allow her this one thing. This one last barrier between Ella and the world we've created for her. I'll gift her this secret.

Which means …

Back in the rec room, I open my laptop. It hums to life, the keys cool under my fingers. It's been off for most of my shift, but it boots up immediately like it's been waiting for me. In a way, it has.

I go into the program that manages the security cameras. It takes a surprisingly small number of clicks to erase the two hours of footage. That footage includes our conversation, me finding the bottle for the first time, and me carrying Ella upstairs in my arms.

Guilt tightens my throat. I don't know what to feel more guilty about—doing my job in an unorthodox way, or the things I'm feeling for the woman sleeping upstairs. It's a storm of guilt. It's an old wound ripped open, over and over again.

When the files are gone, I check the feeds.

Ella sleeps peacefully in her room.

There's no other movement in the house. Damon won't be here for several hours.

Which gives me plenty of time for more research. No matter what I said to Damon, I won't be reading that file. Especially not now when I promised her I wouldn't. The drinking … however, is something I had already noticed from the videos the other night. There might be evidence of a substance abuse problem. It wouldn't be shocking. She wouldn't be the first person in the world to self-medicate.

The initial search turns up nothing. Not even a hint. Nothing indicating the existence of any sealed files.

Searching takes up most of the space in my mind. I don't take my mind off of Ella completely—that would be reckless, and a dereliction of duty. But I do allow myself a calm focus on the search. I ignore my aching cock and my pounding heart and keep typing different phrases and terms, all of them paired with Ella's name.

When nothing comes, I research my options with her. The therapy I once had and the steps I took back then compared to what's available to me now.

All the while, she sleeps. If she dreams, I hope it's of me.

"Morning."

I curse under my breath but manage not to reach for the laptop. "Make a little noise coming in, would you?" I look up into Damon's face, intending to make this a joke.

His usual smile is gone. His expression is dead serious, and his dark eyes travel over me on the couch and my laptop sitting in front of me. "Everything go all right last night?"

"Yes." Now I do reach for the computer and close the top with as much casual indifference as I can muster. "Ella's still sleeping. She slept most of the night after we had a brief conversation. I don't have any other notes."

"You sure it went all right?" Damon's brow furrows a little. He doesn't hide the suspicion in his gaze.

For a moment, I think of telling him. I could open my mouth and do it right now. I could say I was supposed to be giving her emotional support, and I didn't cross any lines. Except in my own goddamn head.

Damon, of all people, would understand. Hell, he's even kept secrets for me in the past. But telling anyone is a risk I'm not willing to take.

"I'm sure," I tell him. "It was an uneventful night."

chapter 10

Ella

Any and all crucial information pertaining to the state of the client must be provided without hesitation to all partners of The Firm by the client or custodial guardian. It is critical that any source of threat or trigger is identified so as to establish a safe space for the client.

IT FEELS AS IF I'VE SLEPT MORE LAST NIGHT THAN I HAVE IN A YEAR. And I didn't take a pretty little blue pill to ensure those hours of sleep. It's the afternoon by the time I finally wake. Although I do so with a migraine that pounds at my temples. It happens sometimes, after a hard night of crying. Yet another reason I despise tears.

Shuffling to the bathroom, I take my time taking two Advil, washing my face, brushing my teeth, combing my hair. All the while last night plays back in my mind as if it were a dream.

It's not until I step out of the bathroom and find my robe folded in half that I register not remembering coming to bed. The image of Zander, laying me down in bed, ignites far too much heat for what it was.

The racing of my heart is also unjustified, since I know it will be Damon downstairs waiting for me, not the man I dreamed about last night.

"What are these?" My brow pinches as my black ballerina house slippers tap on the porcelain floor. Three notebooks lay at my spot at the kitchen island. Damon is always on the left side with me at the right when I start my day. We've developed a sort of routine. And at my spot, piled on top of one another, are three thick binders and a cup filled with colored pens and highlighters. Inhaling a steadying breath, I peer across the island and dare him to tell me he expects me to start coloring my doodles.

Damon's attire is business casual, which is at complete odds with the silk camisole and matching tap pants I slipped on. The only commonality is that we're both wearing black. It's a suitable color as I mourn the state of my headache.

It would be almost comical to compare the two of us. This man exudes strength. I think he could make the cheapest of clothes look expensive. There's even a hint of danger in his deep brown eyes, and a charming smile. The cadence of his voice is far too soothing for a man who could do so much damage.

I'm certain he's broken more than a few hearts in his lifetime. My gaze shifts down to his fingers currently wrapped around the handle of a coffee mug, and I note the distinct lack of a wedding ring. He has most certainly left a trail of broken hearts in his wake over the past decade.

"We don't want to rush anything," Damon starts, "but I thought you might like one of these better."

He gestures to the stack of journals and continues with his normal daytime push for me to consider jotting down any thoughts or feelings that I'd rather not share out loud. Which would be any thoughts or feelings at all. So far, I've only managed to sketch a bit and even that took its toll a time or two.

The first is a deep red and I'm quick to toss it to the side. Damon jokes, which he never does, teasing "next," and forcing a small smile to my lips.

The second has tiny boxes rather than lines in the interior. It reminds me of graphing paper and I'm not a fan of it at all.

The last one is soft leather and my fingertips can't help trailing down the rose gold binding. The leather itself is a pale white, although the pages inside are thick and heavy, and have a tinge of burgundyish, pale pink to them. It's incredibly feminine and the very idea that this man bought it personally … well again I find myself smiling this afternoon with a bit of humor.

"We have a winner?" he asks and I nod, giving in to the acceptance of a new journal but not promising to write anything just yet.

"Can I make you anything to eat?"

Answering him with a "no, thank you," the sputtering at the coffee machine hits me just then. As does the scent of, I think, waffles. From the corner of the island, maple syrup is visible as well as the butter dish.

"Are you finally taking my suggestion to eat here?"

Damon busies himself with his cup of coffee and glances over his shoulder, then says, "You could say that." I'm not sure why, but that makes me smile too.

Getting myself comfortable, I shift up onto the stool. My slippers fall off one at a time, thudding onto the floor. My bare toes rest against the metal bar of the stool. With my elbow on the island and my chin resting in my hand, I wonder more about this man and his relationship with Zander.

"I really like this one," I comment, tapping the soft leather.

"Good." Damon's gaze moves to the journal in question. "If I make you a cup of tea, will you write something today?"

A small laugh bubbles at my lips, and even through my headache that's beginning to wane, I feel a sense of ease. "Is that not coercion?"

Damon's rough chuckle only reminds me that last night I heard Zander laugh, only sort of like that. It was deeper, it was smoother … it's a sound I'd like to hear again.

It's typical for Damon to urge me to open up first thing on the days he's here. Maybe he knows I'm most vulnerable then, when I'm tired and still waking up. I've never been a morning person. He says whatever he can to start conversation, occasionally asking me mundane questions and a piece of me wants to take him up on this offer and ask him more about Zander. At the same time, that's not the game that we're playing. For some odd reason, it also feels like a betrayal.

As Damon builds his case for a cup of tea being a worthy exchange for a page of thoughts, anything at all, I meander to the stack of waffles and make myself a plate.

I like Damon as much as I like Silas and Dane. They are protective, they give me space when I ask for it, they don't judge me like so many others have throughout my entire life. But I don't dream of them at night.

Flutters rise when I remember last night, and how I rested my head in Zander's lap. Shivers threaten at the memory of his hand slipping down my hip.

"What do you say?" Damon questions with a raised brow, raising a glass mug with one hand, tea bag held in the other.

I take him up on his offer, if only to please him so that when I have the courage to ask about Zander, he'll share with me. A little give, a little take.

And so I spend my brief day with Damon ridding myself of a migraine brought on by the hard sobs of last night, but playing out the events without any remorse or regret. With a heavy yet slim pen dancing between my fingers, the ink flowing across the thick pages of the new journal, I daydream of him, but write stories of my childhood. Of what I know I missed, having to grow up so young. But also what I wish I could take back.

I'm far too close to the fireplace. Its dancing blue flames mesmerize me to the point where I haven't realized how warm I am until the deep voice speaks from behind me.

"Damon said you have a new journal."

Even the physical heat surrounding me pales in comparison to what he does to me. Every inch of me is too hot when I lay eyes on him. More than likely it's because his gaze rests on me.

"Did you write anything down today?"

How can he ask something so uninteresting when all I can imagine is picking up where we left off last night, with our hands searching for something to hold us steady and daring to lift my lips to his?

Lying on the hard herringbone floor with a pool of fabric at my feet and two of the cushions from the sofa, one for my head and the other supporting my shoulder, I prop myself up off the floor to stare up at him.

Zander towers over me, a dominating air surrounding him that's only shown whispers of itself before.

"I wrote a few things." I answer him out of respect once the weight of what he's asked me sinks in fully. "I'd rather not talk about it."

Zander takes a step forward, his jeans rustling and when he takes a place next to me on the floor, I notice he's taken his shoes off. His bare feet match the untamed man he is. Sitting cross-legged, and wearing a dark gray Henley, everything feels different between us. There's no melody to dance to any longer. No notes to hide behind. I search his hazel eyes and find the fire dancing in the reflection.

"You don't want to talk about what you wrote? Or you don't want to talk about anything?" he questions so casually with an innocent expression on his handsome face, one would think his inquiry didn't carry the weight of the world with it. The soothing crackle of the fire is the only distraction between us when I scoot forward and readjust some, sitting on my ass with my feet planted on the floor and bringing my knees into my chest.

"I think I could talk today, I just have boundaries."

"Boundaries?" Zander repeats the single word and somehow it sounds sinful on his lips. All the tension evaporates, leaving behind a magnetic pull that I can't resist. "We could discuss boundaries." If I'm not mistaken, at his lips is the hint of a smirk, but he holds it back. "Is that what you want to talk about today? Boundaries?"

I search his expression for the answer to my unspoken thought: *What type of boundaries are you referring to?*

The devilish smirk he'd been trying to hide breaks through. And I find myself wearing a matching simper.

As I rise from the floor, eager to get away from the fire and what is now nearly stifling heat, I contemplate teasing him. Calling him out for the fact that this feels very much like flirting and significantly less like counseling. Just as the words are ready to slip from my lips, Zander stands alongside me, his right hand taking mine and his left bracing my elbow to help me rise.

I've had many social interactions, and I've learned a few important details about seemingly innocent touches. When a person makes contact with you, whether a hand on an elbow or a friendly hug, the longer the contact lingers, the more they want to fuck you. A quick hug and a hand releasing into the air once the connection begins to break, rather than slipping down the small of your back, is very good evidence there's no sexual chemistry.

Which is not at all what happens right now.

The way Zander trails his fingertips along my forearm and then down my torso, splaying his hand against the small of my back as I stand, tells me everything I want to know. My wild heart beats rapidly. I'm not sure if it's in protest, or if it's simply come back to life, but for a moment, I'm caught. Trapped and unable to think of anything other than my heart's existence.

Concern mars Zander's face as he peers down at me, and I struggle to remember what we were even talking about. "Did I already take it too far?"

"Not at all." My lower lip slips between my teeth as I struggle with whether or not I should add, *I don't believe you've gone far enough*. I keep the thought to myself and turn my back to him to make my way to the sofa. "I just thought we should be comfortable for our session."

There's an undeniable electricity between the two of us. Again, I'm reminded of that dance I felt the first morning that we were alone together. I take one corner of the sofa, and Zander chooses a chair across the room, the one farthest away.

"I think we should start with confessions," Zander begins.

"I've never been a fan of confessions," I say, then nearly continue with a phrase that I've said a number of times in my life: "Confessions imply regret. I live my life with no regrets whatsoever." But then I remember. I remember it all and every regret threatens to suffocate me until Zander tells me, "I've seen some videos and I have questions."

"That's your confession, that you've seen videos?"

A nagging thought pricks at the back of my mind. It was only last night I asked him not to look up any information on me, but the slight feeling of betrayal is quickly pacified.

"It was before last night," he says, and vulnerability shines in his eyes. "I want to make sure you know that." The relief is met with cautiousness. He didn't tell me he knew before, but it's obvious that he feels remorse.

The sofa protests as I pull my legs up, resting the balls of my feet on the cushion and leaning back into the pillow. "I appreciate you telling me." The kindness between us doesn't diminish the chemistry. Although I attempt a more casual stance by resting my head on the arm of the sofa, Zander remains professional.

"I want you to know that I meant it when I said I won't look at your file, but I am damn curious and I'd like to speak freely with you."

"Regarding those videos?" There's a hint of a tease there, but also a sadness.

"More than just the videos. You … captivate me."

His confession only adds to my own curiosity about what this man wants from me. About what he could do to me. The nervousness is evident in the tapping of his thumb on the armrest.

"What did you think?" I question shamelessly.

"I searched your name along with a number of questions. By the end of the night, I had double the number of questions."

His boyish shyness he attempts to cover with a loosely formed fist held over his grin makes me laugh.

"These kinds of questions I think I'd like to answer." There's a hesitation from Zander and I wish he'd stop. "You can ask me anything."

A rawness climbs up my throat, but the pain medicine for my headache seems to be helping it as well.

"Would you answer questions about your sexuality from Damon as well or only me?"

He had to ruin it, didn't he? There's a hard pang in my chest. Zander has said the quiet part out loud. Staring at my hands, I trace over the lines of my palms and then peer back up at him, offering him complete honesty. "I wouldn't care for questions like that from him."

"But for me?"

My answer is immediate. "I've dreamed of you asking me those questions, Zander." Swallowing thickly, I don't dare to tame my gaze and I don't dare to leave his when I add, "In my dreams, I call you Z."

I anticipate a humorous response, but I'm met with a serious tone.

"You know I watched videos of you. I believe they were consensual but I'd like to hear it from you if that's the case."

"Very much so. My idea, my … kink. Yes." I remember the first time I shared it. The rush, the desire. "Did you watch them all?"

"Yes," he says and his answer is resolute.

"Then you know that I enjoy many … tastes." Every nerve ending in my body ignites from the way he looks at me. As if he's sizing up his prey. I'll run from him when he's ready, if that's what he wants.

"Would you care to elaborate?" he questions.

"Elaborate on what? I desire specifics." I am far too comfortable with this man, but it feels nothing but empowering.

"Are you bisexual?" he asks.

"I'm attracted to women, occasionally sexually." I elaborate, because there is a difference between sex and partnership when I think about my attractions. "Romantically, the happily-ever-after type of desire … I am not sure. I have always wanted men to fill that role. I'm not sure what that says about me, but I'm aware of it. I feel satisfied and … like I can be complete with a man as my partner. And I do want a partner. A monogamous relationship. But I have always thought women are beautiful, and I enjoy sex with both men and women."

"Understood."

"Do you judge me for it?" I ask, not sure what he thinks of that truth. "In the past, I thought myself to be alone in these feelings. I simply do what I desire and it leads me to want things I don't see people often admitting."

"No. I don't judge you. I understand desire takes many forms …" His fingers rap along the armrest in a rhythmic beat before he continues his questioning.

"Are you attracted to men sexually too? Or just romantically?" Before I can respond, he adds, "Know that I can help you either way. Your answer will only help me to suit your needs better." His statement is direct. His admission … promising things I am desperate for.

Without holding a damn thing back, I tell him, "I'm sexually attracted to you."

"To men," he corrects me, although it's a farce and we both know it.

"Sorry, doctor," I say flippantly, shrugging off my bluntness.

"I told you, I'm not a doctor."

"Sorry, Z," I answer without thinking twice and my treacherous heart hammers at the nickname. Z. Peering up, I judge his reaction. "I didn't mean to overstep." His fingers dig into the armrest, and his lips twitch with a smirk. Readjusting on the sofa, the throw slipping down my shoulder and puddling in my lap, I ask, "Would that be all right? To call you Z."

"I would enjoy that very much," he admits to me and there's a crackle between us, one that hasn't spared us during a single interaction.

"If I'd met you at a bar, would you want me?" I dare to ask him. "I've wondered about it since I first saw you. I wondered if you'd fuck me had we met differently."

"I think it may be a matter to discuss at another time, Ella." Zander doesn't move with me in this step of our dance. My body goes so very still as I feel nothing but vulnerability.

"I'd fuck you, Zander. However you'd like. I'd fuck you." I don't allow my gaze to slip as he holds me steady with his, leading me to divulge a truth we've been tiptoeing around. For good measure I add, "Hell, I've already fantasized about it."

"I am obligated to maintain a professional relationship with you." I have no idea how he can speak so coolly, when his gaze blazes like fire and his tone is thick with desire. There is no mistaking that a boundary has already been crossed. A social one. Perhaps a moral one. And neither of us were affected by it. Our boundaries lie elsewhere.

"What a shame—" I start to murmur, readying myself to remove the throw and tell him exactly what it is about him that fuels my interest in him. But I'm silenced and caught off guard as my head whips to the left.

There's only the quick thud of the door that alerts the two of us that someone's here. Just around the corner. Zander's ease is uncanny. His ability to simply slip on a mask that hides every etched detail of the scandalous desire that was on his face just a moment ago is impressive.

With his back pressed against the chair, no one would have any idea of the seduction that nearly prompted me to do illicit and unwarranted things in return for a pleasure I've been dreaming of.

The sudden intrusion would be shocking this late at night if it weren't for the person responsible for it. Kam enters the room like he always does, already talking and as if whatever it is that he has to say is more urgent than whatever's already occurring. He's done it all my life, and in the past I welcomed it. Currently, I'm grateful for his impulsive ways, given the fact that he seems to have failed to notice the energy of the room. "Could we talk?"

My gaze shifts between the two men. "Of course," I answer and swallow, grasping at any sense of normalcy to ground me back in the real world.

"Stay," Zander commands with a subtle hand signal and steals Kam's focus. "Let me leave so you two can have the room," he states, giving Kam a nod.

If Kam noticed the tension between Zander and me, he doesn't let on.

That doesn't change the fact, though, that I feel as if I've been caught. My rapid pulse and wide eyes give it away, if only Kam would look at me rather than watching a very calm Zander leave the room. I catch sight of his hand flexing on the way out; it's the only indication he gives that maybe he's not as collected as he appears.

I have a moment to fix my expression, and I take it. What's happening between Zander and me is mine, mine alone. I need this and I'm unwilling to allow anyone to take it away. It's only once we're alone that Kam takes the seat Zander occupied only moments ago.

He sits on the edge of it, leaning forward and resting his forearms on his thighs. "I had a meeting tonight."

"A meeting." I mutter the words and already feel on edge. The urgency makes sense. Kam's a buffer between myself and "others." In the past he's negotiated deals, dealt with threats, lawsuits, slander. Anything that would threaten me or my estate in any way.

The times in the past where he's had "meetings" that led to him barging in like this generally meant things needed to change in some form or another. Suddenly all the heat threatens to overwhelm me, and I find myself staring at the fireplace that is no longer lit.

"I've gone over a number of things and I want to start with how to get you back out there," he tells me and that's not at all what I was expecting.

"I wanted to talk about creating routines and maybe ..." He's anxious as he pauses and breathes in deeply, as if what he's about to say is controversial. "Maybe posting again."

There's a small crack in my chest that's raw at the idea of it. It's so very small, though, only a sliver.

"Let's get you together; new hair, maybe?" he offers and I only half smile back at his grin.

"A woman who cuts her hair ..." he begins, and I complete the Coco Chanel quote for him.

"... is about to change her life."

"Just a snapshot, just to tell them you're okay." I nod along with his plan. "What do you want them to know?"

I offer the first words that come to mind: "I'm sorry."

"No, no, no," he says, comforting me. "There is no room for that. You don't owe them an apology."

"I'm trying."

"I love that about you. I love *you*," he emphasizes. His lips form a thin smile and it's contagious, although the sorrow lingers.

"I love you too."

"I know you do."

"I'm trying," I repeat, then offer as a possibility, "I'm working through it."

"Love this." Kam nods and claps his hands in celebration then adds, "They're going to be so happy to hear from you."

"Can I have my phone back?" When everything happened a year ago, Kam took control of my social media accounts, including changing the passwords.

"… I'll be monitoring comments and moderating as needed."

"You know how it can be. And if anyone comments with the … video." I shift where I am, feeling this uncomfortable melancholy. Having to live through that moment was the worst day of my life. Having to relive it on social media for months … well, it almost led to my death.

"If I'm going to talk, I want to talk to my followers. If I write something in that journal, I want them to see it." For the first time in a long time, a burst of motivation urges me to write. "I want to tell them about the ball in the box. It made me feel so much better to know. I want them to know too."

"A ball in a box?" he questions and frustration overwhelms me.

"It's an analogy. More people should know." I've felt the compulsion to post so much in my life, but never so much as I do now. "I can tell them. Even if it only helps a handful of people, I can tell them—" All my life I've shared who I am and what I've gone through on social media. It helped me get through the harder times—most of them—and I know damn well I've helped others get through the same. This is no different. I know there are more people struggling like I am.

"I think right now we should limit what you post—"

"They saw it too. They saw it and other people go through things like that too." My throat goes tight and dry at the visuals that flash in my mind.

"I know they do, love." There's a kindness in his statement, but still a sense of resistance.

"And I want to help them. I want to use my voice and help them get through it. I want to get through it together."

Kam's slow as he takes a seat beside me, making me turn to face him although he's yet to look back at me.

"Kam." I press him, pleading with him. A part of me wants to take back his role, I want him gone and not in charge of a damn thing. I could so easily get the hell out of this house, buy a phone, message someone and they could post on my behalf. He couldn't stop me. He may have changed my passwords, but I'm not locked away anymore.

A chill runs through my blood. Unless I give anyone a reason to send me back. Sickness churns in my gut. "I feel so fucking helpless." The confession is whispered and I look anywhere but at Kam as tears prick my eyes.

"Your love language is acts of service." Kam comforts me, scooting closer to me even though I can't even look him in the eye. "You want to help by doing, but right now, you need to focus on helping yourself."

The sincerity in his message guts me.

"This is a start." Kam's voice is riddled with concern. "Just post to let them know you're trying."

"I want to post about the fucking ball in the box," I practically hiss. I must sound insane; hell, even to my own ears I sound like I'm losing it.

I question why he would silence me. "I've not been on social media for months now. I chose to leave when it was too much. I knew when it was too much for me."

"And then you didn't," he says, and Kam's voice is harsher now. "What if you shared something and you didn't realize what it could do to you … or to someone else?"

"I know there are people who are sad like me. I know that after what happened, I should feel this way. I want them to know I feel it too, and we can get through it together."

"Can we start off slow? Please?" Kam's last word is a whisper, his swallow harsh and paired with a desperate gaze. "I failed you once. I am terrified of failing you again, love. Please. Please, let's start slow."

"With a single picture and a single sentence … it doesn't feel like it's enough."

"Then why don't we record it. Record what you think is enough and we can keep it, we can hold on to it and post it when you're ready."

"When you think I'm ready," I say to correct him, keeping most of the anger out of my tone.

"Not me, someone better than me," he tells me, his voice pleading. "When a professional thinks you're ready, we can share it."

"Like Damon? If I show him what I want to post?"

"I'm not sure—" he starts and as my jaw drops slightly and my eyes widen, he's quick to take it back. "When Damon *and* myself think you're ready. Damon doesn't know the beast people can be online. You know it. You've been through it."

Pulling one leg up on the sofa, I rest my head on my knee.

"Tell me about the ball in the box," Kam urges me. Tilting my head to the side to lay my cheek on my knee, my silence is met with his plea. "Don't hate me, Ella. I love you. And I am just worried."

I take a shuddering breath in and then let the lone tears fall where they may.

"I think we could post both. Maybe?" he says.

"Both?"

"We could post about the ball, and we could post the photo. Just … let me do it, all right? I'll post for you. I'll monitor it."

"I really want you to, Kam," I admit to him and my voice is hoarse. "I haven't wanted to, but it feels so important."

"Then we'll tell them. We will. Maybe write it in your journal and other things you want to post. I'll give you a phone, no social on it, but you can take pictures of it, you can text me. You can record whatever you want to share. I just don't want you in the line of fire.

"You know how people can be." Kam's voice is gentle, but his statement is a wrecking ball. I know exactly how people can be.

"This is good," he tells me, his hand on my thigh, giving me a squeeze although anxiousness colors his words.

"What else?" I ask him, brushing under my eyes and counting the last twenty minutes as a win. I will write for them. And he will share it. It's amazing how much relief I feel, yet there just as much exhaustion present.

"We have new hair," Kam says, then holds up a finger after taking a deep breath, "some social media," and another finger is lifted. "What do you think about a shindig?" he asks, tilting his head.

"A shindig?"

He nods. "A shindig." With my smile, he smiles broadly back. "I knew you'd like that one."

chapter 11

Zander

Any modifications to a client's plan of care will be carefully considered and vetted by multiple members of The Firm, or outside consultants, or both.

HE IS HER CONSERVATOR, I REMIND MYSELF REPEATEDLY AS I leave. He has power over her. He has a vested interest. And he could easily take her away from me. Rage simmers although it's merely a product of possessiveness. I'm all too aware of that. So I get up and go.

What the hell else am I going to do? I nod to Kam like the professional that I am—that I will remain—and get up from my chair. "I'll be nearby," I tell Ella on the way out. I don't know why I say it. She knows I'll be close, and so does he.

I can hear their conversation easily from the kitchen. Hiding just out of their view I take a moment to absorb the submission Ella allowed in our conversation.

Kam clears his throat in the sitting room and starts in on social media. *Posting a photo.* He has options for her … his voice turns to white noise. I don't hear a thing he says. I'm supposed to be keeping an eye on the situation, making a note of what goes on, monitoring her. But I can't. The fact that he's her conservator makes it all the more important.

I need a minute.

I'd fuck you, Zander. I've already fantasized about it.

It's not out of the ordinary for clients to express their fantasies. It's not even the first time this has happened to me. Providing security for a person can heighten their emotions. Protecting a woman … well, it can lead to harmless crushes. In the past, it has always been unwanted and easily directed elsewhere.

This is different. I cannot get her voice out of my head. Ella was so blunt with those words. So bold. I'm hard as a rock. My entire body is tight with the need for release. To pin her to the wall and fuck her raw.

I've always known this situation was different. From the moment Cade described this contract, I'd known there was a higher chance that the client might develop feelings for one of us, or for all of us. But the way Ella looked at me—

That sure as hell wasn't as "a member of The Firm."

She knows. She must have an inkling of what I'm like, or she wouldn't have looked me in the eye the way she did. Like she knew I could indulge her in a D/s relationship. I could take control and let her breathe. I could give her freedom without worry.

Impossible. It's impossible for her to know those things. There are no videos of me on the internet to give her any suspicion. No videos, but … I can taste the words on my tongue all over again. The memory of the first command I gave her lingers. *Don't say that to me. Ever.*

I'd ordered her. Commanded her. And Ella's eyes had gone wide for a fraction of a second. Long enough for me to see the desire there. As well as the complete obedience.

I take another deep breath and do what I've been trained to do. I assess the situation. There are no signs of danger. I assess the immediate needs of the client. She seems to want to be speaking to her manager. I assess my position and I find it lacking. I need to get my shit together.

Rubbing my eyes with the palms of my hand, I commit myself to giving her space to absorb our conversation. I will be more direct, more firm in the next.

So I pour myself a cup of coffee. Ella's been preparing a pot before I arrive. It's always hot and fresh when I walk through the door, the scent of coffee wafting from the kitchen.

I know damn well I should announce myself, but I move slowly through the house as I make my way back to them. Kam's still talking.

"It's just best, babe, if you get back into a routine. Your sponsors miss you, and you know how they are. I convinced them to pause their support instead of dropping you. You have not lost them. Not a single one."

"Thank you, I do know that … well, I know how they can be," Ella agrees. "You think we'll lose them if I'm … if I'm not the same?" There's no restraint in her tone, but she's not pushing back at him, either. It sounds like a conversation between two people who know each other very well. Jealousy pushes out against my ribs. Four-count breaths. I only manage one set of four, but it eases the pressure some.

"You might." Kamden's doing his best not to be pushy, but his best isn't good enough. Why does he want her doing sponsorship deals so badly? She's in the care of The Firm. Adding more to her plate right now doesn't strike me as the best idea. But still, I don't interrupt. I do make a mental note to discuss these changes with Damon, or at least ensure Kam's already communicated this with him.

"I'm not sure what all I can do. I don't want to come off—"

"It won't be the same," he interjects, almost too quickly. "Just a few to dip your toes in and remind them you still exist."

Ella does exist.

She called me Z.

My hand tightens on the handle of the coffee mug. I'd kill to hear her say that again. It was familiar and sexy and totally off-limits. She can't use a nickname like that. That's crossing a line.

I know that, and I also know that if she does it again, I won't stop her. I can't think about what I'll do if she announces she'd fuck me again.

"Finances are still steady?" Ella questions. Have I missed part of the conversation?

"Of course, I've taken care of it all. This is … it's about your security," Kam replies. "It's easier to get sponsorship deals if you already have some. Stay out of the public eye long enough, and you'll be starting from zero.

I won't have it. But they're messaging me. They're asking when they'll see a return."

A low laugh. It sends a shock straight through me, from the top of my head to the tips of my toes. Ella's laugh is a broken thing. Her voice is still damaged. But it has a light, sultry ring to it that makes my toes curl again. "You don't think I've been out of the public eye too long already?"

"No, I don't. Really. I think if you jump in now, you'll be just fine."

It's time. I've been standing out here too long, fucking eavesdropping like a child at the top of the stairs refusing to sleep.

I can see her outline as I round the corner. Debating on entering the conversation is … problematic. It's obvious she's checking to see where I've gone. I watch for it too, the way she watches for me.

It's not good. For either of us. For her, for The Firm.

And …

We're past that.

I know it in the space of a single heartbeat. I know it down to my bones. I know it from the way my heartbeats turn jagged when I think of her in a room with someone else. When I think of the raw truth in her voice when she said she would fuck me. When I think of her arching her back on that video, with another man's hand around her throat.

One last look into the sitting room. Ella looks slightly better than she did that day in the courtroom, but she needs more than sponsorship deals and talks with Damon and regular check-ins with Cade.

She needs more.

She needs me.

And there's a way to do it.

A boulder shifts off my chest as the idea comes to me. It's like that boulder has been split in two by a flash of lightning. The hairs all over my body pull up tight, goosebumps racing over my skin. There is a way to give her what she needs within the boundaries of the contract. Fuck me. A version of me only weeks ago wouldn't believe what I'm considering.

My cock twitches in my pants. It wouldn't involve sex. It could never involve sex.

The next moment, the boulder comes rocketing back onto me.

Only this time, the boulder has the shape of fear and guilt and regret.

Something insidious and deadly. I turn away from the sitting room and go back to the kitchen. I get the coffee cup down without spilling it, which is better than I expected, and then I brace both hands on the countertop and lean over it.

One.

Two.

Three.

Four.

Four-count breaths.

Four sets of them.

Even. Steady.

Gradually, I control my breathing and my sordid thoughts. Gradually, I straighten. I test my grip by taking a sip of coffee. My hand doesn't tremble with the desire to slap her ass again and again.

That was fucking close.

Too close to the past. Too close by half, and I know what set me off. I know exactly what set me off. It's the decision to offer Ella what she needs. The fact that she wants to fuck me—yeah. That did something to me. It set me up, and now I'm going to have to get myself under control the only way I know how.

I'm still going to do it, but another truth rears its head, sliding down my throat with the next sip of my coffee.

I'm going to have to talk about this. Not with Ella. Not with Damon, or even Cade, though it's technically my responsibility to consult with them on matters of care ... they don't need to know this. They wouldn't understand, and they could take her away from me. She needs this. I fucking know she does. Instead, I'll consult a neutral third party.

Adrenaline pumps in my veins. There's only one person I trust for advice when it comes to something as important as this. I take out my phone and send a single text message. It's past nine, but the reply comes a minute later.

It's done. The moment I read the text, the duo makes their way out of the sitting room.

I find Kam already stepping into the kitchen, Ella right behind him.

Kam leaves through the back door. "See you tomorrow?"

"Maybe," Ella says. "I'll text you."

"Okay." He smiles for her, big and bright, and then he's gone, leaving a cool autumn wind lingering in the kitchen.

Ella leans against the counter, her huge dark eyes on me. Her hand flits up to her neck. She's touched it less as the time has passed. It's only a brief skim of her fingertips over the hollow of her throat now, the movement almost suggestive. Almost an invitation for me to touch her there. I almost say it. I almost tell her what I've decided to offer her. What I know she needs. I'm almost level with her right now.

"How are you feeling after that?"

The corners of Ella's mouth turn up at my question and my heart slams against my rib cage. Calm focus. I need to have patience for this. I need to talk this out before I say a word to her about it. "Tired," she admits. "Not like last night." She glances off to the side, looking thoughtful, and then her eyes come back to mine. "It's a simple kind of tired. You know?"

"I do." I get that myself with pills. I wouldn't have it at all otherwise. "Are you thinking of heading upstairs?"

"I'm not sure. Should I?"

The charge that goes through me at her words is just as intense as the one that pulsed through me not even an hour ago. Permission. She's already requesting permission. My sweet little submissive. I remind her, if only to give her more space to consider what occurred and to give myself time to ensure I will do right by her, "We had a session. We've talked."

"We were interrupted."

"I know." We were interrupted at the worst possible moment. Or the best possible moment. I don't know which it is. I might not ever know. "There's no rush to continue tonight," I tell her, keeping my voice as level and professional as I can. "If you're tired, we can always have another session tomorrow."

We will have another session tomorrow. I've already decided it. No matter what happens, Ella and I will have another session.

Her lips part, and I hold my breath. If she says it again right now—

"You're right. I'll head up." Her body shifts toward me almost imperceptibly, but then Ella holds up her hand in a little wave. "Good night, Z."

"Good night, Ella."

I wait until I hear her footsteps on the stairs before I sag against the countertop. *Z.*

I wait another five minutes before I take out my phone, dial, and put it to my ear.

"You've got me." It's Silas. He always says "You've got me" when he answers the phone.

"I want you to look into the manager for me. Kamden Richards." Silas has previous experience with military intelligence, and he's the one on our team who conducts the research that can't be done with a simple internet search. "Background check. As far as you can go. Get me a file on him."

There's no hesitation, only a huff of a laugh. "You got a hunch?" he questions.

"I am … uncertain."

"All right. Need anything else?"

That's the other thing I like about Silas. He's a no-bullshit guy. He does his job, he does it well, and he rarely rocks the boat. "No. Thanks."

We hang up the call, and I bring up the app on my phone that shows me the security cameras. Upstairs, Ella pads from the bathroom to her room and then leaves it. She pauses at the top of the stairs, like she might decide to come back down.

I'd fuck you, Zander. I've already fantasized about it.

After another long moment, she goes into her bedroom and closes the door.

The text comes in while I'm still looking at the camera feed.

Damon: Going through last night's records. Missing a chunk of time off the video. Did you notice any glitches?

I don't answer him.

chapter 12

Zander

Any threats to the client will be dealt with quickly and severely. All legal ramifications will be the burden of The Firm.

THE WAITING ROOM AT 304 PINEWOOD CIRCLE IS THE SAME it's been since the first time I set foot here, in this strip of professional offices. White walls. Black, modern furniture. All of it's comfortable, sturdy, and nonthreatening. No art in frames, just a blue accent wall in the back. I asked Harrison about it at my first session. He said that one of his clients once had a reaction to a watercolor painting, so he stopped displaying art after that.

It takes great effort not to tap my foot against the floor. Moments like this are good for practicing patience. You can't allow the nervous responses to get in the way when you're on a job, and almost no one starts out with enough patience to be that way in high-pressure circumstances.

The soft click brings my attention forward as Harrison opens the door to his office. "Zander. How are you?"

"Good," I answer as I rise, exhaling and preparing myself. "How are you?" I follow him in, nodding at his polite answer. The office is a smaller version of the waiting room, except the furniture is larger and sturdier.

I take my seat in a black armchair, and Harrison takes his seat in a gray wingback. Like always, he appears unflustered and calm. Clean-shaven. Dark, closely cropped hair above a neat white shirt and equally neat tie.

"What brings you in today?"

The words I've been planning to say stick in my throat. Harrison is a patient man. He's one of those obnoxiously tolerant people who will out-wait you no matter how long it takes. It's one of the things Damon told me about him when he recommended I see him—he knows how to shut his mouth and wait, a quality I appreciate in people more than most other things. "I've had a lot on my mind."

Harrison tilts his head to the side and continues waiting. The clock on the back wall is nearly silent. But there's still a steady ticking sound in the room. Punctuated by my heavy exhales.

No matter how much practice I have at being patient, he is better. And part of me wants to crack. It's not that I want him to know the de-tails. The urge to keep this secret is strong. It doesn't seem to matter that I decided to talk to Harrison about this—now that it's time, some protec-tive instinct rears up and tries to keep me from saying a damn word. But it's misguided. This conversation is about Ella's welfare. Her well-being is the most important thing.

"We've got a new job. It's different from our typical clients."

"How so?"

"She's a custodial client," I explain. "Released from a mental health facility into our care. For a case like this, the involvement is significant. Around-the-clock presence in her home."

"And this is outside the bounds of what you've done in the past?"

"Well outside. Normally we're dealing with high-profile security and physical threats. For this client—" I almost said her name. I almost said *Ella* to Harrison. It wouldn't have been a disaster for him to hear it. Everything I say in this room is confidential.

But if I say her name to him . . .

If she becomes part of my sessions as a person in my life and not a client . . .

That changes things.

I clear my throat. "For this client, the focus is mental health recovery.

She was institutionalized for a number of months. This is the stepdown from the Rockford Center."

His left eyebrow raises a fraction of an inch. Harrison isn't the kind of man who's shocked often. Or if he is, he doesn't show it. Could be a trick of the trade, but it could also be his personality. I wouldn't know. I didn't know him before Damon put his foot down and made me schedule an appointment with him years ago. "That type of transfer is unusual, from what I know of the system."

"Highly unusual." There's a strange tightness in my throat, thinking about her standing in that courtroom. "The client herself is unusual, and I think she'll need an unusual approach. If I take that route, I want to make sure I don't cross any boundaries. That I'm seeing the right things."

I'm met with a thoughtful nod.

"And her mental well-being?"

"From what I gather, depressed. Given her medication, suffering with trauma. But very aware, opinionated and independent. She is … working through her pain, but struggling."

"Is she of sound mind?"

"Yes," I answer without hesitation and feel a heat tingling at the back of my neck. There is no indication from my interactions with her, nor from Damon's notes that she is anything other than a strong woman in the middle of a difficult moment. A moment I could hold her hand through. One of the aspects of her case was the consultant verifying that she was of sound mind enough to leave the center … but still …

"What is it you want to see? Something from her?"

"It's not about what I want to see from her." This is harder than I thought it would be. Words are slippery things, and they keep rearranging themselves before I can get them the hell out of my mouth. "It's that I need to look beyond what I want."

"Can you elaborate on that? I don't want to make any assumptions." Harrison doesn't reach for the notepad on the table by his chair. He doesn't so much as look at it. Clasping his hands and resting them on his lap, he waits for me to give him details. He knows better than to write a damn thing down. I don't want any records made of our sessions together. I never have, and I can't allow him to start now.

This is the part I'm going to have to muscle through. Brute force. Rail against. A voice in the back of my head shrieks that this is dangerous, that admitting it is dangerous, that leaning into it is dangerous.

But it's not. Admitting the things I want and need isn't dangerous. What happened with Quincy was a cruel coincidence. It has to have been, otherwise I can't do this with Ella, and I want it.

I more than want it. I need it. And so does she.

"I believe she could benefit from having a stronger hand. Something in line with her previous relationships." He opens his mouth to ask a question, but I speak first. "I'll clarify everything with her beforehand. She's forthcoming."

Harrison steeples his hands in front of him. "What is it that you're afraid you aren't seeing beyond your own desires for this ... would you call it a Dominant/submissive relationship?"

I don't feel anything like embarrassment when he says it out loud. I feel no shame. What I feel is a certainty that he is the right person to discuss this with, just as I'm certain this kind of mediation would be right for Ella. But that certainty, like all other things, is only a feeling. It's not necessarily the truth. If there's an aspect I haven't considered, then maybe Harrison can help me find it. What I know for sure is that I can't do this— won't do it—without some sort of confirmation. I double-check feelings the same way I double-check the details when I'm working security. Flip every lock twice.

"That's what I would call it, yes. A Dominant/submissive relationship to aid her in a positive recovery." A thousand images flood into my mind of what, exactly, our relationship would look like. There are real boundaries when it comes to D/s relationships. Ironclad ones. And they will have to mesh together with the limits of the contract we're both engaged in. "I've observed her closely. I've talked with her. This approach could help her heal."

"And your reservations?"

"She has past trauma," I say, ushering the truth into the silence. It's an easy quiet here in Harrison's office. He never seems to be in any sort of rush. "I'm sure of that. But she's resistant to discussing it or seek therapy."

"Ah. Much like you were," Harrison points out.

"Yes." I was resistant as hell. I was angry. Grieving. Suffering. Pissed at Damon for making me come here in the first place, and for having the balls to look at the wreck I was and call it like he saw it. I was pissed at him for being right, and I knew he was. When my dad died, I learned the consequences of bottling things up, so damn it, I knew he was right. But that didn't make me less furious. The first few sessions with Harrison were quiet, but not like this. It wasn't peaceful. "It's similar to my situation in that way."

"And you're concerned she could suffer if you aren't—"

"If I don't critically consider every aspect of her care. If I miss something because I'm blinded by my own needs."

My own needs have been screaming at me since the day I saw her in that courtroom, and I would be a fool not to admit that and seek caution.

Harrison considers me, and I know he's taking note of everything. The way I sit in the chair. The expression on my face. The tone of my voice. Even the way I dressed for the meeting. "It sounds like you've already come to a conclusion."

"I haven't."

What I have come to a conclusion about is that Ella would respond well as a submissive. With the right Dominant caring for her, she could heal in a way that aligns with who she is. It's written all over her. But knowing it and choosing to act on it are two different things. I haven't yet made that final decision. Harrison furrows his brow.

I'm adamant when I tell him, "I haven't, Harrison."

"You want me to tell you that you'll be critical in all things and see beyond your wants. You want me to guarantee that for you. You should know better, Zander. There are no guarantees."

"I'm not looking for a guarantee." A match strike of irritation scrapes against the inside of my cheek. I know better than that. I know there are no guarantees in life, not ever, and the worst things that happen to a person seem to appear out of nowhere. It's never the thing you're expecting. Never the thing I'm expecting. "I'm looking for a consultation."

"Then I believe your thoughtfulness reflects a high level of concern for this client."

"Is it your opinion—" I pause to sit up straight and tall in my seat, my fingers tapping on the armrest as I consider my next question carefully. "Is it your opinion that I shouldn't do this?"

The empathy in Harrison's eyes is the one thing about this session that presses at some soft spot I keep hidden. Harrison knows about my past. He knows, because after Quincy, Damon insisted that I seek help. What he actually said was that if I didn't go, he would drag me here himself and sit through the session to make sure I talked. I told him it was against every possible policy to barge in on someone else's private therapy sessions. He'd looked me straight in the eye. "I don't care," he said. "I'll do it anyway. Harrison won't kick me out and I'll kick your ass if you don't."

I believed him. And I ended up here, in this office, telling Harrison things I never thought I'd tell another human being. He helped me sort through the overwhelming guilt and shame.

"It could be what she's missing," I tell Harrison, and I hear it—I hear that note in my voice that I hate. It's the one that's craving affirmation. Just one nod from an outside party to tell me that this is not a terrible idea. That listening to my gut instinct is appropriate for the situation. "It could help her sort through the mess. Give her an outlet that's more inclined to her comfort."

Harrison doesn't laugh. "Because Dominant/submissive relationships are bound by the agreement."

"Yes. There can be a release in it for subs. She—" Shit. I almost did it again. I almost said Ella. I almost spoke her name into this room, and I cannot do that. It's one of the hard limits. She cannot become a part of my life like that. Because of the contract. Because of Cade. Because of me. "She seems to need that assurance."

Ella has been holding herself together in a tight grip for a long, long time. It's obvious from the way she stood in the courtroom and those first days at the house. I know if I took her over my knee, I could unwind part of that tension for her. I've never been more certain of anything in my life.

Fuck.

I am not, *not,* going to think about that in this room. Not when I'm in full view of my fucking therapist.

"I'm not saying you shouldn't do it. What I am saying is that if you're going to move forward, it might be worth calling in backup."

"What do you mean exactly?"

"Having a second person in the room, or at least aware of the situation. Someone else on the team, to ensure there's another party present to measure any differences you might not see because you're so close to this situation."

Someone like Damon.

"I'm keeping a professional distance."

"Of course," says Harrison. "Of course."

"If I were to go through with this …"

"It would be wise for someone to be aware, in case you are blinded."

"So long as someone else is watching her?" I leave the question half spoken, knowing full well she has a team taking every precaution to monitor her from her sleeping hours to her weekly weigh-in.

"So long as she is in the right mind to consent … and so long as you maintain your professional distance. You are aware that these relationships can be helpful, but you know they can also bring dependency and other emotions. You must be prepared for that, if that case arises."

chapter 13

Ella

The Firm will work with the client to arrange for the deployment of partners with best endeavors to conduct the offered services. All personnel is at the client's discretion.

EVERYTHING ABOUT THIS MOMENT WAS INTENTIONAL. FROM THE way the skirt lays across the sofa, to how I loosely tie the wrap top to show off a little more cleavage. My long-sleeved cotton dress with a floral print in fall tones is new.

Some of the other details may have been for a photo op with Kamden, like actually applying makeup and false lashes. He's just left, snapping a quick picture before leaving through the back door as Zander strode in. But all of it, I chose with him in mind. It's been a long time since I've wanted to dress up and look pretty. Even longer since I thought of a man while doing it.

"You look gorgeous." Zander's statement catches me by surprise. There's nothing guarded about it. My blush rises up my cheekbones and burns at my temples. The things this man does to me is heady.

"Thank you," I whisper, still taken aback as he takes a seat across from me in our blue room of sexual tension. It's what I've dubbed it now that

I've spent more time in this room with him playing with fire, than I've been in this room with anyone else since purchasing the home years ago.

"You cut it … and it's lighter." The manner in which he gives his observation is comical and offers me a warmth I've missed since I told him to sleep well before going to bed last night.

I shrug, as if this all isn't for him, and say, "Blonds have more fun."

"Hmm." His hum is approving, yet questioning all at once. "You're happy with it?" he asks.

"Yes."

"Then I approve," he tells me and I suck in a breath, ready to toy with him. To let him know his approval is irrelevant and I wasn't aiming for it. I'm certain it would get under his skin and he'd flex that hand of his as he did the other night. Before I can usher out a word, Zander takes his normal seat with a seriousness that silences me.

He's wearing his usual black jeans and a matching tee, but there's something different about the air around him tonight. With his thumb moving over each finger, he cracks his knuckles and tells me, "It's been two weeks. I believe there are benchmarks you could meet so long as we establish boundaries …"

"Boundaries?" I repeat, lifting a challenging brow. I didn't expect him to pick up the conversation right where we left off. Typically he offers me more foreplay than this.

"Yes. And since we're being blunt, I expect you to behave. I expect you to listen to me. Is that clear?" Heat rises through me. Before I can tease him, asking what I'd get out of it, he adds, "I will ensure you are rewarded justly."

"Justly?" I echo the word, feeling suffocated. It's hard to imagine this is happening. That it's real life, this man across from me promising me things only one other man has before. It took ages for James to take me in. Years of occasional fucks, which were enjoyable, but casual, before either of us decided we wanted more. Before we … got together like this. My throat is dry with the memory but Zander's steady voice commands my attention.

"I need you to agree to that. To listen to me."

"Ever the Dominant, to speak of your needs." I utter the word out loud, so there is nowhere to hide any longer.

"Ever the submissive, to require a strong hand."

Barely breathing, I admit with humor, "I am a people pleaser."

His hum of acknowledgment holds a tone of sarcasm. "Why do I think that only applies to *some* people?"

"That I am selective with who I please?" I ask to clarify, feeling the heat rise to my cheeks. He nods and my bottom lip slips between my teeth as I attempt to recall what my dream was this morning. So I can tell him exactly how I'd like to please him.

"One time my friend told me to have some dignity. She thought sex wasn't a morally neutral act," I comment, reeling in the dangerous tension and focusing on the ends of the throw blanket that have frayed over time.

His eyes narrow and I'm not certain if it's because he disagrees with my statements or not. Either way, I focus on picking barely perceptible lint from the blanket and wait for him to say anything at all. I wait for him to tell me what to do. To establish terms. I wait for him.

"Your rewards will be varied. As will your obligations."

"Is that so?" I push back. I only hesitate for a half second before questioning, putting out the word for both of us to hear it in no uncertain terms, "You can't be my Dom, wouldn't that break the rules? It would breach the contract."

"I have no intention of fucking you while under contract," Zander states firmly, although his cock already straining against his zipper tells me he wants to. "That doesn't mean I can't punish you, that I can't reward you."

"Zander," I say, and I hope he can hear it in my voice. The temptation, yet at the same time, the caution.

"If you want to give me your submission, I will take care of you. I will help you. I will give you everything you need and more." I'm floored. I've never told a soul. What James and I had … I'd never shared with anyone. Questions batter me, but I obey, gripping the blanket and accepting that Zander knows more than what I've told him. More than what I've told anyone.

It's a sin to fall so deeply into the depths of desire like this. To blindly want, and devour every promise with such greed. And yet here I am. Wanting nothing but this.

"I'm scared," I admit to him and he repositions himself, his fingers intertwining as if he needs to hold on to them to keep from touching me.

"I will never hurt you. We will establish boundaries and limits. I want this as much as I think you do. Tell me if I'm wrong."

Heat dances along every inch of my skin as I confess, "You aren't wrong."

"Then do we understand one another?" he questions.

"Are you sure you can handle me?" I tease him one last time for good measure, wondering what he'll do to me next time I give him lip. Will he turn me over and redden my ass? Will he lean me over the edge of the sofa and fuck me until I beg him to come?

My toes curl and I reach for the throw blanket, needing to hide myself right now although the additional heat is unwanted. Beggars can't be choosers.

"I love your spirit, little bird. But you will only answer yes or no to the following questions, is that clear?" With shortened breath, I answer him yes, because I want to. I am more than willing to consider submitting to him. *Little bird.* I love it. He has no idea what it means to be called *little bird.* A flightless one who used to sing.

As he leans back in the chair, my gaze slips down to his jeans, specifically his cock that presses against his zipper and down his thigh. He doesn't even try to hide it.

"Have you used hand signals before?" he questions.

"Yes."

"Good. This relationship will be between us and only us. Is that understood?"

"Yes."

"I will use signals when we are with company. And you will obey them as swiftly as possible or receive punishment. Is that understood?"

"Yes," I answer and if I ever had any shame, I'd feel it now at my eagerness. Truth be told, I feel nothing but desperation for us to begin. For the first time in a long time, I feel wanted, I feel excited. I feel a heated pulse that's run cold for nearly a year now.

"Show me the commands," he orders. "You have my permission to speak, but only to tell me the commands as you demonstrate them." His deep, steadying breath raises his shoulders and his hands flex on the armrest before he grips them once again. It's heady to watch a man like him resist his own desires. I want to know what will happen when he gives in. When I do what he says and he rewards both of us, fucking me the way he fantasizes about. I'm desperate to know what it'll be like.

Raising my pointer in the air, the other fingers forming a fist, I make a circle parallel to the ceiling. "Undress." I remember the signals easily. The recollection bombards me with the memories of a handsome man who used to care for me like no one else had before.

My pointer over my lips. "Silence."

My pointer directed at the floor. "Come to me now."

My pointer and middle finger both pointed at the ground and touching one another. "Kneel for me."

My pointer and middle finger pointed at the ground but spread apart, forming a *V.* "Spread your legs for me."

With my chest rising and falling easily, I attempt to recall any others, but I don't think there were any.

"And what of specific kneels, eyes down, hands and knees at the point? What of that?"

Shaking my head gently, I maintain eye contact, and question if I should tell him or if I should remain silent.

"You can speak," he states easily and frees me from the dilemma.

"I have never done any of that, and I don't know what 'at the point' means."

"Was he soft with you?"

Again I hesitate, and my fingers slip to the hem of my dress. "I don't know."

"Did you have lessons from anyone else or observe any other training?"

"No … not really. It's not … It wasn't my kink. I love it, and I loved being his, but all I know is what he told me."

Zander's hand flexes once more, the fingers noticeably spreading wide before he makes a fist. My eyes are drawn to the movement. "It means behave."

A smirk tips up my lips. "Is it a threat of a spanking?" I question and Zander doesn't react. Heat overwhelms me, the nervous kind and I stay perfectly still. His hazel eyes never leave me, and it takes a moment for him to answer. "No. It's a command. I will not threaten you, and I don't like that language."

"So serious," I murmur, all humor leaving the room.

"You enjoy being spanked, don't you? You love it even."

"I do."

"When I tell you to behave, it is not the promise of you enjoying what would happen if you do not obey. Understood?"

"Yes."

"Did you have a safe word?" he questions.

I answer with only a nod, the word stuck at the back of my throat.

"Did you use it often?"

"No. I tried not to use it ever." His expression is unmoving, but his eyes spark with an emotion I can't place.

"I want you to pick a word now."

"Should it be the same as before?" I question without asking if I have permission to speak freely. The fear of disapproval grips me instantly and I'm more than aware that Zander notices. It's the first time since we've started that his expression softens.

"We are not in a scene and I am happy to clarify," he answers, his tone soothing and caressing away the worry. "So long as you are answering or searching for an answer, I am pleased." I only nod, my heart continuing to run away from me.

"To answer your question, the word is yours to choose. It can be the same, or it can be different. It can be as simple as 'stop,' although if you choose that word, you may find that you want to change it later … it's quite easy to use the word when the intensity picks up." With a deeper inhale, Zander's hips move slightly and he palms his erection through his jeans. "I intend to push every boundary with time, but for your word, it is yours and you can use anything you wish."

"Even something like … daffodil?"

He only nods and when I'm silent in response he asks, "Is that your word?"

"No." My gaze drops to the floral print decorating my dress. I didn't anticipate feeling … like this.

"What's wrong?"

I nearly shake my head but before I can complete the action, denying that anything is off, Zander commands, "You will tell me what you were thinking. And you will tell me now."

My throat is tight when I answer, "He told me it was a silly word. He said the safe word shouldn't be … daffodil." I don't know why it hurts so much to remember that. James was good to me. And I loved it. I loved everything that we had together.

"He was soft, and from the sounds of it, it was play for you? It was more than likely play for him with … limited experience.

"Safe words are respected regardless of what they are. Whatever word you want to use, I will abide by. Is that clear?"

"Yes." The stirring of heat in his eyes is echoed at my core under the skirt of my dress. Simply from the way he looks at me, with the darker gaze of a Dominant.

"When you are ready, tell me what your word is."

"Pink." I answer him with only the word and not the reason, praying silently that he won't ask for one.

"Pink." He nods once with his eyes closed before opening them, his dark gaze still fixed on me. "Understood."

"You will use this word often because I will be pushing to find your boundaries. I am not a soft Dom. Know that I don't have any indication whatsoever of your limits. Using your safe word is the only way I will discover them. And it will please me when you use it."

That's so different from before. The way we used it … it was a bad thing to use a safe word. James didn't like it at all, although it only happened a handful of times. I've always thought our relationship was kinky. But now I'm questioning many things I thought I knew well, and we haven't even begun.

"Again, answer me with only a single word. Understood?" The seriousness of his tone is unexpected. For a moment I wonder if this will be too much. If I can handle this, and if this is really what I want.

"Yes."

"For your punishment … spanking, without a doubt, yes?"

"Yes."

"Orgasm denial?"

I hesitate to answer. With my pause, Zander asks, "You prefer it to be saved for greater offenses?"

"Yes."

"Hmm." The deep hum feels like a threat, like he knows how to mold me, how to make me behave.

"Tell me what your limits are. You can speak freely."

"My previous …" I trail off and a tickle runs down my neck as I realize I'm going to speak of James as my Dominant for the first time in my life.

"Your Dom," Zander says, then nods in understanding and there's a note of comfort to his tone I don't expect. There's no jealousy. No judgment. It's freeing, although the sadness lingers.

I can only nod and then swallow harshly. "He used forced silence first. Making me request permission before speaking by resting my hand on his thigh."

With a narrowed gaze paired with his thumb dragging across the pads of his fingertips he questions, "For any offense?"

"My typical offense was back talk."

"How is that not surprising?" Zander offers me a wicked grin that teases the sensitive bundle of nerves desperate for his lips and his touch.

"It is important to me that we speak freely and with respect. I love your mouth and there are a number of things I imagine doing to it. But it would hurt me greatly to silence you."

The seriousness of his admission warrants an "understood" from me.

"If it occurs, there will be physical punishment before forced silence. Is that understood?"

"Yes."

"I imagine your behavior was different when you last enjoyed that relationship."

"Very," I admit and the flashes of a woman I used to be threaten to break me. Before the memories can linger, Zander continues.

"There was more than spanking and forced silence. What else?"

My body hums with exhilaration, and I'm grateful for the distraction. "We played with paddles and whips. I loved the paddles. I didn't like the whips at all. I don't want to bleed."

"He broke skin each time with the whips?" Although his tone is calm, his question is spoken quickly, with an urgency that puts me on edge.

"Yes. We only did it the once and I couldn't handle it."

"Not all whippings break skin."

"I don't want to bleed. That's the reason I don't like whips."

The tips of Zander's fingers tap one after the other in rhythm against his jeans as he considers what I've said. "I think we should eliminate all whips for now, but know they don't all result in what you experienced. He practiced and learned with you; is that right?"

I can only nod, emotions getting the better of me. I don't like thinking of James as lesser. There's not an ounce of me that wants that.

"He didn't want to hurt me. He stopped. The moment I used the safe word, he stopped." The words rush out of me, each one of them trembling.

I'm met with silence and the only sound I hear is the blood rushing in my ears.

"I made you feel you had to defend your former Dom. It's not my intention. For that, I apologize."

The unexpected response only brings about emotions I don't expect. A true sadness and I don't want it.

"Tell me what you loved about it with him. Your scenes, the rewards and punishments. I respect and honor what you had with him. What we have will be different. I will be careful in ways I believe he may not have known how to be. Know that I do not think less of him or of what you had because of it.

"I will find your limits. Tell me now if there are any hard limits. Choking, degradation, fisting, bondage, caning, restrictive discipline, cuckolding, anything at all." My jaw drops slightly from how easily he rattles off the terms.

"Cuckolding is me watching while you're with someone else but not being ... tended to myself, correct?"

He nods, his fist resting under his chin now. "Correct."

"I don't want that. I ... The videos may have made it seem like I ..." Frustration bubbles inside of me. "I am not usually so flustered. I prefer to be blunt."

"Take your time," he tells me. "I'm not in any rush."

"I am possessive. I don't want to be jealous. And I'm not, if it's an equal sexual act. But using another woman to punish me … I am … I don't care for it at all."

"Cuckolding as a punishment is far different from your kink of exhibitionism and swinging or swapping partners. There's a difference in act, in emotion, in intention. I understand that you can enjoy one and despise the other."

All I can give him is a small nod and a whisper in return. "Thank you."

"So … cuckolding is off the table, is there anything else?"

"Bodily fluids in general," I answer.

"Including spitting?" he questions and my body should not at all react as it does.

"No. I meant … I meant …"

"Blood, urine and scat."

Pushing my hair out of my face, the frustration turns to infuriation. I am stronger than this. I am capable of answering bluntly and without hesitation.

"I am detail oriented with this information. I understand if you haven't been asked about this before. There is no shame in that."

Again I nod, my lips pressed in a thin line.

"When we enter a scene, I will inform you if there is anything new to us, or anything we haven't already discussed. There will never be any surprise discipline either. Those are the only times I will prepare you. You must use your safe word or even tell me you are considering using it whenever you feel unsafe or an action is unwanted. Understood?"

"Yes."

"And your rewards will be pleasure. Excessive, freely given pleasure. I will test your boundaries, and I will discover what you prefer myself. That is my reward." His voice is firm, and drips with sex appeal. Any negative emotions are quickly burned away by the primitive need that takes control of every piece of me. "You will not dictate your reward, is that understood?"

"Yes," I answer in a whisper.

"Do you have any questions?"

"When will we do scenes?" I ask immediately.

His answer is unexpected. "To start, always." His rough laugh is subdued and a deadly sound. "You're surprised?"

Swallowing thickly, I nod. "Yes." Although I'm slightly shocked, my body blazes with an eagerness to begin.

"You have your safe word, pink. Now I must find those limits in all things. It is best to stay in play for as long as you are willing and I am able."

Adrenaline rushes through my veins and I find myself picking at the tips of my fingers.

"When do we start?"

"When you no longer have questions and acknowledge that you are now mine. My submissive. And I am yours. Your Dominant."

"There's one. I have … one more question." With his eyes closing slowly, he nods and peers back up at me, still very calm, very soothing in his nature.

"And what is that?"

"Would we record anything?"

He searches my expression, his body stilling. "Like the videos of you I found on the internet?"

"No. Not the … not the punishments and rewards. That's not what I was thinking about. Although, I think that's a separate conversation. I mean our sessions. Where we talk. Can we record those?"

"With what intention? You wish to play them back?"

"I want to share them on my social media. Like us talking through it. Not … not the rewards and punishments. But the therapy sessions. I want to show people how I'm getting through it. The good and the bad. I want to help them too."

"I think we should move through some of the harder topics before we get comfortable with inviting people in. I will consider it, though. I will review first."

A huff of humor that's mostly genuine leaves me. All the men want to review everything. I remind myself that they're protecting me. And I nod although the semblance of a smile slips as I realize something.

"Tell me what's wrong." My focus whips back to him and his stare directed at me holds a possessive intensity that catches me off guard. My answer is immediate and spoken without conscious consent. "My voice."

With a narrowed gaze, I answer more thoroughly before he pries. "It's different than it was before. Scratchier. It sounds different, and they'll notice."

"I see."

There's a small beat in time that passes before he says, "I want you to tell me something about why your voice hurts. Anything at all."

Dread chills any desire I've had over the last hour.

He adds, "I only want one fact but if you want to tell me more, you can. At least one, though. You can do that."

I speak without thinking at his urging, just to get it out there. "I regret it."

"You regret what exactly?" Shifting in this expensive dress on the sofa, I feel cheap and unworthy. "You can change what you want to tell me if you prefer that. But what you tell me must be exact."

"It hurts because I needed surgery after I drank something I wasn't supposed to. I also needed a blood transfusion." I stare at the floor as I speak, focusing on anything other than Zander.

"Look at me," he commands and I do. I obey even though it pains me to do so. "You were aware of what you were drinking?"

I nearly whisper that he told me to tell him only one thing. Just one. Instead the words get caught in my throat, and my eyes prick.

"Good girl," Zander murmurs in a low timbre. Closing my eyes, I do what I've always done, I hold back the tears.

"You have a powerful voice. They will want to hear it even if it sounds different."

I slowly open my eyes to find Zander's expression full of both want and approval.

"If you want to record something, we can. I will be selective about what's saved for you to share."

Pressing my fingers to the corners of my eyes, I comment dryly, "All the men in my life are."

"What do you mean by that?"

"Kam is also monitoring what I post. Damon monitors what I write." For the first time today, my throat feels hoarse and sore; it's definitely gotten better with time. The silence doesn't go unnoticed as I pick up my teacup and drain the now cold tea, leaving behind nothing. It clinks when I set it back down on the table.

It's not until I look back up at Zander that he tells me, "Understood."

Leaning forward in his seat across from me, Zander rests his elbows on his knees and steeples his fingers, resting his chin on the tips of his pointers. "Do you acknowledge that you are my submissive and I am your Dom given the verbal agreements we discussed tonight?"

There is a calmness in his question, but a threat in his hungry gaze.

I murmur, "Yes."

"Say it," he demands.

Swallowing down any hesitation, I give him my submission. "You are my Dominant and I am yours."

He moves all at once, as if my admission opened a lock that held him chained to the chair. So quickly I hardly register it until one hand of his is wrapped around my throat, holding my head against the sofa, with the other on my hip, pinning me to the cushion.

The shock warrants a gasp from me, his touch a smoldering heat.

He stares at my lips as my racing heart pounds in my chest. "What is your safe word?" he questions. "Say it out loud now."

There is no hesitation when I answer him, "Pink." When I swallow, his fingers grip my throat tighter, not constricting, but holding a steady pressure that makes my pulse race with desire.

His right hand moves ever so slowly as he commands me to lift up my dress for him.

My motions are slower than I'd like, but he's patient. The soft fabric glides against my sensitized skin. A low hum that's nearly a growl, of approval resonates from deep in his chest. The air around us is suffocating enough, but his hand on me, controlling me and possessing me, is everything.

I move slowly, but he does not. His right hand cups me through the thin cotton fabric and with his eyes closed he groans, "So fucking wet."

His thumb strums against my clit and I'd throw my head back in pleasure if I could. As it is, I'm pinned where I am.

"You've been a good girl tonight," he tells me, his eyes darkening and holding me still as much as his hand at my throat does.

Pushing the fabric to the side, he runs his fingers along the seam of my pussy lips. Once, twice, spreading the arousal up to my swollen nub where he puts more pressure and runs sweeping circles. Goosebumps race down my arms and then lower.

I struggle to say or do anything, staring at him and for the first time in over a year, feeling wanted. Truly wanted.

When his fingers dip inside of me, not deep, only testing, two things happen at once. My bottom lip drops and I moan from the sudden pleasure. And Zander hisses, "Fuck."

His eyes shut and he stills for a moment. A long enough moment that I question him.

"Do it," I utter and in an instant, he's flipped me over so I'm on all fours. His hand that was at my throat fists the hair at the nape of my neck. His knee is on the sofa, my ass pressed against his jeans. With my back arched, he tugs just slightly.

Again my heart races. He's not gentle with me as he grips my hip, and lowers his lips to the shell of my ear. "Do not test my control, you will regret the punishment immensely."

The battering in my chest is a war drum. "Yes, sir," I answer without hesitation. "I will not do it again."

The desperation for him to reward me, to believe me, not to punish me by denying me this is far too much, far too quickly, is practically palpable. I want him more than I'd ever admit.

A chill meets my backside as he moves away and his grip loosens. For a moment I fear he'll leave me like this, still gasping for breath and wanting. My apprehension vanishes when he pushes his fingers inside of me, curling them and stroking the front wall of my pussy while his thumb brushes against my clit.

My words are unintelligible as I drop my face into the pillow.

His touch is ruthless, and draws out a deep need that's been hidden for far too long.

He finger fucks me until I'm a puddle beneath him, sated and breathless.

I stay as I am, my ass in the air with my dress hiked up and the fabric bunched around my waist after my second release.

The idea of him fucking me consumes my conscience, but he doesn't.

His touch is gentle as he positions me to sit upright. He tells me once again how well I did, then kisses the curve of my neck. My nipples pebble and a shiver runs down my spine.

"Wait here. I have to take care of the cameras for a moment. Then I will hold you and we'll discuss how you'll behave in my absence."

"Hmm?" I question although I have no words and all I can manage is the hmm.

"I'll detail how I want you to fuck yourself and what must happen for you to touch yourself at all when I'm not here.

"We are not done, little bird. We have only just started."

chapter 14

Zander

*Necessary supervision and adjustments to supervision will be a
constant endeavor of The Firm. The client's safety and well-being
will always be our top priority.*

THE AUTUMN NIGHT HAS FALLEN OVER THE MOTEL, LEAVING A trail of burgundy and pinks on the horizon. That's my cue to go back to Ella. I had to force myself to sleep during the day. My overactive mind resisted the pull of the pills. It only wanted her. Planning every detail, reviewing potential lines for the next scene. With my muscles coiled, and my imagination going over every possibility, I hardly slept at all.

My body fought again sleep as much as my mind did. My cock wanted Ella, yes, but so did every inch of me. Every last one. Thinking of her sweet lips and her dark eyes lends itself to a strain I'm eager to explore. It pulls everything into a neat, pulsing tension.

Punishing her will have to be enough. Giving her this release will have to be enough, no matter how badly I want to fuck her. No matter how badly I want her to be mine in every way. It'll have to be enough because these are the boundaries we've drawn. Her life. My job. Those are the circumstances, and part of the challenge is finding a way for it to work so that—

My head spins with the recurring memories.

Fuck. I don't want this challenge. I want to have her under my hands and in my bed, and I can't.

Tugging my polo shirt over my head, I grab the file Silas sent over, tucked into a plain manila folder. It's about Kamden, and it's slim. Too slim. I take it with me on the way out to the car and page through it. Kamden has a squeaky-clean reputation. Absolutely nothing has ever been flagged about him in any database anywhere. Silas told me I'd be disappointed if I was looking for something, because there was nothing.

Something's not right with her conservator. It's obvious in the way he guards himself with her, in his language and tone. He's hiding something and I don't like it. I take another set of four measured breaths and put aside my own misgivings about Kam. Even if I liked him, a completely empty file would be suspicious. Ella's got enough of a past to warrant things appearing on a background check. Kam is with her all the time. One of them has a record, and one of them doesn't?

I pull open the driver side door and toss the file onto the passenger side seat, then climb in. The outskirts of town give way to tree-lined streets. Leaves come down and flutter against the windshield like the feathers of little birds.

My little bird is waiting for me in her elegant, modern cage.

If I'm honest with myself, that's what it is—a spacious, comfortable cage. I've never thought about it in quite those terms before, but now I do. I follow the winding road toward the wealthy part of the suburbs where Ella lives tucked away in the mountains, and let myself consider her dilemma. She needs a cage. That much is clear. Only the house is too sprawling. Not intimate enough. The cage she needs is me. The bounds of our agreement.

The irony doesn't escape me. A cage can set a little bird free.

In that space, with her, the rest of The Firm doesn't exist. Nothing exists except the two of us. She can pick up the pieces of her past and study them from a safe distance.

Maybe that's what I'm doing too. Or what I should be doing.

I pull in at Ella's driveway and steer the car around to the parking in the back. Nobody's in the kitchen. One light is on in the sitting room, but she's not there. Not in the rec room, the formal dining room, anywhere.

There's an anxiousness I shouldn't feel. One I aim to remedy when I find her. She's to wait for me in our blue room when she knows I'm arriving. This tense unease that she's not here, not where I left her, not ... okay— that something is wrong—I don't care for it and it's so easily rectified.

"Ella," I call, keeping my voice calm as it travels up the staircase, but is met with silence. Where the hell is Damon? Distress spurs my steps to pick up.

I climb the stairs. The door to her bedroom is open, but it's empty. *Where are they?*

Did she tell them? Was it too much and she's backing away from me? It's a bitter reality to imagine. Of all the things that kept me up, this wasn't one of them.

Checking my phone, there are no messages from Damon and I'm nearly five minutes early. Still, where the hell are they?

There's only one place I haven't been in this massive house. One place that Kam fiercely guarded when we were doing the modifications. Swore up and down that he'd keep it under control, but we weren't allowed to move anything, to replace anything. So we didn't. Instead there's a rope that's anchored in the doorway of the west hall.

It could've been a mistake, listening to him. That empty file makes me uneasy all over again. I move through the halls to the west wing, ducking under the thin rope and ignoring it altogether.

It's an eerie feeling that surrounds me when I flick on the light. I don't get more than a few steps in before it dawns on me that if Ella were here, she would not be okay.

The clearest demarcation is the art on the walls.

Every piece is wrapped in paper and a thin layer of packing foam as if it's been protected in order to move it, but nothing has been moved. It's all still hanging in place with a thin layer of dust coating it. Like an abandoned house, still filled with its memories and bundled up safely but kept hidden.

The hairs on the back of my neck stand up.

I must have seen this before. I must have. I remember the conversation with Kam, his body blocking the entrance to this hall. I must have looked past him and noted the artwork, but I don't remember it. That was the day of the court hearing, shortly after and before the informal introduction to her downstairs.

I had still been rattled from seeing her.

That's why I didn't notice the artwork. It would have already been done by then.

There's too much packing tape for me to unwrap one and see what needs to be protected like this. Protected—or hidden.

Even the silence is different in this part of the house. As if it hasn't been disturbed in some time, and doesn't like to be disturbed. Not that houses have feelings. I'm not superstitious enough to believe in shit like that. All I know is that the quiet presses in harder the farther I go. Three more steps.

"Ella?"

I call her name, but I already know she's not back here. The first door creaks as it opens. I know she's not here. I can sense it. All the time I've spent working in security has fine-tuned my attention to spaces. They breathe more when someone is there. Small movements in the air give them away. There is no movement here, only a deep hush.

That's when I hear a creak behind me.

The new current in the air reaches me a second before Damon's hand does. A strong hand, just above my elbow. I have just enough warning to tamp down the instinct to subdue him. "We're not supposed to be back here."

I turn to face him, shutting the door as I do, and Damon's expression is more serious than I've ever seen it. Worry flashes in his dark eyes, and a crease in his brow confirms the feeling. I know we're not supposed to be here. He knows I know. So I don't bother saying a damn thing about it.

"What do you know about this wing of the house?"

He releases me and takes a half step back, staying close enough that we can keep our voices low. "Damn it, Zander, why didn't you read the file?"

"Because I never read the files." Irritation is evident in my answer, but it's short-lived. I could have searched other areas of the house before I came in here. "And she asked me not to."

He holds my gaze and I see it—I see it. *Suspicion.* A shiver grips me. Does he know about the arrangement I have with Ella? Has he already figured it out? Damon, of all people, would be the one to notice. He's here at every shift change, since we're paired for this job. He sees me the most. And he knows me the best.

I could tell him, here in this too-quiet hallway with the strange wrappings on all the artwork. That was the suggestion Harrison made, and he had a point. Telling Damon would protect The Firm.

But I keep my mouth shut.

I'll sort through the why of it later, when I'm alone. I'll come up with a plan. But I'm not going to tell him now. Not when I crave her so much that my chest hurts. Not when my hands ache to touch her again.

Not now.

"This is the main wing," he says finally. "Where she sleeps now is the guest wing."

It explains the hotel-like quality of her bedroom. I've noticed the richer the client, the less clutter in general. They can afford a cleaning staff to keep it neat, and the items they buy tend to be fewer but better quality. Still, they have small details that belong to them as people. Who they are and what they cherish most. Ella's room is devoid of almost all the personal items I'd expect. I should have known it wasn't just because of her wealth, or her status. I should have known there was a deeper reason.

She sleeps in a room that's not her own, while her memories are locked away behind packing paper and dust.

"Because all this is too much for her."

"Yes," Damon agrees, although then he adds, "Potentially. The circumstances might have changed. Her progress has been consistent. Ella's taking her meds and having longer conversations. She's more active during the daytime than she was before she was admitted. We spent some time in the yard today, talking as we walked."

"Yard" is an understatement. The estate is grand with a sprawling lawn in the back, fenced in white and bursting with plants and gardens and a chestnut tree. It must sit on at least two acres and backs up to a picturesque mountainscape. I haven't been out there with her much as the fall is rather bitter and she seems to prefer our blue room.

"How did she handle that?" It's hard to picture her out in the sun, strolling with the dappled light in her hair. Her face tipped up to look at the clouds. Her fingertips brushing over a hedge going brittle with autumn.

What I really want to know is if the sun warmed her up. If she seemed free on the outside, or if she was still a little bird in a cage.

Damon can't tell me that.

He nods, considering. "She did well. We took it slow."

He's protective of her too … and for the second time in the space of this few minutes I think about confiding in him. Because the Ella he describes, this woman who needs to move slowly in the yard, this delicate, fragile thing—it's not the Ella who looked me in the eye and consented to spanking with a gleam in the dark centers of her gaze. There are many sides to a person's humanity. Damon is willing to help her, and he can help her in ways that I can't. If I can offer insight, I should. If it will help her. Only if it would help her.

She's stronger than she appears. But also … maybe more broken than I'm seeing.

"And the conversation? Did she share anything I should be aware of?"

"No," he says and shakes his head. "Just small talk mostly. But she's opening up."

"That's good." I force myself to focus and get out of my thoughts. "Where is she now? I was looking for her."

"Resting in one of the guest rooms." I walked right past those doors on the way here. Didn't even bother to look because I thought she'd be in her own room. "She came up about an hour ago. I think the curtains are thicker in one of the other rooms." He shrugs.

I follow him, talking as we go.

"She's been more tired recently," he says.

"She's been staying up later, maybe till two or three."

"Really?" Damon seems surprised. Our footsteps are heavy as we descend the staircase.

"Yeah." I don't elaborate although his gaze is prying. "What time is she waking up?" I question.

"Around nine. I guess that's why she wanted a nap."

"What time did she lie down?"

"'Bout … two hours ago maybe?"

We go downstairs to the kitchen and Damon shrugs on his coat. I try to ignore the disappointment gnawing at my gut. I wanted to see her. I wanted to hear her voice. I want to know what she sounds like when she whimpers because her ass is red and she's falling into that loss of control.

With his keys jingling in his hand, I decide to wait for him to leave and then I'll prepare to wake Ella. We have more boundaries to set. "Wanted to talk to you about something," Damon starts as he pats his pockets, checking for his keys and his wallet. Tension pulls my spine tight. *Damn it.* This is the moment he's going to tell me he knows about Ella. That he saw the way I looked at her in the courtroom. That she spilled to him the details of our arrangement. I brace for it. I'm not ashamed. It's what she needs.

"Go ahead." I hear myself say it, and I'm proud of how normal I sound.

Damon leans against the kitchen island. "I heard you paid Harrison a visit."

Well, shit. I should feel relief, but it's only slight. "Yeah? Did he tell you that?"

"He mentioned that you stopped by. You know he doesn't give details—he only mentioned it in passing. He said he was glad to see you."

"Okay." What is this conversation? "Is there a question in there?"

"Are you okay, man?" Damon's tone is genuine. Empathetic. It's what makes him a favorite of our clients. "We haven't spoken about the hearing yet, and I know it has to be eating at you."

The air sweeps out of my lungs. Of course. The hearing. My gaze drops to the floor as I get ahold of my bearings and then look him in the eye to answer, "I'm doing all right. It'll be better when it's all over."

"I know it won't bring her back, but—" He shakes his head, looking off toward the kitchen window. "She deserves resolution. As much justice as she can get. So do you."

My throat goes dry and I busy myself making a pot of coffee. That familiar ache returns. I'm comfortable telling Damon the truth. That's why it slips out of me now. I'm not used to holding back with him. He's seen me at my worst. "You think she'd want me to have closure? Sometimes I think she wouldn't want that, since the whole damn thing was—"

"Don't say it." Damon holds up a hand. "It wasn't your fault."

He allows us to sit in silence for a moment, the only sound being the drip of the coffee maker. I take a deep breath, then another. Four-count. And then do it again.

Finally I respond, "I know." Don't I fucking know. I've worked through this with Harrison. I'm done working through it. And then a moment like this comes along and all those doubts are back in my head. I remind myself what happened is a ball in a box. "I know. But it feels like the blame should be mine."

"No, man. Quincy wouldn't want that. It didn't matter how things were between the two of you. What happened wasn't your fault. If it was, you'd be the one on trial."

Quincy was good. She was a good person, and I didn't trust her to know what she wanted from me. I didn't trust myself to be honest with her about what I wanted. It's what drove us apart in the end. That and the fact that we just weren't right for each other.

"Look, I'm here." Damon slips his hands in his pockets. "I need to get out of this house and find some food, but—" I laugh at him in spite of myself. "I'm here. You know?"

"Yeah." I clap him on the shoulder. "Get out of here."

He goes, leaving me in the silent house and waiting on Ella so I could feel something other than the emptiness I feel right now.

chapter 15

Ella

*Team members of The Firm will work closely together to
provide a consistent and reliable care experience.*

"IF YOU BROUGHT DONUTS, I'M GOING TO GUESS IT WENT WELL?" The early morning light is still painted with a mauve hue as the sliding back door closes. Kam wears his million-dollar smile, as I used to call it, just as well as his custom-tailored gray blazer with designer jeans. "By the way, you look hot," I add and bring the mug of tea to my lips.

"I would say it went exceptionally well." With his statement, Kamden offers me the pink box of sweets.

Setting down the cup, my smile grows. "Tell me they had the double glazed?"

He speaks as I lift the top, eyeing a half dozen chocolate donuts and inhaling the fresh, sugary scent. It's heaven.

"You know it, my love," he says, then hums and drags out the chair to the left of me, scooting it closer and taking a seat. The extension off of the kitchen boasts large windows. Damon suggested I have my morning tea here to soak up more sun since the weather has turned bitterly cold this week.

Slipping off his sunglasses and folding them, Kamden comments, "I'm surprised you're up this early."

"Couldn't sleep," I answer without thinking. It's the truth that sleep evaded me, but it's because Zander left my mind reeling last night. My nap went longer than I'd have liked and by the time I woke up, he had a list of tasks for me. Starting with me writing down every desire I had for him and reading them off to him one by one after leaving my panties elsewhere. He had me lay the throw blanket across my knees, and then spread my legs. It offered him a view to say the least, but all the cameras would see is me reading from my diary and Zander sitting calmly, asking questions for me to detail more of my goals, desires and fantasies.

He didn't touch me once. Not a single time last night. Instead, after hours, he left me with the task to think beyond what I'd written and focus on what would please him most. Once I write that down, he said I could pick whichever fantasy I wanted.

What would please him most? If I confided in him about what happened. I'm almost certain that's what he wants from me.

The disappointment still lingers I pluck a chunk of the sugary chocolate sweet and pop it into my mouth.

Kam's tone is serious when he asks, "Do you want to talk about it? I can get you stronger sleeping pills, or get the doctor over here to discuss the current medication." As he leans forward without a trace of his humor, the bags under his blue eyes are clear as the morning sun.

"No," I answer with just as much surprise as kindness. "No, no." I wipe my hand on a cloth napkin and shake my head. "It's umm, the medication is working well I think and that's what Damon tells me. It was just a long night really."

My attempt to ease his worries doesn't appear to sink in.

"You'll tell me if you do need anything, right?" he questions and his gaze slips to the old brick of a phone that's capable of making calls, but doesn't have any function for apps. I text him and only him really on it, although I have a small handful of friends I trust whose contact information is on it as well.

"Of course I would. You know if I want to annoy anyone with my bullshit, it will be you," I joke.

He snorts, seeming to relax and leans back in the chair. "It's not annoying and it's not bullshit, but yes," he says and smirks, "I do know how you love to torture me."

I mirror his relaxed posture and ignore my exhaustion as I say, "So, the posts went well."

With his left hand tapping his sunglasses on the table, Kam nods. "Both went well." He emphasizes the first word and it doesn't make much sense at all that I should feel emotional about it. About the knowledge that he did post about the "ball in a box" analogy.

"Was it helpful?" I question, the mug in my hand halting midway as I wait for his answer.

His nod is enthusiastic. "So many people could relate," he tells me and then adds, "There are some comments with other suggestions as well, but I wanted to run them by Damon before showing you." His smile dims slightly, but he holds it in place. "Just to make sure I'm not telling you something or spreading something that could be—"

I cut off his explanation with a wave of my hand through the air. "I get it. You want to make sure it's helpful before I go believing someone off the internet."

His smile turns tight and his gaze drops.

"I should call you Daddy Kam."

"Oh," he says as his brow raises and his voice is playful, "don't tease me." His joke is followed with, "Besides, according to your other post, you've already got a Daddy."

He holds his phone out for me to see.

It takes me a moment to register what I'm seeing. The photo is one that I remember telling Kam I loved. The sight of the floral dress brings back the memories of it being flipped over my waist while Zander finger fucked me. The rumble of his words, do not test my control, nearly has me shivering in my seat.

Focusing on the rest of the photo is much easier.

My caption reads: *I am trying. I am working through it. And I am sending love to all who are working through whatever has stolen their smile.*

I love it. That is exactly the message I would send had I done it myself. Taking a sip of my tea, I notice there are only three comments on the screenshot of the post, which has over a hundred thousand likes on it in the ten minutes that had passed since he took the screenshot.

The first: Sending you so much love back!

The second: I am so proud of you. You can do this, you sexy thing, you!

The third: Whoa, check out the Daddy in the background. I'll work through anything to get to his fine ass.

My eyes widen as I read it and I have to take a look at the photo again. My heart pounds and my blood heats.

Kamden doesn't hold back his laughter at my reaction to the sight of Zander in the background of the photo. The black shirt and jeans he was wearing that day aren't doing him any justice as he stands in the corner of the background through the windowpane. His focus is ahead as he prepares to enter through the back door, so it's a profile.

His stubbled jawline and the power that radiates off of him, even from just striding across the back patio, is sexy as fuck.

"I mean … they're not wrong."

A heat travels across the back of my neck. I'm not certain I can remain composed, so I down the cup of tea before I speak.

"They aren't wrong," I say, my tone less flippant this time.

"You going to start calling him 'Daddy' now? The term going around is 'lover boy,' just so you know."

"Lover boy?" I can hardly get the words out considering the way my breath has been stolen. He's my secret, my safe place. "I didn't realize he was in the picture."

"I think it was one of the last ones I took," Kamden tells me, laying the phone on the table. "It's been great for image. Everyone loves a scandal and even more than that, a romance."

"What did you tell them?" My inquiry comes out more breathy than I'd like, but there isn't an ounce of suspicion from Kam.

"The official statement from your estate is, 'We are incredibly grateful for the professional guidance The Firm has offered during this time of healing.'"

"Professional." I nod in agreement of his wording.

"If you remember, I've always been the professional one. It would be you who would have commented something like, 'Yeah, but is he packing,' along with the eggplant emoji."

The laugh that bubbles up is genuine and given Kam's reaction, the hints of worry diminish quickly enough.

"Now that's a beautiful sound." Damon's comment comes from behind us and I turn to see him making his way over from the other side of the island. His kindness is never unnoticed. The man knows how to make me smile too. I appreciate it and I make sure to widen my grin when I meet his gaze.

"Just the man I wanted to see," Kam pipes up. As the two of them have a quiet conversation, I assume about the comments Kam wants to show me referring to the second post and hopefully not the first, I busy myself with making another cup of tea.

My journal is next to the kettle. Flipping through the pages I find the last one, which I titled: *What would please him most?* It's no coincidence I chose to use a hot pink gel pen for this page. The rest of it is blank.

Damon saw me staring at it this morning. I peek up at him as I wait for the kettle to whistle, and he and Kam are focused on Kam's phone. Occasionally Damon nods.

He told me I was doing well. He said I should be careful not to rush things or judge my progress harshly.

A bad moment is not a bad day. Not being able to complete a task doesn't mean failure.

Staring at this blank page, though, I'm not sure Zander will agree.

chapter 16

Zander

Each client of The Firm will receive regular evaluations to determine whether progress has been made toward their individualized care goals.

ELLA'S HAIR IS WET FROM THE SHOWER WHEN I ARRIVE FOR THE night. I catch the scent of her shampoo the second I walk in the door, and it's all I can do to listen to Damon as he recaps the day. He said it was a lighthearted day but those days worry him. After the highs come the dips, and oftentimes they can feel like falling back when they're only natural.

Harrison once described it to me as a spiral staircase built against a wall. Even though we climb higher and higher, we still hit the wall. We must. It has to occur to move onward.

Making a mental note, I debate on whether or not I should carry through with my plan for tonight.

"Should I aim for an uneventful, quiet night then?"

Damon's head shakes. "Take her lead. If she wants another long conversation, I wouldn't avoid that. It may be necessary. You good?" he asks.

Nodding in agreement that it may be necessary, I continue the movement with my answer, "I'm good."

I send him on his way and find Ella at the archway to the kitchen. I'm not sure where she was before, but she's here now. "Hi," she says softly. The cadence of her voice and the shyness in her posture already have me rock fucking hard.

There is something about a strong-willed woman's submission that is utterly addictive.

"My little bird," I murmur and each word is practically a hum from deep in my chest. I purposefully make the satisfaction audible and I'm rewarded with a slight blush that rises from her chest up to her cheeks.

"We'll start tonight with a scene."

Ella stares at me, her large dark eyes sparking with desire. She nods, and I know she feels what I feel right now. Pent-up need. It's been a long twelve hours without her.

And I am desperate. Combine that with exposed skin revealed by the pale pink silk robe she dons that hugs the small of her waist and cuts off mid-thigh … fuck me.

Now that I've had my fingers in her sweet, tight cunt, it's practically all I can think about. I can and will keep more than one thing in mind at once. Like her safety. Like her progress. Like the way her body moves as we go to the sitting room. But damn does the thought of her enjoying my touch like she did, getting her off and rewarding her occupy every quiet moment.

She takes her seat across from me, perched and waiting for demands like the eager sub she is, and I adjust the lighting in the room. One lamp, turned down as low as it will go. The flames in the grate licking at the crystals in the fireplace. It's intimate, the way I like.

I take my seat. "Stand."

Ella does so without hesitation, getting to her feet in a graceful motion that I want to follow with my hands. The desperation I felt walking in is already waning. It's a combination of the low lighting and the fact that when she obeys me for the first time, we are in the scene, I am in control, and this is right.

It feels right. A 24/7 power exchange is already difficult when there are large gaps of time between scenes. Add in the other men and their own power over her for necessary reasons … every time I walk away there's a prick of nervousness that they won't care for her like they should and that our efforts will be lost. So as much as I'd like, this arrangement is not perfect.

"What are you wearing under your robe?"

"Only panties."

"Take them off." My command, evenly and calmly spoken, is given with my palm up.

Again she obeys, approaching my seat with careful steps and placing them into my outstretched hand. When this is over, she can have them back. Her dark eyes are luminous in the firelight, and she's so close that I can scent her. Fuck, she smells good. Everything about her is intoxicating. It's a combination of her light, floral shampoo and her skin beneath that.

"You can sit down now."

Only a mild hesitation—a fraction of a second before she turns and walks back to her seat. My cock strains against the front of my pants. I ignore it. It's more difficult to dismiss when I'm not with her.

"Good girl." My approval brings back the simper she wore moments ago. "There are things we need to discuss tonight. For this, I'll allow you to speak freely. Understood?"

Ella nods, and I imagine it's because she's conserving her voice, the way she always does. "How is your throat today?"

"Better," she answers confidently.

"Good."

She folds her hands demurely in her lap, resting them on the silk fabric of her robe. Her knees are kept firmly pressed together. I could make her spread them, but I don't.

"You have events scheduled. A brunch, and a rendezvous with executives." I pause, gauging her unmoving expression. Kamden's details are scant. All he noted was that they were friends of hers she hasn't seen in far too long. Damon agrees that she should be socializing. A "rendezvous" isn't a good enough description as far as I'm concerned, but I've been tasked to handle both of them, at Kamden's request.

"Are you looking forward to them?"

"I am." Ella's gaze softens and she seems to doubt herself a moment but then finds her voice I know to be strong. "It's been too long and I miss my friends." The relief that spreads through my chest is unexpected.

I hadn't realized how much I dreaded pushing back on Kamden's request, and Damon's approval, if Ella had been anything other than happy to attend. The idea of her with friends, laughing, smiling and joking … I want that for her.

"It will be a delight to see you among your peers."

"You'll be going?" Ella's surprise forces a smirk to my lips.

"That is correct. You seem shocked."

"I just … I was under the impression Damon would be with me during the brunch, since it will be during his shift. Did you request it?" There's a mix of both hope and worry in the vulnerability that lingers in her question.

Shaking my head once, I admit, "I did not. Kamden did."

"I see."

"Would you rather I didn't?" I question, not understanding her concern and not liking it either.

"It's a relief you'll be there, to be honest. I just … Kamden didn't tell me that."

My hum of acknowledgment is low and short.

"There will be alcohol present at both. It's my preference that you don't drink at either event. Do you agree?"

Ella meets my eyes. Her lips part, as if she's considering disagreeing deeply, but it's several beats before she speaks. This consideration tells me that she's capable of being in this scene. It's something I check for constantly—her ability to consent. Consent, in scenes and otherwise, is never one and done. It can change at any second. At any moment, she could give me her safe word, and this would end. "Yes. I agree." Her voice is so low, so soft.

"I know about the small bottles, little bird."

A frisson of shock moves through the air between us, Ella's eyes widening.

"Do you know which ones I'm referring to?" I ask.

She only nods. "I'd like you to answer verbally."

"I do. Yes."

"I found the bottles, and I reviewed the tapes. I know what you did, and I don't like it. Self-medicating and risking adverse side effects is something that puts you in danger. You're not going to be drinking while you're in my care. I'm glad you agree to the rule. But you should know that I will punish you if you break it." My grip tightens on the armrest when I add, "Severely, and you will not enjoy it."

She nods again. Ella rubs her knees against one another nervously. Her body is tight, not with desire, but fear. "Am I in trouble?" She hasn't experienced a punishment yet beyond orgasm denial. I set her up for that one last night. Tonight I intend to set her up again, but it will be different and certainly not for something she did before she gave her submission to me.

"Do you think you should be?"

"I was … it was a bad moment."

"We also hadn't established our arrangement yet. Had we?" I question her.

Shaking her head, her posture relaxes just slightly. "No, we hadn't started."

Taking a moment to let her compose herself, I shift in my seat, not hiding how very hard I still am for her. I need her to know I still want her. Even if she's done something to upset me, I will always want her.

"Now. We need to prepare for your outings. We will practice."

"Practice?"

"Questions will naturally come up while you're with your friends, or while you're at the rendezvous." Ella changes before my eyes. Her breathing goes shallow, her back straightens and her muscles tense. "They may ask you questions about your voice, or other specifics you have yet to discuss openly and you'll need to be prepared to answer. We'll practice that now."

"They won't ask. They won't." Ella denies the possibility and it fucking guts me how much she truly believes it.

I continue with the scene, I continue my role as her Dom even as the emotions sweep through me. "If they ask you why you hurt yourself, what will you answer?"

"No." Her answer is hard. She struggles to keep my gaze, her head held high in defiance. "I don't want to do this."

What she hasn't done, though, is use her safe word.

"You know what to do if you want to stop something. If you want a scene to end without punishment. You know exactly what to do. So are you telling me no?" I gentle my voice to add, "Or are you saying something else?" She has yet to use her safe word. I imagine the first time will be the hardest for her. This moment, though, this scene, will hopefully not be what does her in, but given her state, I need to remind her that it is available. She has yet to discuss it with me, and it could very well be a boundary and a hard limit for her.

She holds my gaze, the cords in her throat tightening as she whispers, "No."

Good girl.

It does something to me, that "no." That open disobedience. I don't let it show on my face, or in my posture. Her choice tells me how much she wants to heal. That is my good fucking girl. Even if she's going to be punished, I am thrilled with her decision.

"No?"

"I don't—I don't want to talk about it."

The energy in the room feels heightened, almost electric. We're heading toward a line, together. We're barreling toward something new, and I can't breathe for the anticipation of it. I study her. The way she sits, her back straight, her chin lifted. The way her dark eyes never leave mine. Ella knows what she's doing.

"You need to practice. It can't be avoided." It's true. When she reenters public life, the question will come up. More than likely, given her public profile, she will endure it constantly. She must prepare. I need to know she can handle it. I need to know that it won't cause her to break down and erase all the progress she's made. "Are you choosing to disobey me?"

Her chin lifts another fraction of an inch, and then she nods. Definitive. Yes.

"And you're aware of the consequences for disobeying me."

Ella clears her throat. "I'd rather be punished."

I could burst into flames and take this chair with me, and the house, for how much I want her. If I weren't bound by a contract, I'd blister her ass with my palm and then fuck her over the edge of the sofa. Instead, I don't make a move. If she's going to do this, then it will remain her choice all the way to the end. "I won't allow you to deny me indefinitely, little bird. Do you understand?"

"Yes."

I shift forward in the chair to give myself the room we'll need. "Then come put yourself over my lap." Her breathing quickens, audibly so in the quiet of the room, but Ella gets to her feet right away. There's the slightest shake to her body as she crosses the room. She's nervous. Which only makes me harder. My cock twitches with need, begging to satisfy her. Ella hesitates at my knees, and I put a hand on her hip. A professional touch. "Bend."

She does, arranging herself over my lap. I help her into the position I want for a spanking before bracing my forearm over her lower back. She's so warm and soft over my thighs. So nervous. So brave. I slip my hand over the back of her thigh, just above her knee, letting my fingers trail there. The goosebumps aren't my only reward; she shivers and writhes ever so slightly. "You know you can end this," I murmur into her ear.

Ella shakes her head. "No." She swallows. "I want this," she whispers.

I know she does. She's wanted it for a long time now. Her body is begging for this. To have some sort of closure for a pain she can't control. "I know, little bird." I slide my hand up the back of her thigh and under the hem of her robe, and then I flip it up, exposing her ass to the air. She shivers again, and I know it's not from cold—the fire has made it more than comfortable in here. I test one cheek with a quick slap, then the other, rubbing slow circles over the flesh. Her ass is gorgeous with my marks on it. So easily coloring for me. It'll be red by the time I'm done and she'll remember this every time she takes a seat, or even so much as shifts in her seat tomorrow.

Clenching my jaw, I prepare myself. It's been far too long. "Toes on the carpet," I direct her. With the adjustment, her ass lifts into my hand. "You'll keep them there until I'm finished. You can make noise if you need to, but you won't get up, and you won't kick your feet. Understood?"

"Yes."

A breath goes out of her. This is familiar territory. My little bird knows how to do this. I trace my fingertips along her slit.

"Thighs farther apart."

Ella obeys, and it's my turn to take a four-count breath. Her submission brings out a carnal need from me, and it's also more than seductive.

She tempts me like no one ever has, and yet I have to be so fucking careful with her.

I position my palm over her ass so she can feel it. "Thirty swats," I tell her.

"Thirty?" Her whisper betrays her lack of confidence.

Without her able to see me, I don't hide my smirk. "I told you I wasn't a soft Dom. I won't make you count out loud this time, but you should do so in your head."

I give her a beat to process it, and then I begin, sucking in a breath as I slap my hand down on her heated flesh without holding back. She whimpers through clenched teeth for the first three. The next five, though, her mouth drops open and the whimpers are louder, but still short. On the tenth one, her ass is lovely shade of red. It's a dizzying color. The color I've seen in my dreams and my fantasies.

Squeezing her left cheek, I check on her. Wide eyed, she stares at the floor. Her expression isn't scrunched; there are no tears. "Look at me," I command her and she does so. Immediately. Her face is flushed, her chest rising and falling with exhilaration.

"Do you know how many are left?" I question to gauge her ability to consent. Shock can steal a submissive's voice. When she answers twenty, I'm more than aware that she's still with me.

At fifteen she lets out a little yelp, and my cock twitches beneath her. It sounds exactly like I imagined it.

At twenty, her head lifts, and she strains against my thighs, pushing back on my forearm that holds her steady. But she doesn't try to stand, and her toes stay on the carpet. Fuck, it's sexy. I can tell how badly she wants to kick. She's close to crying but not as close as I thought she'd be.

She groans under me and when I ask her again how many, this time her brow pinches, and she can't control her pitch as she calls out ten.

"Good girl," I tell her and reward her by letting my touch fall to her slit. It's a short moment of reprieve. My little bird can take more than this.

But I won't push her tonight. She's already had her first punishment; I would prefer it not to be paired with the first utterance of her safe word as well.

I finish the final ten spanks with the same even rhythm, not letting up, not going soft, but also spreading the blows so they don't land on the same spot too many times in a row. They're hard cracks of my hand on pink flesh, but I'm certain they won't bruise her. Ella cries out with each one but no tears slip from her eyes.

Next time I will be more severe with her. And knowing Ella, next time will come sooner rather than later.

I deliver the final blow and she shudders over my lap, gasping. I pull her upright over my legs so she's straddling me. It's so close to how she'd be if I could fuck her like this. If she was mine. With her robe loosened, her left breast is exposed and I indulge, quickly dropping my lips to her nipple. It's a quick suck that I release with a pop, and then I take her chin in my hand and guide her face up so she's looking into my eyes. "Will you disobey me again?" I ask her even though I'm well aware she will.

My own breathing is heavy, but hers is much worse, it's ragged.

She gives me an adamant shake of her head, and I could kiss her and that naïve, eager-to-please mouth of hers. Her eyes drop down to my shirt.

Squeezing her ass in my hands, I let her small body drop forward as she moans, bracing herself on my shoulder.

"Look at me." Every time she does this—every time she brings her dark eyes to mine—I feel it. An electric jolt. It's deep, in my veins. Ella's breathing is fast, shallow. She needs what every sub needs after a punishment. There's a moment, a moment that's far too short yet suspended in time. And in it, I forget my words. I forget everything except for the way she looks at me.

"Did I do okay?" Her voice quavers, and it's so raw, this thing between us. It's so necessary. And for once I can give a person what they need. For once I'm in the right place at the right time.

I brush her hair behind her back and then run my thumb down the curve of her neck. "You did so well, little bird. That's why I'm going to reward you. Spread your legs wider."

This is for her. But I'd be lying if I said it wasn't also for me.

Her legs are spread over my thighs and I pull her in closer, her forehead resting against the side of my neck. Her body collapses into mine, melting, and I take that moment to skim a hand between her parted thighs and find the heat between her legs.

Ella moans softly and spreads her legs another inch to give me better access. With a rough chuckle, I comment in a low voice full of approval, "Greedy girl."

She's wet. Ready. I don't make her wait long. I push two thick fingers into her without hesitation and she clenches around me. At first she arches her back, and her blunt fingernails dig into my shoulders.

"Steady yourself and fuck my hand." As she does, I make sure I keep my thumb pressed against her clit. I want her to have all the pleasure after getting through her first punishment so well.

Her hips settle into an immediate rhythm, rocking against me, seeking that pleasure. Seeking reward.

"You can have it, little bird. Take it."

"Please," she begs into the crook of my neck, her hips working to fuck my fingers. "Please just let me have you. I want all of you." She stops her movements. "I want you," she emphasizes. She wants my cock inside of her and I'd be damned if I didn't want the same.

I wrap a hand around the back of her neck. "No." It hurts to deny her, but I have to. I'm firm about this. "Take what I'm giving you like a good girl."

I press a thumb to her clit. Three circles. That's all it takes and she's driving her hips forward, fucking my fingers like a wild thing, her face hot on my neck. She comes hard in a series of pulses and flutters around my fingers that I would give anything, anything to feel around my cock.

"Good," I whisper into her ear. "Good girl."

chapter 17

Zander

In the event a client requires more specialized care,
alternate methods may be considered.

I F I'D HAD MORE TIME, I WOULD FEEL MORE PREPARED TO BRING her here. Instead, I ask her once again, "What is your signal?"

My sweet submissive, sweet but defiant, lifts three fingers directly over her lips, the tip of her middle finger resting on the tip of her nose. It would be an unnatural response to yawn, given how straight her hand is and exactly perpendicular to her lips. It is our signal. If she gives it, I will immediately interfere and the conversation will halt.

That is the best I can offer her for when the inevitable questions arise.

For her sake, and her beautiful and susceptible heart, I hope it doesn't happen today. Because she's done nothing but smile all morning when "brunch" was mentioned.

Relaxing the tension in my shoulders, I take a moment, praying that she's right about her friends. I can't control what they say or ask or do. So much is out of my control and I don't fucking like it. If it weren't for the fact that this is my job, I would order her not to attend. It's far too soon in our relationship, but this is not my decision and I already knew our arrangement would come with difficulties.

The restaurant her friends chose is upscale and intimate. We climb the rustic paved steps to the upper floor and enter a sunny room bathed in the golden midmorning sun of autumn. From this height, the picture windows are filled with fall colors. The trees on the low mountain rises have leaves in deep red and orange, with flares of yellow. It's a breathtaking view.

The sight reinforces the stark contrast of the worlds we live in. A woman like Ella will have brunch dates and parties to attend, rubbing elbows with the rich and making appearances for charity. She's a high-profile client for a reason. Her wealth is something I'd nearly forgotten until this morning.

This is her reentering her life. The one she left behind. As I follow behind her, only escorting her for support, Damon texts that he's arrived. He's parked outside next to my BMW 760Li. We each have one assigned to us from The Firm. Black, steel paneled. The security vehicles are unnecessary for Ella, but she did enjoy the leather interior. The car, given to me for the job, is the only piece of luxury I could ever offer her. The thought hits me only now.

"Okay," Ella says and breathes out slowly as she stares at a table in the corner, slipping her periwinkle wool coat down her shoulders. I help her to remove it, but she doesn't let me take it. Instead she holds the folded garment a minute longer, as if it's a shield. Two beautiful women are seated at the farthest end, both smiling and laughing, both oblivious for the moment that Ella's here.

Ella's chest rises and falls with anticipation and I offer her a slight push with my hand on the small of her back. That's the only nudge I give her before her friends notice her and squeal in delight, the chairs pushing back and scraping against the farmhouse wood floors.

With Ella smiling broadly, and quickly joining the women, I text Damon back that we're in location.

Ella described each of her friends to me on the way over. Kelly's the shorter of the two—Asian, with shiny black hair that cascades down to her lower back and the kind of face that belongs in magazines. Her face lights up at the sight of Ella. Trish is tall and blond and wears a playful grin that wouldn't be out of place at a club. From what Ella said, she spends a lot of time partying. Together they all look young, rich and carefree. For the moment.

These are her best friends. Her oldest friends. But I know how it is to go back to the world after you've been away, whether it's mentally or physically. Overwhelming as fuck.

With some friends you can pick up where you left off easily, but even if they're those kinds of friends, where Ella left off is … well, that's where the problem lies. And why I stay on edge, even if her posture confirms that Ella is full of relief and joy.

"Hi," Kelly says, and she wraps Ella into an instant hug. "We missed you."

"We did. So damn much!" Trish wraps her arms around both of them, and Ella is almost lost in the embraces of her friends. "I'm so glad to see you, El. It's been way too long."

Ella clears her throat. "I know."

Kelly blinks; it's only a half second of a response before Kelly corrects her expression. That's the only reaction to the changed sound of her voice.

"Sit, sit, sit," she ushers Ella, pulling out a chair for her and Trish pipes up with, "I was just telling Kelly all about the new guy." They move on without addressing it at all. The atmosphere is lighthearted, the women all smiling still.

It's immediately obvious that these women might not know the full story, but they're not going to push her beyond what she can handle. "Let's sit," Kelly says, giving Ella a last pat on the back. "Let's eat."

"I'm all for that," Ella says and laughs. As they take their seats, I search for a waiter or waitress to ask if I can plant myself in the corner of the room, remaining in sight, but at a distance.

"This one is for you," Trish calls out to me. Half-seated, she perks right back up. "There are four chairs for a reason."

"Come, come." Kelly gestures with her hand, waving me over. "I promise we won't bite," she adds.

Trish side-eyes her with a devilish smile before turning that grin to Ella and saying loud enough for me to hear, "Shh, don't tell him Kelly's lying."

Ella doesn't miss a beat laughing along with the girls and she turns in her seat, brimming with a happiness I have yet to see her wear back at her home. It's a striking contrast and when she asks politely, "Please, would you sit with us," but with wide pleading eyes, I offer her the professional response.

"This is your brunch—"

"Oh no, we insist," Kelly interjects. Clearing my throat, I give them a tight smile and take the seat next to Ella. Heat races along the back of my shoulders. This is what we would do for any other client, I remind myself. This is professional. That is all this is.

Ella's gaze burns into me and rather than looking, rather than giving our relationship away, I reassure her that all is well by slipping my hand onto her thigh. Balancing the professional image with the very unprofessional touch. With it, though, Ella laughs. "You two practically bullied him," she teases.

As Kelly shamelessly shrugs, Trish leads the conversation.

"So." Trish picks up her water goblet and takes a sip. "Who's this, El?"

For a split second, Ella beams at me. It sets my heart racing. Then her expression settles into something more neutral. Good. "This is Zander, one of the men from the private firm I hired."

This is the story we've settled on for when Ella makes these appearances—that she's hired a new security firm. No one else needs to know the details, and no one ever will. The Firm prides itself on confidentiality. "It's nice to meet you ladies," I say to greet them.

Trish shares a look with Kelly, who raises her eyebrows. It's over in the blink of an eye, and I sit back in my seat and stay quiet. It's not long before the three women are talking around me.

This is exactly what I want.

I'm here to observe Ella for signs that she needs to leave, whether it's with her signal or otherwise, and that is all.

Watching her with her friends is a stark difference from the silent woman in the courtroom almost a month ago. She is different with Kam, more laid back and less high energy than she is now with her friends. She is dynamically beautiful, transparently confident, and yet, when no one is looking … I know she has her moments. We all do.

The conversation is easy and light, as are the meals the women eat.

The brunch consists of dainty pastries, a variety of fresh fruits and berries, eggs benedict and sides of bacon, sausage and ham.

Although the women are slim, the platters disappear quickly and I half wonder where they put it away. Ella herself doesn't hesitate to take her share and when the women push it on me to eat, I do so for politeness only.

A half an hour passes without the women concerning themselves with me at all.

Kelly tells Ella about a book she read—apparently she likes fantasy, and she likes it steamy—and only once does she cut a glance at me. "Sorry, Zander," she says, and Ella laughs.

I offer a smirk, again telling myself it's to be polite, although I will admit, I'm fond of the way they treat Ella. Trish whispers, "I bet Z would like it," "there's totally sex in it." Kelly laughs as Trish asks Ella, "What do you think?"

"If I had time to read, maybe I could offer an opinion."

"Oh?" Now Trish is looking at me, and I don't mind it, not exactly. I prefer my focus to remain on Ella, though. "Is this one keeping you busy?"

Heat blazes along the back of my neck and my right hand flexes. It's one of the signals, commanding Ella to behave.

I see an echo of that woman from the videos on the porn site. Not the woman on her social platforms who shared her day-in, day-out life with her followers, but the vixen at night. Her kinky, her less sweet, and much more provocative side.

Ella's gaze falls to my hand, and I rest a loose fist on the table.

"I saw the comments, but that's not what this is."

"Oh," Kelly says and pouts, but Trish doesn't seem to accept it, judging by the way her gaze dances between us.

"I am here only to do my job. I'm sorry to disappoint you."

Ella's reaction is tense at first. I imagine she's wondering now whether she's been behaving or not. The slight flush on her beautiful cheeks gives it away. It takes her quite a few minutes to relax her shoulders and settle into the rhythm again as the women order cappuccinos and lattes. It doesn't go unnoticed that they're quick to turn down the mimosas the waiter offers.

Time ticks by even after the dishes are removed. I don't care if we sit here until the restaurant closes, if that's what Ella wants to do.

Kelly has a constant stream of things to talk about, and Trish chimes in, the two of them a perfect team of entertainment and ease. Ella joins in from time to time. Occasionally her fingers tap her throat and she quickly sips her ice water to squelch whatever pain has come. This may be the first time she's spoken for so long and so loudly. She generally keeps her voice low with me, but it's not at all here. She doesn't say as much as her friends, but it still doesn't seem like they're overpowering her. It's like the three of them are a unit. They know when to give and take.

I like that for her. I didn't expect to feel so relieved when her friends turned out to be good people. There's a sense of jealousy there too—that these women know Ella in a way I might never understand. They knew her before and she has yet to share that with me.

I'm watching Ella's face so intently that I miss the change in the conversation.

"—like James used to do."

Her gaze drops down to the tea bag that sits on the edge of a small porcelain saucer, the smile still in place on her face. "Mm-hmm," she answers.

Trish is still speaking, but I lose the rest entirely. It doesn't matter. Ella runs her fingers through the napkin in her lap and raises her head to continue with the conversation.

I abandon all thoughts of anything other than signs of distress, staying relaxed. I'm not going to give her friends any indication there's a problem—especially if there isn't one yet.

At first I think Ella's lifting her hand to touch her throat again, my body tense and waiting still. But then her fingertips hover over her lips.

My reaction is instant. I take out my phone and study the screen. "I need to step outside for a moment." I speak over Kelly, effectively halting the conversation, saying it with a smile, and Trish and Kelly both smile back. "Ella, would you come with me?" I don't dare glance at the other women, although their objections come with a short gasp from one of the two of them. She nods gratefully, not speaking, and I pull out her chair for her to stand. In her silence, I promise the women, "I'll bring her back in a few minutes."

"You'd better," scolds Trish. It's not lost on me that the two don't speak while we leave. Which is certainly an indication that they will the moment we're off.

With a hand on Ella's lower back, I escort her out of the restaurant. Silently we descend the stairs, although her pace is quicker than my own. She turns immediately to the right and heads through a small alley that lets out to a riverwalk. The river in autumn reflects the colors of the trees, and Ella walks without hesitation to the railing and leans against it.

I should take my hand off her back.

I don't.

Ella lifts her head and peeks at me. "I'm not going to jump."

I think she means it as a joke, but I answer the emotion in her eyes instead of the words. "You're thinking about that? Is that where your head has gone?"

She shakes her head. "No. But I was worried yours might be there."

I assure her, "It's not. And you would fail miserably if you attempted to jump while I was here."

She huffs a small laugh with a smile that doesn't reach her eyes as she gazes over the still waters.

"I just needed some fresh air." She touches the front of her chest, and I know. I know that feeling. Someone says a name you're not expecting and you have a small heart attack. Hurts like the muscle itself has been bruised. I know it so well.

I hate this moment. This grief that she's coping with. But to deal with it in such a healthy way, I admire her. "I am proud of you," I tell her and she peers up at me.

"I couldn't even last a brunch, and you're proud."

"How is this not lasting?" I ask her, pushing back.

"Would you hold me, then? I deserve a reward, don't I?" Her pleas are voiced in a teasing manner, her wide eyes still glinting with vulnerability.

My intention is to pull her in for a hug. But as I reach for her, something else takes over. I don't put my hands on her shoulders. I reach for her face, take her chin in my hand, and pull her to me.

And kiss her.

Right there on the riverwalk.

Ella's lips part for me and she makes a little noise into my mouth, a contented sigh. *Fuck*, she tastes good. Sweet and delectable. I run my tongue along the seam of her lips and she lets me in. It's so easy, and so right, like she was made for me. Like my whole life was dragging me here by the hand.

Boundaries be damned.

My little bird presses close to me, her body warm against mine, and I find both hands in her hair, both hands pulling her in. I don't want her far from me. I don't want her anywhere out of my sight. I want this forever.

And if I'm honest, which I haven't been—not with Cade, not with Damon, not with myself—I want her so badly it hurts. Kissing her shoves the truth out into broad daylight. Punishing her will never be enough. Making her come will never be enough. A quick, hard fuck would do nothing to kill this craving. With her, it wouldn't stop until I'd had my fill. Until I'd tasted each of her boundaries and all her sadness and let her see mine as well. Let her tear them all down.

Ella kisses me back, harder than before, and then she comes up for air. It tastes sweet and crisp, like this autumn breeze. But nothing is as sweet as her arms around my neck. She leans back into my hands, trusting me to hold her up.

"Z," she whispers.

"Little bird."

I untangle her arms from my neck, but it's the last thing I want to do. Reality is setting in. We're out behind the brunch restaurant, where anyone could see. I've lost track of time. I have no idea how long I tasted her. How long I lost myself in her mouth and her touch.

"Are you ready?" I question her. I'll be right there beside her with whatever excuse or escape she needs when we return to that table.

"I want to use the restroom before we go back."

"Go ahead," I tell her. "I'll wait for you by the stairs."

She turns my hand in hers so she can press a kiss to my knuckles. "Are you okay?"

"Are you?"

Her grin lifts up the corners of her mouth, and I can't help myself—I press my thumb to that curve and then run it over her cheekbone. "I'm good," Ella says. "I just had a little moment." With a small shake of her head, a laugh gets away from her. "I'd rather stay out here and kiss you. But my friends will wonder where we went."

"Mmm," is all I can say, and my hum of approval is low and deep. *As would I.*

Ella rises on tiptoe and kisses my cheek, a brief heat against my skin, and then she's gone, moving back through the alley.

I'm about to turn around and let the railing keep me from collapsing when I see him.

Damon.

At the corner of the building, his eyes on Ella as she enters the small restroom beside the alley. My heart pounds. Damon comes to a stop a foot in front of me, and when he looks into my eyes, I know.

He saw.

He saw everything.

Damon slips his hands in his pockets, his jaw working. There are probably a hundred things he'd like to say to me right now, and I tense, waiting for the worst of them. How I've put Ella at risk. How I've been dishonest. How I could truly fuck things up for The Firm, and, by extension, for him. The silence gets painful.

The worst of it is that admitting any of it threatens to take her away from me.

There's no judgment in his words, only disapproval in his expression when he states, "You have to tell your brother."

chapter 18

Ella

While emotional attachments between clients and members of The Firm are expected, these attachments will be carefully managed so they do not compromise the safety of the client or any member of The Firm.

ALL I KEEP THINKING ABOUT IS HOW WELL IT WENT. I HADN'T realized how much I missed them. I missed going out, I missed laughing, I missed seeing the people I love.

There's still a pounding anxiousness in my chest that won't quit. It's been there since this morning and it hasn't left me for a moment, other than one.

When Zander cupped my chin, when he let me deepen the kiss, when he pulled me in close to him and there wasn't a thing separating us.

It all stopped then, and that anxious feeling in my chest … it changed. It's still there thrumming away as I wait for him at the bottom of the stairs.

Picking at my nails, I wonder if he feels it too. I can't help but to worry. He's been different, quiet. Or at least I think he has. Maybe it's all in my head.

A huff of nervous laughter leaves me at the thought.

Damon took me home after lunch so it's been hours now since I've seen Zander, but he should be here any moment. I imagine he'll be wearing what he did earlier, but I've changed. There's a chill that slips up the silk fabric of my pale pink robe as I sit here and without anything under it, shivers grace my bare skin.

I remember this part. I remember falling. To be in this moment and know it is surreal. That fluttering of butterflies dives lower as the rumble of my name reaches me. His timbre is low, seductive.

"There you are," he murmurs and I peer up at him, sitting on the bottom step and feeling so small beneath him.

He towers over me and I'm so very aware of how much power I've given him. How much control he has over my emotions, my actions … my desires.

"And there you are," I offer him in return, attempting to maintain a semblance of confidence that seems blurred in all of this.

"I did good today … didn't I?" I question and if I wasn't his submissive, I'd hate that I'm searching for his approval. If I'm honest, part of me isn't at this moment. Part of me sees a man I'm falling for, and I want him to be proud of me.

"You did exceptionally well."

"I told you you'd like them." Nervous jitters leave me as I reach for the journal. "You'll want to read the part I've bookmarked with the ribbon," I tell him and swallow the knot in my throat. "I did what you asked. I wrote what it was that I thought would please you most."

My heart pounds as Zander takes the journal from me, his fingers slipping against mine as he does and there's an electric knowing that forces me to pull my hand away faster than I'd like.

His stubbled jaw is strong at this angle, his gaze holding something I haven't seen before. *Thump, thump,* my heart wars inside of me.

"You wrote what would please me most?" he asks and I nearly spill it all right now as I stare up at him, praying he'll understand. That what I feel for him is what he feels for me and that even my darkest days won't take away from what we have.

Tears prick at the memory, the memories, the anguish, the shame still fresh in my mind. "I did it. And you said … you promised that I could pick what would please me most if I did it," I remind him. The desperation in my voice doesn't go unnoticed by either of us.

Letting the hand holding the notebook fall to his side, Zander asks me, "And what is it that you want most? What would please you most?"

Standing on shaky legs, my fingers fumble with the tie of the robe, but only for a half second before it comes undone. The moment it opens, I shrug it off my shoulders and let the diaphanous fabric fall to the floor, leaving me bared to him.

His gaze drops to my breasts and he utters my name in weakness, "Ella."

"Take me," I plead. "Take me upstairs and make me yours. Please." My fantasy, what I want most … it's for me to have him, fully and in every way. Not just for tonight, but we can start with this moment.

Staring into his eyes, I pray he can feel how much I need this, especially after today and whatever's changed between us. "I want you," I whisper.

His lips crash against mine and I moan into his mouth. Loving him, needing him. This. All of this. It's everything that I have been missing.

He takes the stairs two at a time. One arm bracing my bare back, his hand gripping my neck to hold me to him, his other arm wrapped around my ass as tightly as my legs are wrapped around his thighs. I'm barely aware of the world around us, it whips by far too quickly.

The second my back hits the door, there's a click of the knob being twisted and it opens behind me. Ushering an approving groan from Zander.

I'm on the bed at once, letting out a gasp. Zander's quick to undress himself as I push myself back on the bed.

And then there he is, a hunter at the end of my bed. Crawling toward me, naked, and his cock jutting out, hard and thick. The heat from his body is nearly suffocating. He is everything, and nothing else matters as licks his lower lip and takes a languid lick of my pussy. He doesn't hesitate to dip his tongue into my entrance, causing my back to arch. His large hands wrap around my inner thighs, spreading me and holding me there for him as he moves his lips to my clit and sucks.

If I gave a fuck, I'd be ashamed of the mangled whimper that leaves me, but as it is, I don't hide a thing from him. I want him to know what he does to me.

Kissing up my body, he leaves me wanting. His shoulders are foreboding as he cages me under him. The head of his cock teases my lips.

I'm ready to beg him, the words on the tip of my tongue, but they don't make it out. He slams inside of me without any further warning. The sweet pain of being stretched steals my breath. His gaze pins me as much as his body does while my body attempts to accommodate him.

He stays there buried inside of me, ever my ruthless Dominant, while I can barely survive beneath him.

Lowering his lips to mine, he kisses me, sucking in my bottom lip as he pulls out slightly and then pushes himself all the way back in. The movement forces me to hold on to him.

He nips the lobe of my ear and groans, "I knew you'd feel like this … fucking perfect."

Pulling back, he looks deep in my eyes and tells me, "I wanted to be controlled for you, I wanted to take it slow." My breath is shuddery as he warns me, "But I'm not going to be able to do that this time." Before I can respond, Zander lifts my hips slightly and well and truly fucks me.

I wanted him to take me, and that's exactly what he does.

Pounding into me as if he needs me as much as I need him.

I shatter beneath him. My blunt nails dig into his shoulders and my body tenses around him. With my head thrown back, I'm lost in pleasure. Zander doesn't stop, he rides through my orgasm and every thrust brushes against my clit, heightening the overwhelming bliss.

The sounds of flesh hitting flesh intensify as my arousal spreads between us. It seems to only spur him on, to fuck me hard and faster, to take from me over and over again. I writhe under him as the intensity climbs again, the cliff I'll fall from seemingly higher.

I can barely breathe as the next crashes through me and my neck arches. With the chill of the air hitting my heated face, I scream out his name as my body tenses and every nerve ending blazes. It starts from the pit of my belly and then rages outward.

Zander sucks and nibbles my neck, as I do everything I can to get a grip, to come back down from the highest high. But I can't. His hips piston relentlessly, never giving me a moment to gather purchase. Instead, he kisses me, he fucks me, and his grip keeps me pinned beneath him, leaving me without any mercy at all.

"Zander." His name is a plea on my lips, one he doesn't take. Repositioning my leg higher up, he slams into me, groaning his pleasure into the crook of my neck. I can't help but to cry out my scream of pleasure as he fucks me deeper. Clawing at his back, the mix of pain and pleasure threatens to destroy me. To ruin me.

I try to plead with him, to call out his name. "Z" is barely a whisper as his pace picks up.

Pink. I nearly cry out pink as he thrusts himself inside of me and leaves himself there, his cock pulsing as yet another orgasm paralyzes me.

My heart hammers and my body trembles. It takes me far too long to release, and he's finished with me that time. Leaving my legs shaking. With his forearms braced on either side of my head, he whispers kisses along my jaw and then down my neck, leaving a trail of goosebumps in his wake.

If I could find my voice, I'd tell him he wrecked me. I've had sex plenty throughout my life, although it's been so long now. I've had lovers and one-night stands; I've had a Dom and a husband who loved me and fucked me thoroughly.

This, though, this shattering and feeling bared in a way that's far too vulnerable … This feels like the first time. It feels like Zander's taken something from me I didn't realize I had to give.

He commands me to spread my legs for him, and I do, although they still tremble. He cleans me and I can barely hear him, his shadow moving across the room and then to the bathroom. Turning to my side, I curl up and still, I can't steady myself.

It feels as if everything has changed. It was so slow this morning, so slow for weeks, and then it happened. In a single moment. He took me there and I know there's no going back.

He climbs back into bed, the frame groaning from his weight. The covers rustle as he lays behind me and then pulls me in close to him. The tip of his nose runs along the curve of my neck, his hand gripping my hip. He leaves a chaste kiss just under the shell of my ear and with the shiver of desire running down my body, I'm reminded of how sore he's left me.

"Zander," I whisper his name, still breathless, still unable to move just yet. His lips are pressed against my hair and he kisses me there before that deep, rough hum rumbles up his chest.

Without turning to face him, without having that much courage I tell him, "I think I want more than to just be your client …" My cadence is shaky when I add, not daring to close my eyes, "I want more than to just be your submissive."

There's a beat and then another beat of silence. And then another. Too much time passes with him still behind me, not moving, not saying a word. Betrayal grips my heart and fears run rampant in the back of my mind.

"We have what we have right now, Ella."

He says Ella, not "little bird."

I only nod, my cheek still firm against the pillow. It takes great effort not to let on how much it hurts. How much pain sits against my chest.

We have what we have. Those are not the words of a man who feels the same as what I feel. I remember falling … and I remember heartbreak just as well.

chapter 19

Zander

Any misconduct by a member of The Firm will be investigated immediately.

S LEEPING WITH ELLA BREAKS DOWN A WALL INSIDE ME.
It's all I can think about. And on this drive back to the motel, it's killing me.

I slept with her. I didn't tell my brother. At this point, I don't know that I will. Damon wouldn't betray me. I'd be a shitty person to put him in that position, but if it's for Ella, I'll draw that line.

Everything is so fucked. And my little bird has no idea.

Selfishly I know I've failed her, but I wouldn't change it. I want to hold on just a while longer, feeling those walls break down.

It's been crumbling for a while now. Probably since the day I saw her standing at the front of that courtroom. Probably since the first time her eyes met mine. On some level, far below conscious thought, I knew I wanted her. All of her.

And I knew it would be different.

It is different.

It has to be different.

My mind can't settle. It's been a runaway mess since I got up from

Ella's bed this morning. There was so much rightness in laying her down in her bed, in fucking her like both of us wanted for so long. Peace, like I haven't felt at any point in my life. And then the heartbroken expression on her face. The tears gathering in her eyes.

And the things she said—

They remind me of Quincy.

That combined with Damon texting me, reminding me that I need to be careful. He says he's worried for me.

It's too much like Quincy, man.
The hearing's coming up. I'm worried for you.
You sure this is for the right reasons?
She could get hurt, and you might not see it coming.

It fucking guts me, to second-guess what I feel for her and what I know she feels for me.

Memories from the past keep sneaking up on me. Quincy's face across the table from me at a wine bar in the city, her blue eyes bright with flirtation and confidence. The disappointment that stared back at me on a street corner, her hand on my chest, those same blue eyes filled with crushing disappointment.

Even now I feel the push as she shoved me away.

Quincy saying, "No. I'm going for a walk. Don't follow me."

I should have followed, but her final statement kept me from trailing after her: "If you don't want all of me, then I don't want any of you."

She was my submissive, but she wanted more. She wanted a "real" relationship.

I hadn't followed her, because she wanted space—and because she wanted something from me that I couldn't give her. What was the point of following, when there was no agreeing to disagree? I didn't want to marry her. I loved her in a way that wasn't that. I broke her heart that night, but it was the truth. She knew when we started that I wasn't looking for more. She said she wasn't either.

She wanted things to progress past sharing an apartment that I barely slept in. Quincy wanted more commitment than a one-year lease. She wanted a ring on her finger, and I couldn't do it.

Not because I didn't love her. I did, in a way. But not in the way I feel about Ella. It was the way you care about a person when you're trying to give them what you want, at the expense of giving up what you need.

Quincy wanted me to be different for her.

Ella just wants me to be hers.

Fuck, it hurts. The worst part of it all is that I am questioning everything. Does Ella truly want to be with me? Or did I take advantage of a young woman who would have clung to whoever had been there for her first?

The migraine combined with the sleepless night is too much as I turn onto the drive.

If she has the same feelings for me as I do for her, then I have to fix this.

It's like a lightning strike, and I'm turning the wheel before I can think about it. Braking. Throwing it into reverse. I'm going back.

If Ella feels that way about me, then I have to make it right, and I have to do it now. I have to hold on to her the way she deserves.

I'm not far away. It won't be long until I can fix this.

Ella's house appears on the side of the road out of nowhere. I'm not aware of the route I took, or anything else. I'm only aware of a fierce pounding in my heart and a twist in my gut.

Again I question myself.

Did I take advantage of her last night?

Did I take advantage of her pain and her desires? Or is all of this meant to be and it's just a fucked-up situation that brought us together?

I only wish I could pause. To take in every detail. To make sure she's all right. To ensure that whatever I do next, is best for her.

Quincy left me that night, and I let her. I let her walk away. What happened next was a tragedy and I've never regretted anything more. If I could go back, I would change it all.

I let her walk home alone while I went the other way. I knew it wasn't safe. Nearly midnight on the city streets. I knew I should have followed her.

But then again, I knew I should have ended it with her weeks before.

I will never forgive myself if Ella doesn't make it out of this well and whole.

I can't be wrong again. I pull into my spot behind the house. One, two, three, four. Again I repeat the breaths. Again. Until I'm calm enough to focus. Until I'm calm enough to walk inside and make this right.

The answers aren't hiding behind my steering wheel. The answers can only be found by seeing this through.

Then Damon comes out the back door with his coat on. Alone.

He sees me, and the corners of his mouth turn down.

And then I'm out of the car, heading for him.

His jaw is hard, the clean cut of his button-down combined with how his shoulders straighten and he stares me down as I approach. Like we're squaring up for a fight. "You didn't tell him," Damon speaks low and deliberately. "You're my friend, but I can't let you do this."

"No, I didn't tell him. I'm coming here to talk to you."

"It's too late."

Betrayal feels like a hot knife in my gut. "You didn't," I grit out from between clenched teeth. "You didn't fucking tell him, Damon. You didn't."

He only stares back at me.

"Why are you out here?" It's too much to come clean to him now, with this storm in my chest. "Is somebody else in there with her?"

Damon shakes his head. "There's nobody inside."

"What the fuck? You know we can't—"

"There's *nobody* inside."

It sinks in then, what he means. I grab for the front of his jacket on instinct but Damon's as strong as I am, and he gets me around the wrist. "You did this."

"I didn't tell him shit. It wasn't me." I let him go and run for the kitchen door. Throw it open. Go inside.

"Ella," I call out.

The house is empty.

I know it, because I can sense it, because it's my job to know. I know this stillness.

I look anyway.

The sitting room is both dark and quiet, without the lit fire, without her waiting there with her gorgeous dark gaze giving me a longing that echoes within myself.

Anger and regret are a bitter thing to swallow. I take the stairs two at a time, checking her bedroom, the guest room, everywhere. It still smells like her up here. I was only gone for twenty minutes. I run back down and grip the doorframe at the sitting room. She's not here. It's empty.

She's not here.

Damon's footsteps stop close by.

"Kamden had suspicions," he says from behind me, an edge in his voice so hard I don't dare look at him. I can't. "He put cameras in the house, Zander. They know."

Dread washes over me. But Damon doesn't stop talking.

"Caleb and Ella are with him now. There may be an emergency hearing." He's pissed. At me.

"Cameras—more than the ones we installed?"

"Yes."

I finally face him. Anger and desolation stare back at me. "Everybody knows what happened." A deep breath. "You're being removed. You aren't allowed to see her again."

My own rage boils over. "You're not going to keep me from her. Whatever you said, whatever you did, you fucked this up—"

Damon stabs a finger into my chest. "*You* fucked this up, Z. You crossed a line. You hid it from everybody. You could have hurt her. You could be taking us all down, so don't try to blame me for your own stupid mistakes."

"You can't do this." I don't know if I'm talking to him or myself. "You can't take her from me."

My oldest friend huffs out a breath and straightens his jacket, disappointment rolling off him in waves. "I didn't do this. You did. Look me in the eye right now." I do it, and he returns my gaze, furious and hurt. When he speaks, it's with an icy clarity. "It's over. For good."

The National Suicide Prevention Lifeline is a United States-based suicide prevention network of over 160 crisis centers that provides 24/7 service via a toll-free hotline at the number 1-800-273-8255. It is available to anyone in suicidal crisis or emotional distress.

hold me

I was born into luxury and used to getting what I wanted.
What I desired most, with my life in disarray, was the man who sat across from me.
He was tall, dark and handsome. Most notably, he was forbidden.

It made every accidental touch more sinful and every court-mandated session more addictive.

So much tragedy had happened and he was supposed to fix me.
I shouldn't have wondered how it would feel to be trapped under his broad shoulders.
I shouldn't have focused on the way he licked his bottom lip every time his gaze dropped from mine and roamed my curves.
I shouldn't have dreamed about him breaking the rules to comfort me the way I desperately needed.

I did, though, and I was the first one to submit.

He was my protector and my confidant, and then he became my lover.
I teased him, tempted the two of us and now there's no way to take it back.
With everything I've been through, I didn't expect to fall for him.
There's only so much heartache I can take.

playlist

"Little Do You Know"—Alex & Sierra

"Me and My Broken Heart"—Rixton

"Mercy"—Brett Young

"Renegades"—X Ambassadors

"Ho Hey"—The Lumineers

"Little Talks"—Of Monsters and Men

"All Your Exes"—Julia Michaels

"Without Me"—Halsey

"Overwhelmed"—Royal & the Serpent

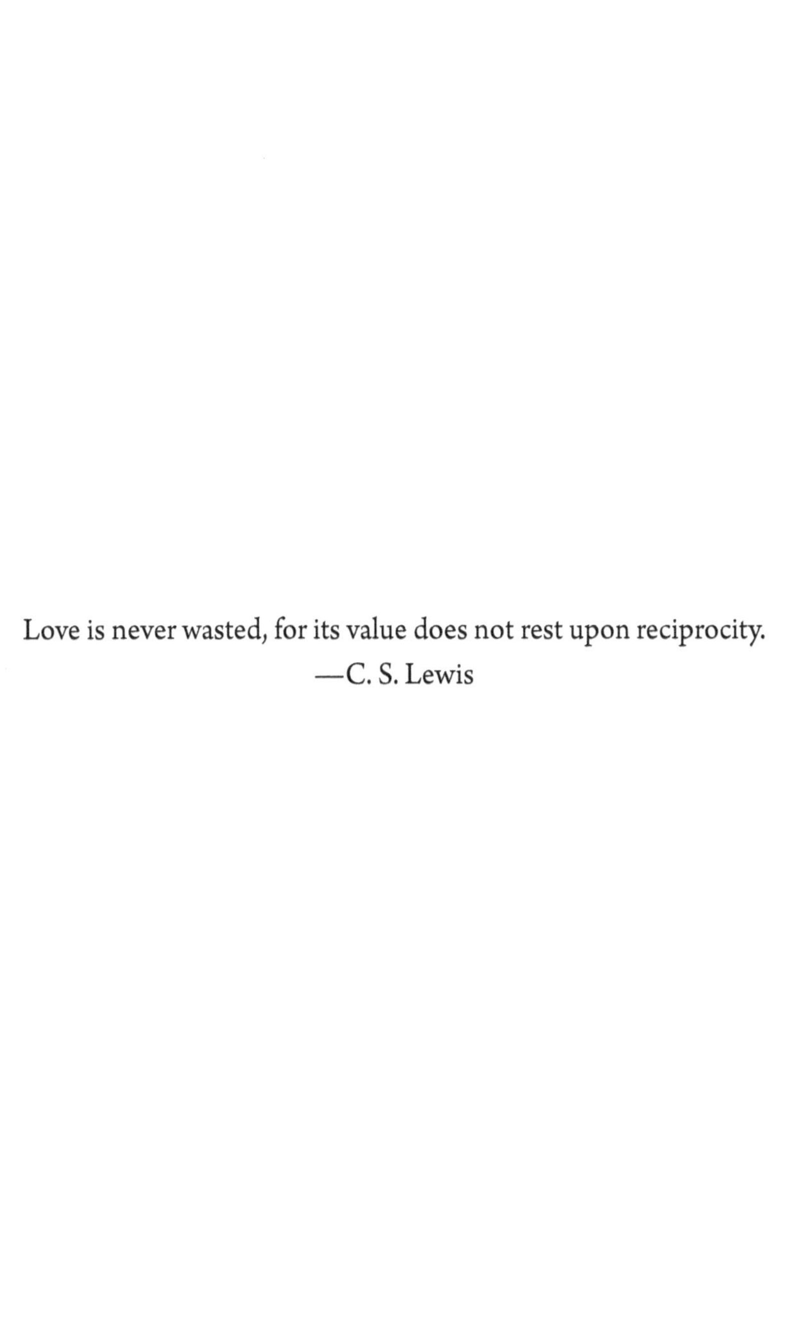

Love is never wasted, for its value does not rest upon reciprocity.
—C. S. Lewis

prologue

Zander

ISTRACTED AND RATTLED, THE WORLD OUTSIDE BLURS BY UNTIL it resembles a seemingly fake movie set. With the driver side window down and the wheels spinning against the asphalt highway, I'm barely conscious of anything at all. Other than her. My Ella.

None of this seems real. I can't help but to think that this can't be happening. My heated palms twist against the leather steering wheel as my fingertips go numb and that sinking feeling settles in my gut. It's as if I could punch the fronts of the buildings and they'd fall down, one by one, until the whole town was leveled. It all must be fake. It can't be real.

With last night's darkness behind me, a pale pink hue settles along the horizon.

The sun's coming up, but it's a cruel joke now that they've made the decision to separate the two of us. I've spent the last three weeks of my life anxiously waiting for the sun to set so I could go back to her. Now I'm caught in a morning I don't want, driving on autopilot back to a motel I know won't aid in giving me rest. Barely seeing the road.

It's not the first time I've felt like this. It's like being forced into the past. It feels as though I'm being forced into another horrific incident that would keep me up at night.

Blinking away the memories, I slow as I come to a yellow light, my gaze flicking to the rearview and I spot Damon, still behind me. Swallowing thickly, I remind myself that I can never go back. It's not possible and even if I could, I might not be able to change a damn thing.

There are things we can control and things we can't. The horrible losses we suffer—at times—come from our own actions.

Last night, I slept with Ella. Thoughts of last night flash before my eyes, images of her beauty stealing my breath, and remembering her soft moan of my name heats my chilled blood. It was against the rules. It was against everything we stand for at The Firm.

I lost control.

Something about her makes me *want* to lose control. It makes me *need* to lose control. I want to lose myself in her and come out the other side a different man. Smirking sardonically, I breathe out heavily and move past the green light as my blinker ticks, ticks, ticks away the thought. It's all another cruel joke from the asshole that is the universe. I'm different now, and I hate this person. I'm running to get away from this morning and the memories of that other morning. Both of them push forward in my mind, tangling up with one another.

A sickness pulls the corners of my lips down as I remember the past I wish I could forget. A past that made me this weakened version of myself.

Bang! There's a loud knock at my apartment door that calls for my attention. Bang, bang, bang. Another three in a row.

"You want me to open it?" Damon's eyes hid the worry he felt as equally as the exhaustion. We'd been up all night at my place. Waiting for her after searching everywhere and calling everyone.

"Mr. Thompson, it's the police." The deep voice echoes in my mind in a way I know I'll always remember.

The leather sofa groans as Damon makes a move to stand. "I'll get it," he tells me as I stare blankly at the front door, a sick feeling running rampant through me. The cops don't show up at anyone's apartment this early in the morning unless something fucking terrible has happened.

It hadn't been twenty-four hours, so I couldn't make a missing persons report. The second I heard that knock and the officer's voice, I knew there would be no report. I knew there would be no search. I knew that much, and still, I didn't want it to be real.

My throat's dry as I turn down the street I've taken for the last three weeks with nothing but anticipation to see Ella. My distraction, my drug, my submissive and … more. Something that's hard to place. Something I don't dare look into, for fear of the depths of its meaning.

I didn't hear a damn thing they said that day two years ago. I was too focused on how numb I felt and how it couldn't be real. How much my heart hurt, even though the rest of me was detached and unfeeling. When the guilt hit, it hit like a sledgehammer. Afterward Damon had to repeat everything they'd said. He was the one who told me about the mugging. About her murder. About what happened to Quincy.

I'll never forget our conversation after she told me to give her space on that street corner.

"I want to be with you." Quincy's blue eyes shone with tears, but she didn't let them fall. She stood her ground on the concrete and looked up at me with her arms folded over her chest. "I want more."

My response was short and immediate. "That's not where I am." The words seemed inadequate, and they were.

"But someday—"

"It's not going to happen." I thought she'd appreciate honesty. After all, it wasn't her fault. I didn't want more and I didn't know if I ever would. But her eyes fluttered shut for a brief second, the pain setting in, and when she opened her eyes they were cold.

"I'm going for a walk." The iron chair grated against the sidewalk, the streetlights outside the bar providing nearly all the illumination in the late night. I'll never forget how they cast shadows down her face. She would be in tears within minutes. I knew it and I hated myself for it.

"I'll walk you. You don't have to say anything to me."

She held up a hand. "I need space, Zander. If you don't want to be close to me, then I need space. Don't follow me. If you don't want all of me, then I don't want any of you."

I didn't follow her. I had another beer, the cool summer breeze and the guilt keeping me there, wondering if she'd turn around. She didn't. After forty minutes, I left, figuring she'd gone home and hoping I'd find her there. The thing I dreaded as I walked was the thought of her packing up her things. Even knowing I couldn't give her everything she wanted, I didn't want to lose her.

I waited for her to show. We'd fight about it, I thought. We'd argue, and she'd make her case, and I'd make mine. I didn't love her like she did me. I didn't want a fairy-tale wedding and children. I wanted what we had and I would be happy to stay there, like we were, for as long as she wanted.

Three hours into the darkest part of the night, I started calling her and then two more hours slipped by. The digital clock of the cable box barely moved as time crept by and I was met with voicemail after voicemail. Every place was closed by 3:00 a.m. There was no reason for her to be out that late. She never answered. Then I called her friends, her mother. I called anywhere and everywhere I could think. Damon and I went out to look for her and came up with nothing. We came up with nothing because by the time we were looking for her, Quincy was already dead.

A car honks loudly behind me. Through blurry vision I move my gaze from the rearview that features a line of cars behind me, to the green light above me. Easing on the gas, I bring myself back to the present.

Back to Ella. To them trying to take her away from me. And keeping me from her.

Unacceptable.

The fact they took her doesn't change the way I feel for her or what either of us wants. It doesn't change a damn thing, except my standing with The Firm. And perhaps The Firm will take a hit to its reputation … but that pales in comparison to what Ella and I stand to lose.

Part of the reason I let Quincy walk away from me that night was because I was too much of a coward to have the real conversation. The one that would end with her moving out, deleting my number from her phone and never speaking to me again. I was trying to honor her wishes for space, but in truth I was acting like a fucking coward because that conversation had been long overdue.

I can't honor anything for Ella, because I don't know what she wants now that they all know.

I don't know if she's imagining I've abandoned her, or that I slept with her and never looked back. I don't know a damn thing and that's also un-fucking-acceptable.

What kind of man would I be if I went back to the motel and left it at that? If I let men who aren't part of our relationship decide it was over because of my professional obligations? What kind of coward would I be?

I jerk the wheel to the right at the next intersection, my mind racing. My blood pumps hard in my veins. This isn't that night with Quincy. This is a different morning. A far more complicated relationship. I didn't know what I wanted with Quincy. I *have* to be with Ella. That is the only thing I know right now.

That's the truth. The one truth that keeps me sane.

In the rearview mirror, I watch Damon's car come after mine, his tires squealing. He's swearing in the front seat, his expression pissed, and that anger won't leave once he finds out what I intend to do. What I have to do.

If Ella doesn't have feelings for me or if she doesn't see any need for me at all, then I'll leave her be. I'll let her go on with her life. I'll step back and allow her the space to get well. I'll never bother her again.

But I'm not going to take anyone else's word for it or allow them to make that decision for her. My heart slams against my rib cage over and over and over. Her manager and the rest of The Firm can claim she doesn't want to see me all they want. I'll believe it when she tells me and not a moment before.

They'll have taken her to one of the properties The Firm hires out in conjunction with every client. We always have a backup safe location in case the need arises. It's typically nondescript. Meant to keep from drawing attention. We still followed this protocol even though Ella is a custodial client and not someone needing strictly personal protection services.

It's a few miles from here. Not far although I've driven a good distance in the opposite direction.

Another sharp right and I'm heading in the right direction. Damon honks behind me. He'll know where I'm going. He doesn't have any choice in the matter unless he decides to crash his car into mine. That's the only way I'll stop.

chapter 1

Ella

THIS SINKING FEELING IN MY CHEST IS ONE I HAVEN'T FELT FOR a long time. A very long time. I'm not unfamiliar with the sickening churn in my gut or the heaviness that presses down on my shoulders, begging me to cave to it and make myself small.

After the last year and a half, I'm quite used to its abuse and the screaming that accompanies it in the back of my mind. This particular feeling, though, is one that used to come often as a child. I imagine so many people feel it. All of us, really. The gut instinct that warns a child they're in trouble. That they've done something very wrong and disappointed the ones they love.

The memory of my father's dark eyes narrowing as I stood there, my fingertips fiddling with the hem of my shirt or my sleeve, forces me to swallow although my throat is dry.

The men surrounding me aren't my father, but they have authority over me and it's not until now that I feel both immense regret in this decision and an anxiousness as I question the consequences of my impulsive actions. It's all too much.

The expression on each of the men who sit across from me tells me disappointment is only one of several emotions. Anger, betrayal … Concern.

Kamden's fidgeting, and his readjusting in the simple black mesh office chair next to me makes me even more uncomfortable.

He's barely looked at me. None of the men have since I sat down. It's eerily quiet and the squeak of the wheels rolling as Silas takes a seat next to Cade marks the first noise I've heard apart from someone clearing their throat.

I woke up expecting to find Zander, but his shift had ended and instead Silas waited for me downstairs. He was polite but firm that I should dress quickly. Silas was my driver to this less than appealing meeting.

He's been vague and his tone far less pleasant than it typically is.

My heart may be rampaging, beating against the cage that contains it, but I endeavor to keep my shoulders squared and my expression emotionless, neither positive nor negative. Even if every man in this room wears a stone-cold expression to match the dark gray of their power suits.

I could have worn black for mourning and to reflect this deep-seated emotion that brews inside of me, but that's uninspiring so I opted for a dark red silk blouse and high-waisted skinny jeans. Red is a color of confidence.

"What's this about?" I question and my gaze is drawn to Cade's throat, the cords of it tightening before my eyes travel back up and he offers me a tight smile.

"It's about your relationship with Zander." Kamden's voice is low, cautious even. There's a ping that runs through me. It's sharp, like swallowing a thorn, and keeps me from answering immediately. That churning in my gut intensifies as I meet Kamden's gaze and then Cade's. It's a horrid feeling that, in this particular moment, can fuck right off.

"What of it?" I reply in a harsher tone than I'd have liked. I've never desired to be a "bitch" so to speak, although I hate that word. I might not be a fighter and I might hate confrontation, but that doesn't mean for one second that I can't defend myself. A side of me that I haven't felt for years returns.

In the silence, I question again, "What of it?" Cade recovers quickly, but I don't miss the shock in his dilated pupils.

The man himself looks worn thin. Bags under his eyes match those of Kamden's, if I'm honest. Silas focuses on his clasped hands in front of him, not reacting at all to anything. If I could read minds, I'd wager a bet he'd rather be anywhere other than here.

With a heat simmering along my shoulders, I wait for any of them to speak. Kamden repositions in his seat yet again and then places his hand over mine. I don't react to the contact; instead I stare at a dull painting of black and gray smears that's hung on the wall behind Cade as Kamden speaks. It's a modern piece that would fade into any room. Surely it's only meant to take up space.

Clearing his throat, it's obvious that Kamden is the one who will initiate this conversation. "Mr. Thompson crossed a line," Kamden starts and that brief sentence grants him my full attention.

My expression hardens and I can't help it. I'm quick to rip my hand away from under his. My bottom lip trembles as betrayal overrides every other emotion. I desperately wish I could control myself more in this moment and not allow the shock and despair to show at all because I know emotion doesn't work with men. In this room, I'm the one who lacks any power at all. My guardians and conservator have all the power they want over me, yet I can't help but scoff, "*He* crossed a line?" In that instant, under Kamden's unwavering expression of concern, I consider, for a moment, that Zander's done with me.

That I was foolish to feel more and think there was more between us. We slept together, he told them, and now he's done with me.

It wouldn't be the first time I thought a man wanted more than just a fling. The thought is an ice bath but I'm quickly relieved of that submersion when Kamden says, "I placed cameras in the living room … I know he took advantage of you."

I feel sicker as his admission sinks in. This is a new kind of hell. A bloody nightmare. One I can't escape.

"You put cameras …?" I can't finish the question; there's no more air in my lungs. *He put cameras in my home? Kamden spied on me? My Kamden? The one man I can remember who I've trusted all my life?* The questions race through my mind. It's not possible. "You wouldn't do that to me."

Cade says something, confidently even, not that I hear a damn word. Kamden's blue gaze doesn't leave mine. We're caught here, staring at one another as we come to terms with our new reality. I hope Kam can feel this, this burgeoning sense of betrayal brewing through me. It's hot and suffocating. My eyes prick and I hate it. I hate that he's done this to me.

I expect a lover to break my heart, but not Kamden.

"Yes. I put cameras in the house to—" His voice is even before I cut him off, although his expression is anything but. There's a sorrow there that I've seen before. Only once, but it's the kind of sorrow that comes with the fear of losing me.

"And you say Zander crossed a line?" It takes everything I have to push out the accusation as I stare at my dearest and closest companion. My bottom lip wobbles again and I have to bite down on it, closing my eyes out of frustration. My hands tremble and I pull them into my lap.

"You know I did it because I love you," he practically whispers and I'd forgotten about the other two onlookers until one of their chairs protests as they readjust in their seat. I'm not sure which one it was, and I couldn't care less. Let them watch. Let them know what it's like to betray me.

"You spied on me." My voice comes out in a low hiss as I raise my eyes to Kamden. I'm seething with anger.

"You … I can't trust … I …" Kamden stumbles over his own words and I struggle not to break his gaze. He does it instead. He's the first to look away and seems to second-guess himself.

"That fucking hurts," I say, biting out the words.

My moral high ground is swiftly taken away from me as Kamden's exasperation reveals itself. "What do you want from me? The last time I left you alone—"

Raising my voice I can no longer control, I tell him, "I wasn't alone!" Heat rolls down my spine. "This time," I add to clarify and lower my voice. "I wasn't alone."

"No. You weren't." Kamden doesn't back down, and his lowly spoken words are harsh.

"It's not like I didn't want him."

"He's supposed to take care of you," Kam says.

"Since when does sex not fall under that umbrella?" My response is flippant and arrogant, and Kamden reacts with equal parts disbelief and outrage.

"Since you tried to kill yourself!"

My throat instantly dries and my attempt to swallow is painful as I lean farther away from Kamden. My lips part to object, but there are no words.

"You aren't … You aren't okay," Kam says, his voice gentler now, and his hand raised as if he's approaching a wild animal. "It was wrong of him to touch you in any way. He was only there to make sure you didn't hurt yourself. That was his *only* job. He crossed the line multiple times and I can't ignore that. You matter to me. Your safety matters to me."

His only job. A sarcastic huff leaves me although my fight has waned. The first time I saw Zander, I wanted him. I was drawn to him. A piece of me needed him. It didn't have a damn thing to do with a job opportunity.

In my silence, Kamden repeats, "He was supposed to take care of you, protect you. Not sleep with you."

Was. Kamden speaks of Zander as if he's in the past tense.

They're going to take him away from me. I can hardly breathe. I would beg them, if that's what they want. I will beg them. It takes a moment for me to gather my composure and my dignity.

Licking my bottom lip, I muster the courage to look Kamden in the eye and tell him, "I'll tell the judge it was all of you."

My words are met with a deafening silence. "I'll tell him each one of you abused me."

"Ella." Kamden ushers his warning in a whisper.

"Not you … but if you make me, I'll tell the judge you knew." If I'm not above begging, I'm damn sure not above blackmail, defamation, or whatever the fuck this is. "You won't take him away from me."

chapter 2

Zander

THE CITY WAS GOING BY IN THE BACKGROUND WITHOUT MAKING any impression before, but now it's in vivid detail. My main priority is getting to Ella. There's an anxiousness I haven't felt for her before. A need to protect her.

I know the situation is complicated, but this part seems simple. Get to her. Get to her. Get to her. I ignore my phone vibrating in the passenger seat; one glance in the rearview and I know it's Damon calling.

Friendship be damned, I won't make the mistake of not fighting for her to have a say in this. If nothing else, she deserves to hear from me and know this wasn't my choice.

With the tires screeching and my nerves still rattled, I pull into the parking lot six minutes later. The office is on the top floor of a two-story building. We chose the location because we considered possible press coverage when we designed her protection plan. She's not unknown to the world, and no matter how slim the chances, we had to prepare for everything. It's harder to take photos of a person when they're not at ground level.

It's then that I consider what exactly I'm about to walk into. I can already feel the betrayed gaze of my brother and the sick feeling that comes with it.

The second the car door shuts with a *thunk*, my name is shouted from Damon's car pulling in beside me. In the shade of the towering building, a chill settles over me and I ignore Damon, I ignore the gut instinct to give my brother space now that he knows what I've done.

Instead, one foot moves in front of the other, but not fast enough.

Damon throws himself out of the driver's seat so fast that the door hangs open after him. "You can't do this," he shouts although there's a pleading tone in his voice. We're both angling for the entrance, and he collides with me as I'm reaching for the door. His shoulder is pressed to my shoulder and I'm met with a desperation in his gaze as I can feel his chest rising and falling with heavy breaths. The momentum takes me a few feet away but I'm determined. "Zander. You can't go in there. You're off her detail." His voice is low and careful, but again, his tone is begging me not to go in there.

For her sake or mine? Maybe both. "Your brother said you can't—"

"That doesn't fucking matter. I'm seeing her, and you can't stop me." With my hand wrapped around the steel handle of the black glass door, Damon's splays against it, preventing me from opening it. The sleeve of his coat slides down his forearm.

"You're caught, man. Nobody's going to let you do anything until Cade figures shit out. We might have to have a hearing if Kamden pushes this, which—to be fucking blunt—I would if I were him. And even if we don't and everything blows over, The Firm can't let you see her." His dark eyes are wide. He presses his free hand flat to my chest, pushing me back and I release my grip on the handle, dropping my arm to my side. He's at least as strong as I am, but he knows better than to square up with me.

More importantly, I want this more than he does. I want to get in more than he wants to keep me out. "We can't let you see her."

Gritting my teeth and reining in as much anger as I can, I push out, "That's not up to you. She has control over her life. You can't forbid me from seeing her."

"We can. As a member of The Firm—"

"Then I'll fucking quit, if that's what it takes. None of you can unilaterally determine that I'm a threat to her if she *wants* to see me. And I'm not going to stop." My breaths are deep and slow, although my pulse is raging in my ears.

Even if adrenaline is coursing through my veins, my mind is clear. I'm only focused on this. Getting to her. To hear what she has to say.

"You know just as well as I do, that doing this could hurt her," I say, reminding him of his duty as her therapist. "Ripping away someone who was helping her."

"Zander …" My name comes out like a warning as he shakes his head.

Damon can pretend it's not in her best interest, but it is. It's a crucial component to her healing. If they keep us apart when she doesn't want that, it could send her spiraling. "If she needs me in there, you're fucked. You know that, right? If taking her away from me compromises her health, you are fucked. Try explaining that to the judge."

"Zander—" I reach around him and he catches my wrist in one hand.

I break his hold. Of course I do. I've trained for this, same as he has, and something in the movement must tell him that I'm serious because he backs off half a step, his hands up. "Did they change the location of the safe house?"

His lips form a thin line. I'm being a dick right now, and I know that. He's not supposed to tell me anything about Ella's location. Private citizen or not. Member of The Firm or not. But we've got a lot of history between us.

"You can refuse to tell me if you want, but I'll just search every building in the city until I find her. I'll search the whole damn world."

Damon lets out a breath, defeated. "They didn't change it. She's upstairs as far as I know."

My next step forward is determined, emotions I didn't expect spurring me on.

"Just—" Damon moves to block me. "It's not good, Z. They've got proof of what you did. This isn't going to turn out well for you, and it might destroy the rest of us. It would be better if you went back to the motel and let Cade handle it. If you did that, maybe there would be a way to figure things out. I don't know."

Swallowing thickly, I nod, acknowledging that I know I put them in jeopardy. "If it goes to court, I'll testify none of you knew a damn thing. That I doctored the security footage so no one else would know about us."

"Just stop—"

"You don't get it. I'm not leaving her up there." My throat goes tight, my heart beating too hard to be contained. "Things aren't finished between us. This is about more than what I want. Hell, what I want doesn't mean a damn thing right now. She tells me to back off, and I will. But I have to know. I have to hear it from her. She gets to make that choice."

"Let's talk about it for a few minutes first," Damon says and irritation rolls through me. He takes a few steps in the direction of the cars, away from the door. "Make sure you're calm. It won't do anyone any good if you go in there with that look on your face."

"What fucking look?"

"Like you'd pull down this building with your bare hands to get to her."

I pause. Hope brightens Damon's eyes; he thinks he might have convinced me to stay out here and have a pointless conversation with him.

"Listen," he says. "You did this, but we can figure out what to do—"

I don't hear the rest. I've yanked the door open and I'm sprinting inside. Punching in a code on the keypad in the foyer. The door clicks open. They haven't changed it yet. Thank fuck.

"Wait," he shouts behind me.

I don't.

I'm halfway professional by the time I get up the stairs, Damon breathing hard behind me. I've at least arranged my face into something I think resembles professionalism. But as I shove open the door, I know how skin deep it is. Underneath I'm feral.

They're arranged around the table of the conference room and there's a deadly atmosphere in the room. The tension is palpable. A reception desk takes up one side of the space. A sofa and two chairs huddle around a bean-shaped table in the corner. Silas on the left. Kamden on the right with Ella beside him. Cade looming over everything at the head. I almost missed Dane, standing outside the conference room. He didn't make an effort to stop me and judging how he's opted out of this meeting, there's something happening with him that I'm not aware of. I don't have time to give a fuck about that.

They're all in suits. And I'm still dressed in my overnight shift clothes. Faded black jeans and a matching T-shirt.

All of it drops away when I meet Ella's dark eyes. They flare wide and my heart aches. She didn't expect me to come for her. Is it surprise in her eyes? Relief? Or maybe horror?

In a scrambled effort she backs away from the table, the wheels of the chair rolling back as she attempts to stand. "Zander," she says, and my name has never sounded so good as it does right now. "Z." Kamden puts his hand on her arm like that asshole is going to keep her in her seat, but she shakes him off. Her legs work to carry her around the table as fast as she can go and she flies into my arms.

The office erupts. Damon curses behind me. "I tried to stop him," he tells the others, and I don't care.

The feel of her body in my arms makes everything and everyone else fade into the background like white noise. It pushes away a number of things I don't expect to feel. I breathe in the delicate scent of her skin, and run my hands over her shoulder blades. Over her back. Her heart flutters in her chest but her arms are tight around my waist.

I want to keep her in the circle of my embrace, where nobody can touch her but me. To protect her and give her the choice of what's next. Cade's warning command to leave falls on deaf ears. He repeats my name and clears his throat. From my periphery I'm faintly aware that he's standing now. There's movement behind me but I ignore it all.

There's something I have to do first.

I put my hands on her shoulders and create the only space I can bear between us. Tipping her face to mine so I can look into those dark eyes, she's trembling but she looks as determined as I feel. Ella's stronger than people give her credit for. Maybe even stronger than I gave her credit for.

"I tried to come back to talk to you this morning. Last night—it wasn't a mistake for me." I have to choose my words quickly, and carefully. I could get cut off at any time. "I want to be with you. I need to know if you want the same."

She pauses, and it's the longest moment of my life. It drags out and out and out until my entire life feels like it's hanging between us. Her eyes stay on mine, searching there, and Ella swallows. It reminds me of the first time I saw her in that courtroom. How quiet she was. But she knew what she wanted then too. And I think she knows now. She gives a single, subtle nod.

Before my brother can make it to us, his footsteps foreboding, I tell Ella to sit, leading her back to the table and pulling her chair out for her. It's silent in the room as she gracefully does as I command. She can't hide the gentle simper at her lips and it forces a heat to run through my chest.

Pulling out the chair opposite to where my brother was seated, I join the meeting like I belong here.

"I fucked up," I announce to the room, but I'm looking at my brother, who's retaking his seat, his narrowed glare not leaving mine. "I crossed a professional boundary. My emotions became involved and I should have told someone before things got this far. I should have come to you."

"You didn't," Cade replies and then swallows so loud I can hear it from across the room. He's shaken and looks like hell. There's an edge to his voice so sharp it lowers the temperature in the room. "You didn't do that, Zander. You had an inappropriate relationship with a client. You can't be part of this anymore."

"I apologize." He breaks the hold he had on me, his gaze dropping to his hands as he clenches his jaw.

"But it would be a mistake to discontinue our relationship, as its purpose has been meaningful to her mental health. I'm certain any one of you can attest to the fact that she has …" It's uncomfortable speaking about Ella while she's sitting next to me, able to hear every word.

"I've been," she says, pausing to take a deep breath, then lifts her head to meet Damon's gaze. "Healing."

Everyone turns their heads to look at Ella, whose cheeks go pink. There's color in her face. A brightness to her eyes that wasn't there when she stood at the front of the courtroom. She's visibly healthier. She's been revealing more about what drove her to the unfortunate place she was. "I'm doing the work that needs to be done," she adds firmly.

"I'm not asking to be in charge of her care. I'm asking to stay in contact.

It's my opinion that cutting off contact between the two of us would have a negative effect on Ella's health. That's my top priority."

Cade arches an eyebrow at me. "Is it?"

"Yes." I've felt how Ella has come alive in my hands, and I'll be damned if I let her go back to that desperate shell of a woman. "Her well-being is my top priority. Same as it ever was. And I know I failed you, Cade. I should have informed you of how our relationship had changed, and I didn't. I knew it was wrong to go behind your back. But it's not wrong for us to continue this relationship."

"What are you asking me to do?" Cade's expression is hard, and admitting that I have royally screwed him over hasn't softened it. But there's something in his tone that speaks to the fact that we're brothers. He won't let my break from protocol be the final determination.

"I'm asking you to give this a chance. To have the conversation about what it looks like for me to stay in contact with Ella. That's what I'm asking for."

ℰ

Ella

"And as I've just indicated before we were interrupted, I'm not above extortion."

"What?" Zander's expression hardens as he stares at the side of my face. I keep my gaze fixed directly ahead on Cade's expression. I wonder if I hadn't just threatened each of the men in the room, how they would have responded to Zander's request.

Swallowing down the anxiousness of Zander discovering what I've just done, I keep my hands steady on the table and remind the room what I'm capable of.

"If I'm no longer able to speak to whomever I want, to see whomever I want, and ..." I say, barely peeking at Zander from the corner of my eye. The five o'clock shadow along his hardened jaw sends a wave of want through me. I've never wanted to kiss him more. "... I'll tell the judge each of you slept with me." I dare to raise my gaze to Cade's, whose own widens yet again before he narrows his eyes at me. "I'll tell the judge you used me, each of you, however you wanted."

"Ella," Kamden scolds in a hiss.

"Well, I'm out of my mind, aren't I?" I bite back at him. "I can't possibly know what's right and wrong, isn't that so, Kam? So if I'm unable to choose who I want to fuck, and how … I can't be responsible for my accusations, can I?"

The condescension drips from my words. "There's evidence of course that I've been sexually active. And apparently a video as well." The last part is reserved just for Kamden.

In the silence, I take a moment to relieve the tension that runs chaotically through me and then meet Cade's gaze.

"You will do no such thing." The drop in Zander's voice and the dominant tone in his cadence send a thrilling heat along my skin.

My expression doesn't betray me. I remain as poised as I can and turn to meet Zander's gaze. It blazes with the threat of a punishment.

We speak at the same time. Him: "Do you hear me?" Me: "Understood."

With my heart rampaging and my lungs refusing to let me breathe, I straighten my back and wait for whatever is next.

Butterflies stir in my stomach when Zander's hand lands at the back of my neck, and his strong grip there is comforting more than anything. Then he runs his thumb along my skin and as he speaks, his words are lowered and meant just for me as he leans closer to me, although I'm certain every man in this room can hear. Zander tells me, "That is—not only—unnecessary, but an act that obviously requires a thorough evaluation when we meet next."

Thump, thump. With the pounding in my chest and a heat pulling at my core, I nod and whisper, "Understood."

It's only when Cade and Kamden both begin speaking that I cut them off to question the room, "And when will that be?"

Glancing to my right, I meet Kamden's disapproving gaze and downturned lips. He doesn't speak and it spreads an uneasiness through me.

"Why don't we all take a moment?" Cade questions, his attention split between his brother and me.

"A moment?"

"Ella," Kamden whispers, competing for my attention, but I remain submissive to Zander.

"I'd like to speak to my brother."

"I'd like to know when—" I begin to say but Zander speaks calmly, interrupting me with an assuredness I desperately needed to hear from him.

"Go, Ella. I will fix this. Go home."

There's a numbness that takes over as he relaxes into his chair, facing his brother as I've been effectively dismissed. He offers me a covert, kind smile as if it's reassuring, but I don't want to leave.

"I feel like I should stay," I whisper and I don't recognize my own voice. It begs for permission.

Zander's hand flexes, the motion drawing my gaze as his fingers spread wide before forming a fist. It's his warning signal for me to behave. Heat flows down my shoulders instantly.

Sucking in a breath, I attempt to collect myself as I stand slowly. It's then that Zander reaches out, his hand meeting my thigh with a tender touch.

"I will be there tomorrow. I promise," he tells me and with that I can finally breathe.

As I prepare to leave, glancing at Silas and assuming my driver here will be the one to take me home, Kamden stands behind me.

"I'll drive you," Kam comments and I turn to face him and his sharp blue suit. It's custom tailored for him and meant to appear expensive, which it does. But Kam looks nothing but beat down.

My gaze drifts between a nodding Zander and Kamden.

My throat tightens as I leave the room, attempting to lead the way, but Kamden opens the door for me.

The clicking of my heels beneath me is all I can hear as I follow Kam in silence. As I climb into the passenger seat of his car, not even the sun can offer me warmth.

I hadn't even considered sitting in the back, as I never have before with Kam—not in all my life—until the seat belt clicks and his keys jingle as he slips them into the ignition.

I can barely stand to look at him without feeling like I've been stabbed in the back. Taking in a shuddered breath, my hair flattens as it meets the headrest and I attempt to relax into it. The gray stone wall shrinks in the distance as he backs out and we leave The Firm behind.

"Nothing to say?" I barely breathe, the words attempting to stay buried inside of me but somehow I pull them out.

All I'm met with is the ticking of the turn signal and a heavy exhale. Another minute goes by and Kamden hesitantly asks, "If he hurt you, you would tell me, wouldn't you?"

Turning my head to give him my utmost attention, I swallow down every emotion and answer him simply, "Yes."

He nods shortly and continues to drive, although the atmosphere in the car is suffocatingly broken.

Ella

The morning after what seems like war feels nothing like victory. Even if you've won. It's as if I'm terrified to drop my guard, ready for the next hit. Taking into account everything that's happened over the last three years up until just yesterday, it's all felt like fate's been toying with me, but also like dominoes toppling. One after the other, each one poised to fall, starting on that day I watched James step onto the crosswalk.

And now I wait on edge for the next piece of the game to forsake me.

Pushing my hair still damp from the shower away from my face, I try to tell myself it can get better. It doesn't have to be like this. A constant spiral downward.

Although sleep didn't come easy, the anxious ball in the pit of my stomach has left. Even after I took the sleeping pills Aiden had prescribed, it still took another hour or so before I had a dreamless rest.

Damon's towering figure steals my attention from the steam of the teacup. It billows out as I blow gently across it, both of my hands wrapped around the porcelain vessel.

"Did you sleep well?"

Giving his suit a once-over, I make a mental note that he's back to business attire. Ever so serious. Damon was the one I was certain would speak up for me. Instead he said himself, he tried to stop Zander.

The cup clinks softly when I set it down on the counter as I answer, "Once I got to sleep, it was a deep sleep." I can't look at him, but at least I've given him the truth.

My father told me once, when I was much younger, that if I didn't want to fight, if I didn't want to feel the blows of incoming war, that I had to stop. I couldn't keep my hands up, prepared for battle, and expect the other side not to react. It's one of the hardest things I ever had to learn: to stop fighting. Although Damon told me it's called decompressing.

Apparently I don't decompress well.

Damon pulls out the stool beside me and the legs of it groan against the floor.

Gently, I push a tray of danishes his way.

"Kamden?" Damon questions and I nod.

"I'm not sure where he is, I've only just come down," I explain to Damon, "but they were waiting for us."

I've already eaten two of the small cream cheese danishes. Damon opts for a raspberry one, taking a piece off with his left hand, holding the rest of it in his right. Before popping the small morsel into his mouth, he asks, "Did you talk to him?"

I turn on the stool to face him and lean my elbow against the counter. Half of me feels nothing but comradery with Damon, and the other half doesn't trust him anymore. I'd like to speak, but instead I shake my head and focus back on my tea.

It's the perfect temperature and has steeped just right.

"Is it all right if I ask if you're angry with him?"

"Yes," I answer quickly, the word raw. Then I realize that only answers whether or not it's all right if he asks me. "I'm very upset."

"Angry and upset?"

It takes me a minute, staring down at my tea before I answer, "Just upset."

Damon nods and I glance over to find he hasn't eaten any more of the small pastry.

I offer him an out. "This can wait, you know? Quiet mornings are one of my favorite things in life."

Instead of nodding and backing off, Damon asks, nearly blurting it out, "Are you upset with me?" His deep brown eyes sink into mine and I'm forced to stare back at him.

I nod and then whisper, "Yes. Honestly, I am."

"I am sorry yesterday caused you distress. I'm sorry it all happened the way it did." His words seem sincere but also professional. As if reading my mind he adds, "I mean it, Ella. When they told me what happened, I was worried about how it would all play out, but mostly worried about you."

Finally breaking his gaze I murmur, "I appreciate that," and return to a now empty tea cup.

It's a bit awkward for a moment, until I pull an open package toward me and inform Damon, "This was waiting for me too."

I take out a chunk of gray crystal. The dark and light grays mingle with a touch of white.

"What's that?" Damon questions.

"It's a rock." Removing the note from Kelly, I read it to him. "Smoky quartz wards off negative thoughts."

As Damon rises, making his way around the counter to the sink, I tell him Kelly sent it and that she suggested I bring it to therapy.

The charming grin on his handsome face grows and that small, amiable feeling takes over. Damon has an infectious smile. "You told me about Kelly? Didn't you?"

As I nod he tells me, drying off his hands, "I like her."

Smiling, I agree with him. "I've got good friends." The admission comes with a sinking feeling that steals the lightness from me. Damon doesn't miss it. Before he can say a word, I tell him, "I think I need a minute."

With a more somber look, although his eyes remain warm, he says, "When you're ready to talk, let me know."

An hour after breakfast the sun sits perfectly in an array of pale coral hues along the tree line. Pulling a blue chenille throw across my lap, I do nothing to stop the breeze from blowing across my bare shoulders.

My satin sleep shirt boasts the same cobalt blue.

It's quiet in the late morning, although I know it won't be for long.

"You brought tissues?" Damon questions, taking the seat across from me on the patio. The outdoor fireplace is to his right but it's not nearly chilly enough to turn it on. Maybe later tonight.

"They're still here from last night," I comment. The square box of tissues and journal sit side by side. Both were used equally last night. Silas gave me space, he's good for that. Quietly watching, checking on whether I could use tea or anything to offer comfort. He's kind and silent. Damon is kind as well ... but never silent.

"I think last night might be a good place to start."

"Last night it is then," I respond and let out a sigh, repositioning myself on the chaise lounge to better face him. I'm caught off guard by his next question.

"Do you think there's any chance that you're displacing your feelings?"

"What do you mean?" I ask.

"Your husband with Zander."

"How is that relevant to last night?"

"It's relevant to all of it, Ella."

"So that's what we're doing today?" I say with mock humor. "We're sparring?"

"We're discussing my one concern." Damon remains professional, giving me a moment to consider my answer.

I don't want to think about it. I don't want to go anywhere near that question. Am I displacing my feelings toward James, my deceased husband, onto Zander? That's a heavy question to begin a session with. "It feels like fencing," I mutter, feeling more uncomfortable by the second.

"Is that what you'd like to talk about?" Damon raises his brow. "Fencing, or maybe we can talk about croquet?"

"Croquet?"

Damon shrugs and says, "It seems like an equally relevant sport."

His comment is rewarded with a short and relatively quiet bubble of laughter I can't control, and I readjust in my seat.

"I know we've talked about this before, but it's okay to sit with your emotions. Right?"

I nod in response, pulling my knees into my chest and making myself a puddle of blue fabric, none of which can protect me.

"Why do you want to come between us?" I question him.

"I don't," he answers without hesitation and he's adamant. With both his hands on his knees, he leans forward in the seat across from me, shaking his head slightly while maintaining eye contact. "He's my friend and …" he pauses, glancing away and trapping his bottom lip between his teeth before seemingly deciding what to say next.

With a deep breath in, he continues, "I have no issues with you engaging in sexual activity." I've never felt such a guard rise between the two of us. Him considering my relationships and whether they're a concern for him creates an unnatural tension that Damon doesn't seem to notice. The only person who should be concerned about who I'm fucking is me. With my fingers tangling together in my lap, I gather my composure. I know his concern is only for my mental health. I know it, yet I struggle with him being involved at all with that part of my life. Zander is mine. It is irrelevant what anyone thinks of us and our relationship. He wants me and I want him. That is all that matters.

Damon's voice, no longer droning, comes back into focus when he says, "I noticed an immediate change for the better when you two began your relationship. I spoke to Zander at length last night. He's updated me on any essential information."

My heart skitters knowing Damon spoke to him, but I haven't. My cell phone sits on the coffee table and I hesitate before picking it up only to find that I still have no messages. To date, the only person to text me or call me on this ancient brick with no camera or apps has been Kam.

"Please know I only asked what was required professionally."

"Hmm?"

"When I spoke to Zander," he clarifies and I absently nod, not liking the knots that sit in my stomach. "There is no judgment from me."

"It certainly feels like there's judgment," I comment, staring back at his umber gaze.

There's a moment, a tick of time between us before Damon tells me, "My only concern was how quickly things changed."

If only he knew how I slowly unraveled since the moment I first saw

Zander. How I felt myself come undone for him before he ever touched me. I question confiding in him, so instead I remain silent.

"How do you feel right now?" he asks.

"Angry." My response is immediate and my throat tightens with it.

"Angry … What size, would you say? A little irritated anger?"

"Enraged," I answer, staring down at my hands.

"You don't seem enraged," Damon responds carefully, like he's testing me.

A well of emotions dries out my throat even further. "Sad … scared."

Damon nods as I answer. "And why's that? What triggered those emotions?"

I put myself in this position. I'm in this place because of what I've done. Tears leak from my eyes and as I wipe them away, refusing to be overwhelmed by them, the back door opens.

Kam pauses when my eyes meet his. His black T-shirt and worn black jeans initiate a smart-ass side of me, as well as a piece still bitter from Kam's betrayal. "Feeling down today?"

I don't miss Damon's ever-watchful gaze as I pull myself together and then stare up at Kam, who glances between Damon and myself.

"Are you?" Kam turns my question back at me. "Am I interrupting?" Kam asks Damon and I'm quick to answer, "No."

I can't look either of them in the eye.

"Just one minute if you don't mind," Damon says, then looks between the two of us and Kam nods, slipping his hands into his pockets as he walks to the edge of the paved patio. With a deep inhale I let go of everything, every wave that threatened to drown me just a moment ago.

"A little homework?" Damon's voice is gentle and low, far too soft for Kam to hear.

"Homework?" I offer him a smirk but then nod, closing my eyes and preparing for whatever it is that Damon wants.

"When you feel overwhelmed or uncomfortable or like you're losing control, like what happened just now," he says without judgment, yet my eyes whip up to his, "I want you to ask yourself, what emotion is it? Take control of those emotions that make you uncomfortable. Because you long for that, don't you? Control over those emotions?"

I can only nod. I don't want them to control me. In this moment I know he understands. Damon understands. The moment he leans back in his seat, it's like a spell has broken and Kam's footsteps can be heard nearing us.

"Are you all right?" Kam's question comes from a place of concern and I shrug.

"A wreck like always," I tell him.

"You're never a wreck." Kam consoles me, taking the chair next to Damon and when Damon begins to stand, Kam asks him to stay.

"I came out to speak to you, really. With Ella's consent."

My brow knits and matches Damon's confusion for a moment. "I want to make it clear that whatever it is Ella wants, whether The Firm stays, whether Zander continues to see her …" Kam's gaze moves to me as he continues, "It's her choice and I will back her up."

Damon's posture remains relaxed although his brow cocks and his head tilts. "Whatever she says?" he asks without amusement. I imagine the threat of extortion is riding through him and I feel bad for the man.

"Kam, I don't think that's necessary."

"I was wrong and I'm going to make it up to you."

Damon's uncomfortableness is more than noticeable in his deep exhale.

Kam continues, "Whatever Ella decides to say, I saw and heard it as well."

"You realize that's not only a crime, it also could be detrimental to her healing."

Kamden doesn't flinch until Damon's concern about my health is spoken.

The defensive tone comes with Kam shifting in his seat. "This is her life. Her decision."

Damon's careful with his response, his posture casual although I'm more than aware he's a master of controlling his body language and speech. "We both want what's best for Ella, and I imagine we won't have any issues moving forward."

"That all depends on—"

"Am I a bit fucked up?" I say, interrupting the men. "Yes." It takes a lot for me to utter the next words. "Watching your husband die only feet from you could do that to someone." Tears leak and I wipe them away. "Seeing the video of it repeatedly every time I turned to social media, having to talk about it constantly, having to beg people to stop … it got to be a little much, I'll admit." The words come out a whisper. Even now, as I sit here, I see it all over again.

The red light, his smile as he waved, leaving me to the paparazzi. He had the most charming smile. The stifling heat of that summer day weighs down on me and it comes with an anxiousness I can't stop. The sound of the truck, the tires locking up, I hear it all, the screams from onlookers and then my scream. I feel the hands that held me back, those fingers digging into my skin now.

My voice is hoarse as I look each of them in the eye and say, "Am I a threat? To anyone? To myself? I don't know but I don't want to be, and I'm trying."

Both of them part their lips to say something, to coddle me, to praise me … To admonish me, maybe. I have no idea, nor do I give a fuck.

"Is Zander bad for me? No. He's not. So stop threatening to take him away. We're adults. We know what we're doing. Stay the fuck out of it."

chapter 4

THE COFFEE SHOP ISN'T EVEN CLOSE TO MAXIMUM CAPACITY right now, but there are a few people at the booths and tables. A couple more lined up at the counter. My brother waits for me in one of the booths. His starched dress shirt is stretched tight across his shoulders. The privacy here is nominal. More than we'd have at one of the tables in the middle of the floor. Far less than we'd have at the motel or at the office. He's chosen a public place for a reason.

For the best, I think. Throughout our lives we've had knockdown-dragout screaming matches a few times. Siblings will do that. This can't be one of those times.

The meeting yesterday ended with Cade refusing to agree to any terms. He needed to speak to his lawyer first.

A coffee grinder whines as I approach the booth and sit down across from Cade, the guilt taking a seat alongside me. Two coffees are already on the table, both black, and Cade stares down at his like it might give him some answers if he looks long enough. His jaw is tight, eyes dark. He's obviously upset. He only glances up from the coffee cup when I reach for my own.

Fuck, I wish it hadn't come to this. If I could go back, though, what could I possibly change?

And then my gut freezes. There's concern in his hazel eyes, but he's made up his mind about something. Cade has spent a long time mastering himself. He's not one to let things slip. So even showing me this concern means this conversation has a real weight to it. I can feel it pressing down on me.

Cade looks away, back down into his coffee. "What the hell are you doing, Zander?"

I'm good at sitting still, but the urge to fidget is strong. It's because I don't have the words to explain myself. How could he possibly understand? I don't feel like we have a shared language anymore. It shouldn't be possible for the two of us to have drifted so far apart, given that we work together. But it happened.

My brother's frown deepens as he looks back at me. "You know how vulnerable she is. And you don't want to admit it, but what happened with Quincy fucked you up. It made you susceptible to this kind of thing."

Rage flares in me, followed by the pang of a deep, old guilt. Not because I felt for Quincy the way I feel for Ella. It's because the mention of her name makes every failure seem worse. All my worst moments stem from that one.

"Don't talk about her."

Cade narrows his eyes. "It's true."

My voice is low, the words coming from deep down in my chest and murmured with an edge to them that could kill. "I said, don't talk about her. Quincy doesn't have a damn thing to do with Ella, and you're not going to sit here in this fucking coffee shop and talk to me about things you know nothing about."

"Fine," snaps Cade and then he takes several deep breaths in a row. His hands flex on the table before he grips his mug again. When next he speaks his voice is level. "I asked you here to tell you that I'm letting you go from The Firm."

Cold shock washes over me. I can't believe Cade would do this. Part of me is stunned that my own brother would turn on me. It doesn't matter that I went against him first.

"You can't be serious." Stress keeps my voice tight. He isn't even man enough to look me in the eye.

His jaw works as he grits his teeth. "If you're going to be with her, you sure as hell can't be on payroll."

A tic in my jaw spasms with agreement. He's right. I have no qualms about that. My relationship with Ella will be strictly what we decide tonight. As I sit here, it all unravels in front of me, a chill running through my blood. It's not about what I want and what could be. It's only about what she needs right now. A Dominant/submissive relationship. She has to know that's all it is at the moment. I haven't forgotten our night together and her emotional response. I can care for her in only some ways. She has to accept that. Until the situation is different, that's all we can be. It's not about what I want, it's about what she needs.

My mind wanders to what I wish we could be, if things were different, until Cade stares back at me, expecting a response.

"I can't be on payroll with the company or for this case?"

"I haven't decided yet." Fresh anger flares in his eyes. "You don't understand what almost happened, Zander. If Kamden had gone to the judge rather than me, you would be in a fucking jail cell, and she would be back at the Rockford Center."

"It wasn't me who—"

"Is that what you want? Ella back at that place, isolated from everyone? Is that what you want for her?"

For her hits me like a bullet straight through the chest. It rattles around my heart and exits out the other side. Cade understands this, at least. I don't want those things. I don't want the Rockford Center for Ella. I don't want her to shrink back into that pale, silent woman.

"No." It untwists something in my chest to say it. It feels honest, and right, even if I'm completely fucked. "I don't want that for her. I did what I could to be careful."

"Bullshit." Cade's grip tightens around his coffee cup. "If you had come to me, if you had informed us, we could have adjusted. You should have waited. You should have told me."

"You're full of shit." My snide response is louder than I'd like and rewards us with an onlooker's gaze. Clearing my throat, I adjust my tone.

"Ella doesn't just want what I give to her. She needs it. There's no adjusting for that. It was what brought her out of her pain enough to even talk to the rest of you."

Cade's eyes meet mine and I have the impression he's looking right through me as though he'll refuse any evidence. Like the truth doesn't matter.

"And what about you, Zander? Do you *need* it?"

Something balls up in my throat, and I can't answer him. He must see the reality in my eyes, though, because he lets out a heavy sigh. Like I've disappointed him.

Cade raises his eyes from his coffee. He's not only disapproving now, not only disappointed. He's worried about me. The instinct grows to brush it off. No one needs to worry about me. But that's not true. I wouldn't have survived after Quincy if it weren't for Damon. Fuck, I don't want to be brought back to that moment. To a place that only offers emptiness or regret. There's nothing else but that.

In some ways, I feel like that now. Everything is fucked. The ground isn't steady, and I need things. It feels unreasonable to want reassurance. I'm the one who's supposed to reassure other people, not the other way around.

It's one simple fact that gives me doubt: they could take her at any moment. There's not a damn thing I could do. The heaviness of that reality is bitter and palpable. I have to be careful, not because of her, but because of them.

I don't say this to my brother. I don't say a word because I'm too damn afraid that if I say the wrong thing, he'll convince me I shouldn't be with Ella. He's right, I do need her. I need her more than I'd like to admit.

He pushes his coffee cup aside and stands. "I have paperwork to do."

My pulse flares in my neck as I flex my hands back into fists. "And Ella?"

He looks down at me, shrugging his suit jacket back into place, and he's hovering somewhere between Cade, owner of The Firm, and Cade, my brother. There's no way to know which version will win out. "If you want to see Ella, go to her. It will not be as an employee of this company. I can't risk it."

My next breath comes easy and the change in my brother's expression tells me he knows how much relief I must feel. My hands are a breath away from shaking. I curl one into a fist on the table, and hold my coffee cup in the other. "Understandable, and I respect that decision."

"That means you'll no longer have the motel paid for."

I don't give a damn about the motel or money. "Also understandable."

"Consider yourself on unpaid leave."

All I can do is nod. For the first time in a long time, I want to stand up and crush him in a quick embrace. He doesn't know what he's given me with this. Or maybe he does. I can't say.

Cade shifts his weight from one foot to the other, about to leave, but then he hesitates. He lets out a breath. "You need to be careful, Zander. You and Ella—you're both in positions to be hurt badly in this. Her more than you. I don't want this to end badly. So if you can walk away, I think you should."

I don't want to hug him anymore. My gratefulness shrinks until it's a more appropriate size. "That's your opinion."

"It is." He's insistent now. Like he knew that it would piss me off to make the comment, but he had to make it anyway. Cade has never shied away from having hard conversations. Sometimes he's taken it too far. I didn't expect him to become a different person over this, and he hasn't. "It is my opinion. But it's because I don't want to see anyone else hurt." He turns to go. "I'll be in contact," he says over his shoulder.

"Anyone else" is another reference to Quincy. With his back to me, he walks out of the shop, the bell above the door chiming as he goes. Leave it to Cade to get that shot in at the last moment. It all starts with her, doesn't it?

But no—no. I take a four-count breath, then another, and sit with the pain in my chest and the surge of guilt. Quincy didn't die because of me. She died because some desperate bastard with a cruel streak mugged her and killed her. What's arguable is whether I should have insisted on walking her home. I should have insisted on seeing her to a safe place, and I didn't. I allowed her to walk away.

I'm not doing that with Ella. I didn't drive back to the motel and head out of town. I didn't take no for an answer when Damon tried to keep me from her. I didn't do a damn thing until I'd spoken to her.

I want to speak to her now.

I want to do more than speak to her. I want to be back in that bedroom with the door shut and kiss her until she moans. I want to feel her body underneath mine. I want to hear the way she whispers my name in her ear.

I reach for the phone in my pocket and pull back at the last minute. That phone belongs to The Firm. There's another one snugged beside it. Mine.

I let my mind wander to her. Her soft skin. Her pouty lips. Her wide, dark eyes. Her trust.

It takes no time at all to pull up her number. To see her name on the screen. She hasn't messaged. I haven't messaged her either, even though we're both aware there's plenty to discuss. It feels as though we're just getting started. It's thrilling, but in a way that's filled with uncertainty.

Be ready for me tonight. I have a few things to work out, then I'll be over like I promised.

There's a slight pause, and then she replies.

Zander?

A smirk pulls my lips up, realizing she didn't have this number. **Yes. This is my number now. Use it as often as you'd like.**

I will. Not another second passes before she tells me, **I miss you.**

It's hard to read her tone from a text message, but I imagine it's soft. Open. She's telling me something in honesty. In more of that trust I've come to crave.

I missed her too.

chapter 5

Ella

EMOTIONAL DAYS SUCK THE LIFE OUT OF YOU. I DON'T KNOW HOW or why, but it's like they eat up all of your energy, leaving you exhausted, yet you've done nothing but drown in the thoughts of your own mind. Ever since this morning, since I asked Kamden and Damon for space, I've stared at my phone and wished it was my old one.

I want to listen to James's voice message I listened to on repeat a year and a half ago. I want to tell my friends I miss him and hear them tell me they miss him too. All of my pictures, all of our conversations. It hit me harder than I thought it would bringing up what happened during that meeting. Every day, I know he died. Every day, I know I tried to kill myself because I didn't want to be alone anymore and I felt so damn alone. It was like the world went dark and the only light I could see was by ending it. It happened quickly, yet slowly just the same. I didn't realize I'd fallen down that path until it was the only one. Everything else vanished and it was all I had left. It was my only escape from grief.

It's a ball in a box. Grief really is an unforgiving ball in a stupid little box.

I stare back down at my phone as I sniffle and wish I could take that text and send it to James. *I miss you.*

Is it wrong that I miss them both? I can tell one and he chooses not to respond. But I can't even tell the other. My first love. The man I thought I was going to spend my life with.

I'm busy pulling the sheet up to my neck, its pristine white silky fabric not coming anywhere near my eyes in case my mascara is smudged when there's a knock at the door.

The shock comes with the knowledge that it's been so long since anyone has asked permission to enter.

"Come in," I answer calmly, lifting myself to sit up on my bed, glancing in the vanity mirror. I meant to change before Zander came, but time has flown by. The silk cuffs of my pajamas are proof I lost it earlier, and I find myself cupping my hands over the bits tainted with black mascara to cover them as he enters.

The door opens slowly, creaking as it does. Zander's steps are measured and he takes his time, closing the door. My heart does a pitter-patter as if a prince has come to kiss my sleeping lips and bring me back to life. What a handsome knight in shining armor he is.

He wears a devilish smirk as his gaze roams down my body. Every inch he takes in blazes with a desperate need to be touched by this man.

Zander Thompson is sin in all black. Black jeans that hug his ass and are faded just slightly, and a black Henley is stretched tight across his broad shoulders.

Then his eyes meet mine and he tilts his head ever so slightly. His expression, though … the seriousness can't hide the desire in his gaze.

"There are things we're going to discuss before I fuck you," he says and his deep voice barely comes out above a murmur, yet I hear every word crystal clear.

Suddenly I'm not so tired. Suddenly I'm not so sad.

I'm needy, though. I've never felt so needy in my entire life as I do now.

The floorboards groan as he shifts his weight.

I can't explain why I suddenly feel like I've done something wrong. "What do we need to talk about?"

"Your punishment." He speaks easily, slowly pacing around the bedroom. Zander loosens his collar first, giving me a perfect view of the masculine sweep of his neck.

Inching backward to rest against the headboard, I'm hesitant to ask, "What exactly do I need to be punished for?"

With his lips pulled into an asymmetric smirk, his deep voice rumbles, "If you don't know, then maybe I should reconsider this arrangement."

"Extortion … threatening The Firm?" I say and can barely breathe, not knowing how he'll react now that we're alone. I've wanted to be at his mercy since he whispered the forbidden word, submission … and now we find ourselves here. It's difficult to maintain eye contact until he says, "That would be it, my little jailbird."

I can't help but to simper at the twist to my nickname.

His approval brings warmth and comfort, although I'm still unsure what's to come. "There's that smile I've been missing."

I could tell him how much I've missed him. How much I don't want him to leave now that he's here. Instead he speaks before my courage comes and says, "We need to decide exactly how I'll be punishing you."

My heart races from how deadly low his tone is. The leather of Zander's belt glides easily from his belt loops as he unbuckles and removes it. All the while his eyes stay on mine.

The pounding of adrenaline in my blood causes it to heat and I swear I feel that pulse between my thighs the most.

With the belt folded in his hand, he turns his back to me before dragging the lone chair from my vanity to the end of the bed, placing it there and taking a seat.

He's far too large for the dainty thing. His brooding stature takes it over.

"I apologize," I say, answering him the only way I know how.

"Good girl," he whispers with a sexed-up grin.

"Edging is what I would typically do in this situation, but—"

"Edging?"

"Orgasm denial for a few hours," he says and leans back, more casual than he was a moment ago. His thumb runs down the stubble of his jaw as he adds, "Until I'm satisfied you've been punished."

Heat simmers along my skin with the threat. James did that before. It wasn't for hours and I cussed him out during. I vaguely remember being on the verge of tears when he finally let me get mine, then he fucked me into the mattress while telling me how much he loved me.

With my heart in my throat, I whisper, "It's what you would do normally … but?"

"But I found what you did made me hard as fuck, so I'll be rewarding you instead."

The blush that rises through me, from the tips of my toes all the way up to the crown of my head, is heated and proof I'm eager for more.

"There's—" I hesitate, my knuckles going white as I stare down at them, biting my tongue.

"Say it," Zander's voice is calm but I still can't bring myself to look up at him, the memory that begged to be spoken playing in my mind.

"Tell me right now." His tone is hardened and my gaze whips to his.

"I don't love the pain." I whisper the confession before swallowing.

His emerald and amber gaze is assessing, and the concern in his expression is apparent with the wrinkles that form around his eyes and his downturned lips.

Swallowing thickly I add, "James had a friend once." It's only once his name is spoken that I realize how easily I've mentioned my late husband. My lover. The only man who I've given everything to. It doesn't feel like the betrayal I imagined it would. It feels like he's given me permission. Like I'm supposed to tell Zander.

"When we were playing and learning things … he had a friend who asked questions. Most of them I didn't really pay attention to." That night was exceptional and a sigh leaves me at the memory, but the warmth that leaves means a chill settles inside of me. Picking at an imperceptible loose thread on the sheet, I peek up at Zander. "We were learning punishments and when James said I was a brat, that I pushed him to be punished, his friend asked if I loved the pain." Shaking my head comes without conscious consent. "I don't like it … not like his submissive did."

Since Zander's come in and seated himself in the chair in front of me, the sun has begun to set and the warm hues seep into the curtains behind him. With the light dimmed, shadows play along his sharp features.

He nods once before commanding me, "Strip. Down to nothing."

I don't expect the embarrassment. With my fingers fumbling at the hem of my silk pajamas, I can't even look him in the eyes. Of everything I thought I would feel confiding in Zander, embarrassment isn't one of them. It's quickly relieved when he tells me, "I'm not a sadist, Ella. I don't love the pain either and I already knew you weren't a masochist."

My heart thuds in a way that denies the space between us, like it doesn't exist. A different kind of heat takes over as he stares into my gaze, unbuttoning his shirt with one hand and tells me, "I want you naked with your heels on the mattress, legs bent and spread, so I can taste you."

With trembling hands I comply to his every wish, not sure if this is the punishment, the reward, or some kind of concoction of the two of them swirled together.

My hair cascades and spreads like a halo around me, my chest rising and falling as I stare above at the chandelier. At the details of the natural, untreated wood and the elegant curves of the iron that shape the sphere.

My eyes only close when the bed dips and groans, and then the warmth of Zander's breath tickles my inner thigh. With his lips pressed against my skin I feel him smile as I shiver.

Looking down my body, I watch as he leaves an openmouthed kiss, teasing me. With one hand, he holds my hip, and with the other, he reaches up and plucks a nipple between his pointer and thumb. Almost carelessly, even though the sensation is directly linked to my clit.

The breath of a moan he elicits only makes me hotter. He nips at my thigh, not hard but enough that my body bucks in response. He doesn't keep me steady; he could have held me down and we both know it.

"You need to keep still," he warns, his eyes darkening. There's a heat that resonates between us, ignited from the intensity in his gaze. I only nod, barely breathing, until he catches my nipple between his fingers, rolling it. The sensation is hot yet there's a pain that comes with it.

I moan my agreement, telling him, "I'll keep still." He releases me instantly, and doesn't hesitate to drop his tongue to my slit. Taking a languid lick, he groans deep from within his chest. The rumble brings a vibration that carries to his lips.

My head falls back and I let my eyes close, focused on keeping myself still. My fingernails dig into the sheets, scratching as I tighten my grip. I want nothing more than to run them through his hair, to keep him still instead of me, to rock myself against his tongue.

A gasp escapes and I'm forced to look down at him as his tongue dives into my heat. He drags himself back up and then sucks my clit. My lips form a perfect *O* and I can't breathe as he causes a heat to dance along every nerve ending in my body. I'm cold all at once, my body refusing to move until the fire engulfs me and a cry of pleasure is torn from me. My back bows slightly, my shoulders digging into the mattress.

The pool of pleasure deep in my belly spreads slowly, outward and toward my limbs. His next statement catches me off guard. It's the demand, the threat that lies there when he says, "Keep your ass down or I'll tie you down."

I don't have a moment to respond before he presses his thumb against my throbbing clit, mercilessly rubbing as two of his thick fingers enter me.

With my teeth clenched, I force out profanity as he fucks me, his fingers curled so every stroke hits the wall where that bundle of sensitive nerves lies. He's relentless, near brutal as goosebumps spread along my skin.

It's beyond impossible to stay still. My legs tremble and before I can get out an apology or an excuse, Zander keeps me trapped in his gaze as he plants a kiss on my quivering thigh.

It takes everything I have to remain motionless and obey. My body begs to buck as the pleasure builds. It carries me higher and higher and I whisper, as if the single letter is a plea, "Z."

Adding in a third, he finger fucks me harder and without any mercy.

"Fuck!" I cry out, my body instinctively attempting to escape the threat of my impending climax.

It hits me just as Zander squeezes my breast. He's not gentle and the hint of pain only adds to the overwhelming pleasure. A cold sweat covers my body as the waves run through me.

My inhale is staggered as I attempt to retake my place and then I'm paralyzed by his next action.

He works his fourth finger in me, stretching me with a sweet, stinging pain. The pleasure lingers and feels especially present between my legs where it's far more tender.

"Good girl, taking what I give you." His groan of approval brings more heat. "I want to give you more."

"More?" I can barely breathe at hearing the word, already overwhelmed and stretched and full.

"Be a good girl, Ella. I want to see how much you can take." He plants a small kiss just beneath my belly button.

His fist? "Are you—fuck!" My neck arches as I scream out, loving the mix of pleasure and pain and feeling this … taken.

He doesn't look me in the eye. Instead he leans down, his broad shoulders forcing my legs farther apart. He takes my clit into his mouth, sucking harder than he did before and my head drops as the sounds of him working his hand promise me that the reality is exactly what I think it is. His fingers bend, his knuckles brutally pushing against my walls, his pace never lessening.

It's all too much. I'm too hot, the pleasure building again, far more this time, taking me higher, to a place where I know the fall will destroy me after it's taken me.

My throat feels raw, the safe word hovering, threatening to be spoken. I feel full, tight, ready to split. A shiver rides up my shoulders just as I feel him press the tip of his thumb in and I can't take it.

I can't take any more. I'm so close once again. Too close. Too full.

"It's too much," I try to speak, but the words are incoherent. "Pink. Pink," I say and struggle, my head pressed firmly to the pillow, my body still shaking. All at once, I'm empty and cold.

"I've got you." Zander's voice is steadying as I roll onto my side. My legs collapse together and the blanket is pulled around my shoulders, the warmth nothing compared to what Z had just done to me. My shoulders shake with a shiver that's only subdued when my Dominant lies behind me, his chest to my back, his arms around me, holding me tightly.

I didn't even feel the tears that had leaked out of the corner of my eyes and rolled down my cheeks until my heart stopped hammering.

"I've got you," he whispers, his lips at the shell of my ear. He shushes me, he tells me it's all right.

I'm barely cognizant of what just happened. When my breathing calms, I realize I safe worded. "I didn't mean to."

My denial is met with a kiss on the curve of my neck. Not too short, an openmouthed version that lingers. "You did," he says. With his lips in my hair, he kisses me again. His arm tightens, pulling me to him as he tells me it's all right.

I recall only safe wording once with James. Only when he cracked the whip and it broke my skin. Only once because of the sudden pain and fear. I was terrified. That was an entirely different experience. He apologized. He held me, but I was crying. The pain lasted and I shoved him away. It was awful.

This … this doesn't feel like that at all. Not in the least.

"You're crying." Zander's voice is full of concern. I wish I could say anything, but I can't utter a word.

"Where do you hurt?"

I can't answer his question because it's not like he could do a damn thing to fix it. Damon said I may be displacing my feelings and I think he might be right. I still love James. I love him and I think I love Zander too, but I don't know how that's possible.

"It's okay, you can cry." I know he's looking down at me but I keep my eyes shut tight. "If you want me to stop—"

"Don't stop." I beg him with quickly ushered words. "Don't stop. Please, Z, hold me."

chapter 6

Zander

Scrolling through the photos on Ella's various social media accounts leaves a longing to know who this beautiful woman used to be. She hasn't posted regularly in nearly two years now but I scroll past flirtatious grins and obvious laughter, past a woman celebrating life and exuding strength with a no-fucks-given attitude. There are pictures of him as well. Her sneaking up on him and laying with him on sunny tropical beaches. Pictures of him kissing her and where she's kissing him. There's an obvious point where her public persona was tamed. Just prior to their wedding photos, she appears wild and free. And then it changes, to bright smiles and "love and light" captions.

There are wholesome posts about her charity work, but it doesn't take much to be certain that prior to marrying James, Ella was known for her partying.

The fireplace in Ella's sitting room is off, adding to the quiet. The blue of the paint is suffused with gray light from the early morning. She's still sleeping upstairs, leaving me alone in the chill of this room.

I came here out of habit. I didn't know what to do with myself when I woke up in her bed. I found a spare toothbrush in the bathroom, still wrapped in plastic among other travel-sized toiletries. She was sleeping so deeply when I finally let go of her that I couldn't bear to wake her. I tugged her blanket up to her shoulders and quietly slipped out to the room that's most familiar to me. We've spent the most time here, in the blue sitting room. And in its silence, I've let my mind wander, I've let the questions repeat themself over and over. *Am I doing the right thing? Is this really what's best for her?*

I'm only her Dom, so there's no reason for me to be here. Not technically. It's storming outside and I watch the raindrops fall against the window. When the wind blows, it's vicious, battering the small droplets against the panes. Unless we're going to have a true 24/7 relationship, then I can't be here all the time.

Even if a part of me wanted to be here, simply because she's most comfortable here, a much larger part of me doesn't want to develop this relationship anywhere other than my own home.

We're going to have to talk about it, and soon. This is a crucial boundary between the two of us. When I'll come over, and how long I'll stay. I need to make clear to her that she was only agreeing to the relationship we had before, nothing else. I'll help her as her Dom. Although I would never make this arrangement with anyone else who couldn't leave the confines of their home. With the only other 24/7 power exchange relationship I've had, the only true D/s relationship, she lived with me. *Quincy.*

Quincy, who has been the subject of at least one phone call this morning. A phone call I let go to voicemail. The hearing's coming up, and I don't want to talk about it.

A larger sheet of rain sweeps across the yard and taps more forcefully against the windowpane. I've never lived in a place like this, with all this space.

All this wealth.

Across the house, the front door opens. I hear it click shut quietly. It's far too early for Silas to switch off with Damon. The footsteps and the jingle of keys is telling. I stay where I am, my jaw clenching slightly. He can come to me.

Kamden appears in the sitting room doorway with my temper barely contained, the anger still palpable. The air between us seems thick. Weighted. He narrows his eyes and watches me from the opening, then straightens up and strides in, taking the seat across from me. He's exaggerated about it. Casual. But it's not casual, and we both know it. From the tight set of his jaw I think he might like to hit me. The very idea begs my lips to pull up into a smirk, but I keep my expression neutral.

It seems we feel the same about one another.

He lets the silence stretch out, and so do I. I've thought about what I'd say to him, but every conversation is different as I play it out. More importantly, I need to be careful. He's Ella's conservator. There is far too much at risk for her to allow my ego to take center stage.

Everything outside of the two of us, is a risk. She isn't in charge of her own decisions. I don't have authority in that aspect of her life either. Pissing off the wrong person could end in me not having access to her at all. Had I not been able to convince Cade and Kamden, things could be very different right now. The Firm, Kamden, even her closest friends. One wrong step and we could be buried in problems I don't know how to get out of.

Wind rushes outside the window now. The rain lets up a little, then comes back down hard. It's one of those fall storms that steals the warmth from the air and makes it feel frigid afterward, even if snow is weeks from falling. The heat kicks on in Ella's house, with the faintest of clicks. Other than the leather groaning beneath Kamden as he readjusts to lean forward, his elbows on his knees, it's the only sound in the room. But not for long.

"If you hurt her, I will destroy you," Kamden says beneath his breath.

I stare at him across the space between us. "That a threat, Kam?" A heat travels up my spine and across my shoulders. Instinctively, my fingers curl slightly, ready to ball into fists.

"It's a promise." His voice is clear, raised so there's no doubt I can hear. "You wouldn't be the first man who thought he could use her."

A crease forms between my brows as my eyes narrow at him. That's fucking rich, coming from the man who installed cameras in her home to spy on her. Fucking rich. Every ounce of anger calls at the back of my throat. Keeping a stone-cold expression I'm careful with my response, knowing full well the power he has over her. I've never hated a soul more than him.

"I'm not using Ella."

"Of course you are." His statement comes with a sadness he fails to contain. If I'm not mistaken, a fear as well. He stares into the empty fireplace, refusing to look back at me. "Even if you don't want to admit it. You're using her."

"You'd know that from experience, right?"

"Fuck you," Kamden spits, his eyes coming back to mine. I've pissed him off enough with that one remark to make color come to his cheeks. "You don't know what the hell you're talking about. She's like my little sister."

I want to call him out on the cameras. Even if Ella were Kamden's little sister, he sure as hell shouldn't have been putting up cameras without asking her. But a guy like Kamden will have come up with a justification for himself. One that I won't be able to change, or counter.

Besides. There are other things I know about Kamden.

"She's like your little sister, but you didn't go to visit her." My tone is deathly low, and wrought with emotion I didn't realize I had for that small fact. I don't bother to hide it, the obvious pain he caused her. "She was alone, locked away, and you didn't visit her once."

All that color runs out of his cheeks, leaving him strangely pale in the gray light coming through the window. Ella told me he never went to visit her while she was at the Rockford Center, and that is definitely the kind of thing an older brother type would do. It's most certainly the kind of thing Kamden should have done.

Kamden opens his mouth. "I—" A subtle shake of his head stops him from continuing. He was going to tell me one thing, and then he changed his mind. His thumbnail finding his bottom teeth as he leans back, once again he focuses on the empty fire. Another few long seconds go by. The rain makes it easier to sit through this conversation. It gives me something to listen to other than the beat of my heart and all my own thoughts. His expression gives me something new to think about; it reads nothing but regret. The longer I sit, the more questions build in my mind.

"I had a relapse," he admits in a whisper and then clears his throat, meeting my eyes. "I didn't go to see her, because I couldn't. I know one of your dirty secrets. Now you know one of mine."

"A relapse?" The leather armrest tightens under my grasp. Kamden stands up and shrugs off his jacket. He's wearing a heather gray shirt underneath with his jeans. He'd look comfortable here if he weren't trying to suppress so much emotion. He tosses the jacket onto one of the other chairs and sits down again.

"I overdosed." Kamden's mouth curves down, his cheeks reddening again, and I'd know that expression anywhere. I've seen it on my own face in the mirror enough times. He settles back into the chair and he's joined by guilt.

Guilt. Real, pained guilt.

That heat I felt before dims instead as I watch him, finding no trace of deception.

Kamden clears his throat. "Fuck you for judging me." His eyes are hard on mine now. He looks like this hurts to say even more than admitting the relapse. "I found her. I'm the one who found her. She'd jumped out of a window. Not this place. I can't go back to her southern home. I thought she was dead. Lying there like a corpse, there was so much blood by her head. I thought she was dead."

The image slams into me like a long-haul truck. Ella, lying lifeless and still on the ground outside some featureless window. The horrified feeling of coming upon her that way. The slow realization. Kamden wouldn't have wanted to believe it was true. Reality would have forced its way in anyway. She had lived. Obviously she had lived. But there would have been a moment when his heart was in his throat, when his mind was screaming for her not to have done what she did. My own heart pounds to imagine it. I have to keep my face neutral with every bit of restraint I have.

It's far more serious than I thought with Ella. I thought she had a moment of weakness once. Only once. "She tried to kill herself more than once?"

"Twice now," Kamden answers and swallows hard. "She was admitted after she jumped out the window. The only thing that saved her that time was the railing. Her ankle caught it on the way down and prevented her from landing on concrete stairs." He readjusts again in his seat, this time opting to sit back, his gaze focusing on the blanket. Like all he wants to do is hide beneath it. As if it could all be written off as a bad dream. "I couldn't do anything about it. The police came. I was in shock. She'd jumped. It was obvious. I wasn't there when they spoke to her when she woke up, they wouldn't let me. They admitted her before I could do a damn thing to help her."

A chill settles between us, dragging the tension down to the ground until it's subdued entirely. All I can wonder is if Damon knows. My mind drifts to the file. Kamden's quiet for another long stretch until he tells me, "And then, at the center, she drank drain cleaner. I've been—" He stops, putting a fist to his mouth, and takes a deep breath. Putting his hands in his lap before he continues. "I've been clean for a decade, but I couldn't stop blaming myself."

"For what? What did you do?"

"I'm the one who left her alone in the first place." His eyes find mine. "She was losing it. Crying, which I expected. But she was angry and hysterical."

This wouldn't have been in the file. Even if I'd read it, this statement from Kamden wouldn't have been in there. He wouldn't be telling me now if he assumed I already knew about it. It comes back to me then—Ella telling me that everything in the file was carefully curated. I thought she meant she did it all by herself, but Kamden must have had a hand too. He must have kept out certain details.

"You left her alone because she was upset?" I shake my head, my own guilt rising again. I did the same thing. I let Quincy walk through the city by herself. I want to convince Kamden it wasn't his fault as much as I want to convince myself, but lies don't help a damn soul.

"No. I left her alone, and I took her phone. So she had no one. I took her phone," he repeats as if the phone is what did her in. "She couldn't call anyone … but she couldn't have it. It was driving her mad."

None of this makes any sense. "Why the hell would you take her phone?"

He's looking into the fireplace again, and I almost wish I'd turned the damn thing on so he wouldn't look so desolate while he stares into nothing. Kamden takes a trip back into his memories and resurfaces with a shake of his head. "They kept posting it. The video. It was all over her social. They kept tagging her, over and over again. Every time she saw one pop up, she lost it."

"Posting the video?"

"Ella kept watching it over and over. Someone would tag her and the whole cycle would start again. She couldn't stop herself. She'd play the video and cry. Gut-wrenching sobs. All day. After a few hours she'd manage to collect herself, but it would only be for a few minutes. An hour at most. And then she went back to the video. Back and back and back. When it was at its worst she would beg people to stop posting, but they wouldn't. Asking them to take it down only made more people share the link. It was vicious. She had nowhere to go. Maybe you don't get it, but sharing everything with them ... she couldn't back away and they wouldn't let her."

I'm missing a crucial piece of information, and for the first time I feel a real, genuine regret that I haven't read her file. I haven't done everything in my power to learn about Ella. I'm against it in general because I think people need the chance to tell their own stories, but this is a part of it that she's yet to confide in me.

I didn't know about the suicide attempt at her old place. I didn't know she jumped out of a fucking window. And Kamden thinks she did that because of some people posting about her. No—posting a video. I've seen some videos, but—

"What were they posting?"

Kamden meets my eyes with deep disappointment. Somehow, the tables have turned since he walked into this room. "You want to make me the villain in all this because you're pissed off at me, but I'm not the villain. You might be, though."

"What got to her—" I stop and take a deep breath. I won't let my anger get the best of me. I won't even talk myself up into thinking I haven't made any mistakes. "What did they post that made her that upset?" It has to do with James. It's the only thing I can imagine. The realization is suffocating.

Kamden looks down at his hands in his lap, then back up to me. "You should ask her." He shakes his head then adds, "No. You should already know."

chapter 7

Ella

I HAVEN'T LOOKED FORWARD TO DAMON AND HIS CHATS. IT'S something I've tolerated because I was told I had to do it. Therapy isn't something I've ever wanted. Until this morning.

Waking up to find another gift from Kam, glazed pastries from a quaint French bakery downtown, and a note from Zander, letting me know he had to have arrangements made but would see me tonight … left me feeling more alone than I'd have liked. Barefoot in the kitchen, that sinking feeling resonated until Damon walked into the room.

"Is there anything you want to talk about this morning?" Damon's professional as always, but I don't miss his subtle change in expression when he glances down at my nightgown. It's the same one from yesterday. I was eager to get downstairs, to find Zander and didn't think much else of, well, of anything else.

"Aren't you the one who's supposed to pick those topics?"

"I could … just thought I'd offer," he says and shrugs. Eyeing him I wonder how this man always looks so professional. Even in only a simple white tee and faded blue jeans, he radiates an aura of strength. Freshly shaven, his dark skin taut over his muscular arms. It's easy to decide that it's just him. It's the air around him. Everything about him reads: authority.

And then there's me. In a wrinkled nightshirt, with finger-combed hair.

Clearing my throat, I hesitantly take a seat at the counter. "I haven't brushed my teeth, let alone begun to think about what we should talk about." Lies. The softly spoken words sound like lies even to my own ears.

"There's nothing you want to talk about?" he questions. Staring past him to the kettle still on the stove from yesterday, I wonder if Z told him about last night. I wouldn't think so, but then again, I'm not a part of those conversations. There's so much out of my own control.

"You seem …"

"Out of it?" I surmise.

"Upset," he says, correcting me. The stool grates on the floor as I stand up and busy myself with the kettle.

In truth, I'm exhausted. I slept so well, yet it feels like I haven't slept at all. With the water running he questions, "Are you all right?"

With a gentle sigh escaping, I tell him, "I'll be all right. Just feeling needy today."

Damon nods, rounding the counter to join me in the working space of the kitchen. He manhandles the coffee pot, finding it empty.

When he opens the canister, the scent of fresh grounds filling the room, I comment on how much I love the smell.

Which he duly ignores. "Is there anything in particular that upset you this morning?" Even though he's facing a now brewing pot of coffee, pretending like he's not watching me, I feel his eyes on the side of my face. That's when I realize I'm watching a kettle, waiting for the pot to boil.

"It's just a ball in a box," I murmur, knowing full well why I'm upset. "I'm still grieving."

Damon's charming smile isn't what I expect to see from him. He nods and says, "We always grieve."

I nod in return and debate on letting it all out. Telling him about last night, but maybe he already knows.

"Did Z tell you?" I whisper the question.

Grabbing his mug of black coffee with both hands, he shakes his head. "Did something happen?"

I scoot from in front of the stove to the counter so I can rest my back against it, gripping the edge on either side. "Last night, I just … I had a moment."

Damon gestures to the breakfast nook to the right with his mug. "Would you like to sit?"

Raising a brow, I ask him, "Would you like to add your sugar and cream?" My sarcastic response grants me an even broader smile. "Sitting can wait until I at least have a cup of tea," I add as he sets his mug down and adds cream and sugar as he always does.

"You know there isn't a story worth not having sugar in your morning brew."

The spoon stops mid-twirl in his mug at my comment, the warmth leaving his expression for a moment as he seems to carefully consider his words. "There is purpose in suffering."

"What?"

"I wanted to wait for the right time, but I feel like you need to know that this morning."

He peeks at me from the corner of his eye as the kettle whistles.

"There is purpose in suffering." He leans against the counter as I prepare my tea. "It wasn't so much that I was caught up in your story, not that I wasn't invested." He adds, "Just … more that I wanted to make sure I told you that."

"Mr. Dwell-in-your-emotions thinks there's purpose in suffering … how am I not surprised by that?" I offer wryly but with a semblance of a smirk.

He takes his time, his heavy footsteps careful as he takes a seat at the small table. After a moment, I join him, letting the tea steep and watching the steam billow.

Since Zander didn't tell Damon, I don't want to confess that I cried last night. But I wanted to get these thoughts out of me. I need someone else to take them. "I don't often feel scared. But I do now. It's alarming how scared I am."

"Why do you say that?"

"At one point in my life I had so much to lose, and yet, there wasn't much at all that I was afraid of."

Speaking the words out loud makes so much of it real. I'm scared. Maybe I'm just as scared as I am upset.

"There was a time that I was scared to be hated. Then someone told me if there aren't people out there who hate you, then it's because no one knows who you are. People with viewpoints are hated; my favorite people are demons in someone else's story. Don't you want to be someone who is known for what they believe in?" I recall the conversation I had, but I don't even remember who gave me the advice. "That's why I wanted it all out there. It's why I love that I got to share my life. I was hated, but everyone knew damn well what I believed in and I found the people who wanted the same in life." Peeking up at Damon I tell him, "I remember I wasn't scared anymore after that. Not like I was."

"But you're scared now?" he asks and my throat dries as I nod. I confess in a whisper, "I'm terrified."

"What are you scared of?"

"I haven't shared much in a long time."

"Kamden said you've started, though," he comments, his voice hopeful.

"Only two posts."

"It's something."

"It is."

"So you want to share more and you're scared of that."

"Not of sharing per se … scared of not sharing where I stand. It's just … it's complicated."

"What are you afraid of now?"

"It feels like I have so little left."

"In this big house?" he jokes in a calm, comforting way. I know he's got a smile on his face and he's watching me, but I can only watch the billowing steam.

In my silence, he presses, "Money?"

"No … money is fine. It comes and goes, but money is fine. … It's just there are things that I want to talk about, and I'm afraid if I share it with them …" I can't bring myself to say it, but somehow I do. "If I share it, somehow they'll make it hurt. They'll make that little piece that means so much, become insignificant and then there won't be anything left at all."

"Well, you know no one has control over you. Only you do. You can only control yourself."

Nodding, my response is cracked when spoken. "I know."

"Maybe you should keep some things to yourself. It's not a bad thing. You don't owe anyone anything."

"It feels selfish in a way."

"Protecting yourself isn't selfish." Damon's adamant, but so is my phone that buzzes with a new text. The cement block that it is, opens to reveal a simple question.

"Everything okay?" Damon asks when I go quiet.

"It's just Kam. He wants to have a meeting soon." Toying with the phone I add, "He asked me when I'm free."

"And that upsets you?" he asks, gauging my solemn expression.

"He's never asked before." Again, that cold, lonely feeling that overwhelmed me when I woke up covers every inch of my skin.

"Things are different now." I swallow down the regret and push my phone away. "Everything is different."

"Different is not only okay. Different is good sometimes."

"I just wish some things could go back to the way they were."

"Which things?" he asks and my answer is immediate. "I wish I weren't so damn afraid."

"What are you afraid of?"

"That I'm going to make a mistake. Just one and I'm going to lose everything because of it." Zander. I'm going to lose Zander. I can't tell him, because even confessing that to Damon feels like it could lead to me losing him. No matter where I look, I think, one step, and it's all gone.

chapter 8

THERE'S A BITE IN THE AIR WHEN I PULL UP BEHIND ELLA'S THE next evening. Sunset comes faster in the fall, and it's almost finished now. Not quite cold enough for a winter coat, but there's a frosty edge to the breeze. The kitchen lights are on, spilling light out onto the porch, and Damon's in there.

Staring down at my phone, I see there are three unanswered messages.

Kamden: Have you talked to her? You need to really talk to her.

Cade: There's no chance in hell that she's moving out of that house. She's under our protection and to the judge's order, it is only under the condition that she stays at that location. And the cameras will be staying. I can't make exceptions and you know that.

Damon: I don't know what happened last night, but you should have been there this morning.

Everyone is watching us. Judging us. Even worse, their approval is an actual fucking factor in our relationship. None of this is ideal.

Another message comes in. This one from one of the lawyers involved in Quincy's case.

Arguments start at 9:30 sharp—wanted to keep you updated. Courtroom will be open if you want to sit in.

For a brief moment, I hesitate in the car. It would be far too easy to tell them all to fuck off. To tell them I'm handling it, that I've got her. It's their intentions that kept me from texting each one of them just that. I'll give Kamden the benefit of the doubt. They all have her best interest at heart. We all want the same thing: for Ella to be healthy and happy.

All day I've wondered what it is I want from this, and all that resonated was the moment in her kitchen when I heard her laugh for the first time. When she smiled up at me with a knowing look. I want that flirtatious look in her eyes. I want her moaning my name. I want her.

Clicking off my phone and shoving it into my back pocket, I settle on not responding until I speak to Ella and decide together what I should tell them.

Damon's message is the one that blindsided me the most. Him telling me I should have been there doesn't sit well with me. If he's pissed at me for turning my back on The Firm, he should say it.

It's not like we haven't had our differences before. If he really thinks I've fucked up with her, though … that's a different story.

I've had enough confrontation for one day. I throw the door open and get out. My duffle is in the trunk; with the click of the key fob, it opens easily enough.

It took me all damn day to find a suitable place to rent close by, to get out of my lease, to schedule the movers and clear out the motel. If I had control like I'd prefer, she would have been beside me.

I spent half the day in the fucking car rearranging my life, and my best friend wants to give me shit over it. I know Ella needs to be cared for. I only left because I trusted him to do just that. Heaving the duffle over my shoulder, I'm more confident tonight than I was last night. I have everything we need for now. I can take it over from here, within the confines this situation allows.

I head for the door instead of dwelling on it any longer. Long, even strides. Like I belong here. Which I do. Ella wants me here, and that's all that matters. What doesn't matter is the prickling under the collar of my jacket and the way my nerves go cold. Seeing her feels so damn flimsy now that I've left The Firm.

Yes, I crossed professional boundaries with Ella. Yes, I did it over and over again. But at least when I was at The Firm I was guaranteed my nine-to-nine shift with her. I could count on it. Now it seems tenuous. One step out of place, and they could lock me out. Move her to a secure location. It's a fine, fine distinction. Any hint from her that she doesn't want me around, and they could escort me out.

It feels as if we're caged in. That's what each step feels like. Like I'm walking into a cage. The only saving grace is that she's in there with me and so long as I'm there, she'll be safe.

Staying calm for her is what anchors me to the ground. It's not a very sturdy anchor. This kind of visiting, where I don't really belong with the company and I don't really belong to Ella, makes me feel like I'm on the deck of a small ship caught in a storm. The waves seem reckless in my imagination.

My thumb runs down the sharp edge of the key, a key only given to me when I worked with The Firm. Staring at the doorknob, I focus on why I'm here.

I want her and she wants me. It's as simple as that.

The moment I open the door, the warmth greets me just as the bright light from the kitchen does. Slipping the handle of the duffle down my shoulder, I set the bag down and gently close the door.

Damon's eyes come up from his phone to meet mine from where he's sitting on a stool by the counter.

The realization I've come to is simple: there's no chance in hell for privacy here.

"You look like hell," my best friend says.

I run a hand over my head. "I have a lot on my mind."

Damon nods, then swipes his thumb over his phone screen and puts the phone in his pocket. From the way he presses his lips together I know he's got things on his mind too.

"I got your text," I tell him, dropping the bag and tossing my keys on the counter. "How is she?"

The question falls into the quiet of the kitchen. Damon huffs out a breath. This is close to how it would be if we were trading off shifts, but I'm not working with him anymore. This is a problem that will keep coming up between us until we solve it. Awkwardness tightens my chest and squeezes the air out of my lungs. Our routines are all wrapped up in The Firm. It's like pricking yourself on the same splinter at the back door of your house. Hurts every time, but until you sand down the wood, make it all right, it'll never let you rest.

His dark eyes meet mine. "I thought that after what happened, she might withdraw. Close up. I was prepared for the scenario where we'd have to start all over with her therapy and with her trust. But she opened up this morning … I think it would have benefitted her to have you here."

"Where is she?"

"Taking a shower now."

"I'm going to go over our new arrangement today." I drag out a chair at the table, taking a seat opposite him.

"What's the plan?"

"I'll stay here. Twenty-four seven power exchange. It'll be easier to be honest, now that I don't have shifts where I'm done."

"Staying here?"

I don't hide my dismay. "We don't have a choice."

Damon's gaze settles behind me by the door, where the duffle bag sits. "You really have feelings for her, don't you?" he asks.

Without my conscious consent, I answer, "Yes." My gaze drops and the pad of my thumb runs down the side of my pointer. "I have feelings for her."

Damon grins across the table and tells me, "Don't look so damn terrified."

"I question if she knows what she really wants. If I even know what I really want. Beyond what we're currently doing."

"What if what you're currently doing is enough?" he asks me.

My smirk in response lacks all humor. "We both know this is temporary." I grind my teeth together rather than adding, *I don't want to fail her.* I'm so fucking conflicted with her. Even my Dom side is holding back. She's fragile, everyone is watching and I don't know if once all of this is over that she's still going to want this. She's still mourning her husband… all of it, keeps me on edge when I think about the idea of us. But then I'm with her, and all I can do is fall.

"Who knows this is temporary? You and her?"

"You and I."

Tapping his knuckles on the table, Damon shakes his head. "I don't know that."

"If she didn't need me, I wouldn't be here, is what I'm saying."

"And when she doesn't need you—"

"Then I'll be gone." I finish the statement for him.

"And what if you become her safe place? You ever wonder that?"

"I still don't know that what I want would be enough for her."

"I think you're lying to yourself."

Rather than engage, I change the subject. "Is there anything you'd suggest I lead her toward today?" Damon cocks his head to the side and looks at me. I add, "I thought I'd spoil her tonight and we can lay out terms."

"Just one thing, be careful."

"I'm careful with her. Maybe too careful."

"Not just with her. Be careful, Zander."

chapter 9

Ella

THE FEELING FROM THIS MORNING HASN'T LEFT.

It's the comedown from the high. I fought for what I wanted, I won … but what is it that I'm left with?

I'm still under a conservatorship. I'm still mandated to be in the confines of my home until I prove my mental stability to someone I don't even know and only when Damon, and The Firm, recommends an examination be done. I have no control over either.

And then there's Zander, a man I intend to give what little control I have left. A man who stirs up a number of feelings that I can barely categorize … especially since Damon made that comment. It won't stop echoing in my head. Maybe I'm displacing the love I had for James onto Zander.

The leather journal with rose gold binding has two sheets filled with nothing but questions.

All I know for certain is that I don't have any answers and that I'm a far distance away from where I want to be. With all of the memories flooding me today, I long to go back more than anything else.

Back to a time before all of this was set into motion.

My phone buzzes with a text from Kelly. You're supposed to hold it.

My gaze shifts to the nightstand where the smoky quartz has sat since Kelly sent it in the mail.

She adds, I swear it works.

I don't have a single comment to make about the crystal and Kelly's hippie-dippie solution to everything. If I wasn't on medication, I imagine she'd have gifted me pot as well.

I'll hold it during my therapy sessions. My thumb hovers over the button, but before I can second-guess it, I send the message.

Perfect! She replies instantly and then asks another question about Zander. What's his shoe size? Her question forces a sly smile from me.

Kam must have reached out to Trish and Kelly and given them this number. All three of them have been texting me today. They've been asking about Zander and anything else … other than the obvious. None of them have asked about what happened or how I'm doing in that respect.

The girls want to know all about him most of all. The secret love interest. If only they knew the whole truth.

I'll tell you tomorrow, I write back and Kelly replies with, I can't wait.

Girls' luncheons are going to be my new favorite, Trish says next.

Kelly piles on with, Seriously, this has been missing from my life. Love you girls. Kisses.

Setting the phone down on the dresser, I wonder how much I should tell them. He's still a secret … at least to most people. They think he's just a bodyguard from the private security firm I hired and I struggle with how much I should tell them.

At that thought, there's a knock at my bedroom door. He's the only one who knocks … as if there's a semblance of privacy in this home. There are cameras everywhere. I call out while peering up at the camera in the corner of the room. It's tucked away, small and insignificant, yet it's one more indication that they're always watching.

"Come in." The door creaks open.

Damon told me Cade added motion sensors above the bedroom door. So they're alerted to anyone coming or going. He not-so-subtly hinted around the fact that when Zander and I are together here, they'll stop watching.

I'm very aware that it will still be recorded. It's odd the sensation it gives me and how it's so strikingly different from when I'm recorded alone. One is troublesome and alarming, while the other is tantalizing.

With only the corner light on, and the evening sun filtering through the curtains, my prince is cast in shadows as he closes the door behind him.

My periwinkle silk nightgown is in complete contrast to his stiff white collared shirt and perfectly tailored slacks. All but the top button is done. It does nothing to hide his muscular physique and the power that lies under the expensive fabric.

"There you are," he comments as if he's been looking for me. I heard him come in. I heard them talking.

"You weren't here this morning," I say and the statement comes out as an accusation. There's a flash in his eyes. I know I've tested him. But it's gone as quickly as it came.

"I had a few things to take care of." He considers me and I do the same to him. His gaze roams down my body and his posture changes, his hand seeming to ache at his side as he flexes it. The door closes then with a final click and he stalks toward me, each step measured and quiet. Like a hunter to his prey.

I can't help what he does to me. How the air heats and each breath is harder to inhale.

Licking his bottom lip, he stops feet from me. My back to the mirror at my vanity, I stare back at him, noting that I'm cornered.

"You're disappointed?" he questions, seemingly surprised with a cocked brow.

I answer him honestly. "I'm not sure what to expect."

"Tell me what you want, and I'll tell you if you can have it." He doesn't let a moment pass before answering easily. Checking over his shoulder, he decides to lean against the dresser, putting more space between us.

"Just tell you and you'll make it happen?"

"If I determine it necessary, yes." His voice lowers, as does his gaze to where the button is undone between my breasts. I'm more than aware that this nightgown leaves little to the imagination when it comes to my chest.

"I want you to be here when I wake up ... at least if we," I clear my throat, composing myself and remembering who the hell I am. "If we fucked the night before, I want to wake up beside you."

The strength in my tone raises Zander's gaze and he nods. "I will make sure that happens moving forward." I didn't realize I was holding my breath until he answers. Nodding slightly, I place my phone down on the vanity next to my hairbrush.

There's something liberating in that simplicity.

In the quiet, he rumbles, "I missed kissing you." The warmth returns with full force. My guard is crumbling; I feel every piece fall and I don't care.

"Is that all you missed?" I say, teasing him without thinking much of it.

"Come here," he commands me in a whisper. It's easy to obey. His hand finds the small of my waist, pulling me in for a chaste kiss. It's simple, all of it is so easy and so bare. Yet I crumble and heat at his touch, feeling more vulnerable with every fraction of a second.

The feel of his kiss still pressed against my lips, my eyes closed and my blood warming, I push out the words that have wreaked havoc on my mind while he's been gone.

"Damon suggested I may be displacing some of my feelings." I push them out as quickly as I can, too scared to open my eyes until the last word is spoken.

He doesn't answer and slowly, I peek up at him through my lashes. The only movement he makes is to run his thumb up and down my side.

"What do you think?"

"I don't know. I know I feel things … I don't know what you feel."

"You're feeling uncertain?"

"Yes."

"Mmm," he says and his acknowledgment is a rumble from his chest. He pulls me forward, into his chest, to kiss the crown of my head, then he whispers, "You still want me?"

"Yes," I answer easily, my eyes still open, staring down at his chest.

"Good," he answers and pulls back, letting cool air filter between us to look down at me. "Even if you don't want me for forever, you damn well better know that I want you right now."

"And tomorrow?" Peeking up at him, I feel nothing but vulnerable.

"I'll want you tomorrow too. So long as you want this, I will be here."

I've never felt so needy before. So fragile with a man. James happened slowly. We were friends first and falling for him was unexpected. The security was there. By the time I realized what I felt, I knew he felt the same. This … this is nothing like that and it's terrifying.

"I'm afraid … you don't really want me. That you're only here because you think I need you."

Zander's inhale is audible, and it's heavy and suffocating all at once. His expression is just as alarming. It's as if the air around him has darkened and a different side of him has taken over. With a single step forward, he towers over me.

"If I didn't want you, I wouldn't be here, Ella." The disappointment is obvious in his piercing gaze. "How could you possibly think I don't want you? It's fucking embarrassing what you do to me. How I can't even think when you're around." Taking my hand in his, he presses my palm against him. "I'm hard as fuck thinking of how I'm going to punish you for that insecurity."

His touch is like fire, the air engulfed in flames around us.

"You missed being punished, didn't you? When you opened your mouth to greet me and instead you complained."

My gaze dances between his broad chest and his hand.

"I'm sorry," I admit.

He smirks at me. "No you're not."

"I—"

"You wanted to test me. To push me. To make me prove myself." My body heats with a knowing feeling as he takes a step forward and I take one back. Then again. And again.

"It's called topping from the bottom." My lower back hits the vanity. I grip it on either side of me as Zander lowers his lips to my ear and whispers, "Did you think I'd let you get away with it?"

"Z." I swallow thickly, not knowing what to say. "I was upset and unsure. I'm sorry." It's not that I fear a damn thing in this moment. Not him leaving, not a punishment. That's not why I'm sorry. I wish I could take it back, because I know it hurt him. That flash in his eyes, that disappointment. "I would take it back if I could."

"You are my submissive, and you were disrespectful." His admonishment is spoken slowly. "Get down on your knees and show me how sorry you are."

I'm almost shocked by his disapproval, by the harshness of his tone. Shocked so much that I freeze until he lowers his lips to mine, his eyes still open, staring through me as he demands. "On your fucking knees right now. Get on the floor."

I fall instantly to my knees, my cheek brushing down his thigh until I'm eye level with his groin. As my fingers fumble with his zipper, he pets the back of my head and then strokes my cheek with a single finger. "That's a good girl. Make it up to me."

In a single yank his cock juts up. Thick and hard, the veins running down his length and drawing my eye. I don't waste a second before licking the bead of precum from the smooth head of his dick. My tongue runs along the seam and the act makes him hiss.

I lick his length for lubricant before wrapping my hand around him. He's got enough girth that my hands are too small to fully wrap around him, so I use both, stroking him and rocking myself as I do.

"Give me that mouth of yours."

With both hands pumping the base of his cock, I wrap my mouth around his head and press my tongue along the bottom side. "Good girl. That's it." I moan around his length, sucking and feeling my own desire build. I'm hot for him.

He groans, "Goddamn," breathily which only fuels me further to please him.

Every little sound he makes, the hitches in his breathing, the deep moans—they all push me to move faster, to please him and get him off.

"Take more of me," he says, pushing himself deeper. I swallow down as much of him as I can, until I gag. Sputtering on his cock, I have to pull away.

As I heave in a breath, he grabs the back of my head. The head of his dick pushes in deeper and deeper. Arching my neck so he can take over, I let him guide himself as my hands move to the back of his thighs to steady myself and keep me upright.

Fisting the hair at the nape of my neck, he keeps me still as he thrusts himself deeper. My eyes sting as he cuts off my breathing. My nails dig into the expensive fabric of his pants.

As he pulls out, I heave in a breath, staring up at him. His jaw is clenched tight as he groans in pleasure.

"Your mouth is good for two things, my smart-ass girl," he tells me and pulls away. Leaving me breathing heavily, with a primal need that stirs a burning fire within me.

"Stay," he commands, backing away, zipping his pants although he's still very much erect.

I'm left alone on my knees on the other side of the bedroom, catching my breath as he opens the bedroom door. My lips part a moment in protest, until he comes back into view, a duffle bag in hand that he sets onto the bench at the foot of the bed.

"Tonight we're going to play," he informs me.

"I want to play."

His short laugh is nearly condescending. "I'm aware you do, my little rulebreaker."

"I'll show you everything I've brought first." He unzips the bag. "You can veto anything you aren't interested in, and I'll make a note of it." He turns to look at me over his shoulder, and it's only then that I realize I've tiptoed up behind him to get a better look.

His gaze is assessing, so much so that I take a hesitant step backward.

"Where did I leave you?" he questions in a murmur, gentle, yet cautioning.

Slowly I lower myself back down, one knee at a time. His piercing gaze ignites something between us. "That's my good girl," he comments with a smirk. Turning his attention back to the unzipped duffle bag he tells me, "I'm looking forward to playing with you tonight."

The first item he hands me is a soft leather blindfold in deep burgundy. It's simple with matching silk ties, but feels luxurious. It's certainly not cheap. His compliment brings a warmth to my chest when he says, "The color suits you."

"Thank you."

Taking it back from me, he sets it gently on the corner of the bed. It's unmade and it's the first time I've even considered making the bed since I've been home. Before my thoughts are allowed to wander, he tells me, "You respond well to praise. It's kept me from degrading you." I don't miss how he gauges my reaction.

"Degradation, like calling me a whore, spitting, and all that?" I question, not sure how it makes me feel anymore. It's been a long time since before James.

"What do you think of all of that?"

I take a moment to consider it. Even in my wildest days, it was mild and I was too intoxicated or well past any limit where I would object. Every touch heightened the high. It was different then.

I've been called a lot of things, like "little slut" and "my whore." I remember a time when I loved degradation, it was a part of the scene. It's a kink that I never imagined would leave me. If a man used it outside of the bedroom, it was obviously different. But within the confines of four walls, it's different because I know I'm going to get mine and when it's all said and done, they'd kiss me and tell me what a good girl I was. That was so long ago, though. A lifetime ago. "At one point I enjoyed it."

"But now?"

"I really just want to please you."

A huff of humor leaves Zander and he says, "Well that makes two of us." He doesn't waste any time pulling out the second item.

"Matching tape."

"Tape?" The hitch in my voice gives away my hesitancy as Zander holds out a roll of shiny tape in the same deep burgundy shade as the blindfold.

"It only sticks to itself," he explains, pulling the end free and holding it out for me to feel.

"It's like PVC tape?"

He nods in response to my question.

"Any objections?" he asks and his tone is neutral. "I know you want to please me, but you should know it would piss me off if you didn't object if you wanted to."

Shock at his darkened tone drops my bottom lip slightly. My eyes widen and he stares down at me with a seriousness. Kneeling in front of me, he drops the roll into my hand, lowers his lips to my ear and whispers, his warm breath trailing down the curve of my neck, "I want to feel you come on my dick as many times as you possibly can before you safe word." My breathing quickens as he leans back, brushing the hair from my face with a casualness that downplays the perversion he just spoke. "It'll make it harder for me if you lie right now."

"I was nervous because it's tape, but it won't stick to me, like duct tape would."

"Not at all."

Gripping the tape tighter, I ask him, "How do you plan to use it?"

"I'll bind your legs, so they're bent and you're easier to position however I want, and your hands and arms … I haven't decided yet." His words drift off and his eyes roam down my body before he looks back up at me. "Or maybe some other binding. Do you have a preference?"

"No."

"Then however the hell I want. I may tie you to the bed frame. Strap you down so you can't move an inch while I fuck you …" Leaving me with the vision of my wrists being cuffed to the bedposts with this tape, Z turns his back to me, fishing for something in the duffle before pulling out a pair of small silver safety scissors.

Nodding, I hand him back the heavy roll, his fingers brushing against mine and eliciting a rush of adrenaline and heat. "Then no objections."

A shiver runs down my back with my hair tickling along my shoulders. Every little touch feels heightened knowing I'll be bound and blindfolded.

The apprehension is an aphrodisiac.

"What should I call you?"

Zander's brow arches. "Like when we're in here … when we're …" A long exhale leaves me, my chest rising and falling with the newly found heat.

"You call me Z," he answers easily. Although I'm well aware he's toying with me.

"That's just a nickname."

"Like 'my little jailbird,'" he comments affectionately. He wears a simple smile yet somehow, there's pride hidden within it.

"I really—" I start to say love. I was going to say love it when he calls me that. Little bird was cute. Jailbird, though … I love it when he calls me that. Swallowing down my admission, I clarify, "I mean, should I call you Sir when we're in a scene … or something else?"

James like it when I called him Sir. And I loved it. I loved being in a room with him, knowing he could do whatever he wanted and that by the end of the night we'd both be sated and even more in love with each other than we were the day before.

"Two things. The first is that we will always be in scene. There isn't a moment where I will hesitate to reward or punish you. Is that understood?"

"Yes." The word rushes out of me with more want than I previously knew existed.

"Second. I've barely touched you, Ella. I only just tasted you last night. Honorifics like Master and Sir are earned. It means something more than … the name of an avatar in a game. It's like a collar."

"How do you earn it?"

"A collar or an honorific?" he questions, the devilish look in his eye turning me on even more.

"We can consider it when you don't hesitate to tell me what's on your mind. When you trust that if I'm asking you a question, it's because I want nothing but the truth. That my opinion of you and our relationship will remain as it is regardless of what you tell me. That I'll protect you from all things, including all that insecurity, all that fear, everything and anything that could keep you from being content."

All I can do is whisper, "So serious." His thumb graces my lower lip, trailing along it until I part my lips as Zander slips the tip of his thumb into my mouth. His pointer curls under my chin and he tilts my head up, staring deep into my eyes.

"That mouth of yours is going to get you in trouble," he warns. Then he informs me, "We're only getting started, Ella. I have yet to break you in and toy with you." A wicked grin plays along his handsome face. My heart pounds harder as he drops his grip and brushes the hair from my face. "You have no idea how much I'm looking forward to breaking you in."

Heat rushes to my cheeks, but even more heat pools in my core. Longing for him to touch me there. No, needing him there.

My desperation urges a soft sound from my lips. It's not quite a moan, and merely an audible exhale. Without breaking my gaze, Zander groans deep in his chest, "The fucking sounds you make…" With a gruff sound he turns away from me, tossing the duffle bag with more force than necessary to the floor. It doesn't escape me that there is more in it, but I'm not given a moment to question what it could be.

Instead, Z commands me, "Get on the bed, I'm ready to play with you."

chapter 10

READY TO PLAY IS AN UNDERSTATEMENT. I'M ROCK HARD, MY adrenaline pounding, ready. Ella is so fucking beautiful with her cheeks flushed like that. So willing. So submissive. I want her under more of my control. I want all of her.

We'll take it slow so she learns what she's agreed to. It hasn't escaped me that she compares what she had before to what we're doing now, and there's no chance in hell that James knew what the fuck he was doing. They toyed around with the idea of submission. I have every intention of training her to *be* my submissive.

It's essential that I don't dive in too deep with her too fast, though I want to. God, I want to. Every inch of me craves every inch of her with a physical longing.

Four-count breaths. Four of them. Trailing along the edge of each of the additional toys I bought just for her, I control everything. I have to be in control of myself before I can be in control of her. I have to stay in control of myself, damn it.

She perches on her knees on the edge of the bed, her nightgown a silk puddle next to her. I approach her slowly so she has time to take me in. To see how I rise above her. How much stronger. How much restraint I have.

That's an easy one. Instead of pushing her back on the bed and abandoning myself to her, I run my fingers through her hair and arrange it over her bare shoulders. The shudder that runs down her teased skin travels lower and hardens her nipples. I'm careful with every touch, and Ella responds to it, her large dark eyes on mine. She trembles under my hand.

I could do this for fucking hours. It's a drug to me. To tease her and immediately receive this reaction. Her shuddered breaths and every small movement as she nervously waits on the bed for my next move are addictive.

Anticipation is an essential part of any scene. It's what adds the tension to the air and the color to her cheeks. With my voice low, it rumbles, giving away my desire that's barely contained. "What are you imagining right now, jailbird?"

"You," she says in a breathy voice. "With your hands on me. I don't—" Her face gets redder. "I don't know if I can give you specifics. So many things. Mostly just the—just the sensation of being—"

"Dominated?"

The air cracks with a heat between us, only inches separating each other. "Yes."

My muscles coil, holding back everything just so I can offer her my thumb running down her bottom lip. Taking one step back, putting space between us, but keeping her gaze locked in mine, I tell her, "You're going to be good for me."

I phrase it as a statement and not a question to fill her with confidence. She can do this, and I believe in her. I know how she needs this.

Ella nods, a sheen coming to her eyes. "Yes," she whispers. "Yes. I am."

It's another reminder that I have to be gentle and guide her into this lifestyle. She thinks she knows what she's getting, but she doesn't have a fucking clue.

"I'm going to blindfold you now. Hands in your lap."

My little jailbird closes her eyes before the burgundy leather even touches her. She's so fucking good for me.

I fasten it over her eyes, testing to make sure it's snug. Ella's nipples peak and I allow myself an opportunity to run my knuckles down her skin, until they run over those hardened nubs. The small moan from her parted lips and the way she attempts to prevent her back from arching are everything I've wanted since I first saw her.

"How does it feel?" I murmur.

Her tongue flicks out to wet her lips. "It feels like everything's been heightened. The air on my skin. The sound of your voice. It makes me question—" She stops herself, shaking her head.

"What does it make you question?"

"That's not the right word for it. It makes me think that I trust you. It wouldn't feel good to have my sight taken away like this if I didn't trust you. And I feel—I feel safe." More color floods to her cheeks. "Nervous, but safe."

"Good." I'm deliberately loud as I pick up the roll of tape from the bed and let her hear me unspool a length of it. She shudders at the sound. "Because I'm going to bind you now."

If I were selfish, I wouldn't bother to bind her. The sight of her as she is, sprawled out and waiting, her pale skin flushed, her lips parted and her chest rising and falling with anticipation is intoxicating.

She would fight the urge and I'd love to see her try and fail. To punish her for not being in control of her body for me. A low groan of want leaves me and I disguise it with a comment.

"Turn onto your belly, legs spread wide and hands behind your back."

There are plenty of toys I could have used instead of tape. Bondage gear and straps. The tape allows me to take my time and it's far less frightening for a submissive who hasn't been bound before.

Her breathing quickens as I draw out the tape, giving her the simple command to lift her chest off the bed. I let her feel it glide against her skin so she can feel for herself that it's not going to hurt her.

It doesn't require much tape at all to bind her, but the sound, the sensation, the prolonged time will make it appear far more than it is. I don't let her know that. I let her sit in the feeling of being helpless at my hands.

I go so slow my cock twitches. Whenever I grab her small body, maneuvering her as I need, she lets out the most innocent gasps. With my erection pressed into her thigh, I lean down and whisper at the shell of her ear, "You're doing so well." With a small peck on her shoulder, I add, "Good girl."

My sweet girl smiles, even through her shaky breath. "Thank you," she whispers, her lips trying to find mine. I could leave her there, not allowing her to seek out a damn thing while we're in this scene. But then I'd be denying myself, and I'm man enough to admit I want to kiss her as badly as she wants to kiss me. She's eager when my lips meet hers, her body arching, although her arms have already begun to be bound.

Tsking, I pull away. "Be my good girl."

Nodding eagerly, she moans that she will as I gently place her back down where I want her, my hand splaying against her shoulder blade, keeping her there so I can continue.

The tape groans as I pull more of it, and every time I do, her body shudders with her instinct to move.

She hasn't set any boundaries when it comes to being bound, but sometimes subs don't know what those are until you're in the moment. Ella's lips part, her body coming alive with more tension, but she doesn't protest. Doesn't use her safe word.

Ella's breathing is heavier and her entire chest is flushed by the time I run my fingertips down her inner thighs after binding her thighs to her calves. The small moans she gives me are fucking everything. She can't close her legs to me, but she tries. On instinct. I know she doesn't want to; controlling a natural reaction is difficult and something tells me Ella doesn't have a damn bit of experience when it comes to that. As I move off the bed to observe her, I give the command, "Don't move," and the words are nearly caught in the back of my throat when I see how fucking wet she is for me. Her seam glistens with arousal.

It takes her a moment to relax into her bindings. As the sheets rustle beneath her, all I do is wait. It's obvious that she's trying so hard to stay still, but not hard enough. She'll learn the way to stay completely still is to submit to it the way she should be submitting to me, with everything she has. Ella's not there yet. I haven't had enough time with her. But I will. My blood heats at the thought of spending hours on this. Days and days of praising her while she gets off on obeying.

Speaking of obedience—

With a hand on each of her thighs, I flip her over. Without any warning, she yelps, the sound high and feminine and all Ella. A rough chuckle leaves me as she lies on the bed naked, legs spread and completely bared to me. Even as she catches her breath I know she can hear my pleasure in the low groan from the sight of her. Hearing and touch are her most prominent senses right now, which means everything I do in those realms carries more weight.

"You're at my mercy now, jailbird," I whisper and then easily flip her again so her arms aren't behind her, uncomfortably supporting her weight. "Do you remember your safe word?" The question is as much of a reminder for her as it is a way for me to ensure she's still in the right frame of mind. Deprivation can play tricks on even the most mentally sound. For a grieving widow … well, I haven't forgotten her struggles.

"Yes," Ella whispers back.

"Good girl."

The first vibrator is ready for me. Ella turns her head so her other cheek is against the comforter, her shoulders rising and falling with every breath she takes. I flip the switch and the vibrations fill the air. I let it go on long enough that it takes over. What else can she hear, other than this? Nothing. I make sure the sound of the vibrator is everything. She waits, patient and submissive. Not that she has any other choice. Ella's helplessly bound, her hands behind her back, her legs spread open for me, and—

When I'm done with her, I'll climb onto the bed behind her and drive myself into her slick wetness until we're both spent. The desire to do that right fucking now is overwhelming. I need her as much as she needs me. Four-count breaths. In and out, focusing on control. On conditioning her to listen and trust, to obey above everything else. Even when the tempting release of pleasure is so very close.

"You will obey me, my little jailbird. I have a set of rules and there will be consequences if you don't abide by them. You need to do as you're told. Do you understand?"

Ella nods behind her blindfold. Her hands open and close again.

Just as my hand raises to swat her ass for not verbalizing her answer, she murmurs, "Yes, I will obey."

With my pulse rising, the adrenaline fueling each of my thoughts, I ask, "Was it like that between you and James?"

Tension runs through her like an electric shock. Ella goes completely still, her breath stopped and her thighs rigid and unmoving. I keep my eyes on her body, every curve down to the detail of how tight the cords in her neck are. Checking every muscle. Monitoring what I can see of her expression.

Did I push her past some hidden boundary? *The mention of his name.* It's hell to wait without touching her, but I do it. This is something that can't be rushed. I'm going to do what any good Dom would do, and what I know to be right.

"Would you rather I refer to him as your former Dom?"

Ella bites her bottom lip. "Either is fine," she whispers and then clears her throat. "And … no. He didn't have a list for me." There's obvious confusion in her tone.

"There is no one way to be submissive and no correct way to be a Dominant. But you will find I have my desires, and that includes control and obedience. Is that understood?"

"Yes." The second the word is uttered from her lips, I press the vibrator to her clit, letting it sit there as she screams out.

With her hands restrained behind her, her legs bound and spread, I use my other hand to press her chest into the bed. Although she cries out in sudden pleasure, the only movements are the curling of her toes and her head thrashing from side to side. Her body is tense and I know that only intensifies the pleasure radiating through her.

"Be still, and take it like a good girl," I command her and she does as she's told, biting down on her lip. As her strangled cry leaves her, her body bucks and bows with her release.

I can barely make out the apology on her lips and I ignore it.

"Did you come?"

Her body shudders and she's quick to nod and then correct herself, staying still as she answers yes hesitantly.

"You are not allowed to come again, not until I tell you that you can. Understood?"

Her answer is delayed, and I imagine she doubts she has the ability to obey. "Yes," she finally says and then swallows thickly, her body finally relaxing.

I hover the vibrator closer to her shoulder, taking my time. Closer and closer and closer until it grazes her nipple that's pressed against the sheet. Ella gasps, trying to resist arching away, but she can't. I've bound her too skillfully to leave her room to wriggle over the bed. "I'm going to make you a list of tasks to complete every day."

This point is easily emphasized by circling her nipples with the vibrator again. I play with the other one, testing its weight in my hand and listening to those sweet moans.

Fuck, I need her now. I can barely think with the sight of her helpless beneath me.

"We'll go over the list tomorrow."

Placing the vibrator beneath her, I let it rest against her clit as I unzip my pants and then drop them to the floor. Her moans turn to breathy whimpers as I climb onto the bed behind her. The bed dips from my weight and Ella strains against the tape. Staring between her thighs I watch as her pussy clenches around nothing, slowly removing the vibrator and turning it off. She gasps the moment it's taken away, as if she's been holding her breath. God, she wants this. And I want it to be so much sensation for her that she has to give herself up to me. She needs to submit more than she already has. She needs to learn to do it, damn it, because that's the only way I know to keep her present. It's the only way I know to heal her.

I notch myself to her slick, hot entrance and thrust home in one stroke.

Hard. Possessive. Like she's mine.

She is mine, and her clit is mine too. I reach the vibrator around her and press it directly to that bundle of nerves again, although I'm more than aware it must be overly sensitive now. Ella cries out. This is intense for her, and I know for certain because her body has made it intense for me. Her muscles squeeze me, going tight and tighter. She can't actually change her position. The tape keeps her in place.

She has a safe word and she knows it.

Ella has never been more beautiful than she is with all her weight pressed against her bindings. It's a fucking gorgeous struggle. Her muscles tense as she tries to stay still for me because I ordered her to do it, but she can't let go. The vibrator is driving her to a new, expansive pleasure as her walls tighten around my cock, forcing a tingling need up my spine.

"Wait," I tell her through gritted teeth. "Wait, jailbird. You don't come until I tell you to."

"No," Ella says in a breathy voice, and quickly adds in desperation, "Please." I won't punish her now because she doesn't even know she's said it. It's pure begging, pure pleading, and I don't give in.

I angle the vibrator more firmly over her clit. "Good girls come when they're told to come." She clenches around me at the praise. She loves it. She can't get enough of being told what a good fucking girl she is. New arousal coats my cock as I lean down to whisper in the curve of her neck, letting my warm breath trail there, "Good girl. My perfect jailbird. It's so hard not to come, and you're doing so well."

A shiver runs down her back and her pleas turn to whimpers that she buries in the sheets.

I brace one hand on the bed and fuck her with deep, long strokes. All the way in. All the way out. Every thrust presses against her inner walls, with no more room to spare. Stretching her. I don't want this to be over yet. I don't want to be finished with this pleasure. It's mine too. It starts in the base of my cock and spreads outward along every inch of me. Up my spine. Down my legs to my toes. Every muscle works together to fuck her harder, but not faster. I've never concentrated harder than keeping this vibrator on her clit. Practice in obedience for her. Practice in domination for me.

It makes me feel almost drunk, this power. A few words is all it takes to get her to stop an orgasm for me. Ella's mouth opens, trying to get air to cry. She's close.

"Please, Z," she begs. "I'm trying to be good."

"You need to come?"

I'm being harsh, and I know it. Pleasure is just as intense as pain. They're two sides of the same coin. "Yes," Ella answers, her voice rising. "I need to come."

"Please," she cries out again when I don't answer. Her head thrashes once, barely tugging the blindfold up.

"I can't stop it and I don't—" She bites down on the sheets and I fuck her slower, moving the vibrator up just slightly. Her breathing is heavier.

It gives her a moment for her orgasm to lessen slightly. I barely hear her beg me again and then reason, "I don't want you to be unhappy with me."

God. Such a perfect submissive. She tries and tries and tries. I couldn't have asked for better.

I remove the vibrator, and instantly Ella collapses away from me as much as possible. She can't move much. The tape is too strong, but she tries. I give her three long seconds of trying to live without the vibrator and push it against her clit again while thrusting into her harder and faster.

"Come for me, jailbird," I say into her ear, and she explodes around my cock, gripping me as she shudders and shakes. It's a cascade of pleasure and heat and it almost makes me come.

But I'm not done fucking her.

I drop the vibrator, turn her over, and drive my hips between her spread legs. I'm conscious of her hands behind her back, and her arms, and I keep it in mind while I fuck her with primal need. Her body is so pretty, arched for me this way. Her neck is exposed. Her breasts. I take one of her nipples and roll it between my finger and thumb. Over and over and over. It's not a particularly unforgiving movement, not really, but if I do it enough, she'll—

"Oh." The sound stretches out and out and out. "Oh," she says again.

Her voice almost pushes me over the edge, but I pull away and flip her over again. I want to be inside her heat. It seems like the only thing keeping me on earth. Her hot, wet pussy trying to get me further inside.

I circle her asshole with a fingertip. She's helpless to stop me, and Ella shivers when I do it. "Have you been taken here?"

"No," she whispers.

I work a finger into her pussy beside my cock. And then I bring it back to that tight little hole. Ella groans when I push my fingertip in, lubricated with her arousal, and gasps when I give her the rest.

And then I grab the vibrator.

One touch to her clit and she's off, crying out, crying hard. Coming yet again. Her pants fuel me to keep playing, toying with her, pushing her boundaries slowly yet steadily.

I pull myself free from her as she comes down. Giving her a moment, I take out the scissors after cleaning off my hands with a wet wipe.

"Stay still." The safety scissors easily cut through the bindings within seconds, releasing her body to fall onto the bed.

She's still unsteady from the aftershocks so I have to prop her up with my hands to get her on her knees. "Take off the blindfold."

Ella pulls it down with shaking hands, leaving it around her neck.

"Hands and knees, jailbird. I want you to watch the mirror now."

She gets to her hands and knees, still trembling, her dark eyes locked on me in the mirror as I climb behind her, line myself up, and take her again. She's a gorgeous sight. Her hair a messy halo, her cheeks flushed. Every thrust shakes her. Her breasts sway with the motion of my hips. I fuck her like I've wanted to since she first talked to me, hard and unforgivingly, until I'm close to the edge of my own pleasure. Seconds away.

I need to see her face. I turn Ella and position her on my lap as I fall to the bed. Her small hands land on my chest to steady herself. My hips thrust up and she's far too weak to keep herself upright. She drapes her arms over my shoulders and holds on for dear life.

And she kisses me.

Her lips capture mine with a need that's unexpected.

What that single kiss does to me is a shock I hadn't anticipated. It strikes me how obvious it is that she was desperate for it. She tastes both sweet and sinful.

"Fuck," I grunt into the crook of her neck as my orgasm tears out of me.

She holds me just as tightly as I hold her as she finds her release with mine.

As she's lying lifeless on top of me, I kiss the crown of her head and whisper without thinking twice about it, "You don't know what you do to me."

chapter 11

"Awash and wave?" Kam comments. "And I like the all white," he adds before I can respond. His four fingers do a half wave as he gestures toward my hands.

"The manicurist suggested it." I peek down at my nails as the waiter arrives with a tall skinny glass of unsweetened tea. "Thank you," I manage to get out in time for him to give a smile and nod.

The Fooleries has been remodeled since we were last here. Seated on the outside balcony, there's a heat lamp already blazing in each of the corners. The balcony only has three small circular iron tables, fitted with a robin's-egg-blue tablecloth. Everything else is white. The menus, napkins and single candle burning in the center of each table.

"You really like the white?" I question before popping one of the almonds from a small bowl of mixed nuts that was on the table into my mouth. Kam loves the walnuts, so I leave all of those pieces for him.

"Very in. Very chic … Angels and virgins wear white, but I've always thought it looks just as good on the sinful."

Kam's comment gets a laugh from me. "I wasn't sure at first," I say and shrug, lifting the glass up, "but I like it." The last bit comes out raspy and my fingers press against my throat before I sip the cold beverage.

When I set the glass down and peer back at Kam, his expression is riddled with concern. "How are you feeling?"

An anxiousness sweeps through my body at the realization that the pain I felt was a reminder of what Zander did to me last night. More specifically, my cries and moans for him to fuck me harder, but for Kam, it's a reminder of something entirely different.

"Fine," I answer easily, reaching for the cloth napkin and laying it across my lap.

"Well, you look beautiful. You look—" His words falter and I'm not sure what he planned to say, but what comes out after an exhale is only a reiteration of his first statement. "Just beautiful."

"It was Zander's suggestion," I confide in him in an attempt to usher the conversation away from wherever Kam's carefully navigating. I know my throat, my voice even, has to be a reminder of what I did while at the center. "He said I should get my hair and nails done today. This morning he handed me a credit card, then told me he made appointments and that Silas would be driving me, so I should get my ass ready to go and be pampered." I add for good measure, "And if I wasn't ready on time, he'd spank me."

Kam's movements stop midway as he was picking up his napkin and the silverware clangs on the table. I can't help but laugh.

"Well I'm glad one of us is smiling," hc chides.

"Oh please," I admonish him in return, a genuine smile pulling up my spirits. "Since when did you become such a prude?"

Humor lights his eyes. He even smiles as he rearranges the cutlery and places the napkin across his lap as I have. "He's controlling."

"Like James was," I reply without considering what I was saying until the comparison left me. Another wave of that anxiousness comes over me, but it quickly vanishes.

"And I told you to dump his ass too." There's a fondness, a nostalgia in Kam's comment.

"I remember that," I say and my smile falters only slightly. The rawness in my throat comes back but this time it carries a prick to the back of my eyes as well.

"I mean, obviously I was wrong about that one," Kam says offhandedly and I realize we're speaking about him. Talking about James in the past tense. I don't have long to dwell on the thought. "He went from a *good time*," Kam adds, lowering his voice at the insinuation, "to taking all your time."

I can't help but smile, even if there's a painful longing in my chest. "He took his time, though." I roll my eyes at the thought and resort to picking up my iced tea once again. It's tart, making my lips pucker after a sip before I reach for the sugar.

"What was it? It took him what, a year?" he asks me, and it's easy. It turns easy, thinking about how we came to fall in love. How he went from a man I wanted and enjoyed the occasional fling with, to a man who only wanted me and who I couldn't imagine living my life without.

"Every third Saturday for …" I trail off, peeking up past the heat lamp and spot a small blue jay on the roof. "Maybe four months it was just that one night?"

"At Monet's, right?" I nod in response, the memories filtering back to me. It was a good time. That's all *he* was. We ran in the same circles. Knew the same people. One night, after I'd been avoiding him, teasing him, leading him on … we hit it off and had a romp in the sheets. It was a fling, a damn good fling. I thought it would only be that one night, but the next month, at the same gathering, he made it known in no uncertain terms that I'd be with him again that night.

"And then it was house calls and almost nine months later is when he got in that fight with Taylor."

Kam's brow raises and he lifts his coffee mug and then says, "Oh yes, and that would be the moment I told you to dump his ass."

Biting down on my lip I remember that entire ordeal as Kam continues, "He couldn't call you his girlfriend, but he could start some shit with Taylor." Taylor's no one really. He's the son of a hotshot, who's hot as fuck himself. He got through life on good looks. He's nice enough, but he wasn't looking for anything more than a good time. Which was fine, 'cause that's what I was after too. I figured James only wanted me the once, or else he would have called. He would have reached out. So I made my move for Taylor and that's when James intervened.

With a one-shoulder shrug I remind him, "I might have been the one to start it … technically."

Kam's laugh is as genuine as it is enthusiastic. "That's right," he says and his smile is contagious. "Now I remember that reporter with the press article that we had to pay off."

I hum at the memory. "The truth was much better than fiction." As the waiter brings the avocado caprese salad, which looks divine drizzled with a thick balsamic vinegar, I lean back in the chair to give him room.

"The truth always is better than fiction," Kam comments and then smiles up at the waiter to thank him. I don't miss how the waiter gives Kam a longer glance than he gave me.

Speaking of hot men, I think as I watch the tall young man, he's got to be no older than midtwenties. In other words, way too young for Kam. And it's quite obvious he's interested in Kam.

"Flirt," I speak beneath my breath and smirk at Kam the moment the waiter has left us.

Kam has the audacity to deny it as the blush reaches his cheeks. He's freshly shaven so it can't hide behind stubble.

My fork spears through the ripe tomatoes and I let Kam pretend that I've forgotten. The bird I saw a moment ago flutters in a way that steals my gaze. He's a vibrant blue, perched on the edge and more than likely waiting for scraps.

"So," Kam gets my attention before asking, "is Zander your boyfriend then?" He raises a single brow in question.

With a thump in my chest, I don't know how to answer him so I retreat to draining the rest of my tea. Twirling the straw forces the ice to clink against the glass. After an awkward moment, I ask him, "I thought we were going to discuss selling my properties … and you know? Moving on." I hate the term. I'll never move on. Damon says you move through it, and there's a piece that's always there. I prefer that.

His expression drops as he nods, his tone more serious. "It's not the best time to sell, so we could wait, and sell when the market's better. Or if you'd rather just be done with it, we'll still get a good deal, just maybe not a great one. Either way, whatever you feel comfortable with, we can maneuver."

Whatever I feel comfortable with. His words repeat in my head as the memories filter back. I can't stop them. Just thinking of our home together, of the furniture, the majority of it his, I can barely keep myself composed when I remember how we broke in the dark gray Old English-style sofa of our first place together. So many firsts happened in that house.

"Let's sell them." I push the words out. "The main home and the two vacation properties down south."

"And the belongings?" Kam's question is gentle and I nod in response, picking up my drink to find it empty. I shake the glass, rattling the ice and with the straw I drain the tiniest bit of tea until there's nothing left.

"And what about where you're currently staying?" he asks cautiously. "The lodge?"

"We can keep it," I answer him. "We were barely there together." Fuck. It's not like ripping off a Band-Aid at all. Not when the wound is still raw and bleeding.

"And the west wing?"

His answering question hangs in the air between us.

"What of it?" I say in a whisper. I don't want it mentioned.

"We still have it closed off . . ."

When all I have is silence, he offers, "Maybe we redecorate it?"

I focus on pushing around the remainder of the food on my plate. Staring at the crumbs and remembering how that's what hurt the most. Laying in a bed we shared, and waking up alone.

"Did Zander suggest anything else?"

"What?"

He gestures toward me, his tone relaxed and casual. As if he could disguise the fact that he's attempting to change the subject since the current one has turned heavy. "Hair and nails. Does he want you to go to the spa too? Maybe to a lingerie boutique?"

Although his tone is humorous, my response is flat. "He wants me to create a new normal that would make me happy." I force a smile, remembering how we went through the checklist two days ago. He sat with me while I made the necessary arrangements and Silas accompanied me to them, acting more as a chauffeur than anything else.

"A new normal?" Kam's back straightens, his reaction not at all contained.

"We made a list," I say after taking a deep breath in and leaning back in the chair. My appetite has vanished.

"A list of what you want your normalcy to be?" Kam questions and I nod. He nods along with me. "So what else is there, other than nails and hair?"

Chewing the inside of my cheek, I keep myself from reaching into my purse to take out the list and instead tell Kam only the ones he needs to know.

"Things like, make my bed in the morning and practice yoga before noon like I used to." I'm quick to add, "I have daily affirmations."

"What affirmations?" Kam asks, and judging by his expression, I know he's still wary of Zander. I get it. I do.

"I will allow myself to feel grief and then let it go," I tell him after inhaling slowly and Kam's eyes widen slightly. "Damon approved it."

Kam nods as he looks away, obviously uncomfortable but he says, "There was an affirmation I was using a bit ago."

"Really?"

He meets my gaze to tell me, "When Gerald broke up with me." His expression sobers. They were engaged and I still don't know what happened; all I know is that I wasn't around when they broke up. I was at the center.

Sucking in a breath, he tells me, "I give myself permission to do what is right for me." He swallows thickly.

"I like that one. I really do."

He pouts at my smile, a goofy expression on his face. "You should add that to your list."

"I think I will."

"Yoga, affirmations, anything else he wants in your new normal?" He returns to picking away at his chicken caesar wrap.

Shaking my head, I don't tell him the hair and nails, and even my chosen outfit for the day, is all Zander's choosing. My grooming and appearance are to please him. It's a requirement for every day.

Along with accepting a list every day of what I should accomplish while he's gone. He's busy arranging everything in his new place nearby.

I haven't seen it yet, but he said once he has everything in order, since things have gotten chaotic with his leave from The Firm, then I can come see and maybe stay if Cade will allow it.

Kam asks in a humorous tone, "What about daily blow jobs?"

His last question is spoken at the same moment the waiter returns to refill my tea. I can't help the grin that slips across my face at the sight of Kam's embarrassment.

The waiter remains professional, although he's obviously heard and has a hard time keeping a smile from creeping onto his face that would match mine. "Anything else I can get you?"

Kam asks for the check and I'm grateful he seems to forget about the list after the young man leaves.

"Speaking of blow jobs," I murmur and prod him. "Anything new in your dating world?"

My playfulness falls flat. Kam's lips are pressed in a thin line. "Gerald wants to get back together. He called a couple of nights ago and again last night."

I'm surprised by how happy his admission makes me. "You two were so good together."

Again the optimism does nothing but faceplant on the table.

"When you were away … he didn't do things he should have. Not like I needed him to."

My throat dries and once again, I'm left with an anxiousness that comes with those memories.

"Enough of that," he says matter-of-factly. "To a new normal," Kam offers in cheers, his tone a little more upbeat. It only takes me a moment to force a smile and my glass of water, since the tea is empty, meets his.

"To a new normal."

And so that's how time passes, checking off a list daily, letting Zander fuck me into contentedness and pretending this new normal feels right and not like I'm counting the days until something inevitably goes wrong, very, very wrong and entirely out of my control.

chapter 12

Zander

It feels like several lifetimes have passed since I let Quincy walk away from me into the night. Time seemed to drag on forever after she was murdered. Guilt is a heavy, relentless emotion. It makes the body move slower and time crawl, except during the moments when you think it might be lifting. It always comes back, though. The guilt is never resolved. No amount of therapy has been able to free me from it. I'll live with that guilt until I die.

If I had stopped her and done what I wanted to do, done what I know she needed, she'd be here. She'd be alive and happy. Probably with someone else, but she'd breathing.

I know all the things to think, and all the things to say. I know how to organize my thoughts from the physical world around me to the emotional world inside my mind. I've practiced holding these things at arm's length and observing them without sinking into them. But no matter how many times I logic my way around Quincy's death, I still end up at the same conclusion.

I bear some responsibility. It's not all my fault, of course, though it felt like it at the time. The man who murdered Quincy bears more of that burden. He's the one who mugged her and then killed her. He took her life.

I can't describe the hate I have for him to senselessly take her life.

I'm still not ready for the hearing.

It takes a disgusting amount of time for these cases to work their way through the courts. She's been gone two years and we're just now reaching the point where the case is before the judge.

Ella and I move gingerly around each other in her house before it's time to leave. The guilt feels so heavy on days like this. No reasoning my way out of it this time. I have to sit with it, and sit in the knowledge that something new will happen today with Quincy's case, regardless of whether justice is served or not.

"Are you nervous?" Ella asks me in the car on the way over. I don't miss how her black heels slip against one another nervously. I haven't told her much. Only that Quincy was a good friend turned lover and a former submissive, and that she was murdered. Her only comment was whispered, *so you're mourning too*, which I didn't respond to.

"About the outcome of the case?"

"Yeah."

"No."

She watches me with those beautiful dark eyes, her expression open. "Do you think it's already decided, then?" She's gentle with her questioning, which is different for her. It's a careful tone, like she's afraid that it'll hurt me.

It warms something inside of me, knowing she cares. She is good. All things good in this world. My hand lays on top of hers, my fingers slipping between hers to hold her hand loosely.

"There's more than enough evidence. The DA told someone I know that he's hoping for a lesser sentence if it looks like he'll get off. He wants to plea it down." I keep my eyes on the road and my breathing steady. "No amount of prison time will bring her back. But this is how she gets her day. Other people will be—" I cut myself off with a deep breath and I pull my hand away to pull onto the highway. "Other people will hear about her today, what happened to her, and that seems right. That her death will be acknowledged." My throat's tighter than I'd like and the car is warmer than it should be. "It's a two-hour drive," I tell her, "so get comfortable, little bird."

I turn down the heat and we drive mostly in silence.

She holds my hand, though. Every chance she gets. Hers is small in mine, but her grip tells me she's not going to let go unless I want her to.

When we get to the front of the courthouse and I let go to take her tweed coat, her cheeks are still flushed from the chill of the short walk in here.

It's nearly ten degrees colder here. I fucking hate the cold.

I'm picking up my phone from the bin at the courthouse metal detectors when the text comes in.

Cade: You doing okay?

It's the first real communication we've had since the coffee shop and my immediate instinct is to ignore him. He knows that I don't want to talk about it. It also pisses me off that he hasn't asked about Ella. Not once. Although it's possible he's been keeping tabs on everything through Damon. More than likely actually. The last thought softens my resolve.

With Ella's heels clicking on the marble tile, we take our seats near the back of the courtroom and Ella scoots close to my side while I answer Cade. When she reaches for my right hand to hold, and sees the phone, she politely withdraws, but I make a point to move my phone to the left and take her hand in mine. I can feel her gaze on the side of my face, but I don't say anything. All I do is run my thumb over her knuckles as I text my brother back with one hand.

Zander: I'm doing all right.

Cade: I know Ella came with you for the hearing.

Cade: I think it's a good thing.

The defensiveness that spiked at his first message is quickly dissolved by the second. It's unexpected for him to approve anything at all that has to do with Ella. It's a relief that he's being agreeable about this. It's like one brick in the wall between us is showing cracks.

Zander: I do too. I'm glad she's here.

Cade: How is she?

Zander: Quiet, yet full of questions. My response makes me smile and I glance over at Ella, this beautiful woman by my side who's taking in the courtroom and watching each of the people who file in. I recognize a hand-ful of them, Quincy's friends and family who offer me nods, quiet hellos and a squeeze of my shoulder from Quincy's father.

I don't say much and neither do they. They all notice Ella, though, and their hesitant smiles offer me only a modicum of comfort.

She wears a simple black sheath dress that still manages to look ex-pensive, her hair in a twist behind her head, and she looks exactly as prim and proper as the day I first saw her. Exactly as elegant. Some things are different, of course—there's a light in her eyes now that wasn't there be-fore. She's not so silent. But anyone looking at her now would never know what she'd been through. They'd see a gorgeous, delicate woman wearing a serious expression and sitting at my side. No more, no less.

There are many sides that people show. The broken man. The loyal brother. The confident Dom.

I'm not any of those today. Not completely. I've healed enough that I'm not going to lose my shit in the courtroom, but I can still feel the cracks in my heart that were left when that policeman showed up at my door.

I add, after a moment with him not responding, She's good.

Cade: Let me know how it goes and if you need anything.

The proceedings begin, and it's mostly a bunch of legal bullshit, the opening arguments and requests for changes to this or that. Which piece of evidence can be admitted. Who is representing whom. It all seems very clinical compared to the reality of the situation. No one mentions what the night air felt like on my face as she walked away from me. No one de-scribes the reflection of the streetlights in her hair or the angry set of her shoulders. All of this is encapsulated with a few quick sentences. A state-ment from her then-partner Zander Thompson.

Of course I'm mentioned, but that amounts to nothing, just like my relationship with Quincy did. Other than her murderer, I was the last per-son to see her alive.

Ella stiffens at the mention of my name. I'm quick to move my arm around her, pulling her in and retaking her hand. She molds against me, warm and with a remorseful expression. My name is mentioned again, but those sentences are swallowed up by what happened after. I'm not on trial in this case, and neither is Quincy. It's her murderer who's on trial. A guy who's been rotting in a jail cell since his arrest two years ago. I feel no pity for him. Let him rot forever.

Was Quincy thinking about our conversation when she died? That's what I want to know. Before the murderer approached her, what was she going to do? Was she going to storm back over and scream at me for not wanting to get married? Was she going to apologize and tell me she loved me, even if I couldn't say it back?

No one mentions this, either. It's not part of a legal proceeding. Quincy becomes the body her assailant attacked. No mention of whether her face flushed with anger when he attacked her or went pale with fear. No mention of whether she screamed, or what she said. *Signs of a struggle. Lacerations on her temple and collarbone. Fifth metacarpal fracture.*

They can't see her, but I can. She took a swing at the guy. It wasn't enough.

My throat dries and I have to readjust, keeping back the emotions that threaten to overwhelm me. It's been two years, but there's no amount of time that could pass and make this right.

I take so many four-count breaths I lose track of them. Ella holds my hand tightly through the whole hearing. It's the longest we've touched each other. She refuses to let go and I'm grateful for her.

Quincy ended up in harm's way because she wanted more from me than the D/s relationship we had, and I didn't want that. I couldn't feel the spark for it, even though she was beautiful and smart. Something in my gut warned me away from that deeper commitment. And now I'm here with Ella, who also wants more than domination and submission. She wants it, even if she hasn't admitted it. Of course she wants it. She's been married before. She knows what it means to commit like that.

And with her—

My chest seems to expand with how much I want that too. The vision blocks out the court proceedings. If Ella were mine, she'd have my ring on her finger right now. I could feel it while she held my hand. It wouldn't be her home, but *our* home, somewhere else. It would be the two of us looking out at the world together. But then again … would she ever want to move?

Peeking down at her, I know she was someone else's first. Someone she misses. Someone she hasn't let go of. I know it all too well.

There's also the logistics and legal blocks that would stand in our way. If Cade allows me to return to the company, there's no chance in hell I can be married to a former client. A current client. Trust is our main currency at The Firm. If potential applicants can't count on us to protect their lives and well-being, then we don't have a job. My brother's business will be destroyed. All kinds of suspicions would follow all of them everywhere.

The prosecution has brought out more evidence. Pictures, this time. Of the street where it happened, a yellow arrow pointing to where Quincy's body was found. Another photo. Another yellow arrow. This is where it happens.

Photos of Quincy.

The rush of blood fills my head, and Ella's grip on my hand tightens. I'm not going to lose control. I'm not going to sink into this firestorm of guilt and hate. I can witness it from a distance, the way I have to witness these photos. Rage slowly consumes me. *Breathe. Breathe.*

"Do you want to leave?" she murmurs into my ear. Both of her hands firmly around mine.

I offer her the single word although it comes out harsh and ragged. "No." I don't want to stay, but I'm not walking out now. I won't walk out now. I have to face this as much as Quincy's murderer does. I have to look at the consequences of my actions. Forcing myself to restrain every emotion, I tell her calmly, "We'll stay."

"Okay." Ella sounds even and sure. She's not disappointed that I want to stay, though I do glance over at her face in profile. Should I have brought her here? She's under the care of The Firm because her past caught up with her. Overwhelmed her.

"What about you?"

Ella's eyes come to mine, and I don't see an ounce of indecision there. "It's hard to look at," she says, keeping her voice low. "But I want to be with you for this."

I bring her hand to my lips and kiss her knuckles.

I'm so damn grateful she's here, and it brings back that overwhelming sense that she should be mine. In every way possible. Using the D/s relationship as the only framework for us seems like a cop-out, in a way. Saying that's all we can have is a lie. It's not true. There can be more. Another layer.

If Ella wants it. If she really does want it, once all of this is over and she's not in The Firm's care. Not a minute before.

There's a brief recess where Ella insists I eat a granola bar, and then we're back in the courtroom for the defense to respond.

And that's when I see this is going to be different.

Murder cases like this often have trials that stretch out for days. Weeks, even. There's a shift in the energy in the room when we come back, the defense attorneys consulting in low voices at the front of the room. One of them approaches the bench, and the judge listens. Nods.

"What's happening?" asks Ella. "Can you hear?"

"No. But we'll know soon enough."

We do know soon enough. What happens is that the defense puts the murderer on the stands.

He's a tall guy, too thin and pale, with dark bags under his eyes. He's lost weight since they put his picture in the news for killing Quincy. I'd expected to feel pure fury when I saw him on the stand, but looking at him now, all I feel along with the rage is …

Emptiness.

I've been staring at the back of his head all day, and seeing his face doesn't change anything. It doesn't change that Quincy is gone and never coming back. She'll be dead forever, and it will always have begun with our conversation.

Justice can be healing, though. We have to own our actions, but we cannot own anyone else's. This will change something. It will bring a sense of closure. There will be no more open case, no more phone calls, no more text messages. Quincy can rest and her name will be spoken by people who knew her beyond those photographs. The memories of her smiling will be the context of those conversations. And I'm ready for that. Fuck, I need that.

No more of this.

There's a brief back-and-forth between the murderer and the judge, and then the defendant, her murderer, a man named Elijah Edwards is holding a sheet of paper in his hands, staring down at it.

"Your Honor. Jury. Ladies and gentlemen in the courtroom." He sounds tired. "We're all here today because of what I did, and I won't sit in front of you and deny it. I killed Quincy Davis."

My next breath fails to come. A cold sweat breaks out along my skin as I sit still, barely contained and listen to him speak.

"I was high, on meth, when I encountered the young woman on the street that night. I don't say that to make an excuse, but to offer an explanation. I wasn't thinking straight, and I killed her. I—" He covers his mouth with his hand, then drops it down again. "I am truly, truly sorry for the pain I've caused to her friends and family, and I know that nothing I say here will ever make up for that. All I can tell you is that I live with the horror of what I've done every day. That I became a person who would take a life under the influence of drugs. It's not what I intended, and it's not the way I hoped my life would be. Your Honor, I understand that I don't deserve a second chance. All I ask is that you grant me mercy when you make your decision. I was in the grips of something I couldn't control." He puts the paper down. "That's all," he says. "That's all."

chapter 13

Ella

I KEEP EXPECTING HIM TO CRY. I DID. TEARS SPILLED HELPLESSLY once we were back in the car. If anything were to bring him to the brink, it would be the tombstones to the left of us.

"She's buried over there." He motions as we sit at the red light. His knuckles rap on the window although his focus is on the street.

"We could go, if you want?" I offer Zander, who shifts in his seat. Staring out of the window at the rows of headstones.

"No," he says and his answer is gentle, more composed than he's been. I learned today he's short when he's emotional. He's also quick to check on me once he realizes he's been blunt.

All I can do is to keep holding his hand.

I don't think souls stay in cemeteries. There's nothing here but stone, dying flowers and grass that needs to be trimmed but with the chill in the air and fall turning colder in the mountains, it'll probably stay like this until spring.

"Are you all right?" he asks me yet again. The ache in my chest is the most vulnerable I've felt in so long and it's directly linked to the way he looks at me. And the question I keep wanting to ask him, but my heart refuses. *Did you love her?*

Instead I nod, saying that I'm all right, and question, "Did you come this way because you knew she was buried over there?"

"Yes … Are you sure you're all right?"

"I'm fine. I haven't gone to where James is buried. I just don't think he's there. Have you been … since she's been gone?"

"To the cemetery?" he questions, slowly hitting the gas and putting it in our rearview. "I used to. In the beginning."

I debate on whether or not to tell him something I haven't confided in anyone yet, but I settle on the truth, on speaking what's on my mind. I'll feel it, whatever the memory brings, and then let it go. "I would go to the bar a lot. When James first died."

"The bar?" he asks for clarification, and he peeks at me a moment before returning his attention to the road.

"There's this bar down by the trolley in the city we lived in; it's the first floor of Monet's. It's where we first met." I smile at the memory as the car moves and the world blurs around us in a beautiful hue of greens and blues. The trees are only just starting to turn to auburn shades. Licking my lower lip, I continue, staring out of the window. "I knew of him, of James," I say, correcting myself. "I knew he slept around. I'm sure he knew I did the same."

I can feel Zander's eyes on me, but I don't look back at him. Instead I remember the din of the bar and the way James smiled at me, like I would jump at the chance to fuck him. I'm certain I roll my eyes now just like I did back then. "He was cocky, came from money but invested in a few companies at the right time.

"Rich Prick is what we used to call him."

"Sounds like Prince Charming," Z jokes and I finally turn to him, letting him see how happy that comment made me. His strong hand lands on my thigh and I place mine on top of his, not wanting him to let go as I remember the first time I spoke to James, years ago.

"He wanted my number when I turned him down."

Z looks back at me, curious without an ounce of jealousy. His thumb travels over my hand as I tell him our story.

"He said he'd change my mind." My heart does a painful flip in my chest remembering the timbre of his voice. "There wasn't a chance in hell

I was going to sleep with him. I was getting over a different guy. So …"
I take in a deep breath and huff it out as I lay my head back on the seat.
"So when he asked for my number," I say and smirk when Z's eyes meet
mine, "I gave him my ex's number. To piss two men off at the same time."

The low, deep rumble of Zander's laugh spreads a much-needed
warmth through me. "That's one way to make an impression."

My smile is dull, but it's there. It lingers along with the grief that comes
with the past.

"So you were always a smart-ass, stubborn woman?"

"You mean a bitch?" I question and Zander's quick to say, "I'd never
call you that."

"Well, I would. I could be a bitch when I wanted to be one."

"I don't want you to call yourself that." His admonishment is a simple
statement and as he turns the wheel, he has to remove his hand and along
with it goes the warmth. Dom Z has returned it seems.

"Yes, Sir," I murmur sarcastically.

"Don't make me pull this car over and spank your ass because of
your mouth." The warning on his lips changes the atmosphere of the car
instantly.

His tone heats every nerve ending in my body at once. I wonder if he
knows how much power he has over me.

"I'm sorry," I say and pull the hem of my black dress down. With my
pulse quickened, I change the subject, back to Zander and Quincy.

"Do you have any stories?" I ask him.

"Stories of what?"

"Of you and Quincy."

He's quiet for a long moment, too long. An awkwardness slips between
us. "You don't have to tell me if you—" Just as I'm offering the both of us
an out, he speaks up.

"I was drunk and wanted to pick a fight." He peeks over at me, smirking, and his hand returns to its rightful place on my thigh. "It also started
at a bar."

His gentle smile picks up the corners of my lips. His jaw is strong, covered in a five o'clock shadow as I gauge his expression in profile.

"I was pissed. I'd gotten into a fight with my brother over our parents.

He wanted them to go live with him. I wanted them to move down south where it was warm. It's what they wanted really."

"Why did they want to move?"

"Mom had chronic pneumonia and … well, things had to change. Pops had a hard time taking care of everything although he wouldn't admit it."

"Did he love her?" My question throws Zander off and I almost feel compelled to explain myself. "I don't remember a time when my mother was alive, really … only moments and they were fighting."

"Yeah," he says and nods, taking my hand in his and kissing my wrist before setting both our hands back down on my thigh. His thumb moves in soothing circles. "He loved her and she loved him."

"They're gone?"

He nods slowly and says, "Yeah, they had just passed. One after the other and my brothers just made things worse."

"I'm sorry."

"You don't have to keep saying that, my little bird." I swear he almost says something else but stops himself. "She passed quickly. My father died later that year."

I have to bite down on my lip to keep from apologizing again. "How old were you?"

"Twenty-five. And angry."

"So you went to the bar," I say to remind him of the start of his story.

He sucks in a breath and nods. A moment later he has to turn the wheel again, but he makes do with just his one hand.

We're driving slower now and on a back road I'm not familiar with.

"I was angry at the world, but Cade got the most of it."

"Well … if it's any consolation, Cade is an ass."

He chuckles. "Why do you say that?"

I shrug, shyness overcoming me. "Because I want to make you feel better."

This time he lets out a bark of a laugh and I love it. I love seeing this side of him. "You're sweet, Ella." His thumb taps, taps, taps as he pulls in the side entrance of a long lot with a row of brick buildings. At the very end is a larger building with parking all around it. I imagine that's the restaurant we're having dinner at.

"I wanted to pick a fight I guess, and she was there at the end of the bar."

"Don't tell me you fought a woman," I say, dropping my voice to be comical.

He doesn't laugh. Instead he gives me a sad smile. "No, we didn't fight." His voice is hoarser but he keeps going. "She made me laugh. I hadn't laughed in a long time."

He stops then. Not speaking as we pull into a parking spot. The car sways slightly and he keeps it running as we sit there.

It hits me then, that he loved her. I thought he did when we were in the courtroom. He looked like a man who'd lost his love. Seeing him now, there's no question. He loved her.

"How long were you together?"

"About a year and a half." He doesn't hesitate. That little fact tells me more than anything.

"You loved her?"

He shakes his head once, but he doesn't speak. He doesn't say it out loud. "We were lovers."

My heart breaks in this small way watching him deny it. Suddenly I feel like a mistress, like an imposter posing on his arm. And I don't want it. Glancing at the restaurant and then back to the man denying the obvious, I no longer have much of an appetite.

"Did you come here with her?" I don't want to be here if that's the case.

"No. No, this place is new. But my friend suggested it." He doesn't pick up on what's come over me, thankfully. I don't understand it fully myself and before I can think much of it, Zander kisses my knuckles.

"Thank you," he says between kisses and then stares deep into my eyes. "For coming with me today."

I melt for him, for the side of him he doesn't want to accept. The side that loves and breaks. The vulnerable bits that turn us crazy and allow us to fall into a well of emotion we can't control. I ache for him. Because I feel it. No one can deny the fact that I feel every bit of it. And then there are people like him, men who pretend they don't when it's so very obvious that they do.

I wonder if he would ever admit that he loved me. If he ever did fall for me. Would he say it? Would he tell me, or would I just have to know it and be complete with that?

"You're certain you want this?" he asks as he finally shuts off the car. "Knowing I'm a little fucked up too?"

"Yes."

"Show me," he commands and leans across the console of the car, taking my chin in his hand and kissing me deeply. So passionately it shocks me at first, my lips parted, granting him access and my world tilted. All because of him. Because of what he does to me.

Not a damn bit of it I can control.

chapter 14

Zander

T HE DAYS PASS EASILY. IT'S BEEN WEEKS NOW OF SPOILING ELLA and enjoying her in bed … as well as discovering her boundaries. One thing I love is taking her out, and watching her light up a room when she doesn't even realize it.

Ella looks gorgeous in soft candlelight. She looks gorgeous in every light really, but the candlelight at the Italian restaurant does something special to her features. It catches in her silky hair and makes her dark, sultry eyes shine.

And it makes me want to do filthy things to her.

I feel lighter after the hearing, and somehow heavier. Lighter because this part of my history with Quincy is closed. There are no more hearings, other than the formal sentencing. Heavier because I want Ella so much. My feelings seem much more intense than they should. Which makes me question them. More specifically if I'm using her emotionally because of what I went through with Quincy.

We go to dinner nearly every other night. Just like tonight.

She hasn't stopped talking since we got in the car, and only occasionally stops to take a drink and touch her throat. She's worlds better than she was only a month ago.

Tonight, she talks to me about surface-level things, things that don't hurt, things like what decor style she likes and how much of the garden she'd have to take out if she wanted to change the landscaping in her yard. It's a busy night and the waiter takes a few minutes to arrive.

It's all seemingly mundane, but the truth of the matter is that Ella's been discussing plans to redesign most of her home—never the blue room, though. She's told me repeatedly she loves that room as it is. Every plan she's made has fallen through. She ends up making some excuse as to why it isn't good enough and vetoes it all.

Damon mentioned it as well. It's a process, whether she realizes it or not. I'll be here through all of it.

Ella glances at her empty wineglass. It's late, getting later by the minute.

"Are you thinking about having a glass?" I ask her.

She readjusts the napkin on her lap. "No. Damon told me it's not the same when it mixes with the medication. It could make me feel lower than if I wasn't taking anything at all."

"Come here."

She listens. Of course she does. She's out of her seat in a heartbeat and sliding onto my side of the rounded booth a moment later. Close enough to touch, but not so close she's actually sitting in my lap, though I'd love that. I'd love so much with her.

I place my hand on her thigh. "Tell me more about the garden."

"Well—" Her cheeks flush, and she looks so beautiful against all this red fabric and the cream walls. All this dark wood and candlelight. "One of the beds is overgrown, so I'd probably have—"

I brush her dress up with the back of my hand, the silky deep red fabric gliding easily up her thigh, and Ella sucks in a little breath.

"Keep going," I command.

With her lips still parted and her voice breathy she whispers, "But I thought maybe a raised bed would be nice."

Another inch toward her waist, then another. It's entirely inappropriate. At the very last moment I slip my hand under the fabric and toy with the waistband of her panties. Her cheeks turn a deep rose. All the while, my focus is on the thin paper menu held in my left hand.

"You know what to say to stop this if it's too much," I murmur.

Ella bites her lip, and I dip under her panties to graze a knuckle against her softness and seek out her clit. She brings her hand up to cover her mouth, trying to make the movement seem natural, and I do it again.

"Good evening," the waiter greets us, and I feel her body stiffen. "Please forgive me for the wait. What can I get started for you tonight? Drinks?"

I don't take my hand away. I brush my knuckle over her clit as slowly as I've ever done it. "I'll have a cider. Whatever you recommend. Ella?"

I keep the pressure light, but I don't stop.

"I would—" Ella takes the drink menu in her hands, then lets it fall to the table. "A mocktail. Anything, really. Just something sweet."

A smile from the waiter. "I know the perfect thing."

He leaves, and I hold the menu in front of Ella while I play with her. She's hot, hotter than she's ever felt, and her breathing is shallow. "Have you done this before? Discreet play?"

She shakes her head. "The most outrageous thing I've ever done, you've probably seen. The … swinging, recording, and uploading—"

"Exhibitionism." I add a little more pressure, cutting her off.

Ella gasps. "Yes—yes. We stopped when we got married." Discomfort presses out at the boundaries of my chest. I don't love hearing about her marriage before, but I won't order her not to talk about it. It's part of her past. It made her who she is today. "Our lifestyle changed. Our relationship changed."

"Do you miss it?"

I can tell how hard it is to follow the conversation against all the sensations. She's having to struggle to keep her ass on the seat instead of rocking into my fingers.

"I don't know what you mean, exactly." Dark eyes on mine. It's intense for her, and it's also intense for me. Her heat. Her closeness. The fact that I can't fuck her in this booth, as much as I want to. "Z," she begs me, her hands on mine, but I don't let up.

"The exhibitionism. Do you miss it?"

"I don't know."

I pretend to study the menu again. "What if something were to be leaked? Would that be upsetting? Exciting?" There's a low moan as she closes her eyes and reaches for her glass of water, but doesn't drink it.

"Little bird, I asked you a question."

A simper plays across her lips, and it takes most of my restraint not to push her down onto this booth and kiss her until she can't breathe. "I can't imagine anything being leaked that would be upsetting. It only excites me."

Goddamn. There isn't a part of me that's ever been intrigued by the fetish, until she refers to it as "exciting."

The waiter returns with my drink and something red and sugary in a martini glass for Ella. When he puts it down in front of her, I take my hand away.

"Oh," Ella says, clearing her throat and sounding so disappointed that my cock twitches. I can't help but to smirk.

"Would you like something else?" The waiter is genuinely concerned, his eyebrows knitting together. "I can get you anything else."

"No, no, no." Ella offers him an apologetic yet somehow bright smile. While he's still watching, still trying to gauge what was wrong, she sips it. "This is delicious."

I order my meal for the sole purpose that I know I'll be able to pick up a piece of the tagliata and slip it between her lips. The thinly sliced steak is simple, delicious, and I can already hear how she'll moan from the tender taste.

Ella orders next. All the while, Ella makes sure to give the waiter special attention. Beaming up at him. It would make me jealous if I didn't know she was only doing it to smooth things over. One thing I love about her is that she strives for those around her to be comfortable, her friends especially, but even people she'll only interact with once as well.

The waiter steps away, and as soon as he's out of earshot, Ella's eyes go wide and she scolds me in a whisper, "You stopped." How fucking adorable for my little submissive to show her disappointment.

"I did."

She pouts, that plump bottom lip tempting me to nip it.

"Did you think I would give you an orgasm before our food arrives? That would be too early into dinner, don't you think?"

I've never seen her face redder than it is right now.

With my forearms on the table, I lean over to speak directly into her ear. "You keep your thighs apart for me, jailbird. I'll tease you as long as you're good."

"Tease me?" Her voice is breathy. Oh, she can't hide how needy and desperate she is. Her eyes consider me for a moment, the reality sinking in. With her fingers toying with the napkin on her lap, she questions, "You're not going to let me come?"

"No."

The corners of Ella mouth turn up, almost as if she doesn't believe me. "I can't believe you'd do that. Tease me to the brink and leave me …" she licks her lips, glancing away at the martini glass before concluding, "unwell."

I huff a laugh at her word of choice, but that's all she gets.

A bread basket arrives, dropped off by a passing server, and I wait until Ella has the first bite in her mouth before I touch her again. She's spread her legs under the table just like I told her to. She swallows the bread as I brush my fingertips over the softest part of her.

Petting her until her eyes go half-lidded.

"That bread must be fucking delicious," I tease her in a low groan. I'm hard as fuck watching her enjoy this without anyone else knowing. We're in a corner, and there's no one who can see. So long as I keep an eye out for the waiter.

Ella, in all her stubbornness, says nothing, merely rocking into my touch.

"You're going to keep talking to me, jailbird. No matter what I'm doing to your clit."

"I think," she says, her voice breathy and light, "I'd like to visit a bookstore."

Her statement comes out of nowhere, and a quiet laugh leaves me. I don't stop, though, not my petting and not the conversation.

"Why's that?"

"I haven't replaced many of the books in the house in a long time. I don't want to feel like I'm living in a staged apartment." Her lips part as warmth rises to her cheeks and her eyes beg to shut so I drop my fingers lower, no longer concentrating on her most sensitive bundle.

With an exhale of relief, her shoulders drop and she reaches for her drink. "You know?"

"I don't know." Waiting for her to have a sip and place the glass down, I circle her clit, and her body tries to get more of my touch, which I deny her. "Your books aren't yours?"

"I don't have many on the shelves. I was into a more minimalist—a more minimalist design before. But now I think I'd like to read. What do you like to read?"

"I don't have a lot of time for it." Her eyes dance over my face. "I listen to music in the evenings, or podcasts. If I have time to read, I like science fiction and thrillers."

I stop touching her.

Ella bites her lip, but she doesn't push me on it again. She seems to sense the power between us. I'm controlling this, the way I do everything else. And I will reward her immensely for having the pleasure of teasing her like this.

"Good girl," I murmur into her ear, rewarding her with my hand back between her legs. "You're letting me play with you as much as I want. Following all the rules. You are being so good for me."

She lets out a shuddering sigh and when I dip down to her center, I find her hot and wet.

I toy with her all through dinner, and Ella turns down dessert when the waiter is still mid-sentence. Very much on edge and in need of getting the hell out of here and into bed. It's a good look on her. My insatiable smart-mouthed, yet obedient submissive.

Good. Because I'm wound tight too. I'm so fucking hard it hurts. I need her. I have to be careful when I stand, opting for discretion.

I escort her out of the restaurant with my hand on the small of her back. A stiff breeze greets us as we head toward the parking garage. Ella walks quickly, doing her best to keep up with my long strides. She's out of breath by the time we get to the third floor of the parking garage. "How do you do it?" she says as she hurries for the car. "How do you wait? Because I want you so much that I—"

"I'm done waiting."

I get one flash of relief in her dark eyes, and then I have my mouth on her. On her lips, and the side of her neck, and her collarbone. Fuck any-one who happens to walk up here. I've never experienced this desire Ella has, but I'll share it with her. A fast, hard fuck where someone could see. I'm careful as I push Ella's back against a concrete pillar, and she wraps her legs around me as if she's done it a thousand times. Hanging on tight while I deal with my zipper and push the fabric of her panties aside.

There's no mercy for her as I slam my cock to the hilt inside of her, knowing she's been ready for almost an hour now. "Fuck me," I groan in the crook of her neck. She feels like heaven.

Ella moans, her tightness enveloping me, her hips rocking back and forth. I've never felt anything this soft or sweet or hot, and I want to fuck her like this all night. The chill of the night wraps around us but it's no match for how warm and wet she is. I brace one hand against her ass and work the other between us to get to her clit.

"I'm not teasing this time," I growl into her ear. "Come for me."

She comes hard around me, squeezing tight, her cries echoing off the parking garage. The adrenaline rushes through my blood, my pulse racing. Nothing else matters in this moment except Ella.

chapter 15

Ella

THE WEEKS PASS IN A BLUR. EVERY DAY CHECKING OFF A LIST. Greeting Zander on my knees seems to be a favorite of his as time goes by. It's the first item on the slip of paper he gives me in the morning.

I love those moments.

The days, though … they come with ups and downs. Small moments where I feel so much lighter and then darker times where I close my eyes and remind myself: Grief is a ball in a box and it's okay.

The thoughts barely stay for long, because Zander's there or Damon. Even Kamden has been coming more frequently, making arrangements for me to attend different social events if I want to, all of them already approved by Zander and Damon.

They say I'm getting closer to a new normal, but almost every night, I glance down the hall no one talks about. When we lie together in bed, sometimes I forget and I think I'm in bed with James down the hall, being held and kissed and loved by him. Then I wake up, and it processes slowly.

I haven't told anyone. Not Damon, not Zander. Because if I said what I'm thinking, maybe they'd think I'm crazy. I think James wants me to go down the hall. I think he wants me to go back into our bedroom. Even if it's just to say goodbye.

Maybe he wants me to know that he's okay with everything that's happened. Maybe he's trying to tell me he still loves me, even if I'm in bed with another man. Maybe he wants me to know he misses me. Maybe it's all in my head.

The low rumble of an approaching thunderstorm drowns out the rustling of the trash bag at my side. It's easier to handle than the damn cardboard box I found in the garage, so I settled for it. The gray skies and increasing winds of the incoming downpour feel right for the occasion.

We loved the storms. One step at a time, one breath out and one in, I bypass the thin rope blocking off the west wing and flick on the light. Ignoring everything in front of me, I remember laying in James's arms on the porch of his uncle's house, under the tin roof, listening to the rain.

I can still hear him laugh as the bedroom door creaks open, the memories and the present moment colliding.

"One day we'll have a tin roof porch," he declared once. He said it like a joke until I told him I'd love that. I love the storms.

The next exhale is more difficult, because it hurts even though it shouldn't. Simply existing shouldn't cause pain like it does when you're missing someone.

"You lied," I speak into the quiet room. It's colder in here. Unlike the hall, nothing in this room is covered. Roughly two years ago, I closed the door and told everyone not to enter it. And that's how it's remained. The heat clicks on as I drag my finger across the dresser. It's dusty and musty. I suppose that's what happens when a room is closed off for as long as this one has been.

With the trash bag still in my hand, I sit on the edge of the bed. It doesn't protest in the least. A thought crosses my mind that I didn't expect.

I wonder if Zander did this. If he cleaned out drawers he didn't want to ever open. I wonder if he had someone else clean up the traces of Quincy, the ones we're not supposed to leave around because it prevents us from "moving on."

I'd ask him, but just like this bedroom door was a moment ago, I think that conversation is a place Zander doesn't want to go. That it's something that's quite firmly locked up. Placing the bag on the bed, I focus on the other item that was balled up with it, the ancient phone that only texts.

I'm going to put some things aside.

It's odd to feel relief and accomplishment, sitting in a room, proud not to be losing it.

What? Kamden texts back. What things? Do you need help?

His messages come quickly, one after the other.

Let's just store them until I'm ready—My thumbs hesitate and I can't type the rest of the sentence so I hit send. The idea of typing, to get rid of them, disrupts the small moment of ease, the hope that I am strong enough for this.

I hope he doesn't ask, "Ready for what?"

Thankfully, he doesn't.

Okay. We can store anything you want for however long or indefinitely. Can I come over?

Staring down at his question, I don't know how to answer him. I think I want to be alone for this, but I don't know that I can be.

I have a meeting but I'll be done soon if you can wait.

No. The word is typed and sent before I can think twice about it. My breathing picks up as I push myself off the bed, taking in the abandoned room.

His texts don't stop and with each one, I know he doesn't trust me. He doesn't think I can do this. Insecurity weaves its way through me. What about the girls? We'll make it a cozy night in—we can watch Hocus Pocus and Kelly can read our tarot cards?

In an effort to reassure him, I tell him, Damon knows. I'm surprised by his response.

Where's Zander?

I lie and tell him, Zander will be here soon.

But where is he, did he tell you to do this?

No, it's just a part of me getting back to normal. It's such a lie to minimize it as a line on a checklist. But there's truth in it too. As my phone continues to vibrate with message after message, I pick up a silver frame from my old dresser. Sweeping off a thick layer of dust that clouds the photograph with my thumb, I peer down at a memory frozen in black and white. I used to call it "our photograph" because it's the one nearly every gossip column and media outlet used when it came out that we were seeing each other.

In the photo, I'm lying against his chest; I can still feel the stubble lining his chin that rested in the crook of my neck. His teeth are perfect and I remember joking with him that it could be an ad for a dentistry practice. We look happy. "We were so happy," I whisper to no one. Although my eyes gloss over, I hold it back and it's easier to do than I anticipated.

Kam continues texting and I let out a small laugh that surprises me. I'm not sure where it's come from, but I'll take the lightheartedness over the heaviness that's come over me.

I'm okay, Kam. I promise I'm okay.

If I text you every five minutes, will you be mad?

No ... I think I'd be okay with that.

Good. I'm here for you.

Through the parted curtains, I'm given a view of the storm raging on, the rain rampaging against the panes and a crack of lightning in the distance.

The frame makes a small clunk as I set it down and let out a heavy breath to steady myself. His clothes. I remind myself that it's not the furniture, it's not the visual reminders like that photograph, or anything like that that should be stored or donated. It's his clothes.

That's the only thing.

Naturally, I turn my back on his dresser and move to my nightstand. The lavender lotion is still there; picking it up, I find it's nearly full. A vision appears in front of me: the last time I remember using it. In silk pajamas with boy shorts and a matching tank top. I climbed into bed, under these sheets, and he was there, waiting for me.

I'm less careful dropping the lotion and then think it should be something that I toss in this bag, but I don't. Instead I spot the room spray from our honeymoon. I bought so many bottles of it but barely ever used it. Without touching it, the scent hits me as if bathed in it. The tropical scent of the Riviera Maya.

A sad smile crosses my face when I remember he told me I'd never use it. It was expensive and James couldn't have cared less. He was right, but he told me to get it, because it would make me happy.

It's not fair how many little things that are meaningless can bring on so much emotion.

Tears well again, but I hold them back, forcing myself to open just one drawer and get it over with. Just one drawer, clothes that should be donated. Clothes that I don't need to hold on to anymore.

The lightning strikes closer, and there's a louder rumble this time. The rain beats down as the drawer scrapes open. It's a long drawer and I get down on my knees to go through the few pieces that lay in the bottom.

There aren't many pieces at all. This was our vacation home. We were barely here, so it shouldn't be surprising but somehow it is.

The first three garments are easy. I toss the shorts and jeans into the bag and I'm able to go through the entire drawer. There's nothing to keep. Nothing that should stay here.

Sitting on my heels, I lean back and look at the pathetically empty bag and then open the next drawer and the next.

It seems easier and easier as the rain pours down and the lightning lessens, until I get to one piece. One rugby shirt that I hated. God, it looked awful on him. The fit was all wrong, the fabric too thick. I never hated a shirt more.

The storm carries on as I hold up the orange shirt, still not seeing the appeal. I remember how he laughed about how much I hated it. I'm surprised to even see it here. Just as I'm thinking he never wore it, or at least I don't remember him ever wearing it, I see the tags.

It's brand new. He had it for years and never wore it.

"You're not wearing that. It's awful."
"You're a little small to be so bossy," he joked, smiling down at me.
"Seriously, I'll dye my hair if you put that thing on."

The moment takes over, his hands on me, how he backed me up against the wall.

I don't realize I'm crying, hot wet lines running down my face, until my phone goes off with a text.

Laying the shirt on my lap but not letting it go, I answer the phone with my other hand and see I've missed three texts from Kamden.

You okay?

Hey babe I just need you to message me, okay?

Please, Ella. I'm a PITA but I love you and anything will do.

As I'm reading them, another comes through. Don't be mad, I messaged Damon.

Shifting so my ass is on the floor, I let the shirt go and respond. I'm here. Just had a moment. It's not so ladylike as I wipe under my nose and consider using the damn shirt as a tissue. A small laugh leaves me at the thought, but then without warning, I sob. Crying into the shirt with fresh hot tears.

"Oh my fucking God what is wrong with me," I murmur in between wiping at my face with the shirt. *Feel it and let it go.*

Even as I tell myself to let go of the emotions, I don't want to let go of the shirt. I don't know that I'm ready. I don't think I'm ready.

Focusing on my breathing, I quickly text, Kam I don't think I'm ready to throw anything away.

That's okay, that's totally fine.

My fingers fly across the keys. I mean the houses too. I don't want anyone to touch them.

Even as I send them, I know it's unreasonable. I know it is. I just want to stay still for a moment. I'm just not ready for it to change.

I text him again adding, Please, but I can't explain why.

I spend too long staring down at the rumpled trash bag and wrinkled-up shirt, with my hands trembling. It's not until Kam tells me no one will touch anything and that he'll make sure of it that I'm able to consider pulling myself together.

Shame creeps up my spine at how easy it was for me to fall apart.

I couldn't clear out a dresser of clothes.

"Ella." Zander's voice carries through from the cracked bedroom door. It creaks open; he doesn't wait for me to answer.

I'm sure I'm a sight to behold. There's no doubt my mascara has run, my cheeks are tearstained and I'm sure my nose is red. Taking in a steadying breath, I slowly rise to my feet, not bothering to hide anything at all.

"Ella," he repeats, saying my name with a gentleness, a comfort that's unexpected. I suck in a deep breath, meant to make it all right, but instead my expression crumples and my throat goes tight. He's quick to wrap his arms around me, bringing me back down to the ground, nestled in his lap as I cling to his shirt. I fist his cotton T-shirt, burying my head in his chest.

One deep breath after the other as he shushes me, rubbing soothing circles on my back and rocking me slightly. Back and forth as the waves of chaotic grieving dim.

With my eyes closed, I breathe Zander in, his unique scent. It's masculine but clean. Like fresh open water.

"I thought I was doing good," I whisper, opening my eyes to see the light shining off the silver frame. My gaze drops until Zander grips my chin between his thumb and forefinger, bringing my eyes up to his.

The world pauses. All my thoughts, all the sorrow just as much as the battering of the rain when he traps me with his emerald and amber eyes. He doesn't see through me, he sees all of me. Every last piece and I can't breathe.

"You did very well and I'm proud of you." He's the one to close his eyes and when his lips meet mine, I close mine too. His kiss is bruising, taking without remorse and consuming me in a way I'd forgotten I could feel.

The only way I can think to describe it is safe, cherished, wanted … I don't know that any one word is enough. It feels like it'll be okay. Maybe even that nothing else matters. As long as I just stay right here.

He lowers his head again and my eyes close, eager for him to do that again. To make it all go away. To make me his and nothing but that.

My lips mold to his until he nips my bottom lip. A gasp leaves me at the sudden hint of pain.

"Good girl," he whispers against my lips and then kisses my forehead.

I hadn't realized how tired I was until I rest my cheek on his chest.

"Did I interrupt you?" he questions.

A knot forms in my chest and I readjust to sit up, to feel the cool air against my heated face. "I think I did all I should for today."

I peek up at Zander to find him considering the bag of clothes. He doesn't question anything, he only nods and then pushes the drawer shut to lean against the dresser, keeping his arm around his waist to pull me along with him.

With his legs bent on either side of me, both arms wrapped around me and my head resting against his shoulder, he sits with me, in this room that doesn't belong to either of us.

It belongs to what once was.

My exhale shudders out of me. Unsteady and daring me to let my thoughts wander.

"You came in with a purpose. I will stay until you've done what you wanted." I tilt my head back to peer up at Zander, who takes his time to look back down at me.

"What are you going to do? Follow me from room to room?" I don't hide the incredulousness from my tone.

His answer is as simple as it is definitive. "If that's what you need."

"You have more important things to do than to babysit me."

"No, Ella, I don't."

For the second time in only moments, I feel caught, but safe. Seen and protected. All at once, it's suffocating and I tear my gaze from his. Staring across the room, I tell him, "I had planned to do one drawer."

"It looks like you did that."

I can only nod, my snide thoughts telling me I should have stopped while I was ahead. "I did."

"Next time I'd like you to tell me." His strong hand wraps around my thigh. "Poor Damon was standing outside of the door not knowing what to do with himself."

Surprised, I turn to face Zander, who grins at my shock.

"No he wasn't."

He laughs slightly, his broad chest shaking as he does. He nods and tells me, "He was."

Brushing at my knee, I stare at the thick accent rug, feeling guilty. "I didn't mean to make him worry."

"We can't help but worry," he tells me. His thumb runs along my cheek, as if he's brushing away tears that no longer exist. "I want to be here for you. Don't deprive me of that, my little bird."

My heart thumps, loud and heavy. Refusing to go unnoticed. Three words nearly slip from my lips, reckless and nothing but raw emotion. The moment I catch them, I swallow them down. I haven't forgotten Damon's comment about displacing my feelings.

Zander stands slowly, holding his hand out for me. "Come." He towers over me.

There's a question that lingers, that begs to be spoken. Asking if we'll ever be more. With my small hand in his, I consider asking him, letting it out and seeing where the chips may fall.

"You did well today. I'm proud of you," he tells me. Like a Dom speaks to his submissive. Matter of fact.

"Thank you," I whisper and the chill of the room creeps over my shoulders.

The question goes unasked. We've both already loved. I'll never be the woman he met in the bar who made him laugh. And he'll never be the man who wanted me so desperately that he wouldn't take no for an answer.

He's only my Dom. And to him, I am only his submissive.

It's only when we're leaving, the bag and rumpled rugby shirt staying where they are, that I notice the rain has stopped.

chapter 16

Zander

Ella's doing well. The sessions with Damon, the new coping habits—all of it is everything I could have hoped for when The Firm took over her care. But something makes me suspicious. Like it's going too well.

Like she might be hiding something, or burying something. Separating from me in a way I don't like. But then, of course, that's the whole point. That Ella will grow to a place where she doesn't need any of us anymore.

Except … I want her to need me. The way I'm coming to need her. Or maybe it's only a powerful desire.

I am so fucking conflicted with her. She's still grieving and I have no idea what she truly wants. A Dom or more. Let alone what she's capable of committing to once her life goes back to what it was.

We're in her sitting room in the middle of all that blue, and I can't keep my eyes off her. Ella is curled into a chair with a book on her lap, and all I can do is sit here and stare at her. Marveling at her progress but hesitant to let my guard down.

It's a cold, dreary day. We could spend days like this in a hundred different ways. Like in my dungeon, for instance. I want to show it to her, but I don't know if she'd approve.

It's one thing to have this relationship in the comfort of her home. It's another to pluck her away and toy with her like I truly want to do.

I don't know if it would meet her standards. Ella's house is a testament to her wealth. She's swimming in it. Drowning in it. Would she even accept the lifestyle I want? I don't realize I've started looking out the window at the thrashing trees until she speaks.

"Z?"

"Yeah?"

A hint of worry in her dark eyes. "Would you hold me?"

I open my arms to her, and she drops the book to come to me. Her only stop is by the fireplace to hit the switch. It springs to life in the grate, filling the space with orange flames, and Ella crawls into my lap. It'll be winter soon. The snow will blanket us in. It's different from my place in Pennsylvania. Everything is different here, and I'm not sure how the two worlds fit together. I'm not sure if they can.

It's all going well, but can this be sustained?

Ella rests her head on my shoulder, and I tuck a blanket around her on my lap. There. This is the way to sit in silence together. With her so close I can feel her heat.

Hypothetically, how would I live without her? I can't exactly picture her in my house in lower Pennsylvania. It's significantly smaller than her place. Substantially less in nearly every way and I have never wanted to live in a home that feels … expansive and impersonal. My home doesn't have a separate sitting room and a rec room and an enormous backyard. It doesn't come with gardening staff and people to take out the flower beds if you want them redone. Ella lives in a world surrounded by people to support her, care for her, and work for her. It would just be me in Pennsylvania. I don't have any desire for this life.

I can't even be sure I'd be with The Firm anymore, and I have to question myself—really question myself—about whether my desire for Ella is pure desire for her or if it's strengthened by the fact that I've given up my job for her. For a long time, The Firm was the steadiest thing in my life. The jobs we took under my brother's direction provided a shape to my days, a way to make good money, and a reason to get up in the morning.

I'm not questioning if Ella would be enough. She would be—I know that by the way she fits into my arms. By the way her scent makes me feel, which is powerful and peaceful at the same time. But would I be enough for her, if I told her I didn't want this?

I breathe through the thoughts in my head. They are just thoughts, and having them doesn't make any one of them truer than the others. I hold my emotions at a distance and try to consider them with an impartial mind. I'm obviously unsettled about how things have been left with The Firm. I'm wishing for more solid footing in my life, and not having it is causing some fear and anxiety. But mostly, overriding everything, is how much I want Ella. How much I care for her. I can't keep that feeling at any kind of distance. It's too close.

"Would you ever want to live with me? To continue our power exchange in my home, rather than here?"

Her head comes up, curiosity running through the shades of amber in her dark eyes. "Yes."

"Even if it wasn't all of this?" I gesture around us and the obvious wealth. "I can take care of you, but this is not a lifestyle I ever imagined for myself."

She pushes herself up to look into my eyes. "Would you ever want to live with me, then? Even if it *was* all this?"

I smirk at her to cover the instant twinge of uncertainty that burrows into my gut. "I don't think I could maintain this lifestyle for you."

"You wouldn't have to. I've never had to work a day in my life. When my father died, I got everything. There wasn't anyone else to inherit a thing. Even his business partners and everyone else suing for this and that and claiming rights …" She lies back down, as if comforted by the memory and explains, "Kam took down every single one of them and I got every dime to my father's name."

There's something … off about the manner in which she delivered that statement. Like she's used to the vultures, used to litigation.

"Did you expect that? That when he died, you'd have to fight to keep what he left you?"

There's a sad smile that graces her lips as she peers into the fire. "In this world, there is always someone wanting what's yours. I remember once, I …" she hesitates and I tell her to go on, to tell me what she's thinking.

Swallowing thickly she admits, "Kelly, Trish and I, we were as thick as thieves."

"You still are from what I can tell."

Her hair rustles against my chest as she readjusts in my lap, getting more comfortable, still staring at the fire as if it's playing back her memories. "We are. Because of the shit we got into. Drugs, alcohol … we were given invitations that no one should ever give minors. And I didn't have a father or mother to tell me no. I had Kamden. Who was used to getting himself and his sister out of trouble."

"I've seen your record."

"It's a colorful résumé, isn't it?" she sighs, not with nostalgia, but with regret. "I'm thankful for Kam and what he did for me. If it weren't for him, I might not be this version of fucked up, but I would be a hollow shell of …" She breathes in deeply before clearing her throat. "What I mean is that, all of this, is forever mine. There's no needing support from anyone. So if you could want this, then it's no bother."

"I imagine—this—comes with Kam? Kamden was there for everything?"

"Always." Ella skims her finger over the collar of my shirt. "Ever since I can remember. Our families have known each other forever. You know Kam's sister, Trish and I, we got along from the start. That's the way it is in this life. There are so very few people you can trust. You tend to stick with the ones you know, and we always knew Kam's."

I had friends growing up, though none were wealthy and there was never a threat of trusting the wrong person. Family friends, of course. My family had those. But they came and went and came back. It was easy. Society fears were never something I concerned myself with.

"Why did you choose him to take custody of you back then? When your father died and you were sixteen." I'm surprised by the spike of needless jealousy. I can't go back in time to be in every part of Ella's life, as much as I want to. And even if I could, I don't know if I'd do it. The way Ella and I are together is only possible because of the people we are right now, and those people were shaped by the past.

She frowns, her eyes going distant. "I knew he'd do anything for me. He took care of … a lot of things. So it made sense."

In the space of this one sentence, her tone has changed. It's off, and her body stiffens in my arm.

"Don't withdraw from me, jailbird. We're in this conversation until it's over, unless you want to use your safe word."

Her eyebrows go up as color darkens her cheeks. "I can safe word out of a conversation?"

"You can use your safe word at any time," I remind her. "It's not just for when I'm fucking you, or when you're bound. It's for any time. Because our relationship is twenty-four seven, so is your safe word. Do you feel like you might need to use it?"

Ella considers it for a moment, like she should. I'm proud of her for not immediately saying no. Some submissives become convinced that using the safe word is a kind of weakness, and that it makes their Doms happier if they don't use it. That's not the case at all. I need her to know she can use her safe word at any point, because otherwise I can't adjust my methods. It's crucial to be comfortable with using a safe word. I've always thought that a reluctance to use it is a sign that the Dom hasn't done his job. I'm going to do well by Ella. I won't let her down.

"No. I don't need to use it." She takes a deep breath, steadying herself. "When he died—my father, I mean—there were a number of people in my life I didn't trust. I knew I could trust Kam."

"How did you know you could trust him?"

"He knew things I'd done. And he knew things about my father. He knew everything." Ella swallows, meeting my eyes. "You can trust someone who knows all your darkest secrets. You know?"

chapter 17

THERE IS PURPOSE IN SUFFERING. DAMON'S PREVIOUS declaration has wreaked havoc on me since I woke up in the middle of the night and struggled to get back to sleep. With my eyes feeling heavy, the questions roll around in the back of my mind.

What the fuck purpose is worth what I went through? The tragedies that so many people endure have purpose?

The question sticks to my tongue as Damon takes his seat on the patio chair across from where I'm lying. In high-waisted jeans and a cream sweater, I don't have to worry about covering anything from him.

"Enjoying the fire without me?" he jokes, leaning back in the chair. The fire burns bright behind him. Damon's gotten back to his more casual, friendly banter with me. Any bit of tension or uncertainty since The Firm found out about Zander and I has subsided entirely.

But why would he tell me there is purpose in suffering? The more I think about it, the more it almost seems cruel. The question is still there, but I swallow it and answer, "It's the perfect day for the fireplace out here, don't you think?"

"There's a nice chill out here, I'll admit."

What purpose could be worth *this*? I've been thinking about it all day. He said there was purpose in suffering, but what could possibly be worth the suffering that comes with loss?

"Something on your mind?" he questions and I run my teeth along my lower lip, considering him.

"Did Z send you out here to babysit me while he left?"

With a shake of his head, Damon crosses his ankle to his other knee.

"You look like a therapist, you know that?" I point with a chipped nail and add, "Especially in a collared shirt under that sweater."

"You sound like a patient avoiding meaningful conversation."

I huff out a laugh and ask, "What's it called when you keep thinking about the same thing over and over?"

"Obsessing?"

"No." I'm quick to dismiss that suggestion. "When it's things that make you sad."

He nods and says, "Ruminating. Excessive thinking about negative feelings."

Snapping my fingers, I point at him and say, "That's the one."

"What are you thinking about?" he questions but then corrects himself. "What can't you stop thinking about?"

I watch his foot tap on nothing in the air.

"Missing James," I confess under my breath and I let my expression show the sadness I've been concealing as I add, "Don't tell him. Please."

"Zander?"

Swallowing thickly, I nod.

"He knows that you miss him. But I won't tell him anything in our conversations. It's only between the two of us."

"I can't stop thinking about how if James had looked, even though he had the right-of-way, or if I'd seen it quicker and yelled."

"That must feel heavy."

I murmur without looking back at him, "Endless loop about my current suffering."

"I have to be honest." He waits for me to peek up at him before he tells me, "I'm not a fan of that loop of yours." He offers me a kind smile and raises his brow.

"That would make two of us."

"But I'm happy that you're talking about it."

"I want it to stop," I confess to him, not hearing whatever he's just said. "How do you make it stop?" The question reeks of desperation.

"Recognize that you are ruminating. Acknowledging that it's not productive."

"I do that. When I go there, I realize it's happening at least."

"Good. Good."

"And then I'm angry that I'm thinking about it again and reliving it. I get so frustrated with myself … it doesn't stop."

"I need you to know that we are not our thoughts. Separate the feelings from the thoughts."

"I thought you said there was purpose in suffering." The words race out of me, nearly sounding accusatory.

"The purpose of suffering is not *to* suffer. The purpose is knowing why you feel that way and then what you can do, if you can do anything. In your case, you can't."

"I wish I could."

"That's understandable."

"Help me make it stop," I practically beg him, praying he can understand how much it still hurts. "Please."

"Tell yourself it's just a ball in a box. The button was pushed. Was there something that led to it or not? If there's nothing to do, nothing to control, let it go."

"Okay. Let it go."

Damon makes a show of looking at his watch. "Well, we dove right in, didn't we?"

I let out a small laugh, laying back into the pillow.

"Do you know what triggered it?"

The bedroom. I don't answer him, though. "I think I'd rather talk about something else."

"We can do that."

My lips perk up into a soft smile. "You're easy to talk to, you know that?" Damon's broad smile is comforting. I add, "And you have a beautiful smile."

"Well, now you're just buttering me up for something."

I don't say anything, I return my attention to the lone loose thread on the knee of my jeans. *Just let it go. Feel it and let it go.* The advice resonates but it's too simple. At this moment, I'm not sure how to feel about its simplicity.

"If you don't want to talk about James, maybe we can talk about Zander?" Damon suggests.

"What about him?"

"Have your other relationships been similar? Romantically or sexually?"

"As in, have I had other Doms in my life?"

Damon nods.

"Only one. My husband. But it wasn't the same."

"Do you want to talk about it?"

I shift again, feeling colder as the breeze sweeps my hair in front of my face. "I … feel uncomfortable comparing the two of them."

"Remember that it's okay to be uncomfortable. There are no good or bad emotions. Only comfortable and uncomfortable, and there's nothing wrong with either."

"I don't want to talk about him right now."

"I understand. Let's go back a bit, shall we?"

Nodding, I clear my throat. "Okay."

"Back on the topic of sex, sexual empowerment, is that what you called it?" He references a conversation we had the other day.

"Yes."

"You said something about having all the money in the world, but you choose to use your platform for sexual empowerment."

"My social media following." Yesterday and the day before, I went on little rants mostly. Apparently Damon wants to hear more of my "I am woman, hear me roar" movement.

"That's right."

"How far back did you go when you looked through my social media posts?" I question him nearly comically, although it doesn't reflect in my expression or tone.

"To the beginning, skimming," he admits which is shocking. "I wanted to make sure I understood what you meant about using your platform for empowering women and sex positivity."

"Being called a whore and slut for years will do it, I guess." Those types of comments started the moment I wore my first bikini … I think I was fourteen. I know my dad was still alive, so I was young, just posing with friends at the beach.

"I did notice when you got engaged so did the amount of overt expression in your posts."

"I like posting things that make women more comfortable with their bodies and sexuality. I always have but I had to be careful. I didn't want to sound bitchy or judgy … I just wanted women to know it was okay to want sex. To have sex. To wear what they want and to say no if they didn't want to do something. That it didn't make them "less than" to want some *activities*."

"Was your mother an active role or voice in that subject?"

My snort is exceptionally unladylike. "No. No, not at all. I don't remember much about my mother except …"

"Except what?"

"Fighting."

A cool breeze blows by and I emphasize, "They were *always* yelling."

"You were young when your mother died, but you remember them fighting?"

"There are very few memories I have of her," I tell him and moments flash in my mind. "In nearly all of them, she was fighting with my father."

"Do you want to talk about what happened with your mother?"

"You know what happened." My blood chills and the sun starts to set, dimming the natural light far too quickly.

"Are their deaths, the trial, their fighting something you think about often?"

Staring blankly at him, I wish I could speak as easily as I just have when talking about my upbringing.

"Do you remember how you felt during those harder times?" Suddenly the topic of sex no longer seems important. Damon watches me like he's gotten to something he'd like to dig up.

The screaming is what I remember most. I'd wake up from them screaming at each other. "Scared, angry … like any child would be." With another breeze blowing, I brush my hair from out of my face and cross my arms.

"Guarded?" Damon pokes fun and I tsk him. "It's just cold." My heart does a little tap in my chest that's uneven. Yes. This conversation makes me very guarded and I wonder if Damon saw posts or comments that he shouldn't have. Kam said they were all removed.

"Did it ever get physical?"

"Yes." I nod, my throat going tight and dry. "I can still remember the sound of him slapping her so hard she fell to the ground."

The tapping in my chest continues, intensifying and quickening when he asks, "Do you remember how old you were?"

"I had to be in middle school."

"I imagine that was difficult."

Enough. Enough. We're not supposed to be talking about this. "I don't see how any of this relates to anything at all."

"Conflict resolution is a learned behavior. How did you learn to handle your emotions when you were dealt such severe ones at a young age? You just told me you know that you're ruminating, but don't know how to stop. You've told me a number of stories where you struggle with your emotions."

"I think that's normal."

"Just because it's normal doesn't mean it's healthy. I want to help you, so tell me."

"Tell you what?"

"What happened when they fought?'

With a deep breath in, I answer him, "That's something I haven't thought about in a while." He starts to say something, but I cut him off. "You know how we started this conversation with ruminating? I used to stay up at night, thinking about their fights and if I could change anything."

"And how did you cope with those feelings?" he questions and the events play in my head. Kelly, Trish and Kam … the plan. Uncovering the truth and then covering it all back up. How did I cope? I did something I shouldn't have.

"I think we should go inside," I whisper.

chapter 18

THE TWO OF THEM ARE SITTING IN THE BLUE ROOM IN FRONT of the fire, and I know right away that the session has pushed Ella to one of her boundaries. Or to a place where she needs someone else to act as a boundary for her. She needs me. Her face is pale, and her eyes shine, but she's not crying. I pull a chair directly in front of her so I can take her hands in mine and look her in the eye. Damon watches from his seat, his face neutral.

"What's wrong?"

Damon begins to answer. "Ella and I were discussing her past with her—"

"Wait, Damon. Quiet." My tone wasn't meant to come out the way it did. "Please," I add for good measure. "I want Ella to tell me what happened." I stroke a lock of hair away from her cheek.

Her only acknowledgement is to scoot on the sofa and make room for me to sit next to her. There's a sadness that doesn't leave her gaze, which flicks between the mine and the fire.

"She has a voice, and I want her to use it. Tell me." She knows a command when she hears one, and her body settles into the sofa a bit.

"There's a lot," she admits, and her voice is soft and slightly shaken.

"I have a lot of memories. Some of them I wish I could forget … and today," she pauses to take in an unsteady breath, "I'm just remembering a lot right now."

"We're going to go over them now, in a safe place." I don't want to push her past what she can take, but because Ella is a submissive, I make the decision for her. She still holds the power over the conversation. She can use her safe word at any time. "I'm listening."

"James—" Ella lifts her chin a fraction of an inch. "James knew about it. He knew about what happened, and I wish—" Now her eyes brim with tears.

It's obvious how difficult it is for her, and I've never wished for anything more than I wish she didn't have to remember these things. I wish she had a clean slate, and that her life had been the fairy tale she deserves. "I wish you already knew so I didn't have to say it out loud."

"You will say it out loud, and I'll hear it, and then I'll know," I reassure her. "It won't have so much power over you once you've told me." I hope it's true for Ella. I kept what happened with Quincy bottled up from as many people as possible, but it all had to come out eventually. Otherwise I couldn't have survived it. The longer you let a secret fester, the worse it gets.

Ella takes a shaky breath, and I run my thumb over the back of her hand. "My father abused my mother. He—he beat her. Not just once or twice, Z."

"And you saw?"

"Yes. I saw it. And it didn't seem to matter if anyone knew. He knew I saw, and that only seemed to make it worse. If he caught me looking, he would make it worse for her." Tears spill down Ella's cheeks. "Watching was dangerous, and so …"

"So what? What were you going to say?"

"I don't know. I like people to know, I like them to see what's really there. I want them to know it all … and see it all."

"I'm not sure this is—" Damon pipes up and makes his hesitation known. Whatever conclusion Ella's come to, he doesn't necessarily agree with.

"So maybe with James and other men, I liked for people to see me. It's wrong to even talk about those things one after the other—"

"It's not wrong," I say, cutting off that line of thinking, although I'm still not entirely sure what she means.

"I think I like people to see and hear it all, because I wish they knew everything I knew back then. So ranting about what's on my mind … fucking whoever I want on camera, whatever it is, I want them all to see it. They're going to judge me anyway, so let the facts of my judgment be crystal clear and out there in the world for all to see."

"Each part of your life affects every other part. If being a witness was wrong in your childhood, then being witnessed can be a way to take back your control over that. It's okay, jailbird."

The name slips out before I can stop it, but Damon says nothing. I'm going to have to ask Kam about all this shit. This is much darker than I thought it would be. Than I ever imagined for Ella.

"Maybe I wanted to be seen back then, because it wasn't dangerous with James."

"Do you think it would be dangerous to be seen with me?"

"I don't know." She doesn't take her eyes off my face. Doesn't glance in Damon's direction. But the color has come back to her face and she leans closer to me, her breath quickening with anticipation. "I want to feel powerful enough to show everyone what really happens," she whispers. "I want them to see what my life is really like."

I take her face in my hands and pull her in for a kiss. Hard. Deep. Like I don't give a fuck if Damon is sitting there. The truth is that I don't. If Ella wants power, I have one way to hand it to her—by taking it from her. That's the game we play, at its core.

With tearstained cheeks she peers up at me through her thick lashes and murmurs, "Do you still want me? Even if I'm this fucked up?"

There isn't a second I hesitate. I stand her up between my knees and strip off her jeans and panties together at once, consumed with her body. With the delicate, elegant frame under a soft baggy sweater. It means that even when she's naked below the waist, she's still partially covered. Ella reaches for me over and over, not wanting to break the kiss. I let her kiss me for as long as I can stand it, and then I push her back into the sofa. I know Damon's seated in a dark blue armchair behind us, and the angle in relation to Damon will keep her partially out of view.

But not entirely. My heart rages in my chest, wanting her to know I want her all the more for confiding in me. More than I care about anything else.

He still hasn't moved, and I know he's not going to. If he wanted out of this, he could have gotten up at any time. Still can.

Either way, I'm going to fuck Ella exactly how she wants to be fucked.

I spread her thighs to the edge of the chair. Her chest rises faster, and I slide my hands between her thighs and lean in close. It's only an illusion that we're having a private conversation. Damon can hear every word. But I do it anyway. "You can use your safe word at any time."

Ella gives the tiniest nod of her head. Her breathing is slower and heavier.

"He can see you," I tell her.

She takes in a quiet gasp, her head tipping back against the chair, and I can feel how much she wants this. Her thighs are already trembling beneath my palms.

It only takes one movement to switch places with her. Pull her out of her seat, take her place, and pull her into my lap. I undo my pants as soon as I'm underneath her, gripping my cock and use my hands on her hips to guide her down. Ella reaches for my shoulders, her cheeks reddened. She lets out a small moan as the head of my cock meets her opening and I pull her down hard.

The gasp she gives me, with her lips parted and her eyes wide, is fucking everything.

Her pussy is wet for me, and the only resistance she offers is that she's so tight. I curse softly into her ear as she buries her face in my shoulder and rides me. I'm going to keep her moving, keep her fucking me with the rhythm I want. She wants this too. She wants it so much that she can't relax into my hands. Ella's hips move faster in my grip. Almost frenzied.

In a quick glance, I note that Damon hasn't left.

"He's still looking," I whisper at the shell of Ella's ear. "He's watching while you fuck me. Do you wish you knew how much he could see, jailbird?"

She doesn't answer me; instead she struggles to say, "I'm going to—"

Her pussy clenches, and I know. It happens again and again, the pace picking up. "I'm going to come—"

"Good girl. Come for me."

Ella's orgasm is a pretty, shuddering thing, her face hot on my neck and her hands fisted in my shirt.

When she moves to slow down, I stop her. I'll lift her up and down myself if I have to. "You're not done, jailbird. Not until I am. Keep going."

All's quiet at Ella's house the next morning, except for the sputtering of a coffee pot. She's still sleeping when Damon comes in through the back door for his shift.

When I was done with Ella, Damon had left and Silas was in the rec room, his shift having started. I messaged him a number of times, dancing around the obvious.

I'm at the countertop with a cup of coffee in my hand, and when he sees me, he cocks a brow, closing the sliding door with one hand. I wish I could say I didn't feel the heat of slight embarrassment.

"Morning," I tell him.

"Morning to you too." The awkwardness is only slight.

"About last night …" I start and he finishes.

"I figure I won't address it unless she needs to be reassured that there is no judgment from me?"

I'm slow to nod, considering his expression.

"Her coping mechanisms are," he says and breathes in, "apparently compatible with yours." The grin against his cleanly shaven face is humorous. I huff a laugh, picking up the mug to take a drink.

"Apparently so."

"Do you think she'll need reassurance?" he questions in a more serious tone.

I consider him, and the situation before answering. "I think she needs more reassurance that it was all right to cry, more so than anything else. I think she needs to know that whatever happened back then, is okay to put in the past."

Damon nods, pulling a stool out from the counter to sit beside me. "So, listen. I did some research last night on Ella's father like you asked me to."

"Did you find anything that could be helpful?"

"There were some records of her father's abuse, all sealed and don't ask me how I got them."

I nod and tell him, "I won't ask Silas either."

"Good. But the records only contained statements and evidence of his abuse toward his first wife, not his second. She tried to press charges once, but they were dismissed on the grounds that she was mentally ill and filed a false report. When she died by suicide, no one questioned it at first."

"Suicide? I thought—"

"Evidence came to light years later on that. The allegations that Ella's mother was responsible. It wasn't suicide, it was murder."

"Do you have the records of what the evidence was?"

Damon nods his head. "I can send you the file, but keep it to yourself." He meets my eye. "It was also sealed and it looks like …" He struggles with what to say next. "Whoever sealed it didn't want it found, is all I'm going to say."

"So whatever he did to his first wife, he might have done to the second?"

"Potentially, although she never hinted at abuse herself and she certainly had a reason to speak up when she was tried for murder. She also … died by suicide in her cell before the trial was over."

"Suicide. Ella's mother committed suicide. Do you think there's a genetic—"

"Ella's on antidepressants. But more than that … with what's in that file, I would be surprised if her mother really killed herself."

My friend shrugs off his jacket, getting off his stool to hang it up by the door. "The court cases mostly focused on Ella, from what I can see. It's like she was used as a distraction in some ways."

"To garner sympathy for her mother?"

"No." He frowns. "Sympathy for her father."

"That's … interesting."

"Everything that's documented is odd. Half of it doesn't appear to even appear to be legally relevant."

My gut churns. "How old was Ella?"

"The trial lasted two years and started when Ella was only seven."

Damon grabs a mug and gets his own cup of coffee, stirring in some sugar. Then he goes to the fridge and adds milk before coming back and taking his seat. "Cases involving the wealthy are generally pretty calculated." He tests his coffee, then looks over the mug at me.

"Anyway, I thought I should mention it since you asked me to look into … whether he'd hurt Ella or not, or rather the extent of it."

"What do you think?"

"I wouldn't put it past him."

The air turns stale between us as we each drink in silence. Glancing at my phone, I turn on the security app and check to see Ella, still sleeping soundly in bed.

"You're not supposed to have that anymore."

I peek up to find Damon tipping his coffee mug toward me.

"Do me a favor, and pretend like you didn't see."

He doesn't respond to that request, although he doesn't comment on it anymore either. "How are things going between you and Ella?"

Damon did just watch us fuck last night, I contemplate reminding him just to fuck with him. But there's more to it and we both know that. I don't know what to tell him. I have feelings for her. Obviously I do. But I've also been gentle with her, too much perhaps. I'm aware that she's still grieving and coping with things that have happened to her as well as how she's handled them. It's heavy. With her, it feels easy, but everything surrounding us is troubled.

"She said she'd live with me," I tell him.

His brow shoots up higher than they did when he first walked in. The surprise is genuine on Damon's face. "You're moving in together?"

"Only under the parameters of our current relationship. And we also hadn't exactly decided one way or another on where we'd live."

He snorts, almost spilling his coffee in the process. "What are the parameters?" He uses one hand to make air quotes around parameters. "That you'll just have your power exchange and never ever fall for each other?" There's an air of sarcasm that coats his guess.

"Something like that."

"Bullshit. You and Ella, moving in together, and it's not something more? I don't buy that for a second, Zander. You're really going to try to pull one over on me?"

"I'm not pulling anything over on you. That's all we talked about. We didn't talk about a romantic relationship. We're a little too old for boy-friend-girlfriend titles don't you think?"

As if everything I've done with Ella hasn't felt romantic to the core. Even when I'm punishing her.

"Sure," Damon says with obvious doubt. "No romantic relationship. Got it."

I don't want this conversation with Damon. She isn't ready. There's no reason this should even be a conversation.

If I start talking about how I really feel, about how serious this could get, then it'll be real, and then there will be no turning back.

chapter 19

Ella

Kelly's thin, arched brow hasn't budged an inch and it doesn't escape me that her gaze is firmly fixed on Zander's ass. I scold, comically, "You're shameless."

Her murmur is just as humorous. "And you're fucking that hottie?"

My lips pull up as Trish laughs into her glass and the waiter comes by to drop off our appetizers. Ruze has an impeccable variety, from spring rolls and buffalo cauliflower, to steak tartare and caviar.

I've always loved this place. It's laid back, with garage doors that stay open and let the breeze in. If I had to describe the style I'd say it's botanical boho somehow mixed with a brewery. It's high end and expensive as fuck to attract and keep the clientele … well, the rich and famous.

"The rumor mills were true then?"

"Kind of sort of, maybe." I shrug and pop a bite-size crostini with crab into my mouth so I can't say any more. We talked about heading to his place later this week. It'll be the first time I'll see it. He's unpacked and settled in now and if I'm honest, that makes me nervous.

I'm not sure I want to leave. I'm not sure I want to give up my lifestyle because it's something he isn't sure he wants.

"So … what's the deal for real? We know he was fired."

"How the hell do you know that?" I question and my tone is harsher than I anticipated. Trish's widened eyes are evidence that she's taken aback. "Sorry," I whisper and lean forward, snatching another bite from the plates.

"Is it serious?" Kelly asks, choosing a few pieces of deliciousness and sorting them on her small plate.

"How can it be if he doesn't even have a job?" Trish says, piling on.

I don't consider Trish's sentiment emotionally, only logically when I answer, "He has income and it's not like I'm after anyone for their money."

Trish doesn't bother hiding that she's staring, lifting the martini glass to her lips.

"Well, honey," Kelly says and tilts her head, reaching for a spring roll, taking her time to dip it in the accompanying sauce, not looking me in the eye, "it's not *his* money that we'd be worried about."

There's a bit of a chill in the air all of a sudden. "How did you know he was fired?"

"You know how people talk."

"Well, what else are people saying?"

Trish answers first. "That he's broke but into you."

Broke. In social circles, the word *broke* is blood in the water. "How broke?"

"Just not … not someone who could afford your lifestyle." Chewing the inside of my cheek, I let her comment sink in. I've never really cared to talk about money. There's a knot of guilt that twists in my stomach when I consider the hand I was dealt. I was born into wealth and then everything was left to me when my father was buried and I was only sixteen years old. The cherry on top is that Kam took over everything, keeping me safe, wealthy, and guiding me through a chaotic world of parasites who were after any cent they could suck from me.

I settle on a simple truth. "I hadn't thought much of it."

"I mean it's not like you need Mr. Moneybags, but it's just something to consider." Her tone reflects the high society's guide to staying elite. In other words, don't marry someone who could be after your money.

"I don't plan on ever getting married again." I decide on another comment to keep my friends, as well as the rumor mills, away from the subject of Zander's bank account. "We're fucking and enjoying each other's company. But this bill," I say and gesture to the meal. "He's paying for it and for all the nights we've been out."

As Trish's expression turns concerned, Kelly states she's getting this tab since Trish got the last.

"How?" she asks bluntly and is rewarded with a jab in her ribs from Kelly's elbow.

"Ouch!"

"The fuck is wrong with you," Kelly hisses in a murmur.

I can only laugh, although that sick feeling remains. Before I can answer Trish, she changes the subject.

"There are other rumors too. Like Kam isn't really your conservator and it's a cover-up. You went to rehab."

I don't say a word, but my eyes are locked on Trish's. "Don't worry, my love, there are so many rumors no one knows what's really going on … but the biggest rumor is that you tried drinking and fucking your way through mourning, and it ended up with a rehab hangover."

"Your social being quiet since you came back is throwing people off, though." Kelly's comment once again holds a tone. She's good at saying things without actually saying them. The hidden message: I better start posting and filling people in so they stop talking.

"You haven't seen anything, have you?" Kelly asks and Trish answers, "We know Kam isn't showing you the articles. But trust us, it's a good angle."

"What are most people saying?"

"You took a trip down to a private resort. A few do think you went to drug rehab. No one really believes the conservatorship is real. There's a seal on it and since Kam knows the judge and Kam's been telling everyone to mind their damn business and let you enjoy some sunshine … really people are just wondering if you're mad at them. You've never been quiet before and most people miss you."

"It's just us who know, right?" Trish questions although I'm sure Kam has filled her in.

I nod.

"And what about that hunk over there?" Kelly asks.

Peeking over my shoulder, I catch sight of Zander just as he was glancing at me. Butterflies stir and when he winks at me, I blush violently. It's a sin what this man does to me.

With a simper I tell them, "He's my secret. Anything else out there is PR."

Kelly questions, "So the bit about him getting fired because you were fucking?"

I laugh into my drink, some cucumber mocktail the waitress whipped up. "Well, sometimes PR does reflect the truth."

"Mostly people are just happy to see you back and happy that you might be seeing someone else. Like, that's the chatter. You're back from wherever, you're sober." She looks at her mocktail and playfully clinks it with mine. "And that you're fucking around again and causing all sorts of problems with your security team that you hired to keep people the hell out of your life."

Trish nods with a half smile. "It's a good spin on it, I think." Then she asks me, "If we take a pic, can I post it?"

"Selfies with our mocktails?" I lift my drink in pose.

"Girl gang, bang bang?" Kelly offers the caption.

"Fuck yes."

"Will Kam be all right with that?" Kelly asks and I shrug, quickly popping a cherry into my mouth before saying, "Yeah. I'm sure it'll be fine."

"And what about Playboy?" Trish's question brings my gaze to hers. "Can I get him in the background?"

Another one of him in the background?"

"You know what they say …" Kelly says in a singsong voice.

Spotted once could mean anything or nothing. Spotted twice together means everything.

"Yeah," I say, pushing the word out with more excitement than I anticipated I'd have.

I wonder when he'll see. Who's going to tell him. I want to know what he'll think of it the most. Maybe I should be more careful, but it excites me that they'll know he's something to me.

"Don't tell him you asked me," I whisper to them.

"Feeling cheeky?" Trish murmurs as she applies a fresh pat of powder to her face.

Shrugging, I tell her, "He looks good."

"He looks damn good," she agrees and snaps her compact closed.

"Smile," Trish says as she snaps a photo. I pop in another cherry garnish just as Trish says, "Wait, one more." Back in position, with a cherry at my lips I pose humorously and then pull it out to smile.

"Hell yes," Trish says and grins. "Check them out."

"Oh, post both those," Kelly suggests.

For a moment, there's nothing but an easy happiness, like nostalgia and old times. A row of hot guys in the background at a bar, one of them I'm enjoying the best sex of my life with. Delicious food at an exclusive local restaurant, with damn good company. Not everyone has as good of girlfriends as I do. With secrets that always stay just that—secret.

"I'm still mad at Kam. Not wanting you to post. I miss your daily rants." Trish's admission is spoken beneath her breath as she types out the caption on her phone. "Done. Posted." She nudges Kelly with her teeth sinking into the bottom of her teeth, placing her phone with the screen facing down on the table.

"I bet every comment is going to be about the cherry and Playboy in the background," Kelly surmises, her gaze pinned to her phone. She barks out a laugh not ten seconds later. "Told you," she states, pushing the phone in my direction.

She is so fucking him.
*Omg that cherry *laughing emoji**
Our girl is back
BangBang is right! We see you ladies!
Check out who showed up in the background.

The comments filter in with tags to gossip columns and celebrity outlets, dozens by the minute. There's a flip in my chest and anxiousness I hadn't anticipated.

"Come on," Kelly says, shifting her weight to the other hip. "This has to make you smile."

"It does, it does." I force my tone to be more upbeat. "Just … just wish I could post it too." I don't know why I lie. Maybe it isn't a lie. Ever since the other night, there's been a churning in the pit of my stomach. Like I sent something into motion.

"You're the one who pays Kam. If you want to post, post."

"I agree with Trish. Tell your man over there to get you a phone and just come back. You are back. So … if anyone says shit online, block, block, block, block, block."

"I get why he doesn't want me to … Just the thought of being hammered with questions and seeing that video or pics of us …"

"Kam can filter that out. He has his team."

"I know … I don't know why he is so damn adamant."

"I think it's time you put your foot down." Kelly's seriousness takes me aback. "Or I can put my foot down for you."

Trish has far more compassion, but she doesn't hide the fact that she has her qualms when it comes to my PR. "Everyone failed you; you paid them, and they failed."

"I'm still here, aren't I?" My comment sobers the mood too much, too quickly. "I do want to keep up with everyone again. It's just, I feel like I should be careful … maybe. I don't know. It's … it all feels different."

"Look, I didn't want to say anything but the way they handled James's passing was shit. That fixer bitch was dumped from Conntelex."

The temperature of my blood plummets at the mention of that company. They're the most sought-after company for "fixing" situations, images, for planting rumors even. I know Kam still has them on retainer.

"Cynthia, right? Like literally the day you woke up from … your fall," Trish says, lowering her voice. I didn't fall, I jumped, but I keep that correction to myself. They know what happened. She just doesn't want to say it. "That next morning, she was fired."

"It wasn't her fault that I—"

Kelly's small hand lands on mine. "She handled it poorly. Every step of the way. She was supposed to fix it, and her choice was to ignore it in the hopes it would blow over."

Trish huffs, shaking her head as she taps her phone against the table.

I fumble with how to express anything at all from what happened that night. "I wasn't in the best mindset—"

"You shouldn't have been. You paid people to protect you. And they failed you."

Kelly adds in a whisper, "Even Kam." When my eyes reach Kelly, riddled with shock that she'd talk about Trish's brother like that, she's quick to add, "It wasn't his job and I don't blame him. He was relying on the fixer. What the hell was her name?"

"Cynthia. I'm sure it was Cynthia," Trish states slowly, and then adds, "Even Kam will tell you he made a mistake and he wishes he could take it back."

"Given how easily you two are talking about this—"

"Yeah. We've talked about it behind your back, but only because we love you and we're mad on your behalf. It's not in the tabloids; cross my heart."

"Kam did his job there," Kelly chimes in.

"You should have your fucking phone is all we're saying." Trish's statement is final. "And I've told Kam exactly how I feel about it."

"It wasn't just your phone. It was access to support you had all of your life. They snatched it away. What the fuck did they think would happen?" Kelly's eyes brim with unshed tears and it doesn't go unnoticed that everyone is speaking in whispers now.

"We need chocolate."

"Could we?" Trish says while waving down the waitress, motioning to our drinks.

They're quiet, and in that moment, I remember that night, like it happened just yesterday.

"If she can't stop going off, what else is there to do?"

She wants me to keep asking them for space. Just ask for space, as if they would listen.

Kam's spoken up for me, but he's nervous. He hasn't been this nervous since... well since everything with my father. "You don't know her. She doesn't want space."

It's like I'm a child again, scolded, scared, and watching them fight through a cracked door. I can't even bring myself to move to the bed. Instead I stay on the floor, staring at my hands that won't stop shaking.

"You're supposed to fix this!"

"She can't do what she's told," Cynthia says and she doesn't bother to hide her irritation. "She's not supposed to comment."

"They shouldn't be there for her to comment on."

"Kam, I just need it back." My fingers are still shaking. I call out from my bedroom, not leaving where I am. "Kelly just messaged and she said—"

"Okay baby, but not right now." He brushes me off … like a child. Like I'm something that can be handled.

I stress, "Kam, I want to look at his picture again and—"

He cuts me off, not even listening. "I just need a moment."

We practically speak over one another as I plead for it back. "I won't comment. I swear. It's just they tagged me. They keep posting it and tagging me and I—"

"We're going to fix it." He tries to shush me.

"Kam! It's my fucking phone." My voice is raw and it hurts. It hurts from crying, from screaming.

"I'm trying to protect you, Ella," he says, emphasizing each word, his face pained.

Gripping onto his hands, where he's holding my phone hostage, I try to pry his fingers away. "Give it to me."

"No!" Kam's wide eyes look down at me as I fall to the floor, both palms hitting the wood with a loud thud. "Kamden," I cry out, feeling so fucking alone.

"Jesus Christ," Cynthia chides in the background. "Give her another Xanax and take her fucking phone away."

I feel so fucking alone. I don't know what's wrong with me.

I don't hear what Kam tells Cynthia, but whatever it is has her offering a snide rebuttal as the door closes, leaving me sobbing against the drywall.

James. James wouldn't be okay with this.

I've never felt so alone.

chapter 20

MY HOUSE IS A COMFORTABLE TWO-STORY STANDALONE WITH a brick front in a neighborhood where the houses are separated with space and tress. It's not that expensive, but it's private.

I chose it for the privacy. It's close enough that we could enjoy each other's company at either house, while having our own spaces.

Damon suggested space, given how quickly things have developed and how their sessions have been carrying on. Space is good. There are times when I won't be there for her and she should know to behave in my absence. She should be strong in solitude, if for no other reason than it would please me for her to do so.

So tonight, she'll sleep without me. Silas has already been informed to be more vigilant than normal. I keep reminding myself that this is best. That she will benefit from this.

And if not, she has my number and she will tell me. That is the only item on her list while I'm good. To keep her phone on her and use it if necessary.

The sound of heavy footsteps on the back deck, draws my attention.

Damon comes in through my back door, rubbing his hands together.

"Damn. Cold out there tonight. And you have me out in it for a card game." He takes a moment to look around before saying, "Nice place."

"It's not even snowing." I pull open the fridge and hand him a beer as soon as he's got his coat off. "How's Ella?"

"Already miss her?" he teases with a grin.

"Fuck off. How is she?"

"You can't always be there for everything, Zander. She needs to be okay without you, you know?"

"I assume that means she's doing just fine."

"Last I checked, she told me she was zoning out with a box of chocolates and some new show Kelly told her she needed to binge."

I nod first and then thank him. "I appreciate it," I tell him before patting the threshold and showing him around the new place.

"It's minimal," he comments.

"I like a modern style with clean lines." Glancing around, I can count on both hands the number of purchases I made for the dining room and living room combined. There's functionality in the gray suede modular sofa. The set of modern chairs with leather backing and black coffee table were on display in the furniture store, as was the abstract black and white with dark blue faded six-by-six canvas. The dining room is even more bare, with simple clear chairs and a dark walnut table that boasts a knot of a single chunk of wood on the surface.

"Downstairs is where it's at," I tell him, avoiding the hallway and in it, my master bedroom, along with the playroom for Ella.

The dungeon is tucked away in the back half of the basement, and I second-guess whether or not I closed the doors as Damon follows behind me on the newly finished stairs.

"This place is nice. You're renting?" he questions.

"Maybe buying," I half answer, more focused on the closed door than his question.

The first thing Damon says is, "Nice," running his hand down the newly felted poker table. "Dartboard in the back."

"No bar yet, but I'm planning one," I tell him. It's a typical game room although all I have in here at the moment is the table and the hung dartboard. "There's still a number of things I'm looking to add." My gaze wanders to the dungeon but I'm quick to correct it.

Before Damon can say any more, his phone goes off. As he checks his phone, I check mine and a text comes in.

Ella: Do you have Silas spying on me?

I text her back, I'm always spying on you my little rulebreaker.

Ella: I miss you.

Damon comments that Silas just updated him. Ella's doing well. He must have just checked on her, prompting her to message me.

Ella: It's quiet in this house without you.

Zander: If you feel empty, I have ways to fix that

Ella: You're so dirty!!

Her mock scolding makes me grin.

Zander: Be good, I'll be watching you.

I put my phone in my pocket while Damon fills me in on his drive. We set up the card table with two decks. I've been back here more often over the past months ordering furniture, making necessary arrangements and debating on whether Ella would be comfortable here or not. It's starting to feel like home again, like my old place I rented, though I'm beginning to think it will never feel completely right without Ella.

With my mind occupied, Damon moves on to other topics. We're setting out a heaping bowl of chips when Damon asks beneath his breath, "You find anything else?"

"Anything about what?' I ask him.

"About Ella's father."

"Yeah." I've been doing more research on Ella's family history, focused on the media surrounding the trial. "There's a theory that it wasn't her mother who killed her father's first wife. It was the father."

Damon nods. "Sounds plausible."

"There are a number of conspiracy theories out there. Ella was so young, I can't imagine she would know anything."

"I think it would be best to let that part of her history go, unless she's the one who wants to know more?" he questions.

"I haven't told her. It was just … something just doesn't feel right."

"Are you done looking now?"

"Not until I figure it all out," I tell him. Maybe I shouldn't dig, but there's a prick at the back of my neck when I think about how she reacted to talking about her mother and father. There's something there, I know there is.

Damon's tone breaks me from the thought. "No murder theory talk while the guys are over for cards."

It's like he's summoned them, because there's a loud knock on the front door. Hustling up the stairs, I get to the door just as there's another knock.

Opening the door wide, I tell them to come on in as Damon's coming up the stairway.

"Damn, nice place," Thomas comments before he's even fully in. Glancing around the place, I think it's nice in some ways, yet cold in others.

"I've got boxes to unpack still, but the game is set up downstairs and there's plenty of beer.

Alex, Thomas, and Ethan file in one by one, shouting and greeting us with slaps on the back. I've known these guys since high school. Damon had a front-row seat to when I lost my shit over Quincy, but they were there too, in a way. Not so much in my apartment, or guiding me through healthy ways to deal with loss. Just in the way they always have been. They checked in on me, invited me out even when I kept declining. They were simply there and that made all the difference.

We've always been there for each other.

"My girl practically kicked me out," says Thomas when all of us are in the kitchen, choosing our first-round picks for beer. "Begged me to spend a night with you assholes."

Thomas and his girlfriend have been together at least six months now.

"When you popping the question?" Ethan jokes, "She sounds like a smart one."

Thomas just smiles wider, not reacting to the taunt. The way he talks about her, always bringing her up, always smiling when we ask about her … it's telling. He really cares about her.

"Mine was excited too," says Alex. "She said she wanted to binge-watch this romance show on Netflix. I said I'd watch it with her, but she said she wanted to experience it the way it was meant to be experienced, whatever that means."

"Means it's going to be hot," says Ethan. "So hot she won't want you there to see it."

Alex frowns. "Why wouldn't she want me to see it?"

Ethan comments dryly as we make our way down the stairs to the table. "'Cause if it's one of those historical shows, then you'll have to witness how horny she is for a guy in a tricorn hat." The laughter ricochets in the stairwell and the guys keep it moving, finding their place at the table and twisting off the caps to the beers.

"It's about time we had a poker night," says Damon. "How long has it been since the last one?" Damon was the last one to join this group. When he took me in, I took him in. Now he's one of the crew.

"Too long," I say. Months, at least. I used to love cards. We used to play once a week, and I looked forward to it even when I was with Quincy. It's one of those things you walk away from feeling good. Like the world is right.

At that thought, I check my phone, searching for a message from Ella but find nothing.

As the guys chat and catch up, I open up the security app to find the living room empty. There's a nagging twist in my chest, and I'm quick to search before finding her in her bedroom.

It's too early for her to be in bed.

There's the crack of the deck being shuffled as I tell them I'm headed up to get another beer. The guys are passing around pretzels and making a fucking mess of my table, and only Ethan is in need of another beer.

"I'll get you one."

Taking the steps two at a time, I text Ella.

Zander: Spread your legs for me.

Watching on my phone, I see her get the message and then peer up at the camera before doing as she's told. Each heel digging into the mattress and her legs bent and spread wide as she lays back on the bed.

Just as she's texting me, I test her.

Ella: Like this?

Zander: Fucking beautiful.

The fridge opens, delivering a cool sensation and the two bottles clink in my left hand as I text with my right.

Zander: Pet your pussy for me, I want to watch you come undone for me.

The quality of the camera and the app make it impossible for me to see with enough detail to fully enjoy this. Which is for the best, considering my current company.

I don't have to have an up-close view to know my little bird is being greedy.

Zander: Not just your clit … I want to see you squirm.

I'm slower in my descent downstairs, satisfied that at the very least, my little bird is focused on pleasure now. She's thinking about coming and obeying, about pleasing me and what rewards I'll give her for being a good girl.

Zander: Good girl.

The sound is off, but as I retake my seat, her back arches on the bed.

Zander: Come for me, but be still.

My text goes unread for a second and then another.

Just as I'm ready to admonish her, she sees and stills, getting back into position after stripping off her nightgown.

Glancing around the table, all the men are looking at me.

"What'd I miss?"

Thomas fills me in. "I asked about your new place and if you got rid of the one down Route 40?"

"Yeah, it was a rental." I peek down at my phone and smirk at Ella, still playing with herself.

Zander: Dip your finger in. Just one.

"We gonna get back into it?" Ethan questions. "I know you've been busy with work and all. Is this more permanent?"

"I'm not sure yet." With my phone in my lap so I can see, I decide to give her a few minutes to enjoy herself.

I've been vague with the guys about the details with Ella, and The Firm. Too much is still up in the air to get into a real discussion about it, and I don't want to spend a poker night talking about it.

"Once a week sounds good to me. Or every other week." I take a good look at Thomas. "You think every other week would be better with your ball and chain?"

I barely hear his answer as I text Ella to come like a good girl and then clean herself up.

"I like every week. The drive wasn't too bad either."

"Lindsey would binge-watch her show once a week," Alex says. "Especially if you're telling me that tricorn hats are hot now. I don't know if I get the appeal of those kinds of hats."

I offer a short chuckle, focused on my little bird's lips making a perfect *O* as she finds her release on the bed. Fuck, that's hot. I run my hand down my face. I'm hard as fuck.

"You're going to have to if you want to keep up with her," Tom jokes, and it's another round of easy laughter.

"You all right?" Ethan asks.

"Just work," I answer and when I look up, Damon's brow is arched, his phone tapping on the felt surface.

"Yeah, sometimes," he says. "It would be nice to get a heads-up." His tone is dry and I force the humor to stay in my chest at the realization that Damon just got a scene he probably wasn't prepared for. Or Silas did and informed Damon.

Either way, it's one more reason that they need to leave her to me.

"Just don't go being quiet and ignoring us," Ethan says.

Thomas agrees and I have to reassure them that it's not going to happen. My phone vibrates in my lap.

Ella: Did I please you?

Zander: Always, my little bird. I'm looking forward to fucking your pretty little pussy tomorrow.

Ella: That makes two of us.

Zander: If ever I'm not with you and you want to enjoy yourself, I give you full permission to do so, understood?

Ella: Understood. Thank you, Z.

Zander: Are you going to sleep?

Ella: Yes. I'm so tired.

Zander: Sleep well and dream of me.

Ella: You too, Z. xoxo

"I mean it. You're being weird again. Moving and not telling us until after."

"It's a girl, isn't it?"

"Tell me it's a girl, fucking please. God, just tell me you're getting laid again," Thomas groans and the guys laugh at my expense.

"I'm not ignoring you guys. Just …" I contemplate my next words. "Just a bit busy with a client and I had to make some last-minute arrangements."

"Is 'client' a code word here for something else?" Ethan questions.

Running my thumb down my jaw, I decide to admit it. "Possibly, yeah."

"Damn."

"Holy shit."

"She has you moving and everything?"

The guys make their comments and I let them, not giving them much information at all. Damon's the only one who's aware of my preferences.

It feels damn good for them to know about her, though.

"I'm just glad it's a chick and you aren't avoiding us again."

"Not avoiding you, and let's aim for every other week?" I offer and after a few comments while Thomas shuffles, we all agree to keep game night going.

I pulled away from everyone the hardest after Quincy died, and that's why the card games were so erratic for a while there. It felt fucked up to think about sitting around the table pretending like I was all right when she was gone. It still feels a bit wrong, if I'm honest. The fact that I get to enjoy this, and she doesn't, it'll always carry a certain weight. But if I've learned anything, it's that withdrawing from your whole damn life is as good as being dead yourself.

That's no way to live. Not for me, and especially not for Ella. She has to have her life back, and not just with me. All of it. Friends at her house. Dinners out as often as I can take her. A life.

It doesn't take long, maybe an hour or so before my stomach growls and I realize I forgot about dinner. "Anybody else want pizza?"

"You didn't order the pizza yet?" Damon shoots me a look. "Order it. Now." He points me out of the room with a stab of his finger, and Alex laughs.

"Somebody got hungry," I say, and throw down my cards.

I go back into the kitchen to order the pizza and end up wandering down the hall while I'm on hold. All the way to Ella's playroom.

There are windows high up on one wall, thin ones to let in a bit of light, but otherwise it's equipped with necessary and custom furniture for play, along with a large antique dresser that I use to store toys in.

I have … a collection. Some of the more severe instruments will stay in the dungeon in the basement. Two locations for two different purposes. I'm hard again imagining Ella spread across the burgundy padded spanking bench.

I chose that design just for her. It looks expensive as hell and having her perched there, with her ass reddened as she pants, is going to be picture fucking perfect.

The St. Andrew's Cross is in the dungeon, although I debated having it in this room. I think it'll serve us better for punishment.

I took my time, making sure it would be perfect so when she enters this room all she'll have to do is enjoy it.

Still on hold, I meander to the dresser and pull open the top drawer. Counting each accessory in the row of vibrators and dildos. All sizes. All intensities. I could spend an entire day using these on her. In fact, when she comes here, I *will* spend an entire day using them on her. It'll take a few days to truly indulge.

Checking on my phone, she's fast asleep. I hope it'll be a deep, easy sleep for her. offering her nothing but comfort.

The other drawers are filled with riding crops, clamps and restraints. I have a separate rack for the longer implements.

Again it strikes me how torn I am with my little bird. She's delicate in a way that holds me back. The first day we agreed, I would have shown her this collection. I would have already toyed with her.

There's so much about her, our situation, about us in general that conflicts me.

Even the idea of bringing her here isn't as easy as it would be with anyone else.

It would have to go through Cade. Until the courts dissolve her ruling, everything would require his approval.

If my brother agrees, then there's a process we'll have to follow. The Firm will have to modify my house to fit the judge's orders, which I've taken into consideration, but cameras would be necessary.

However, the toys could fall into a different category regarding her physical health and access to any items that could be harmful. They would need to be involved to make sure no stone is unturned for every item in the establishment she resides in. It's the same thing we did for Ella's property, only I can't do it myself, because it will have to be in compliance to the last letter. There would be no room for error if we made a change of this magnitude.

Shutting the drawer, I'm not clear on how this particular room would fare in that investigation.

We'd also have to request a full psych evaluation for Ella. Cade will need documentation proving that it is her choice, and that she made it of her own free will. He'll also have to attest that he thinks it would be in her best interest, which might be a hard sell.

It's one thing for me to be with her in her home, which has already been vetted and cleared and is a familiar location for providing care. It will be another thing entirely to move The Firm's base of operations here. Even if it is only for a night here and there.

It's a massive inconvenience, in other words.

"Nico's Pizza," a voice says on the other end of the line. "You there? The connection doesn't seem great."

"I'm here." Clearing my throat, I remind myself that my friends are here, that tonight is a night where I don't have to think of all these things. I can't help myself, though. All I can think about, all night, is Ella and how best to handle her. How best to proceed with the concept of "us."

chapter 21

Ella

"**S**O WOULD YOU SAY YOU'RE HAPPY WITH HOW THINGS HAVE been going?" Kam asks as we stop in front of the large paned windows so I can peek into the boutique shop.

The tissue paper peeking out from the thick, pearly black shopping bag tickles my wrist as I sway to face him.

He nods toward the bag. "Not the shopping. I already know you're happy about the shoes for this weekend's social."

Damon, Kam and, more appropriately, Kelly and Trish said I need to get back on the scene. So long as it goes well, everything else should fall into place. Kam said this weekend is the first piece. If my life is back to what it was, if everyone sees me and there's no sign or evidence that I'm unwell, the judge should be moved to dissolve the initial ruling.

Hopefully. The weekend is step one and I'll be wearing Manolos for the occasion.

"Seriously though, gorgeous." I'm on a mission to pick out a dress that will knock Zander on his ass too. I also bought a small riding crop. It's harmless enough and mostly a gag gift, but I intend to be playful after the party. I'm not exactly sure, but I imagine he'll allow me to amuse myself and then show me what he can do with that riding crop.

My cheeks heat and I nearly trip in my heels. "It been ages," I say, defending myself against Kam's smirk when he catches my arm. "Leave me alone," I answer playfully.

"So … are you happy?"

"Am I happy? I am."

"With everything … are you …" he hesitates but with a deep breath, he presses on as we continue our walk down the storefront. "How are you doing with James's …" He doesn't say death. He doesn't say it, but I hear it.

To anyone else it may seem like we're a well-dressed couple, out for a luncheon or perhaps they can tell we're only friends. To me, this feels like freedom. Although some thoughts and emotions still feel imprisoned.

"More than I have been. It still … it still hurts sometimes."

"Are you nervous about anyone bringing it up?"

"Zander will be there," is all I can answer.

"Right." Kam nods. "He'll take care of you, but I want you to know you're handling it well on your own too."

I wish I had a retort that wasn't sarcastic. As it stands, all I'm thinking is that I can now add "grieves well" to my resume.

"If all goes well, we should be able to request a psych eval."

His statement stops me in my tracks, although the bag hanging from the crook of my arm continues to swing.

A thought hits me that I haven't considered. "The Firm would leave?"

"When you pass the eval, two things will happen. The first is that the judge can order their dismissal entirely."

"What about Damon?"

Kam's brow scrunches, not understanding for a moment. And then my concern registers, his eyes widening when it does.

"I want to continue my sessions. I'm not a fool. I'm doing better because of him."

"We can continue their service even if it's not judge ordered.

"The second thing … we can request a hearing on your conservatorship."

"When would we schedule that?"

"Not until you pass the mental health check and The Firm agrees to their dismissal without complaint."

My heels click on the sidewalk as we near the end of the row, with Tiffany's perched on the corner and the sweet smell of pastries from a Brew & Cap coffee shop we just passed surrounds us.

"One thing at a time."

Nodding, I feel more at ease.

"I'm glad we'll be able to continue with Damon."

"Of course."

"Then he can keep monitoring the weaning."

"Weaning?" This time it's Kam whose pace is troubled.

"From the antidepressants," I clarify.

"I didn't know you were stopping them," Kam states, his voice lowered and obviously bothered by the discovery.

"Damon said some people renew indefinitely as long as there are no side effects since withdrawal can create more … well, it can make things much worse."

"How are you feeling about that?"

"Good," I respond in the same chipper voice although he arches a brow like he doesn't believe me.

Stopping where we are, with the city at our back and couples surrounding us without seeing us at all, I grab ahold of Kam's hands. "It's all going so well. Just let it happen."

"One last thing." Kam's business tone makes an appearance.

"Uh-oh, my PR is mad with me?"

He huffs a laugh, slipping his hands into his black jean pockets, an attempt to appear casual I would think.

"About Zander," he starts and my pulse drops as a chill I hadn't felt yet creeps through my tweed jacket. I pull it tighter.

"What about him?"

"Everyone loves a love story and you two are cute together."

His comment is unexpected and the smile it brings me is genuine.

"Is he on the same page as you?"

"What do you mean?"

"I saw Kelly and Trish's post, Ella." He tilts his head down, his brow raising, like a father scolding his daughter and I laugh.

"Does he know that you're hinting you're together? Does he want that too? This life and … the things that come with it."

Memories are a fickle thing. They creep back to me. I remember James confiding in me one night and then I told him everything. For us, it brought us closer. But he knows how it is.

"If you want to come out at this party, you can. If you don't," he says then sucks in a breath and looks off into the distance to the mountains, past the shining windowpanes of boutiques and designer shops. "Just make sure, whatever you decide, that you're on the same page."

"What if I want him to stay a secret? Or he wants that?" My heart does a painful flip. Just the thought of having this conversation with him makes me feel sick. I don't know what Z will say.

"That would be a first."

"We could say he is, without it being real," I offer, taking another peek inside the coffee shop and tilting my head toward it.

Kam nods, leading the way, although what I've just said seems to concern him.

"He's not really my boyfriend. You know?"

"I know. But no one knows that other than you and Zander, plus The Firm, who are bound by a contract. Because of their … purpose."

His purpose has passed. He stayed because he wanted to. He stayed for me. The need to defend him rises inside of me, but I don't. Instead I swallow it down and settle on something more simple.

"It's just … for me … it's more."

"And for him?" he questions.

"He's been blunt. He's my Dom." I'm surprised how much it pains me to say it. At the same time, I don't think Zander is honest with himself. I think he's holding back. No. I know he is.

"Have you asked him about being more?" I keep my lips firmly in place as I stand at the end of a three-person line, pretending to read off the list of cappuccinos like that's more important. The truth is, I think if I push Zander for more, I could push him away and I don't think I'll be okay if that happens.

Kam presses me, saying, "Maybe you should ask him. You know others will be curious, they'll pry. It's important you're both on the same page."

chapter 22

Zander

THE KEYS JINGLE IN MY HAND, THE CAR ALARM CONFIRMING I've locked it as I make my way to the back door by the kitchen. The pressed jacket feels stiff, but it's tailored and, more importantly, Ella chose it. I allowed her to pick my outfit for this occasion. It's a sharp look and well dressed. With black slacks, a dark brown belt, black collared shirt and the gray-blue jacket I'm wearing in this single look, the cost is equivalent to an entire paycheck.

But I promised her, I would stay on her arm, I would escort her and I would wear whatever she wanted.

It's well past sunset and I'm eager to see what she's chosen for herself. Checking my watch, I know we have some time in case she's still running behind like she texted she was.

The lights are on in her kitchen and I let out a sigh of relief that surprises me. I understand what Damon meant about Ella needing time to be alone, but it's damn good to get back to her, to be present and know I'll be kissing her, touching her in ways that'll make her shiver. It's addictive and simply walking in the back door is like getting a hit of my favorite drug.

Every single time. I don't think I'll ever get tired of this.

The moment I close the back door, Kam enters the kitchen, none too quietly. It's intentional, almost as if he was waiting for me.

"Kamden," I say, greeting him with an easy tone that's just as intentional. He opens his mouth, looking like he wants to question me, but I have one first.

"I've been meaning to ask you—when Ella was younger—you two were close?" Standing at the threshold between the small nook and kitchen, he stills, his eyes narrowing. Taking a few steps in, I meet him halfway. "I know she was good friends with your sister. Is that why you took custody?"

He blinks. "I took custody because she needed someone and our families have been friends forever. It was a great tragedy." His mask slips on easily. Public relations 101. "I wasn't about to let just anyone step in. You never know what will happen when someone gets control over a young woman like Ella was … and her assets."

"Control?" My hackles go up, but I remain poised as he assesses me. Taking a few steps, I stop behind a chair at the table and grip the back of it.

"I mean regarding her assets. Custody is a tricky issue," he tells me, pulling out a seat, but not yet taking it. His gaze reaches mine as he adds, "When you have as much money as Ella does, it's shark-infested waters."

"That's understandable." I've been waiting to ask him this, and it spills out of me before I can stop it. "Do you know if there's any truth to the rumors that there was foul play with her mother's death?"

Kamden shakes his head like this is the most bizarre conversation he's ever been part of, which can't be true. "Not at all."

"There's a number of theories—"

"Why would you look into that?" His voice is slightly raised and he seems to shake it off, laughing slightly although he doesn't look me in the eye. "That doesn't have anything to do with—"

"There were theories. Rumors that caught my attention after what she said the other day."

That statement makes Kamden pause. He swallows thickly before looking back at me, his mask back on and firmly in place. He knows something. He damn well knows he does.

Ella's kitchen is warm, and Kamden lets out a breath. He leans against the counter and looks at me. "People love a scandal. You know what I think?"

"I don't. I would appreciate it if you told me."

He chews the inside of his cheek. "I think it wasn't her mother who killed her father's first wife. I think *he* did it. I think she took the fall, and he had her murdered in prison." Kam's eyes narrow and his voice lowers. "I also think … that I'm glad he's dead."

"Zander." Damon enters the kitchen, mid conversation. "Am I interrupting?"

"No," I say and then swallow, not wanting to involve Damon in this. "We should talk later, though," I tell Kam, my grip white knuckled on the back of the chair. There's a cold sweat on the back of my neck.

Whatever happened, I'm almost certain Kam knows every detail. And a part of me wonders, what does Ella know?

The other night, she was anything but okay remembering her mother. If someone hurt her or coerced her … I don't know what I'll do, but it takes everything in me, in this moment, to calm the rage that simmers inside.

"I wouldn't look too much into it." Kam attempts to reassure me as Damon rounds the corner of the kitchen, opening the fridge and disappearing behind the door.

"Just seemed like there might be something I should know," I say, keeping Kam's gaze as he slips on his jacket.

"We're on the same side when it comes to this. And the part that matters, is that it's over. It's long dead and it should stay that way."

There's a moment between us, but the moment Damon closes the door to the fridge, bottle of water in hand, it's gone.

Kamden addresses Damon first, and then me. "I'm on my way out. Have a good time at the party tonight."

He leaves, and I watch him go.

"You all right, man?" Damon questions. Relaxing my posture and letting out a deep breath, I decide to keep what just happened between Kamden and me. That conversation isn't over.

"Yeah, I'm fine."

"Don't worry about the party. It'll be packed and might be intense for the both of you. But you can always leave." I stare at Damon, unblinking.

"You're my therapist now?" I ask deadpan and instantly the tension in my shoulders lifts.

He laughs, setting the bottle down. "I'm just picking up on the tension is all. You look sharp, she's excited and I think she's ready."

I can't help but to smile at the idea of my little bird being excited. Everything about her is fuller, lighter, happier than she was when I first saw her in the courtroom. Nearly everything. The vulnerability is still there and she's still so very breakable.

Damon adds, "There's no reason to be concerned."

"I'll have a better time when it's over and everything goes well."

The thought of the party doesn't thrill me. There's a delicate balance between us right now and I'm certain she has the upper hand with what to expect with this party. This is necessary, though.

"She told me tonight could set a precedent for the order to be dissolved?"

"That's the plan that Cade and Kamden have agreed on."

"What exactly are they looking for?"

"Returning to normal documented behavior and presenting it to the judge."

"Good." I nod along with the plan. It's ideal. It should be straightforward. And it aligns with what Ella told me, so they're being transparent with her.

"How's she been today?"

"She's been … seeking pleasure." Damon doesn't look at me, and there's a tilt of his head.

I don't understand at first. "In her journaling?"

"No. Not in her journaling." Damon looks me straight in the eye.

Oh, fuck. *That* kind of pleasure. The kind of pleasure I ordered her to have. Just the thought of her enjoying herself makes my cock stir. *That's my good girl.* "Thoughts on that?"

"It's a good sign that she's doing better."

"That makes me happy to hear."

Damon nods in agreement. "You seem lighter," I comment.

"I think tonight is going to go well. We talked about it earlier. Ella is ready and looking forward to it."

Before I can say a word, he adds, "She asked me about drinking tonight."

"Drinking?"

"It's a social event. She said she'll most certainly be around it and be tempted."

"What did you tell her?"

"She's weaning off the antidepressants. She should use her best judgment, but a glass would be all right. Maybe sticking to only one drink would be best."

"Sounds good." It does not sound good. I want to close the kitchen door behind Damon, take her upstairs, and strip her clothes off. I want nothing between us but air. And then I want to figure this out. It would be easier if I could breathe her in. Taste her.

Protect her from any pressures that would move her too quickly, too close to dangerous territory.

"You sure you're good with going to the party by yourself?" There's no hint of judgment in Damon's voice. None at all. "I could go, if you want a second pair of hands."

"Silas will be in the parking lot, won't he?"

Damon nods. "He's already there, waiting. I'm off duty and you are officially her chauffeur."

I huff a laugh at my job description and already feel relieved knowing Silas is in place. "I'll be fine. I doubt things will go too late."

"I'll have my phone if you need anything." Damon slaps me on the shoulder on his way past. "Any time, day or night."

"I know it."

"I'm headed out. Seriously—you'll call if you need anything?"

"I'll call."

"Okay. Have a good time."

With the door shutting behind him, there's a feeling that takes over. A need to go to her, to kiss her, to brush her hair to the side and tell her what a good girl she's been. I call her name into the house, and a soft noise from upstairs answers.

She's in the bathroom in her bedroom, the light slanting into the hallway from the open door. I'm drawn to it, and it seems for a second that she's the light source.

The glow inside the bathroom caresses her hair, which has been gently curled and cascades down over her shoulders. Ella leans in close to the mirror, her hips pressed against the countertop, and an animal urge claws at me from the inside out. I could take her like that. I could brace her hips in my hands so they wouldn't get bruised on the counter and command her to watch how beautiful she looks in the mirror while I fuck her.

With my grip on the threshold, I stay where I am, watching her instead.

The light shines off the silver tube of lipstick in her hand. Red, to go with the black dress hugging her hips and skimming her thighs. High heels lift her legs into a criminally beautiful stretch. Is my heart even beating?

Ella finishes and presses her lips together, then blots at the color with a tissue. I have the oddest feeling that I'm watching something out of the past. A memory come to life, right here in this house. This gorgeous woman, in her former glory.

She looks at me over her slender shoulder and shoots me a sultry look as her gaze roams down my body. As if she's the huntress.

How utterly fucking adorable.

"Hey, Z."

"I'd punish you for not greeting me on your knees, but it'd be a shame to wrinkle that dress." Color rushes to her cheeks and there's a glint of mischievousness in her dark eyes. "You look gorgeous, Ella."

"Are you ready?" I ask her.

"I'm as ready as I'll ever be."

It's quiet as I lead her downstairs, her hand tightly holding mine.

The spark between us is magnetized, the air electric as I help her into the car. She's graceful but most of all, quiet.

"Z," her voice murmurs over the hum of the car before we've even left her house. "Whatever happens tonight, just ... you'll still want me, won't you?"

"Why do you say it like that?"

"People will ask questions."

"People are irrelevant when it comes to our relationship."

"You say that," she says and brushes a stray hair from in front of her face. "But what about when they ask if there's anything between us?"

My pulse races with the way she looks at me. As if saying the wrong answer now will stay with her forever. I'm weak in this moment. Weak for her and the thought of her walking away.

"I'll be there when you answer, and whatever you tell them is what I'll say."

"What if I tell them that we're together. That we're … an item?"

"Like I said, whatever you tell them, I'll agree with."

The host, a socialite in the elite circles Kelly entertains, lives at another ritzy house a twenty-minute drive away. Not quite as expansive as Ella's home, but it's up there.

And it's crawling with guests. Expensive cars are parked along the half-circle drive. Music pours out into the front gardens. Chatter is heard from the house and even those gallivanting in the yard. It's a sight to behold. The sheer luxury and expense of the evening doesn't hide behind a curtain. It creates a spotlight for itself.

We haven't been out of the car thirty seconds when my phone buzzes for the first time.

Damon's name is displayed on the screen. I don't have time to check it this second. I need to be aware of what's going on around us and aware of how Ella's behaving. And at this very second, she's ahead of me, in the chaos of the crowd. The sky is pitch black and with everyone around her blurring, she peeks over her shoulder, eyeing me with a happiness I haven't seen from her. One that lights up everything around her.

The phone buzzes again a second later.

Cade.

"Z," she calls out, turning around but not stopping her stride. As she twirls back around, she reaches out for me to take her hand. Hers slips into mine and my phone slips in my back pocket. Let us at least get settled. There's nothing to report just yet.

"How are you?" I check with her as she squeezes my hand.

"Excited," she confesses with a beautiful smile, her teeth sinking into her bottom lip. "You?"

"I'm happy you're happy."

There's a photo op at the front entrance and Ella poses without me, then pulls me in behind her for a shot. A photographer calls out, "Who's the gentleman?" She ignores the question, choosing to wink at him instead.

"Cheeky girl," I tease when she takes my hand again. She's delighted, mischievous and it's a thrilling sight.

As soon as we've relinquished our coats at the door check, a clutch of women I don't recognize descend on Ella, greeting her with shrieks and hugs and so much touching that I angle myself closer to her to give her some breathing room. Her face is lit up with exhilaration, color in her cheeks and a glint in her eyes.

She glances at me. I put my hand on the small of her back and lean down to speak into her ear. "If this is too much, give the signal." Three fingers directly over her lips, the tip of her middle finger resting on the tip of her nose, means I'll immediately intervene.

"I know," she whispers and takes a step ahead of me. I stay back, letting her readjust to something that I'm sure has been familiar all her life. It's almost as if she's the client once again. I'm here to protect her, to shield her. I'm here to offer her comfort if she needs it.

And judging by the sweet laugh that she utters from her lips, she doesn't need me. Not in this moment.

As she looks up at me from under her lashes, my phone buzzes again.

There are more people than I expected. I try to refocus to keep an eye on all of them in relation to Ella.

Another message. I glance down at my phone and see both Cade and Damon are checking in. There's no emergency, nothing to cause alarm.

I text them back, everything going as planned.

A light touch on my arm draws my attention. It's Ella, her dark eyes searching my face. "Can we go somewhere and talk?" Something's off.

"Of course." My answer is irrelevant. Ella's attention is quickly drawn away.

"Ella!"

Trish pushes her way through the crowd to get to Ella's side and wraps her up in a giddy hug. "People are waiting for you. Come on, let's go."

"Who's here?" Ella asks.

"Old friends, new friends … and everyone worth showing off the new you to."

Trish leads Ella up a flight of stairs and toward the back of the house. I stay a few steps behind but I don't miss how Ella checks on me. Each time she peeks over her shoulder I offer her a calm smile.

"You good?" she mouths at me. As if she's the one who should be worried and not the other way around.

I eye her in a way she should recognize and then tap her ass to keep it moving. Her shy smile and the way she bites her lip are everything. They go out through a set of open double doors. It doesn't make sense that the doors are open—it's too late in the year—until I step out after them.

It's a massive heated porch. On the other side is a long bar.

The partying on this level is far more intense. Trish and Ella join up with a crowd near the bar.

Someone hands her a drink. Someone I don't recognize but Ella obviously does.

"Cheers," the woman yells over the loud din from everyone one else out here, and Ella drinks from her glass. It's only a sip at first, but it doesn't take long for more people and more sips until it's drained along with the rest of them.

"Zander," calls Trish over her shoulder, and I step forward so she can introduce me to their friends. I don't hear any of the names she says while I shake hand after hand, looking into one glazed-over pair of eyes and then another.

They're wasted. Every person here is drinking heavily and as I'm politely shaking hands. Ella accepts another drink. Red flags. This is a sea of red flags.

chapter 23

Ella

THIS PARTY FEELS LIKE A FUNHOUSE AND I'M IN THE MIDDLE, distorted by all the mirrors, too hot and drunk and a mess.

"Like I said, whatever you tell them, I'll agree with."

It didn't quite hit me at first when he said that in the car, or maybe it did and I just played it off. But the more time passes, the more upset I get. A drink down and he's not beside me. He's staying back and it feels like I'm here alone.

There's a heat, a longing, a stirring of anxiousness that's just getting worse and worse.

I want another drink and then another.

He can't even agree that we're an item? I shouldn't have come in here without dealing with it first, but here we are.

He's stayed back and behind me, not by my side. He's there, though, I remind myself. He's here, we're just … I don't know what we are.

With two drinks in, I'm already feeling it, and every passing second he's not by my side, I feel more and more betrayed.

"You good, girl?" Kelly asks, clinging to my side before kissing my cheek.

"Just pissed," I whisper and it takes a second for her to register it, more reading my lips than hearing it over how loud everything else is.

With her brow knitted she asks why, and I nod toward Zander.

All I asked him was what if we were to be called "an item" and he couldn't say that we were. It hurts. I tried to pretend like it didn't, but alcohol has a way of making lies go quiet. I haven't forgotten what Kam said. I haven't forgotten what Damon said.

"Fuck him," Kelly murmurs and then peers across the patio to a hoard of men. Some of them I know, one of them I know-know, and others I don't.

"I don't want them. I want him," I tell her and she nods.

"Maybe a little attention from them and Zander will shape up?" she suggests and I shake my head. "I'm not … no. I don't know." My head is fuzzy.

Minutes pass and more people gather. Only one person mentions James. With everyone talking over each other, it barely registers. I only know it was spoken to me because the group around me goes quiet. I stare back at a tall man, his hair cropped back and his tie loosened around his neck.

"Just, I'm just … I wanted to give my condolences is all."

My heart does that pitter-patter thing. Before I can even answer, Zander's on one side of me, telling me someone named Arthur is looking for me and Kelly's on the other side, a flute of champagne that was in her hand, being pushed into mine.

"Drink up, baby."

It feels like stumbling, as I turn my back on the group, Zander's arm around my waist as he leads me away.

"You all right?" he questions and I throw the flute back, letting the bubbles worm their way down my throat.

My eyes prick and suddenly everything isn't so great and wonderful.

"It fucking hurt," I say to him and breathe out, but not daring to look him in the eye. If I do, I think I'll lose it. The one night of all these nights where I need to simply be and be seen, and this has come over me.

"I know," he says and then I realize he's talking about James. Fuck, it's a knife to the chest. I struggle to respond at all. In a sea of people, I glance around them, feeling the cool breeze against my hot face, and I feel alone. With the exception of this man.

"Do you love me?" I ask him, barely breathing.

His striking eyes hold me for a moment, and I think he'll admit it. He has to feel it, doesn't he? He speaks his words carefully. "Ella, you're drunk."

I've felt my heart break before. I've felt it shatter. It belonged to someone else back then. Someone who would never dare to hurt it. "Don't do this. Not here."

"Right," I answer him in a single breath, attempting to compose myself. Swallowing thickly, I push it all down. All I can hear are my heels clicking on the ground as slow as my heart beats.

With my heart beating faster, I walk with him and accept the bottle of water. "No more drinks," he orders. "Only water."

Fiddling with the cap, I nod in agreement.

Why does it hurt as much as it does? It feels like the rain has poured down around me.

All because he couldn't say we're an item?

No. No it's not that. It takes me minutes to register that I asked him if he loves me.

He knows. He must know, that I love him. Fuck, I am drunk. I'm far more than tipsy.

The conversation plays on repeat. Then the one with Kam insinuating we aren't on the same page. Then the one with Damon, and how my feelings may be displaced.

"We're going to steal her, if that's all right." Kelly's voice rings clear over my head in the dark corner behind the bar that Zander's cornered me into.

"I think it may be time for us to head out."

"You just got here." Kelly's objection reflects both her shock and disappointment.

"I'm not leaving. I'm fine." My voice is clear and my decision firm as I look Zander in the eye.

"So … about stealing her away? I think she should see some people.

Some influential people Kam mentioned?" she tells him. Asking *him* permission and not me.

He doesn't answer her, other than to nod. There's a concerned look in his eyes and he tells me, I'll be right behind you.

"I'm not letting her out of my sight," he warns Kelly who only laughs, a sweet friendly sound before whispering to me that whatever he said he can shove up his ass and that she loves me.

"Should we hide in the bathroom?" she asks me and I shake my head. Half of me wants to leave, while the other half wants to feel it, and let it all go.

"Smile on," she says and like a ghost taking over, I grin entering the room and hollowing out to let the former me show. That's what this night is about. This is for me, not him.

As the clock ticks by, and hour passes easily, I laugh when everyone else does. I smile for the cameras. I accept hug after hug and give comments to the gossip columnists when they ask for one that would make Kam proud. I've been through hell and back. If Zander thinks his commitment problems are enough to break me, he's the one who's got a new thing coming.

I'm fine. I'm better than fucking fine.

He's barely approached me, watching from a few feet away as if he's merely security. He must know he fucked up. He called in backup. I spotted Silas across the room and nearly rolled my eyes. It's yet another betrayal. It fucking hurts. It feels like a breakup. Like I did the one thing I knew I would do. I pushed him and he refused to move with me.

I have issues, yes. But so does he. And it's not my responsibility to take his problems on. That's what I tell myself anyway, as I'm looking at my ex from another life.

That … and to do what Kelly suggested, to show Zander why he needs to commit.

John, a handsome lover from years ago, circles the edge of the crowd, his face disappearing and reappearing as people talk into my ear and ask me the same stream of questions over and over. *How are you? Are you set-tled at the lodge? We missed you.*

I just wish it didn't hurt so much to be here hearing how much they missed me and being reminded over and over that I was gone. Being re-minded of what happened.

Suddenly, the music feels like an assault, and the crush of their bodies close to mine, and the heat of all that skin so close by. The autumn night can't compete with the number of people here and it's too much. It was easy to be irritated at Zander before, when he kept pointing out that we could leave any time, when he insisted on going over our signals again and again, and now it turns out he's right.

I hate that. It feels like a rock at the pit of my gut to be wrong about this. But if I'm being honest, it's not the party that feels like such a raw, open wound. It's him. I had him in my bed, where I thought he belonged, and he didn't choose me.

Tears prick at the corners of my eyes but I blink them away before they can fall.

"You need another drink." Trish's face swings in close, her eyes bright.

"Hell yes I do." Zander's order be damned.

She throws her arms over her head and cheers, and I echo it. My voice is too weak to do it justice but it doesn't matter. The music is loud enough to cover it up. The music is loud enough to cover everything up, except Zander.

I can feel him watching me. His eyes on my skin are a palpable burn, even when I can't see him through the crowd. I know he can see me.

I don't look at him at all. It's one of the more difficult challenges of my lifetime, keeping my eyes away from his. Screw him. I don't want to look back at him and see all that emotion in his eyes. It's bullshit. It's not for me.

Trish comes back with two shots and we knock them back together. Oh, it's a bad idea. She pulls me into the circle of friends and into an ar-gument about which shots are better, and who would rather have a full mixed drink, and who's really a wine girl.

"Wine," I hear myself say. "I know I just took a shot, so it doesn't make any sense. I love wine at the end of the day."

Trish agrees with me, and it becomes reality—I'm still a woman who loves a glass of wine at the end of the day. It's a lie. It's not true. There's no wine in my house, and even if there was, drinking too much of it makes my throat hurt. I love the idea of having wine at the end of the day but I don't love the reality. Which thing is more real?

I love the idea of being with Zander but not the reality of him rejecting me. Of him choosing to guard his heart over protecting mine, or his past over me, or whatever he's choosing.

Maybe he loved Quincy so much, he'll never love again.

Maybe I should be like that. Maybe James should be my one and only love.

"Another shot!" Kelly calls out and I don't hesitate to down it.

I thought Zander would choose me. I thought he wanted me. I've been over his lap, I've had his hands everywhere on my body, I want it now.

I want it now.

I want all of it. The conversation floats around me and none of it sinks in. I'm pushing past comfort for my voice, so I stop answering questions and put on a big, fake smile.

No one notices.

Not a single person notices that I'm broken, and that I'm desperately sick of being broken. I'm so tired. It's a tiredness that sinks into my bones and weighs me down to the floor. I'm so damn heavy with it.

"Hey, sweetheart."

John. My ex. He's not like Zander, not dark and handsome. He's blond and beautiful and an all-American kind of guy who could be in a men's magazine. I tip my face up to look at his. "Hi."

We broke up a lifetime ago, right after college. Two different people going two different directions, we said. It took me by surprise, though. I'm always the one who's surprised. I never see it coming. But who cares about all that? He's standing in front of me right now, and Zander's not. Zander didn't want to be in that place.

"It's been a while since I've seen you out. How are you?"

"Better now that you're here to talk to." I touch his wrist, a little flirtatious touch, just so Zander will see. "Some of these conversations." I roll my eyes.

"I know." John shakes his head.

This is how we were. Other people had conversations, and we were better. Up until the day John decided he was better than me. Times are different now. I'm the one with all the mystery. I could cry from how ironic it is. The worst things in your life end up making people more curious about you. I had money before, but now I have whispers and rumors and the ability to turn heads just from walking into a room.

"You look like you could use a drink."

"I do need one."

Another lie. Lies on top of lies on top of lies. When is Zander going to step in? When is he finally going to choose me? I know I'm pissing him off every time I put a glass to my lips. I know it, and he's not doing anything at all about it. I edge closer to John and let him take me to the bar for another shot. I let him lift it to my mouth for me and put my arm around his waist when he tips it up so I can drink.

Choose me.

Just choose me.

He doesn't.

John starts talking to me about his job, about all the bullshit conversations that go on there, and I make up a story. I make up a story where I'm not under care in my own home, and I'm not struggling every day to keep my head above water, and I'm not suffering through this party with a broken heart because Zander didn't want to be with me the way I want to be with him.

Zander doesn't enter into it at all. I never mention his name. I don't say that he's the man who's been watching me this entire time. I don't say that it's foolish of me to want him the way that I do, because it's not allowed. Because he's always been forbidden. I don't say any of it.

I bottle it up and touch John's arm and his waist and I throw my head back and laugh at his stupid jokes even though it hurts my throat to do it. I take another shot even though I'm already too drunk, already past the point where I should have stopped and gone home.

A dark-haired woman who looks put together and not very drunk at all steps between John and me, getting his attention. She has perfect red lips and a dress that's cut low in the back. She looks hot, and I'm a mess. I'm a mess who wants Zander and wants her life back and maybe I'll never get it. Maybe I'll only have Zander in my bed and I'll never get to have him and I'll always be this person who wants what she can't have. Who wants it so badly she breaks her heart every day of her life thinking about it.

"Sorry about that," John says. "You all right?" he asks with humor in his tone and a short laugh. He cups my chin, and his touch is warm.

"I'm fine," I whisper and then clear my throat.

"You look sad that I left you."

I lie. "I was."

His shoulders rise with a pride and wanting I've seen from him before. He leans in close to whisper in my ear. "I guess I shouldn't leave you alone again then."

Alone.

Zander's so far away that he left me alone.

My heart tinks.

"I need some fresh air." The air in this covered patio isn't enough for me. It's too warm and too full of other people. On one end of the bar there's space. The gap between the bar and the railing is so narrow here that the bartenders can't fit on this side. Oh—one of those L-shaped bars. I see it now.

"Remember how we used to let it all go?" I ask him, eyeing the edge of the railing.

John grins and asks, "You want to?"

I only nod, feeling my heart race.

It was a different time and for different reasons. But right now, it's all I want to do. Let it all go.

John helps me hoist myself up on the other side, abandoning the shot glass I've been holding, and stand up.

I'm so hot, and I can't be hot anymore.

"You ready?" he asks at the same time that I hear Zander shout out. As I close my eyes, he's there, staring from so far away.

All it takes is two steps.

One step to the edge of the bar. The next step to the railing.

Two steps. One jump, and I'm sailing through the air, off the side of the railing, going down fast.

chapter 24

Zander

"**E**LLA!"

She disappears.

Drops out of view.

One second she's there, the next she's gone, and I lose my mind. I don't know who it is that I shove out of the way. One guest, maybe two, and then the bartender.

"The fuck are you?" some prick questions as I fist his shirt and shove him back. He's the one who helped her up, some asshole she decided to punish me with.

No one's screaming around me. The air isn't filled with terror. They're cheering. Pure delight electrifies the air.

My heart is in my throat, caught there along with my voice.

I can already see the blood when I reach the bar and hurtle around. My legs slam into the railing on the side of the balcony. My hips connect. I lean out over the drop—I have to see if she's still alive, and …

It's a pool.

There's a pool down below. Ella floats in the middle of the pool, kicking her feet and pushing her soaked hair back from her face.

My beating terror screams itself into anger.

"It's a fucking pool, man." The asshole who helped her up dares to fucking speak to me.

Gripping his collar with both of my hands, I look the son of a bitch in the eye and warn him, "If you ever touch her again, it'll be the last thing you do."

What the hell was she thinking? My hands shake as I storm my way down, ignoring the gasps and onlookers.

I was already counting the ways I'd redden her ass. I was already cursing myself for taking it too easy on her. For not being more forceful. I'd let her push and throw her tantrum. I'd let her get it out of her system and when we got back home … I'd show her who she belonged to.

If she wants me to say it, I'll fucking say it. I want her, I need her. I have love for her that I don't anyone else. I can't lose her. Yes. I'll tell her I love her.

My blood rushes in my ears. My hands fisted and every muscle in my body is coiled.

I let her get away with too much all because I was waiting on Damon or Cade to get their asses here. Why the fuck did I listen to Silas and wait for The Firm?

She's mine. She misbehaved. I'll be damned if I let this situation get in the way again.

Taking the stairs as fast as my feet will carry me, not a single thought in my mind is spared for anyone else at this hellish party. Not one. All I care about is getting to Ella. I need to secure her safety, I need to get her out of here, and I need to punish her for what she's done. I need to make her understand what she's done to me.

It's cold out by the pool, with heat from the water rising into the air.

And I'm not the first one to arrive.

I don't know how the hell that fucker got here, but there he is, helping her climb out of the pool and laughing. Peering up at the house, I see an iron spiral staircase down just on the other side where the bar was.

The two of them laugh like this is funny, like my heart hasn't been ripped out of my chest and beaten. They're a pretty match like that. A young couple, in each other's arms, pretending that life is a joke. One of them hasn't been wounded. One of them doesn't feel like a madman.

None of it matters. I can't stop. I get there just as he's leading her away from the pool and take her by the shoulders.

"Fuck off," I spit out. "I told you to stay the fuck away from her."

"Hey man," he says and reaches for Ella who doesn't spare him a glance.

"I thought you didn't want me," she says. As if I've ever not wanted her.

His eyes go wide, darting between us. "Have you fucked him, El?"

I'm dimly aware of cameras around us. Cameras and phones. Recording. We need to get the hell out of here. "It's not like that," Ella says. Her voice is soft at the margins. She's been drinking.

I lean in, looking him dead in the eye. "She's mine."

"Z," she says and her voice is broken. I know I didn't say the things she wanted. But I'll be damned if I don't fight for her to give me a chance to make it right.

She's fucked up. I'm fucked up, but together we work.

"We're leaving." I see the opening in the crowd and move us toward it with Ella tucked tight into my side, my arm across her shoulders.

Her pace barely keeps up with me. If I didn't think someone would call the cops, I'd throw her ass over my shoulder.

"Zander," she says, her voice barely audible over the noise from all these people talking, talking, talking. They make so much noise. "Zander, stop."

"Not a chance in hell."

It takes forever to get us through the house. The crowd seems to have multiplied and all of them want to be in our way. In my way. Ella's not helping. Every time she turns her head, she sees someone else she wants to talk to and tell them it's fine. I can't find the words to make her under-stand the situation we're in. She jumped off a second-floor bar and into a pool below.

She could have died.

She could have *died*.

Cade and Damon both said the same thing. Don't make a scene. They said they'd be there after she took the first shot. A fucking half an hour and a goddamn heart attack later and they still aren't here.

"Zander," she protests as I pull her along, her long legs and heels not keeping up with my strides. I swear I'm two seconds from throwing her over my shoulder. I can barely contain myself.

I can feel myself falling into that old spiral. It's the same thing that happened after Quincy died. I questioned every action I ever took, trying to figure out which one would have kept her alive.

I can't do this again. I cannot fall into that shit again. It almost destroyed me the first time.

"We need our coats," Ella says as we make it to the front entrance. "Coats!" she yells out and everyone around us takes notice. "You're acting like a maniac," she scolds me under her breath.

Soaking fucking wet, dripping from head to toe, somehow still gorgeous, she dares to tell me that I'm the one acting like a maniac?

My exhale is long and audible as I stare down at her. "We need our coats," she repeats clearly and I swear I'll lose my mind if I don't get her out of here and across my lap in the next five seconds.

There are dozens of coats here now. Maybe over a hundred. I park Ella at the door of the coat closet and dig through them.

"We don't have to leave," Ella says from behind me, her arms crossed, onlookers watching her calmly berate me. *I swear to God.*

Cade and Damon's directions about not making a scene are fucking hysterical by now.

My coat appears and I toss it in Ella's direction. It's another fifteen coats before I find hers. Step over to her. Put it around her shoulders. I take my own coat by the collar, and take Ella by the arm.

"Z," she says and the single letter is a plea on her lips.

"I'll deal with you when I get you alone." I'm too loud and too obvious, and from somewhere nearby I hear the click of a shutter. I don't care. Anyone who takes a photo right now is taking a photo of a bodyguard doing his job.

"Zander, please calm down," she insists, her voice getting rougher. It's been too much. This night out has been too much for her. At least the last round of shots were water, courtesy of the hefty tip I paid the bartender, but still. I should have put a stop to it earlier. The second she asked me if I loved her, the words slurred on her lips, we should have been out the door.

The only thing that kept me here was the fact that she needed this. She needed everyone to see her. It was going so perfectly. Fucking hell.

I guide Ella out the front door and down the steps. Maybe it will look like a jealous man taking a woman out of a party before she's ready.

I'm not jealous. I'm beside myself.

Ella doesn't say a word on the way to the car. The cold is setting in. She shivers under my arm, wrapped in her coat. Her teeth click together as we reach the car. I bundle her into the passenger side and run around to mine and throw myself in. Start the car. Turn the heat all the way up.

The tires screech as I back out of the parking spot. I don't bother to call or text a soul seeing as Silas is standing right there at the exit, watching us leave.

The radio plays along as I accelerate into the road and get us out of the neighborhood, thankfully, Ella reaches over and turns it off. I usually took city streets between the motel and Ella's, but tonight I take the first available turn onto the highway that skirts the edge of town. Stars shine above the mountain in clear skies. *What was she thinking, jumping off that bar? What the hell did she intend to do to me?*

Ella huddles in the passenger seat, her teeth clicking together with her shivers. Her arms lock tight around her stomach. "I'm so cold."

I try to turn up the heat some more, but it's already at full blast. "That's probably from jumping off of a balcony into the pool when it's freezing outside."

I don't take my eyes off the road for even a moment and focus on not losing it. It doesn't matter. I can still feel her watching me.

"Are you mad at me?" she whispers as the night whips by us.

Mad does not begin to describe what I feel right now. It's such an intense storm of emotions that I hesitate to open my mouth. There are no words to describe it. Mad doesn't encompass the terror and the relief and yes, the anger.

It doesn't describe the need.

Because right now I am in a state of need. I need her to understand. I need an outlet for all these things I feel. I need to be in control.

I don't answer, and Ella doesn't ask again. She stares through the windshield as we sail through the night, headlights from the oncoming traffic gliding across her face at uneven intervals.

We pass the exit we'd have to take to go to her house.

I feel Ella notice it. Her wet clothes shift against the seat. But she doesn't ask the question. On some level, she already knows where we're going.

The exit that leads to the motel looms out of the night, and I give all my attention to driving carefully. To steering us off the highway and going the speed limit and not fucking up another thing tonight.

We're here. The mom-and-pop motel is a strip of rooms on a quiet road off the highway. It was closer than my house, closer than hers. And we'll have privacy.

Lights burn on the outside of each door, keeping the night at bay. I think it's meant to be welcoming, but right now it's more than welcoming. It looks like safety. There's no one outside the rooms.

I park, and leave her where she is.

"Stay while I get a room," I order and she nods. For a moment, a tic in my jaw spasms until she answers, "Yes."

Once I have the key, I open my trunk to take out a spare bag that stays there. Most of it is useless, but there's a dry undershirt and pair of boxers that will do. Grabbing them, I go around to her door. Wordlessly, I open it and offer her my hand.

Ella hesitates.

Then she puts her hand in mine.

That hesitation does something to me. I know she's delicate. But I also know had I been stricter, this shit wouldn't have happened. She wouldn't be questioning a damn thing between us.

I hustle us to the door, take the key out, and let us in.

The room seems too small to contain me in this moment, but there's more than myself to focus on. "Get out of those wet clothes."

Ella stands by the door, still and silent, and I unbuckle my belt. As I pull it apart, ready to slide it through the belt loops, I see she hasn't moved an inch.

"Little bird."

Her eyes snap to mine.

"Get out of those clothes."

I don't know if it's because she's responding to me or because it's cold that Ella's fingers go to work on the buttons of her coat. She strips it off and tosses it across the table, then goes for the hem of her dress. Anger surges through me again. She could have died, and then I would have been there with her broken body and my broken soul. She could have died and left me to live through the aftermath.

Ella has her dress over her head, her bare breasts perky, her nipples pebbled. She's not entirely steady. Probably still drunk, and how the hell did I let that happen? I told her there would be punishment for drinking. She knew that going in. And she did it on purpose.

Which could mean—

I don't know what anything means anymore.

The rest of her clothes come off, and Ella stands naked by the door of my room. I stalk across the too-small space and grab a clean towel out of the bathroom, then return to her. "Dry yourself off."

She follows orders with a sullen set to her chin. Ella's got a lot of nerve to be pissed at me in this moment. Like it's my fault that she threw herself into a pool on a cold night. Like it's my fault she threw herself at her ex-boyfriend.

Ella hands me the towel with that same tension in her chin.

Handing out the spare shirt and boxers, I tell her, "Put these on."

When she's pulling the clothes on, I sling her coat over the radiator.

I turn back to find her looking at me, her eyes huge and questioning and pissed. "What am I here for, Z?"

"You know why we're here."

"Why don't you just drop me off at home and leave me?"

"Leave you?" The incredulity is palpable.

"You don't want me. I know you don't."

With a deep, steadying breath, I dare her to call me a liar. "I want you more than I want anything, Eleanor."

My words bring her lips to part and a shuddering breath leaves her. I close the space between us, splaying my hand against her back. "The fact that you question that at all tells me I failed you. But my little bird, you are here because it's time for a punishment that I don't want anyone to see. I intend to fuck you into the early morning, and it's only for us. Everyone else needs to get the fuck out of what we are until you know damn well that you're mine."

Her breathing picks up, her chest rising and falling chaotically and her beautiful gaze caught in mine. My heart beats wildly, knowing that look and that need. Knowing this is exactly where we're supposed to be.

"Z," she whispers.

"You need someone to fuck the wild out of you," I growl, and it's wrong. I know it the second I say it. Ella's eyes fly open, her lips part, and the shock on her face tells me I've screwed this up. I've stumbled over a hidden pain I didn't know existed.

As she pushes me away, my phone goes off.

I ignore it. "You okay?" I question her as she crosses her arms and moves toward the bathroom, everything changed. Something's wrong.

She nods, but doesn't speak it.

"Ella," I start and my phone goes off again. Again I ignore it.

"Ella, look at me," I command her and she does as she's told, her wide eyes staring back at me. "Are you all right?" I question, already knowing she's not.

My phone rings in my pocket and I reach for it without thinking. "What?" I snap into the phone.

"We have a problem," Damon says. "There are photos of you and Ella at the party and—"

"I need tonight, Damon," I cut him off.

I turn my body away from her, as if that will give me any privacy. As if it will stop her from hearing this conversation. "We need a moment. We can talk—"

"Photos of you two. At the party. They're on social media. There's a story already posted. Several outlets are picking it up. She's not nobody, Zander. What happened? You need to tell me what happened so I can figure it out." Damon's worry amplifies a different concern, one I wish had waited.

Wood knocks against wood, and I whirl around to find the space by the door empty, the door banging against the frame.

Fuck! I run out of the room, dropping my phone and race to the end of the hall. I could have gone left or right, I chose left and I chose wrong. With no one there I race to the other side and find that empty too.

"Ella!" I cry out, desperate for her to come back. *Fuck. Fuck.* "Ella!"

Ella

"I'm going to fuck the wild out of you, El." James's whispered words echo in my mind. Tears stream down my face and I can't stop them. Huddled into a ball in the corner of some utility closet, I don't really know, it's so dark, I'm rocking back and forth. All I can do is cry, grieving for a man who loved me truly and deeply.

My hands tremble, my body's shaking. With my hair stuck to the side of my face, I let the cold seep in. Needing to feel anything at all. I've gone numb. Numb all over.

I feel it happening again, this darkness that takes over as I gasp in air and wish it would all stop. I'm slipping backward faster than I ever could have imagined.

In the distance I hear Zander calling my name. Once, twice, then it fades. At least it gave me a moment to breathe.

I don't want to be this way.

It was a moment. Only a moment.

There's only one truth that I know as I sit here in the cold dark. I'm not okay.

The National Suicide Prevention Lifeline is a United States-based
suicide prevention network of over 160 crisis centers that provides
24/7 service via a toll-free hotline at the number 1-800-273-8255. It is
available to anyone in suicidal crisis or emotional distress.

love
me

From *USA Today* best-selling authors W Winters and Amelia Wilde comes a sinful romance with a touch of dark and angst that will keep you gripping the edge of your seat … and begging for more.

He was mine. My protector, my lover.
My second start at life.
The man who promised me there was more than this.
He gave me hope.
Until my world fell apart again.
It was bound to happen. It's all life has given me.

Maybe he won't break his promises.
Maybe my heart won't shatter.
All I want … is for love to be enough.

This is book 3 of the Love the Way You series. *Kiss Me* (book 1) and *Hold Me* (book 2) must be read first.

playlist

Airplanes - B.o.B. featuring Hayley Williams

Ho Hey - The Lumineers

I Wanna Be Your Slave - Måneskin

Nothing More - Here's to the Heartache

Riptide - Vance Joy

AJR - Bang!

Pumped Up Kicks - Foster The People

I Love It - Icona Pop featuring Charli XCX

What Ifs - Kane Brown featuring Lauren Alaina

Somethin' Bad - Miranda Lambert and Carrie Underwood

prologue

Ella

Four years ago, before tragedy struck

"You know I care for you, don't you?" he questions and there's a hint of something I can't place. Something in his tone he's never given me before. We've been on again and off again for years now. Something tonight is different.

"Of course I do." During all that's happened, he's always cared for me. God knows I've been to hell and back with a bottle of tequila, and he's been there all through the night and in the morning. He's cared in other ways too. Ones that give me this insecure feeling I can't shake. The wind blusters in, shifting the curtains and the moonlight stirs in the expansive room. There were boundaries before tonight, boundaries that seem to disappear when he looks at me like that.

James is the only lover I've ever had who's kept my secrets … he's the only one I've told the darkest ones to.

"Then why won't you talk to me?" he asks.

As a chill sweeps along my shoulders, I pull the covers up higher, settling deeper into the bed.

"I think I love you," I tell him, although I'm reluctant to admit it. I roll onto my side as I do, pulling the satin sheets with me and ignoring the groan of the bed. I'm still sore between my thighs and I have to hold back a sated moan of content. The fan revolves in the silence and I turn from looking at the shadows it casts on the ceiling to stare at the man who's making me remember too much, making me feel too much.

James … my on-again, off-again lover I can't resist.

His lips quirk up into a cocky smirk as he props himself up on one elbow and then moves a hand beside me, so that he towers slightly over me. Still silent, not giving an inch and only finding amusement in my statement.

A humorless laugh leaves me, and I press against his chest but he doesn't move. He continues staring down at me, watching and waiting. For what? I don't know.

"Leave me be, you sex fiend," I tease. "Sleep is tempting me and I'd like to take it up on its offer if I can." He knows how hard it is for me to sleep. Insomnia is something that bonded us. Oddly, with him in my bed, I sleep so much better. Rolling onto my side I pretend to ignore him and he lies down beside me, then nips the lobe of my ear, making me squeal. I can't help that the slight pain sends a ripple of want through me, reviving the pleasure I felt only moments ago.

"You think you love me?" he questions with a hint of awe in his tone and I'm forced to look at him over my shoulder.

It's hard to tell if he's toying with me. If he's playing around like we do with each other or if he's being serious.

"I have feelings for you," I whisper back, unwilling to be open and vulnerable until he is first. For some reason, when I look at him, refusing to give him what he wants, my chest aches. There's a tenderness for him I haven't felt before.

"Tell me you love me," he commands and my bottom lip drops, my body already wanting to give him anything he demands. It's dangerous, though. Especially for a girl like me. Kamden's warning is there on the tip of my tongue. Money is a drug that people will do anything and everything to obtain, and it can leave you with nothing. Love doesn't change that and my name alone is worth enough money that no one outside of my inner circle can ever be fully trusted. But Kamden knows James, and he knows what James knows.

That chill comes back again.

James's eyebrow cocks humorously. If he knew the thoughts racing in my mind, he wouldn't think it was so funny.

My expression slips before I can stop it and he moves to hover over me. "What's wrong?"

Pushing away from him, I wish he would stop. I wish it would all stop. "I don't want this life anymore. I don't—"

"El, I can give you whatever you want."

"Promises, promises," I whisper with my eyes closed, not wanting to think.

"I can promise you the world," he says with such sincerity my throat closes.

They're the same promises my father gave my mother. The assurances that fool women into trusting men and leaning on them, into loving with everything they have. It's all too much.

"I don't need you to promise me the world, James," I tell him as if he needs reminding.

I smirk at him, and the spaghetti strap of my black silk cami falls down my shoulder. James's gaze follows it and there's a hunger there, a lust … but when he looks back up at me, it shifts.

My heartbeat pauses, frozen where it is. As if it too wants to know if that's love in his gorgeous eyes.

"You don't need promises," he scoffs at me before kissing the tender spot on my neck. Whispering at the shell of my ear he says, "You love it when I fuck you like I did tonight, though, don't you?"

I can only hum in response, my body instantly responding to his as his warmth covers me. "You know why I love fucking you like I do?"

"Hmm?" is my only answer to him, as if I don't care, as if it's not a thought that keeps me up at night. He doesn't answer until my eyes are on him.

"I love that I tame you."

They say he fucks the wild out of me. He has me on a leash. I don't know how or why, but he does.

"You're saying love an awful lot tonight," I murmur.

"Is that really why you're acting differently? Because you love me?"

"Because I'm scared to love you." Before he can respond I add, "To love anyone."

"You can love me, Ella. I promise," he tells me. "I'll protect you, provide for you."

My gaze drops to the moonlight spilling across the bedroom floor. I can't look at him as the memories flash through my mind.

Promises, promises. Men give them out like candy. James whispers promises just like my father did to my mother.

Those promises he gave her that she fell for.

The promises he told before he killed her. And before I killed him.

chapter 1

Present time

Tᴀᴇ ᴍɪxᴛᴜʀᴇ ᴏғ ᴀɴɢᴇʀ ᴀɴᴅ ғᴇᴀʀ ᴀʀᴇ sᴏ ɪɴᴛᴇɴsᴇ ᴛʜᴀᴛ I could never calm myself. It's impossible to feel anything other than rage as my hands tremble. My feelings won't make any difference in the end, though. I'm going to do what I need to for Ella even if my heart is pounding so hard it threatens to leave my chest.

It hasn't stopped since I left the motel. This unwanted concoction of emotions threatens to consume me.

All I need to do is gain control over this situation. And that means getting to Ella. The sound of my footsteps echoing on the staircase is foreboding as I climb up to the next floor. My ears burn knowing everyone else knew where she was before me. The fact she called Kam over me is something I'll have to deal with later.

Speak of the fucking devil.

As I round the corner to the hall, Kam stands outside the door to her bedroom, his arms crossed over his chest. His irritation darkens his eyes and furrows his brow. The closer I get, the more palpable his anger is.

I'm thankful now for all the years on the job. Difficult clients and high-stress situations. High-risk scenarios. Nothing has ever felt like this before, though. Like I'm on the cusp of losing her. Losing everything. All my experience with The Firm means nothing if I don't have Ella. Kam can be pissed all he wants; he can't make me feel any worse than I do right now.

Kam draws himself up to his full height as I stop in front of him, the wooden floor creaking slightly. "You have no idea how badly you fucked up, do you?"

He squares up with me like he wants to fight and as much as I'd love to oblige, my feelings on the matter are irrelevant. Still, I sure as hell don't want to get into a discussion of whether or not I fucked up, let alone how it all happened. I want to get to Ella. I *need* to get to her. I will make damn sure she never runs from me again.

If Kam weren't her conservator, I'd ignore him entirely. As it is, she called him. I can't ignore that.

"Is she okay?" I ask in as level a tone I can manage, bypassing Kam's question to discuss the only topic that matters.

Kam lets out a breath. He's obviously pissed, but wary as well. His expression slips, revealing he's more scared than anything. Fuck. I didn't think I could sink any lower, that I could feel fear any more than I did the entire drive here.

"Is she all right?" I demand.

"Right now? She'll be okay," he admits finally. "I ran her a bath. When she's finished in there, she needs to get some sleep."

I can breathe again with a hint of relief. But only a hint. He continues, "Damon checked her out, and there's nothing wrong, but she needs rest. I was just stepping out to get her some water. She's … not sober. I'll stay with her tonight."

"I'll be staying with her tonight."

"Zander, no. I—"

With my shoulder to him, I go around Kamden toward her bedroom. It's a good five feet away and I eat up the distance with him trailing behind me.

I half expect Kam to argue with me. He could try to drag me away from Ella's room, and I wouldn't put it past him. If I were in his shoes, I'd be doing the same. Both of us are trying to beat the other one to be the first to the door.

It doesn't really matter who's first. I'm going to go in. *She's mine.* This problem is mine to fix.

As we take the final steps to reach Ella, the fear comes back. I'll never be able to get those images of her out of my mind. The way she seemed to get more and more distant as the night went on. The panic I felt when she fell from that ledge. Leaving me in the middle of the night in a strange motel.

Something I did triggered her and led to her spiral. I saw it happening and I hung back thinking I could catch her at any moment. I failed her.

A cold sweat lingers on the back of my neck as I grip the glass doorknob.

I'm genuinely afraid to lose her, yet we've been reckless. I regret that. I should have been more careful with her. I also should have made a few things much clearer. I'll be rectifying that immediately.

That's the danger of falling in love. You break rules. Find excuses to justify your actions. She has clouded my judgment from the first moment I saw her. I knew better from the very beginning with Ella, but I couldn't stop myself. I felt too much for her.

In my own weakness, I risked losing her because I didn't have the strength to tear myself away. Now it's too late for that, even if Kam made a real attempt to stop me. There is nothing that will keep me from her ever again.

Kam grabs my shoulder and turns me to face him. His expression is dead serious, the anger in his pale blue eyes cold and menacing.

"Listen," he says in a low voice, nearly a hiss, his hand still gripping my shoulder. "If you don't take control of this situation, then I will." His eyes search mine, his lips pressed in a grim line.

This isn't like him, but Kam's been pushed to the limit tonight. I see my own fear reflected in his eyes. He grits his teeth and continues. "Nothing that happened tonight can ever happen again. If you fail her, I'll destroy you."

The strength of conviction in his tone only makes me like the man more.

I can respect the protectiveness Kam feels right now, even if I think it should be solely my responsibility to care for her.

He could never take me from her, though. Not unless he killed me.

My first priority is Ella. It will be for as long as I'm alive. "Understood," I tell Kam. My tone isn't as even as I wanted. The tension in the air thickens. My muscles are ready for violence. It would at least take the edge off if we came to blows. Muffled sounds of Ella moving around inside her bedroom can be heard. She must be finished with her bath.

If we're going to fight, it'll have to be later. Kam seems to realize that at the same time I do. "Good."

He releases me and I release the knob, opting to knock on the door first. "Ella?"

There's no answer from the other side. I do a set of four-count breaths to calm the fuck down and focus, followed by another one. Then I open the door.

My heart races again the moment I cross the threshold. All of the terror that had been dampened from going toe to toe with Kam comes back full force.

Ella's sadness hangs in the air inside her bedroom. The space is clean, containing muted tones and decorated with expensive furniture. The mood isn't a neat and tidy one, though. It's heavy. Pervasive. Almost as if it's hard to breathe.

Ella leans against her dresser; the mirror is still one made of polished metal rather than glass. It's a reminder of what happened to her before.

With damp hair clinging to her back, she turns her head to look over her shoulder at me. Those beautiful chestnut eyes reach mine and there's longing there but something else too.

The sight of her makes my breath hitch. Wrapped only in a towel, her face is flushed from crying. Her cheeks are tearstained and her eyes rimmed in red. She's the epitome of sadness, and appearing so small in the expansive room, it only emphasizes how alone she must feel. Ella's home is beautiful, but it doesn't change the heartbreak in the woman standing in front of me.

Relief hits me harder, shocking my heart. There she is. She's alive, her heart still beating. She's still my Ella.

"Go away, Z." Her voice shakes as she tells me to leave. The sorrow shifts to something else as I close the door behind me. It shuts with a foreboding click.

I take a step toward her. And then another. All the while she stares at me, not daring to command me to do a damn thing.

With every step, a piece of me returns that she desperately needs. It's for her. Every fucking thing I do is for her.

Ella clutches the towel tighter to her chest. I take another step, reaching out a hand until my fingertips meet her skin.

Her strength begins to crumple at my touch. Ella's shoulders curve toward me, and I fold her into my arms. This is all I wanted when Kam was blocking my way in the hall. Ella in my arms where she belongs.

Cold droplets from her hair soak through my shirt, but her warm body molds to mine. She leans into me, letting me hold her. I can't help but kiss her temple, telling her in as soothing of a voice as I can, "That's better."

"Z, what are you doing here?" she questions, her face still pressed to my chest.

"Did you think I wasn't going to come?"

She pulls away slightly, enough to look up at me and whispers, "It might be better if you go."

"Who am I to you?" My voice is harder now, and it's exactly what she needs.

Ella's breathing grows ragged as her eyes shine with new tears. I knew she'd be afraid. I knew she'd question whether I was going to come for her. It's what caused her to melt down at the party. Her uncertainty is something I have to be patient with. Something I need to tame.

"Who am I to you?" I ask again.

Ella's expression falls. "You should go—"

"Ella, answer me. Who am I to you?"

I emphasize each word, leaning closer. The heat between us is intense enough to burn my skin. She takes a rough breath but doesn't answer.

Ella's shoulders tremble. It's a sign her walls are coming down. It's what I'm waiting for. I'm not going to back off until she's okay.

Sadness, hurt and guilt coat the back of my throat. I did wrong by Ella. I should have stopped her or stopped myself. I should never have let us reach the point where she felt like this.

I know now. And I will fix this. If it's the last fucking thing I ever do, I will fix this.

She meets my eyes, and Ella's softening now. Giving in.

"Z," she says softly. Her heart is broken. I can hear it in her voice.

"Who am I to you?"

"My Dom."

"That's right. Act like it." She stiffens.

My heart pounds viciously as I gentle my tone to add, "I'm sorry."

Her eyes widen as we stand in our embrace. "I should have caught you and stopped you from running. I should have been stricter and transparent at the party," I say, lifting her chin with my forefinger, forcing her to look at me when she attempts to look away.

"Tonight was my fault, but you shouldn't have run and you better not push me away."

She swallows thickly.

"Who am I to you?" I ask for the final time, running my hands down her shoulders in a soothing motion. She's fragile right now. Far too fragile to punish how I'd like.

More tears glisten in her eyes, and she releases a heavy breath. The horrible distance I felt when I came into the room fades. I'm relieved as all hell. I couldn't have lived with myself if Ella put up more walls or, God forbid, ran away from me again. I've survived plenty of things, but that's the limit.

"You're my Dom," Ella says confidently and calmly.

Those words out of her mouth are all I need to know it'll be okay. At least for tonight.

"Are you done, jailbird?"

Ella steels herself. "You … you should probably go. I don't want you to see me like this."

"It's my wants you should concern yourself with. Let go of every other thought. I want you right now. Fuck, no. I need you right now. I'm not leaving, and neither are you." The confidence comes easy now. We're in the roles we're meant to play. I'm her Dom, and she's not going to send me away. "You're going to get into that bed, and I'm going to hold you until you close your eyes. You're going to sleep off the alcohol and every other messed-up thought you just had. And when you wake up, and I make sure you're all right—"

"Z," she says, her voice nearly breaking into a whimper.

"After that." I lower my voice and pull her face close to mine. I want my jailbird to hear every word. She might not be certain of us right now. She might be too shaken to realize that I'm never leaving. But for tonight, she's going to know exactly what's coming next. "You're going to pay for what you just did, Ella."

She makes a soft sound.

"Your ass is going to feel that punishment. Your cunt. Your mouth. I'm going to claim every inch of you until there isn't a single thought in that pretty little head of yours other than that you belong to me."

With a hand over hers and the other on the small of her back, I lead her to the bed, gently but demanding. "Under the covers," I tell her, pulling back the sheets.

She doesn't hesitate to get into bed, but she doesn't lie down. Instead she pulls the sheet to her chest and peers up at me with wide eyes brimming with emotion. "Will you stay with me until I fall asleep?"

"The fact that you asked me that tells me I haven't done the job I need to." I didn't think it was possible to feel such a drift from her. She's pulled away, but I'll pull her right back and hold on to her forever.

Pulling my shirt over my head, I tell her to lie down. I kick off my shoes and strip down to my boxers before climbing into bed, pulling her back into my chest and kissing her hair. It only takes a few minutes before her shoulders tremble and I know she's crying.

I soothe her and hold her, rubbing her back and kissing her over and over.

"I'm sorry," she whispers and I tell her it's all right. She has nothing to be sorry for. I do, though. I'm sorrier than she could ever imagine.

chapter 2

Ella

EVERYTHING IS DIFFERENT THIS MORNING. IT'S LIKE THE FOG HAS cleared and now each destructive thought and the resulting consequences are highly visible. It's hard to describe this unsettled feeling, but the way I'd put it is that if the barred door to my gilded cage were wide open, I wouldn't move an inch from where I sit. Not because I don't crave freedom, but because I'm terrified of what I'd do with it.

The wind carries a slight chill that whisks across my arms and I'm quick to pull the gray crocheted throw blanket up around myself more. I breathe in the brisk woodsy air and sink back into the porch chair.

I wouldn't move an inch and I don't have to. It's something Kam has always reassured me of. I'm okay here and I can stay safely inside for however long I want; the door is always open and he'll be there to hold my hand if needed. Inside or outside.

He was there for me before. And then there was James.

The thought tightens a vise that's soldered to my heart. Zander is only feet away inside the house, more than likely watching the session. And yet here I am, reminded of what once was. The past that he'll never fully know because I'm incapable of speaking of it.

"Your voice sounds much better than it did only weeks ago," Damon comments. His teacup is empty but he keeps picking it up as if he's going to take a sip from it.

Absently, the tips of my fingers graze my throat as I watch him. I wonder if it's a sign of anxiousness on Damon's part. I've never seen him fidget like that before, repeatedly lifting the empty cup and setting it down.

Even through the heavier conversations, he's usually still or taking notes. Today has been relatively quiet so far and as the teacup clinks against the saucer, I imagine he has something he'd like to discuss but doesn't know how to start.

"My throat feels better," I comment idly. "It feels a lot better actually." Everything is better, depending on how you look at it.

My gaze shifts to my left, peeking over my shoulder to the living room where Zander may be sitting. The thick curtains are mostly drawn shut and looking through the tiny slit in the middle I can tell Zander's not there. The leather chair is empty.

Nervousness pricks through me.

"Is there anything you'd like to discuss today, Ella?" Damon presses as he lifts one ankle over his knee and sits back in his chair as if it's a casual conversation.

He knows what happened. That I drank too much, I made a fool of myself … I had a moment.

Dread comes over me. I don't want to talk about it.

James and Zander compete in the back of my mind but they both tell me I have to talk about it. The knowledge chills me as if James is here, as if he wants Z to command me to say the words out loud. I have to get everything out of me or it will kill me.

That's one thing I imagine they'd both agree on. It's going to eat me alive.

"Can we talk about James?" Damon says, moving the conversation forward and all I do is nod, staring off into the distance.

"I didn't know love until James." My statement is a murmur, but Damon hears it. His pen clicks and I glance to see his pad open.

"Why do you say that?" he questions, his dark eyes on me holding nothing but compassion.

"My mother used me as a bargaining chip, my father did the same when I was old enough … the things he made me do I'll never forget or forgive." Glancing down I find I'm picking at my nails. Readjusting myself in the seat, I get more comfortable and pull the throw blanket up again. Practically hiding under it although my head remains poking out.

"He was your first boyfriend or—"

"No," I answer honestly and I'm certain Damon is already aware. "Every lover was only a partner for sex. There's no family to speak of other than my mother and father." Trish and Kam and Kelly flick across my memory at the mention of family.

Damon comments as if reading my mind, "You had your friends, though. You've been close with them for longer than you were with James, haven't you?"

"Yes. Yes, and I love them. It's just a different love."

Damon nods thoughtfully. "Well, that makes sense."

I do love my friends; they know this game as well as I do. The lies and the depths to which others will go. And they've been there for me as I was for them. There was that … partnership, that dependency …

But then there was James.

And now … Zander is bringing up things he shouldn't. He's making me feel things he shouldn't. I don't know how to simply turn it off.

"Do you want to tell me what happened?" Damon presses.

"I had a drink and I shouldn't have," I answer mildly, picking at the throw.

"It's me, Ella. You can talk to me."

"What if I don't want to talk?" I'm surprised by how blunt my answer is. He's only trying to help and I'm more than aware of that. A part of me desperately wishes to tell him everything. But I don't understand it. I don't know why I can't turn it off.

"You don't have to talk to me, but you may want to when I'm not here and I'm here now. I'm worried, Ella," Damon tells me and that anxiousness shines through. His teacup sits unattended on the table. It's his tone that gave it away.

"I'm worried too," I answer him and my throat goes tight. This time it's me reaching for my cup and finding it empty.

"Grief is a ball in a box … is love like that too?"

"What do you mean?" he asks and his head tilts. For such a strong and dominating man, Damon has a tenderness about him. A thoughtful caring that coaxes out the conversation I want to keep buried inside. The one I'm not ready to have.

"I remember how much I love him, or loved," I answer softly and then swallow thickly.

He's gentle, but quick to answer, "You never stop loving someone. You can use it in present tense."

Tears prick my eyes and I dab the corners of them as if they don't fall recklessly at the memory of James.

I will always love him, but I love Zander … And dare I say I love him more?

Sniffling, I ignore the fact that the trickle of tears turns to sobs. My hand shakes too hard to gently dab so I bring my chin to my knees and press the throw blanket to my eyes instead.

"I'm not okay," I admit to Damon.

"You may think you aren't, but I'm looking at you and I know this is okay. I know you are going to get through this. Are you thinking things that aren't okay? Ella, are you thinking about hurting yourself?"

Shaking my head I say, "I just miss him." At the admission, surprise courses through me enough that the tears stop. I'm not thinking of that at all. When everything first happened, I was plagued with thoughts of driving down the highway and plummeting off a bridge. Or taking a long hot bath and drawing a knife down my wrists. Those ideas are what got me sent away to the Rockford Center, because I truly thought of suicide almost every waking hour. Just ending it.

"I don't want to kill myself," I tell Damon.

"Did you last night?"

"No." My answer is easy and spoken only in a breath. "I was shocked and worried because I felt the loss all over again, but I didn't want that."

"When's the last time you've had those thoughts?" he asks.

"Since before … since I was in Rockford."

"I just want to be very clear and make sure I understand. Are you thinking anything that would be alarming? This is a safe place, Ella. We won't make you go back or do anything outside of your comfort zone.

Know that before answering this question. Are you thinking about hurting yourself at all or in any way?"

"No. But I'm thinking I wish I was with him."

And that makes me feel like I'm cheating on Zander. Like I'm a truly horrible person. He deserves so much more and so much better than a woman who misses her first love. Who will always miss him.

"He shouldn't want me." Not when I'm so thoroughly broken by what happened with James. "Zander shouldn't want me." James said he would ruin me and I swear he did. I love him. I do, but I love Zander more. Even if it makes me an awful person.

"I don't understand it and I'm scared."

"Scared of what?"

"Scared that I'm undeserving."

I love what he does to me, though. The control and the heat that burns between us. Last night comes back in full force and I swear I can feel his warm breath in the crook of my neck. My eyes become heavy and desire along with something else floods into my blood. He feels that too. I'm able to give him that at the very least and I'm certain he enjoys it.

"He knows what he wants and he wants you as you are."

I stare back at Damon. "Has he told you that?"

He answers my question with one of his own. "Hasn't he told you that?"

"Has he told me …" It takes a moment to put the pieces together. "Has Z told me he wants me?"

Damon nods and waits for me to answer.

"He has," I say and the admission is a whisper. "He makes it very clear what he wants." My heart thumps hard in my chest, painfully so. I've told him I love him and he hasn't said it back.

Maybe that's a good thing. My gaze drops and I grab a tissue, blowing my nose and getting over the sorrow I feel for myself when I'm the one causing so much pain for everyone else.

I TYPE OUT ONE LAST MESSAGE TO THE GROUP CHAT ON MY PHONE and send it: I'll take care of it.

End of discussion. She's had time to process. Spoken to Kam and Damon. Now it's my turn.

Cade and Damon have been texting nonstop in a whirlwind of discussion. They have their wants, their preferences, and their concerns.

But I'm the only one who knows what Ella requires. What she desperately needs and it's time that I give it to her and in return she'll give me every fucking worry she has.

I've heard all I need to hear from my brother and Damon and Kam. And Ella for that matter.

"Everything okay?" she questions. Her dark eyes are soulful and inquisitive. She is still shaken from the events of her breakdown, but surer of herself now.

"Of course, jailbird."

I take her hand in mine and lead her to the room down the hall. To a door that will lead her to punishment and pleasure. To a room where she can let it all go. And give it to me.

Ella looks at the closed door, her breathing shallow. I take a minute to step back and assess her. She is anxious, possibly from the thought of her punishment. Better than last night for sure. We can do this. This is the next step.

"Open the door, Ella," I tell her.

With a heavy inhale she obeys. Her eyes widen slightly and her chest rises with shock at the newly decorated room.

"It's different," she whispers with a touch of awe in her voice. A smirk gently lifts my lips, but it comes and goes before she can see it.

"I ... redecorated."

It's the BDSM room. A playroom. Silas helped move everything from my place to hers. We worked while she slept last night and put the finishing touches on while she had her session with Damon. I haven't slept at all, but this was needed.

My equipment has been arranged around the room. The air is cool, not too cold. The window lights the room from behind a thin curtain although I can pull the thick drapes shut if needed. I want her to see this, though. Every piece is placed with purpose. The traditional armoire with paddles and whips rests beside the padded bench. The horse has the addition of knee support, I imagine she's going to love that piece, given how much pleasure she gets when I take her from behind.

The scent is of freshly polished wood and leather. It's faint and not overbearing.

I watch her move around the space, fingertips reaching out to glide along the luxurious furniture. My heart races again at the memory that I almost lost her. My fear slips in with the anger, and I breathe it out. Never again. She will regret ever leaving me in a moment of chaos.

She turns to face me, hesitant, waiting. As if realizing her punishment is imminent.

"You are in need, Ella," I tell her. "And you will not stop me from providing you with what you need." Her breath hitches as a flush creeps into her cheeks. "Understood?"

"Yes, Z."

"Good ..." My gaze drifts to her silk nightgown and my cock twitches with desire. "Take off your clothes."

She does as I tell her. Her curves are quickly unveiled as the silk slips into a puddle around her feet. Her lace bra and panties are next, joining the pale pink fabric on the floor. Then she faces me, hands clasped in front of her, her naked body beautiful before my eyes.

Heat floods through me. My hand flexes with the need to feel her skin redden beneath it.

"You had rules before," I state, my body already responding to hers. I'm hard and ready to take her. However, I'm not focused on myself in the slightest. All my attention is on her. "Today, you're mine, and from here on out, no other rules matter. Not the company's rules, not Kamden's rules. No formal rules except the ones we make right now. Even the fucking law is irrelevant. Is that understood?"

"Yes, sir," she says breathlessly as I round her, pacing and making certain she hears everything crystal clear.

"Give me your wrists." Ella offers them to me with sweet submission.

I take them in mine with one hand and lead her to the bed. With the fireplace crackling in the corner, she'll be warm here, but not too hot. Her body temperature, like everything else, is important to me. I don't want her to overheat. I also don't want her to shiver.

Nothing but pain and pleasure. Punishment and security.

"Lie down on the bed," I say, loosening my black silk tie, leaving me in gray suit pants and a button-down that will both be on the floor in a matter of time.

Ella lies back on the bed, her body spread out before me, and I turn to my next task.

I tie her down slowly, like it's the most important thing I've ever done. It *is* the most important thing I've ever done. Each new moment with her becomes the most important. All of them will build on each other until she's whole again.

With her hands secured above her head, tied to the headboard, I put a spreader bar between her ankles. The clicks of the restraints resonate in the room. Fuck, she's gorgeous.

My jailbird is completely exposed to me now. She's completely vulnerable to me. Bound to the bed by my own hands. As I complete her bindings, I speak to her, adding one light kiss to her lips.

Otherwise, I don't touch her. Only necessary touches that leave goosebumps in their wake.

I won't touch her until we've discussed the rules and she acknowledges them and agrees. The kiss was the only exception.

"Rule number one, Ella." Her eyes come to mine as she waits silently. "You will not leave my side unless I agree to it. Ever."

I swallow thickly, knowing how extreme it is. Given what occurred, it is a requirement from here on out.

A second passes, her eyes on mine. She listens, she hears it … and ultimately, she agrees.

"Yes, sir." She's eager to please me. As a reward I slide my fingertips over her soft folds. Her back bows slightly and a soft murmur spills from her lips. She's ready, slick for me, but not as ready as she will be when I'm finished. I stroke her clit with my thumb. A few seconds. That's all. Reinforcing her obedience.

Her chest rises and falls with her heavy breaths. Standing beside the bed, I slowly unbutton my shirt. "What's rule number two?" she whispers.

I reach into the side table, taking out a butt plug and the small bottle beside it. Applying adequate lube, I warm it for her. "Rule number two. No alcohol again. Ever. Unless I give it to you."

Ella's friends say she doesn't have addiction issues. Damon agrees there's a difference between misuse and addiction. Right now, she's not allowed to use alcohol as a crutch, though. If she's triggered while inebriated … she will spiral faster. I have to contain her.

The bed groans as I place my hand on it and lean to tower over her. I look deeply into Ella's eyes. "Is that understood?"

"Yes, sir," she answers without hesitation.

A moment passes as I move to the foot of the bed so I can do as I please. I angle her hips slightly, lifting the spreader bar and twisting it enough to give me access to what I want, and push the plug gently inside her. Ella gasps a little, her hips rocking back and forth. I rub a small circle over her clit as her reward.

"That's my good girl," I tell her.

My praise and small touches have Ella close already. I can see that in the trembling of her muscles. Part of me wants to let her come, but I pull away. Her hooded eyes snap to mine.

"There were boundaries you and James had, correct?"

She blinks, seemingly startled by the question. Perhaps by the mention of James. I don't miss how the cords in her neck tighten as she swallows. "Yes," she replies slowly.

"What are they?"

"I'm not sure I can remember them all." She gives a small shake of her head as if she's reluctant to even try.

"You know some of them, which brings me to rule number three. When you discover another trigger, you will confide in me immediately. You will run to me. You will cry in my arms. You will break for me and me alone. I share your pleasure, jailbird, and that means I also share your pain. Is that understood?"

"Yes, sir," she answers.

"Can you remember some of those boundaries, Ella?"

"No talking about our families." She squirms uncomfortably on the bed.

I'm quick to rectify her discomfort, kissing along her curves. "Is there anything else?"

She shakes her head although I'm almost certain she'd prefer the pleasure. "Ella, what are the words you don't want me to say?"

"Wild. Don't call me wild or say anything like that. Or tame." The request flows beautifully from her lips, without hesitation.

"Anything else?" I question and then kiss her breast.

"No. Just … that."

"What about mentioning James?" I ask.

She hesitates, thinking it over. "I want to tell you about him."

I smile against her lips before kissing her.

"That would make me very happy," I confide in her. "Thank you for being such a good girl for me."

I push my fingers into her. With even strokes she comes quickly. Ella clenches down on my fingers and cries out with her climax. Her moans are low and sweet as she struggles against her bindings. I keep her restrained with my knee pressed down on the spreader bar.

Ella's completely at my mercy. Her face is red and flushed, her hair a messy halo.

"You're so fucking gorgeous when you come," I praise, my voice low.

"I'm going to blindfold you now," I tell her before flipping her over, maneuvering her delicate weight in my hands with the spreader bar. Ella yelps in surprise. Her wrists are crossed now. The restraints are tighter. I slide a pillow under her belly, angling her how I want, then get up, leaving her alone. Until I return with the blindfold, carefully tying it into place.

"Z?" she says, her voice trembling.

"I'm here," I reassure her.

I open the bottle of water left on the dresser, then open up a pill bottle next. The Viagra goes down with a sip. This session is going to last a long time, and I need to last with her.

"Repeat the three rules back to me," I say.

She takes a deep breath. "I don't leave your side unless you consent. I'll never drink again, unless you give me the drink. And ..."

"Keep going."

"And I'll tell you the moment I'm aware I'm triggered."

"What else, Ella?"

"You'll punish me however you see fit, for however long you want. Do I still have my safe word?"

"You'll always have your safe word."

I lean down and press a kiss to her lips. "Thank you," she whispers.

Desire makes me harder. "You know I care for you, don't you?"

Ella nods.

"Good. Remember that today, and tonight, while I fuck you like my personal whore."

With every detail laid out and agreed to, I climb on the bed and position myself. Precum leaks from my cock and I use it to stroke myself. Ella speaks again. "Z?"

"Yes?"

"Do you ... want me?" she questions.

I know what she's asking. Do I want her more than just a game? As more than just a Dom/sub relationship?

I more than want you, Ella. I love you.

The words are on the tip of my tongue, but Ella lifts her head and I lean down to kiss her lips, whispering to her that she should know just how much I want her. Every fucking moment of every day and night.

With my reassurance she rests her head against the pillow and I move beside Ella, readying myself for her punishment.

"You scared me, Ella. You left me alone and refused me."

Her breath comes in ragged pants now. "I'm sorry," she says.

"Twenty for that, my little jailbird. You'll count." I bring my palm down on her ass, over and over again. Each time I strike a different area, starting from her upper thigh and moving higher. She whimpers, biting down on her lower lip and cries out my name but doesn't protest.

Ella counts each one and I don't stop until her ass is red.

Then I move behind her and push my cock into her.

It takes everything in me not to come instantly as she pushes back, eager for that reprieve of stinging pain. "Please," she begs me and I lean forward, kissing her neck as I fuck her ruthlessly. This is the part that's fucking heaven.

I let her come twice before I move to her ass. I play with the plug, toying with her and listening to her moans. Her head thrashes from side to side and I know she's close.

I grab the small bottle of lube, letting the cool liquid drizzle down her heated skin before replacing the plug with my cock.

Ella shudders as I take her tight hole inch by inch. The sight of her biting down on her lip to quiet her moans is enough that I lose myself. Coming doesn't matter, though; I'm still hard as a rock for her. It's impossible to hold myself back. She belongs to me and being buried in her is all I've wanted all day.

Her body is tense as I rock into her. Slowly at first, letting her adjust until finally I take her fully and fuck her ass mercilessly.

Another orgasm hits her as I spill myself into her again.

But I'm not finished.

Pulling out, I spank her again and again and again, making sure every inch of her ass is red, reminding her that she's mine. Squeezing her reddened skin, I heighten the pain-pleasure threshold and then fuck her again.

For hours. Enjoying her however I fucking want.

"Have you been taking your medication, babe?" he asks me with one brow cocked and a smirk on his lips. The look he gives me is comical and it's one I've seen a thousand times.

I smirk back and say, "I have." My silk nightie rides up under the covers as I pull my knee up to rest my chin on it. He can't see a thing, but still, I tug it back into place and cock a brow in return as I tell him, "Medication and dick work wonders for a girl like me."

Kam's smirk widens to a grin and mine follows with a nonchalant shrug. Even that small movement reawakens the soreness between my thighs and I bite down on my lower lip to stifle the moan that begs to spill from me.

There's no polite way to say it: Z fucked the hell out of me.

And I loved every sordid minute of it. I haven't slept so well or felt this content in … well, I don't dare to remember.

Kam plops down on the other side of the sofa from where I'm sitting in the living room and the sofa offers a groan in response.

My tea is the perfect temperature and as far as I know, Zander is still sleeping soundly. Silas and Damon are in the other room, giving me privacy in the early morning. It's all comfortable now.

As if everything has settled and all is as it should be for the moment.

"I think most of life's problems can be solved with a pill or dick," I half-heartedly joke and hope the comment hits as intended.

"Or money," Kam chimes in and I'm quick to agree.

He toys with the thin black tie he wears; he must've left his jacket in the foyer. Without it Kam looks so much younger, yet the wrinkles around his eyes seem to have worsened. The last year has aged him immensely.

My gaze drops and apparently Kam sees it as his cue to pipe up. "So … how are you really?"

Chewing the inside of my cheek, I pause only a moment before I answer honestly, letting the truth slip out easier than it has recently. "I feel guilty … moving on—" A chill drenches me as I admit it.

Kam's head shakes immediately as he cuts me off. "First, no guilt allowed. And second, you aren't moving on."

My throat tightens and I shake off the prickling sensation that runs down my arms.

"James would want you to be loved thoroughly … and quite often," he jokes and it lightens the mood.

With a short huff of a laugh, I nod but it doesn't stop the bits of pain I feel whenever I think about James.

"So don't feel guilty. Or I'll have to tell your … your … what do you call him? Boy toy?"

A genuine laugh bubbles out. "Z is my boy toy?" I question humorously.

"Well, what is he to you? Just your Dom? Or …?" he asks.

Heat blazes across my skin and a tension settles through me. I could see him being more. So much more. But just the idea is stifling.

"Or rather, what should I call him?" Kam shifts the question and then pats my leg as he readjusts to face me more directly. "I suppose I could always just call him Zander, and not complicate it?" he offers and I'm quick to agree, releasing every ounce of apprehension that threatens to overwhelm me.

Before I can verbalize my answer, Kam says, "So if you're feeling guilty, I'll have to tell Zander to fuck that out of you, or spank it or … whatever kink you two agree on." He gestures in the air with a comical expression on his face that soothes so much of what ails me.

"Sex … no guilt," I say, summing up the conversation.

"That's right."

"Got it."

"We've had this conversation before," I comment and remember sitting on a sofa similar to this one a little over a year ago, promising I would stop feeling guilty, that I would stop thinking about all the dark things. It was just after the first time I tried to kill myself.

Kam had tears in his eyes then. They were raw and bloodshot. I'd never seen him like that.

"We have definitely had this conversation before." He nods in agreement and just as guilt starts to trickle in he says, "And it's okay to have it again. There's nothing wrong with that." He leans in closer, lowering his voice to jokingly add, "It would be great if it was the last time, but you can be a slow learner." I can't help the laugh. It's genuine and so out of place, but also so very needed.

A moment passes that settles everything. He lays his hand over mine and I flip mine over, so my palm is facing up and touching his. I give a gentle squeeze and he returns it.

His head falls back and he stares up at the ceiling. "Last time instead of guilt we were going to drink, but this time I think maybe instead of guilt"—with his head resting against the back of the sofa, he turns just slightly so his eyes are on mine to say—"we just have sex."

At my laugh he smiles, his pearly white teeth showing off how charming and handsome he is.

"Is that your way of telling me you've found a new boyfriend?"

"Ah, yes, I have a new boy toy."

"Really?" I shift to face him. A giddiness comes over me at the thought of Kam falling in love again, especially after things didn't work out with Gerald, his ex. If ever someone deserved a happily ever after, it's Kam. He's dedicated his life to our circle of friends and made whatever sacrifices were necessary. Ones we aren't supposed to mention. Some I wasn't meant to know of at all.

Just as I part my lips to ask who he is, he presses on about Zander.

"Let's talk about yours, though. About Zander."

"What about him?"

"The media reaction is exactly what we wanted and it also offers you a choice. Whichever you make, I'll support."

I pause, waiting for him to say it out loud although I can already guess what the options are.

"You can keep him or leave him. Our reaction determines what they perceive and given his position with The Firm, as well as legally … there won't be any issues either way."

"Do we have to make any statement at all?" I question, thinking pragmatically. Silence is golden. That's my mantra and it's been my mantra for years.

"Not at all. It is good timing for public relations, though. The spotlight is on you, babe."

"Mm-hmm," I hum in understanding. Picking at my nails, I struggle to think of anything I want anyone to know. It's all too fresh and raw. I just want more time before I give them anything at all.

"If you want him to stay, he stays. If you want him to go …" He gives a little wave, his hand making a rolling motion. I know what "go" means.

It's been ages since Kam last saw to a relationship ending. Prior to James. It's a final decision and one that can't be undone without extensive damage control.

"You can take time if you need," Kam starts. "I can keep him away if you want space to think—"

"I want him to stay." My statement is firm and Kam's lips lift in an asymmetric grin, giving me a sense of peace at my answer. Good. With that look I know everything will be all right.

It will be, won't it?

"I thought you'd say that. I thought you might tell me you love him." His gaze is locked with mine as he stares back at me expectantly. I can't answer, though. It seems more final to admit it to Kam than to Zander himself.

I can't do it. Not when I don't even know how Z really feels about me. Not when I don't know if this is going to last.

"Keep your secrets," he says, throwing his hands up with his lips pressed into a thin smile and then he breaks eye contact to look away. "You don't need to tell me anything more."

He readjusts on the sofa and I can only watch him until he looks back at me. Déjà vu comes over me and the theoretical clouds rumble in the distance.

"Just let me know if things change, all right?"

"Right. You'll be the first to know."

"And I'll take care of it."

He did the same for James. It's as if history is repeating itself. At that thought, chills run down my spine. I can barely swallow but before the intense emotion takes hold, Kam distracts me with an odd fact.

"Did you know that sex can occasionally result in transient global amnesia?" Kam tells me.

"What do you mean?"

"You can forget for a couple of hours."

"Forget what?" I question.

"Forget anything … everything," he says jokingly and I have to smile as he gives me a grin.

It's quiet for a moment and I sink back, feeling as if I'm either in the eye of the storm, or the dark gray skies have passed and I'm just not aware of it yet.

After a moment, he breaks the silence.

"Your friends are worried about you," he tells me softly, patting the back of my hand and giving me a somewhat sad smile, but more like one with empathy.

"I'm worried about me too," I admit and consider jotting down some thoughts in the journal Damon gave me, the one with the rose gold binding. When Kam leaves, I think I'll do just that.

"It may sound odd, but that's a step up from last time." Kam nods as he speaks. "A good step," he adds, continuing the nodding. It's what he does when he's decided on a plan and is content with it. Those little nods provide so much comfort. More than he could ever realize. "You're worried, and I'll take that. Plus you're getting laid, so that's a good sign."

A huff leaves me. "It'll make me forget."

"Exactly."

"We have so much to forget, don't we?" My tone is slightly somber, which follows the path my mood drifts.

"Hmm …" he hums as if truly considering and I nearly laugh. "Not that I can remember," he jokes back.

chapter 5

Zander

SEATED ACROSS FROM ELLA IN THE BLUE ROOM, I CAN'T HELP BUT come to the realization that's been following me since our last session.

It didn't just change things for her. It changed things for me. The way we were together unlocked something buried deep down. The fire crackles, keeping the expansive room warm even though the chill of late fall has set outside.

That one truth, that something has shifted inside of me, is something I've been keeping at bay with four-count breaths for months now.

I couldn't really admit it to myself.

But now, looking at Ella …

I know.

Everything has changed and it can never go back to what it once was. It's not only that I want to share myself with her. It's that I'm finally ready to stop carrying the burden of these thoughts by myself. I've been attempting to give Ella some of the same relief about her own past. How can I do that when I won't do the same for myself? I know she feels this is one sided. Damon told me that she even claimed she was undeserving.

It's because I haven't leaned on her as a Dom should. It works both ways. If anyone knows that, it's me.

It's hypocritical to not confide in her, and I don't want to be hypocritical with her. I want to be myself. And these thoughts, these ideas, are part of me.

It's only right to share them with her.

If Ella knew, then I wouldn't be the only one. I wouldn't have to carry it all by myself. It's time to let this go. The only way I can do that is by confiding in her.

"What are you thinking about?" Ella asks me from her place in the armchair across from mine. She's delectable this evening, in a cream silk slip designed just to taunt me. Her dark hair is swept over one shoulder, revealing her slender neck which carries a faint mark from last night as I nipped her in the heat of the moment. "Hmm?" she presses and her chestnut eyes pierce into me.

I want to deflect and move on to another topic. That's been an old habit of mine. But I force myself not to do it.

"I was just thinking that I wanted to tell you something."

"Oh?" Her voice is even but her brow raises and there's a worrisome look that I don't like.

Smirking, I add, "It's like you could read my mind."

She huffs a small laugh at my comment.

"It's about Quincy," I warn her, testing her boundaries. She doesn't shift, she doesn't react in the least other than to nod, as if to tell me to continue.

"I think Quincy wanted me to tell her that I loved her," I admit, my throat feeling sore around the words.

"The night she died?" Ella's voice is soft and accepting.

I nod. "And before that, there were so many times she wanted me to say it. I knew she wanted that, and I never did." Deep regret pierces through me.

Ella glances out the window, looking thoughtful. My heart beats faster. "You'll tell me if you'd rather not discuss her."

"I want to." She's quick to quell any second thoughts about confiding in her. Moving from her seat of solitude, she comes to me. And I make room for her. Just this, her soft touch and warmth, is enough.

Nestled beside me, she looks back into my eyes. "Did you love her?"

There's no judgment in her tone. Only the desire for truth.

"Yes," I admit. "I did love her. Maybe not in the way she wanted and not in the way I craved from a partner, but I still loved her." I wrap my arm around her waist to tell her that it doesn't affect what we have. I'm not comparing the two of them.

"I know what you mean."

A weight lifts off my shoulders. Saying it out loud, even to one person, feels so much lighter. I can't believe how heavy it felt to treat that information as a terrible secret. I can't count how many nights I've lain awake wondering if I'd told Quincy what she wanted to hear, if I'd allowed myself to acknowledge it, would she still be alive?

What-ifs have never healed a damn thing, though, as Damon would say. "It was a different love than what we have," I say, realizing what Ella might think and feel in this moment might be the complete opposite of what I'm experiencing.

A smile curves her lips. "I know, Z," she murmurs. Ella maneuvers herself and drops into my lap, but I can feel in the tension of her muscles that she's insecure.

My jailbird belongs to me. Now and always. She shouldn't feel insecure for even a second.

"Come closer." I wrap my arms around her.

"I'm already sitting in your lap," she says with a playful laugh.

Tension thickens between us. A new tension. It makes my heart pound loud in my ears. I brush a lock of her hair back from her face and tuck it behind her ear. Ella's expression turns serious.

"What is it, jailbird?"

I can see the fear in her eyes. She thinks there might be more. Another layer of secrets when it comes to me and Quincy. But she's not able to verbalize the question. I understand. I couldn't talk about this for so long. The longer I went without saying it, the less I believed I could.

"I love you, Ella. I need you to understand."

The fear slowly retreats from her eyes, and she turns pink in the cheeks. The last thing to arrive is a small, trusting smile.

"Now," I say, "be a good girl for me."

"Z," she says, quickly. "I love you too, but—"

"There are no buts." I'm firm, but cut her off before she can complete that thought.

Ella cannot doubt me after everything she's been through. I won't let her do it. Her happiness is mine. Her sadness as well. That means her uncertainty is also mine.

I stand up and gently guide her to remain on the couch. "Lie back."

Ella perches on the edge and leans back, stretching her body out before me, her eyes glinting. I'm slow and deliberate, testing and teasing her as I go. The fire crackles behind my back and it reflects in her heated gaze. With a single kiss, I tell her that I love her again.

Ever so slowly, I push her slip to her hips, letting the silk ride up her thighs. She shivers from the contact and her nipples pebble under the thin fabric. I groan as I pull her panties to the side and put my mouth between her legs, taking a languid lick. Her fingers splay through my hair and her back bows slightly.

It's more of the connection I've been craving since I decided to tell her. I needed this. The taste of her is everything I needed.

I'm overwhelmed with a sense of peace. It was the right decision to tell her. I've made it my business to know as much as I can about Ella. While I may be her Dom in the bedroom, that doesn't mean we're unequal. Some people new to the lifestyle can make the mistake of thinking that subs are lesser than Doms. That they have less influence in the relationship.

It's not true. She's just as important as I am. Even more so. Sharing myself with her is as crucial as Ella sharing all her deepest secrets with me.

Licking and sucking her clit, while she gasps and cries out, sends even more desire through me.

Ella's slick and hot, and her thighs clench around my shoulders.

It won't be long now.

Her fingers wind through my hair.

This is the best life has to offer. There's nothing I'd rather do than make Ella come.

I lift my head from her pussy and speak to her as I reach up and pull down one thin strap of her silk slip. Her full breast fits perfectly in my hand and I massage her, commanding her, "Come for me, jailbird."

The second my tongue touches her again and I pinch her nipple ever so slightly, Ella comes in a burst of pleasure. She hangs on to the couch cushions for dear life. Her nails scrape against the fabric as she cries out my name.

She's still coming when someone steps into the room. The footsteps only resonate with the sound of, "Shit, fuck. I'm sorry." The words all tumble out rapid fire. It's my fucking brother.

Ella gasps, curling up into a ball to cover herself and I turn, wiping her arousal off on my shirt to face Cade.

"I'm sorry," he says with his hands raised, "I didn't see anything."

His widened eyes tell me he's lying. "Out. Get out." A possessiveness I haven't felt before comes over me. Damon's seen me fuck Ella. But I knew he was there. There was permission. There was pleasure given to my Ella. This was not that.

"Of course," he says and turns abruptly. Cade leaves the living room, his footsteps quickly growing quieter.

I gather Ella into my arms, put her on her feet, and rearrange her clothes. "Go upstairs, jailbird. Wait for me in bed. I need more from you than that."

"Z," she says, her eyes darting to the threshold of the room.

"It's all right." I take her jaw in my hand, pull her face to mine, and kiss her hard. She moans as she tastes herself on my lips. The connection burns between us, strong and raw.

After she's upstairs and her bedroom door has closed, I go to find Cade in the kitchen. He's leaning against the counter, his hands in his pockets.

"You need to contain yourself, Zander."

"No," I snap. "I'll be fucking her on every inch of furniture. On every inch of the floor. I'm going to make that woman feel alive and loved and wanted."

His eyes narrow, but there's a thoughtful expression behind them.

My anger is as hot as my love for her right now. It's even stronger now that I've had a chance to let go of the bitter grief I've been holding onto for so, so long. "I mean it, Cade. I'm going to fuck her whenever I want. Wherever I want. Until all her sadness is gone and the past takes its claws all the way out of her. And as for *you*, you need to send a damn text before you come over."

Cade stares for a moment, shaking his head as if I've lost my mind. His expression shifts and he nods, slapping a stack of papers down on the kitchen counter. "Fine. I can send a text. I'll send a text next time I'm going to stop by, but you need to see this."

I go to his side, forcing myself to calm down, and look at the papers. "What are these?" I flick through them. They appear to be medical reports … news articles. It's a mix of papers with several lines highlighted. Including "strangulation" but then "death by suicide."

"What the hell are these?"

"This is what you asked Silas to research." He folds his arms over his chest. "Ella's mother didn't die by suicide."

We both look down at the documents together. The awkwardness of the past moment is forgotten. I flip through the papers, then again.

"There are a lot of things that don't add up," Cade says to my right as I read.

I'm reminded of the conversation I had with Kam a few nights ago. "Kamden told me he thinks her father did it."

"Why would he tell you that?" Cade sounds skeptical. He's rarely ever thrown off his game, but this is bothering him. "And how, exactly, would he know that?"

The front door opens, then bangs shut. "Hello?" Kamden calls.

The fact is, I don't know what's going on. But Kam's footsteps come closer by the second. I use the time to lean in close and murmur something to my brother. "I think it's time the cameras came down."

Kam steps into the kitchen then. Crossing swiftly to the island, he drops a box of pastries onto the counter. Cade locks eyes with me and gives me a single, silent nod.

chapter 6

Ella

I T'S A ROTATION.

Damon, Zander, Kam, Zander, Silas, Zander. Occasionally Dane. Zander is a constant but gives them space. And they take shifts watching, questioning, and observing every little thing I do more often than not.

Men revolve around me and I'm held accountable to each of them. Any slight stress from any of the men monitoring me is immediately alleviated by Z.

In a past life, I'd have resented all of them. I'd have pitched a fit and fought tooth and nail for privacy and freedom. Even Kamden for interfering, for being overbearing, for not leaving me the hell alone, would be on the receiving end of my wrath. But this go-around? I look forward to the sessions, the questions, the appointments. Maybe it's because they're all I have left. Or maybe it's because Z is there at the end of all of them, rewarding me and reminding me that none of this matters.

As I stir sugar into my tea, Kam shuffles the papers on the counter next to me. He has stacks laid out along the granite. This is cup two for me and the steam billows outward as I blow across the top. The mug itself is a present Kam gave me only two hours ago when he arrived. A pearl blue iridescent mug that's limited edition from Tiffany.

"I can't help but think you're trying to butter me up."

"I wish," Kam answers absently as he shuffles through the papers. He doesn't look back at me, very much consumed with the next line of business.

Shifting on the stool, I'm careful to gather the fabric of my skirt so it doesn't bunch. It's a classic navy blue high-waisted number and I paired it with a simple short-sleeved white blouse that's loosely tucked in. I decided to attempt to look as if I'm prepared for business, even if in reality I won't be leaving the house and I could have stayed in my pajamas from yesterday.

I rock gently to and fro on the stool, watching Kam squint at the papers until he pulls out his glasses from his shirt pocket.

With the slacks and thin wire-rimmed glasses he reminds me of his father for a moment. He was a hedge fund manager and as Kam gets older, he looks more and more like him. Not that I would tell him that. He hated his father and for good reason. For similar reasons that I hated mine.

"We have three offers but we shouldn't take any on the beach house. The one in LA you may want to consider, but I wouldn't say yes to anything yet."

His statement makes me pause the easy motion of back and forth. "I'm sorry, did you say 'offers?' How do we have bids if we haven't put them on the market?"

His glasses clink as he closes them and then he passes me three papers. I don't bother looking at them, he'll explain it well enough. "We haven't put them up on the market, but some realtors have contacted me. There's clear interest but I thought maybe we should wait until you can see them one last time. Make sure that you are set on selling them?"

My heart does a little tumble and my fingertips go numb. I take a sip of tea, allowing it to warm my hands instead of replying.

If I were to go to those homes, especially the beach house, all I would see are memories of James. Even now, without stepping foot on the premises, I see him.

"I'd rather just sell them," I tell Kam with finality and set the mug down. Memories flood in and I can't shove them away.

"You don't want to say goodbye? Have a look around? We'd be selling fully furnished and I don't want you to regret that. Or regret anything."

I remember the moment James and I bought our first house together in LA. I remember the snapshot we took, how he kissed my cheek and whispered, *I love you, my wild girl.*

Tears prick as I imagine never setting foot in the same bedroom where he made love to me, the same kitchen where he told me he loved me for the first time.

"Is it bad if I don't?" I ask Kam and steady myself. I'm not going to cry. Not over houses and furniture. This is the home we spent the least amount of time in. We bought it because of the bedrooms. We wanted a family. And that family will never happen now. It was only hopeful wishes that lived here and they have since been replaced by reality.

"Not at all," Kam is quick to answer and then offers, "Do you want pictures of any of them?"

"Pictures?"

"I had a photographer take photos of everything in the houses … if you want to see them to have a look over? Especially the items left behind. Is there anything at all you can think of that you don't want sold with the properties?"

My answer is immediate. "There's a picture by the bed in the beach house."

The moment the statement leaves me, Kamden gives his complete attention to a manila envelope and takes out a bundle of photos held together with a paper clip.

I glance, but just as quickly return my attention back to the mug in front of me. The nervous energy doesn't leave me alone. Neither do all the memories.

"This one?" he asks, handing me a printout of what could be a home decor magazine cover. I forgot how much we spent decorating that house to make it perfect. I forgot how luxurious it looked. The painting by James's bedside was a gift I gave him the weekend before we got married.

He wanted to elope on an island off of the coast. I didn't and he caved easily, telling me we could do whatever I wanted. The weekend before the wedding, which was set in an expensive hotel in Maui, we took a jet out to that island where in a simple white sundress, I told him my vows and

Kam married us. Trish snapped the photo and my artist friend made it into a painting.

We both got the wedding of our dreams and none of our guests beyond our inner circle knew there were two.

That painting is a secret and a memory and it's exactly who we were as a couple.

"I just want that painting, please," I whisper to Kam and touch ever so gently at the corner of my eye, willing the tear not to fall. I remind myself that I am okay and there's no reason to cry. It's fine. Everything is fine.

"Of course," Kam answers and he can't hide the sympathy in his voice.

That's what does it; the damn tear falls. "I think I want to see Zander," I manage to get out with my throat tight. Rule three. Rule three.

"Okay … is there something I can do?"

"Just get him, please," I plead with him as my shoulders tremble. I don't want to cry anymore. But if I must, something inside of me simply needs Z to hold me while I do. When he holds me, it ends when the tears stop. If he's not there … I spiral.

"I would do anything for you."

"I know. I would do anything for you too."

"Okay, let's go see Zander. The rest of this can wait."

With deep breaths, I push the stool out, the legs scraping against the floor. "Let me help you," Kam offers with a hand on my elbow at the same time that the front door opens and Trish can be heard calling out, "Honey, I'm home!"

"Shit," Kam mutters under his breath and then reaches for a cloth napkin, handing it to me to dry my unwanted tears.

"Do you want me to get rid of her?" he questions beneath his breath as her keys jingle closer and closer to us. "Anyone home?" she calls out.

With a weak smile, I shake my head no. "No. It's okay. I'm okay," I'm quick to push out the words, all the while sniffling and trying to shut down the sudden grief.

I'll have to tell Zander, though. He needs to know. My thoughts are cut off by a concerned voice.

"Oh my God … are you crying?" Trish stands in the opening to the kitchen, keys in one hand, a box from pastries from my favorite local bakery in the other with her purse dangling from the crook of her elbow. In white skinny jeans and a simple navy top with a white minimalist logo, we actually match. It's the same colors, just inverted, and I'm uptown while she's downtown chic.

"I like your shoes," I answer her and then shrug at her question. She takes a peek down at her pointed toe navy heels before looking back up to me. "Oh, my love," she says and pouts. "No deflecting. Tell me, what's the matter?"

"I'll get tissues until you two are ready for retail therapy," Kam says and leaves the two of us to hug awkwardly with Trish's hands still full.

Wiping my eyes and sniffling I tell her it's the same old, same old.

I let out a weak laugh as she unloads on the counter and then she hugs me for real. One of the strong kind that can hold you up when you want to collapse.

"I swear I'm all right," I tell her, blotting under my eyes with the tissue Kam gives me and then accepting another for my nose.

"You had a moment," Kam says and looks to his sister. "It was just a moment."

It's odd how the smallest things set me off. "I wish I could just stop it."

"It'll come and go, babe. There's no stopping grief."

I nod as he talks, feeling calmer by the second. Trish stares at me and I can feel her gaze, but I focus on deep breaths.

"It was a fast moment," Kam adds and this time I say, "That damn ball in the box."

All Trish says is, "Fuck that ball," in the driest, most sarcastic tone I've heard in a long time and I can't help but to laugh. "I don't know anything about it but it can fuck right off."

Her comment makes me laugh and Kam pats my hand.

"Does my makeup still look okay," I ask her and she tilts her head slightly, taking the tissue from me. "Let me just …" she says and I chuckle again.

"I'm such a mess."

"You okay?" she asks with an empathetic pout, rubbing my back once the laugh is over.

Nodding, I crumple up the tissues and tell her, "Yeah. I was just …"

"Just grieving," Kam finishes for me and I nod again in agreement.

"I have a distraction if you'd like," Trish offers, pulling out the stool Kam previously sat in. She misses the comical glare he gives her and I nearly laugh again but it's cut off when she says, "Did you see what the tabloids said?" Without waiting for me to answer, she turns to her brother to ask, "Did you tell her?"

As he shakes his head I ask deadpan, "Am I the reckless rich bitch whore again?"

"Not quite," she says and passes me her phone.

"We didn't make a statement, right?" I clarify with Kam and he nods, confirming, but then says, "They decided no statement was a sign that there's love in the air."

The first reads: *Crazy Meets Crazy, Heated Forbidden Romance!* and then I swipe right to read the second one: *He May Be Her Bodyguard but Her Body Isn't Guarded From Him …*

Just beneath the second headline is a picture of me, soaking wet from head to toe, my bra visible beneath my dress as I grip onto Z and he looks down at me as if we're about to kiss.

Did we? It was at the party; tensions were high, emotions even higher. I barely remember that moment. From the picture, though, it looks as if it's a still from a romance movie. As if we're about to kiss against the wall.

His expression is everything. It reads pure devotion.

"For real I thought he might have fucked you against that wall right then and there in front of everyone," Trish jokes.

"If you could refrain from that, the PR team would appreciate it," Kam comments dryly.

Trish laughs first and then I follow. For a moment, for one small moment everything feels like it used to. Then I hand her phone back and I remember it's nothing like it used to be.

"You looked like you might be in love," Trish says but her tone is slightly defeated as she watches me war with myself. I know my expression doesn't hide a thing.

"So … are you two in love?" she presses lightheartedly and Kam mutters beneath his breath for her to leave me alone as he stacks all the papers on the counter back into one pile.

I don't answer her but I know the truth. I love the way he makes me feel and I want him to feel this way too.

"You good?" Kam asks.

I hesitate to answer, glancing at Trish and then back to Kam. "… I'm better."

With a rap of his knuckles, Zander stands on the other side of the glass. Tall, dark and handsome, in gray slacks and a thin black tie, he peeks in the window waiting rather than pulling back the sliding glass door beside him. I huff a small laugh as he looks through the window and signals by pointing to his chest. It means: *Do you need me?*

I blow him a kiss back. It's our code for: *I'm all right.* There's a sputtering in my chest as I'm caught in his gaze. It strikes me that he could have walked another few steps, but where he's standing would be the first place he'd be able to see me.

"Your knight in shining armor for real," Trish comments.

"I might have messaged him," Kam admits. He adds, "I can keep her occupied if you want to see him?"

"I'm 'her' now?" Trish jokes at the same time that I respond.

"I'm good." Z smiles at me through the window, gives a short wave and then goes back to the deck where he's been talking with Damon. They're making plans to present paperwork to the judge. Something that has to happen for the conservatorship to dissolve. It's all so heavy and I wish it was just over with legally.

"That's cute that he checks on you," Trish states and then opens up the box from the French bakery I love downtown. She offers me a tiny cupcake but I wave it away. As does Kam. With a shrug, she leans back and bites into her morsel.

The emotions swing so wildly, I don't know what to think anymore.

"It's going to be okay, isn't it?" I question Kam because he knows it all. He takes a moment, observing me and not answering right away. "I don't know why I feel like this," I admit out loud.

"Do we need to—" he starts and I can see the panic and worry in his gaze.

I cut him off, not wanting to cause him more stress than I already have.

"This is me telling my friend … I don't know why I can't trust it. I think the moment I'm happy it's going to be ripped from me."

"Nothing is going to be taken from you," Kam says, attempting to comfort me but it doesn't work.

"If I let myself fall for him and then … something happens and he's gone …" I can barely get the words out. It's the first time I've said it out loud. "I can't go through that again."

Kam's answer strikes me hard, although his voice is nearly a whisper. "What happened to James was an accident, Ella."

"I know. I know."

"It was a fucking tragedy," Trish adds.

"You deserve to be happy," Kam tells me with a gentle firmness. "He makes you happy, doesn't he?"

"He does," I answer.

"And he loves you," Trish points out.

"He does," I say with a simper, letting the warmth flood me. Not fighting it and knowing it's true. He does.

"You love him?" Trish asks.

"I do."

Kam steps in, placing a hand on each of my shoulders and says, "Then be happy. For fuck's sake, Ella, be happy. That's all anyone wants and you never know when it's all going to change. One moment and everything falls. We've seen it so many times. We recover, we always do. I will always make sure you get back up. But you're up, babe. You can be happy now. I promise you."

chapter 7

Zander

Ella's been doing exceptionally well. Much better than I ever could have imagined that first day I saw her in the courtroom. She still has moments, but she acknowledges them, embraces them and then gives them to me.

She's fucking perfect.

All I've done today is praise her in the playroom. Anticipation coats the air. All of the equipment is arranged as it usually is. Ella stands naked in the middle of the room, preparing herself. It's like other scenes we've done.

The difference this time is that there's a camera. The steady red light from atop the dresser indicates everything we do is being recorded.

I've ordered Ella not to look at it. I want her attention solely on me.

Still, it's like another person is in the room with us, watching.

Her chest rises heavily, lust evident in her expression. She loves this. And I can give it to her so easily.

It's not my kink, to be watched, but I can't say that it doesn't thrill me. She loved it when I fucked her on that chair with another actual person in the room. The camera is a stand-in for that feeling, yes, but it's also serving another important purpose.

I want this documented so that she can see.

Ella deserves the right to see everything we do together the way I see it, or the way an onlooker would see it. By using the camera, I'm making that possible for her.

The new addition makes the session feel more charged, like she has a willing audience ready to play into her exhibitionist tendencies. Even if nobody's watching on a screen in another room.

It's also an avenue for something she's unaware of. It's for me to delve deeper into territories that may be uncomfortable. Things I may need Damon's help addressing.

I have her body. I want all of her, though. Every bit and that requires asking questions that may trigger her.

Swallowing thickly, a paddle in my hand, I stare into Ella's dark eyes and steady myself. She breathes heavily, her face flushed from already having pleasured herself. A vibrator is on the floor at her bare feet.

Slowly, I tie her hands and attach them to the hook above her head as I speak. "I'm going to ask you questions. You remember your safe word, don't you?"

"Yes," she answers easily, her warm breath tickling my neck as she does. I kiss her hard, my hand falling to her waist.

"What is it?"

"Pink," she says. Taking one step back, I tell her she's a good girl and then I ask in a clear and controlled manner, "What would James tell me about you if I asked him for advice about being your Dom?"

She swallows hard, and I wait patiently. Talking about James is difficult for Ella, but she's been getting better at it. What I've learned about painful topics is that staying silent about them doesn't work. Not in the long run. I learned that from talking to Ella about Quincy. Repetition and exposure are the only things that make it easier. Not less painful, really, but easier.

James shouldn't be a dark secret. Not between us. No dark secrets belong in a relationship like ours. Doing this will only bring us closer.

A faint smile comes to her face, and inwardly I sigh with relief.

"He would say ..." Ella begins slowly but thoughtfully. She rests her weight on the cuffs at her wrists, and I can tell she's weighing each word as well. "He would say that I respond well to praise."

That's right. She does. I give her a nod of encouragement.

"And he would say that maybe a little degradation works too. He would say that I need a firm hand." She smirks slightly, still looking at me.

"You do need a firm hand," I agree. "You test my patience sometimes, don't you?"

"I did in the beginning but I could do a better job of that now," she teases me and my cock hardens.

"Oh, don't push me right now, my little bird, not when I have a new … kink to test with you."

Her dark eyes brighten. I don't put a collar around her neck. Not yet. I use my hand instead. "Do you trust me?" Her pulse is hot against my skin.

Ella seems to relax into my grip. "Yes, sir," she answers.

"Do you remember your safe word?" I ask again.

"Yes, sir." Her voice is soft, almost a whisper, but she doesn't falter with her words.

I add pressure to my grip, careful to avoid her windpipe. Some think choking is about the throat. It's not. That's dangerous and more than a little damaging. I only put a small amount of pressure on her carotid artery. It'll make Ella light-headed, and heighten the pleasure. "Eyes open and on me," I command her, barely squeezing, only testing. Her dark gaze stays on mine as I add a bit more pressure.

Her nipples pebble and a blush flushes her skin.

"How much do you trust me?" I ask.

"With my life," she says.

"You know that's in my hands right now, don't you?" I ask.

"Yes, sir," she says.

"Do you like that feeling, jailbird?"

"Yes, sir," she whispers, but I already know she does. Her body writhes as she hangs helplessly for me. Bending down, I flick the vibrator on and I press it between her legs. Her back bows slightly.

"Be still, Ella," I command, leaving no room in my tone for argument, "and keep your eyes open." She does as instructed and the moment I find that sweet spot, I know it. Her bottom lip drops and strangled moans leave her. I murmur, "There it is."

With my left hand controlling the wand and the right back at her throat, I give her pleasure like she's never felt before.

I put a little more pressure on until her pupils expand and she struggles to stay still. "Come for me, Ella," I whisper, holding her gaze.

"Oh," she says in a breathy voice and her toes curl, making her entire body sway as she loses her balance.

"Light-headed?" I ask, checking in.

"Yes," she says. "I almost feel …"

"High?"

"Yes," she answers. "It feels good," she adds and she's far too calm, so I turn up the vibrations with the press of my thumb. As her lips form a perfect O, I question, "Being choked?"

"No," she struggles to answer and then pushes out the next statement in a rush. "You having so much control."

I arch an eyebrow at her. "Sir," she finishes, the one word a pitch higher as her head falls back. I keep the pressure steady, feeling her pulse pound beneath my fingers and let her come. And she does, so beautifully. My cock twitches with need at the sight of her, lost in pleasure.

She heaves in a breath after I take my hand away from her neck. "Now stay still, my good girl."

I step back and watch her struggle to compose herself. She's already come twice and I imagine a third is going to wear her out. I'm aiming for four, though.

Pulling a small silver clicker out of my pocket, I tell her, "One click equals one spank." Her eyes fly open wide and she readjusts herself, paying attention. I raise the clicker in the air and press my thumb down. "There's one. I told you to be still."

This is a simple game, but it'll be difficult for her and we both know it. I'm setting her up to fail, but she will love being disciplined and it keeps her from being tempted to talk back, to disobey in any way. She'll enjoy the sweet pain of punishment as often as she needs.

Because I will set her up to fail. She needs it.

Ella attempts to stay still, but she bites at her lip watching me. "There's two. Keep your eyes on me," I tell her, releasing the bonds from above her head. "Stay still with your arms at your side." I lower each, rubbing her wrists as I do.

Her hands are resting loosely by her sides, but as I watch her, as I take in her beautiful naked body, one of her fingers flexes. "There's three," I say and she swallows audibly.

I make her stand there for three minutes as I pace around her. Kissing where I'd like and checking her wrists and throat. It must feel like an eternity. For the person trying to stay still, of course it does. Staying still isn't a hardship until someone else orders you to do it. It's easy until you have to.

By the time the three minutes is up, Ella is trembling. I don't count that against her. That's just her muscles. In all, she's earned herself thirteen spanks.

The bed groans as I sit on the edge of it, my cock eager to be buried inside of her. I could have her ride the horse or the bench, but I crave her like this for tonight.

"Now come here," I say. She nods and does as she's told, her bare feet padding against the floor. When she reaches me, I pull her over my lap. "I don't want you to count," I tell her. "I'll keep track. You take your punishment like a good girl."

Ella gasps loudly at the first swat, her hands fisting. I don't hold back but I soothe the spot the moment it's done.

That small touch is rewarded with a moan, reminding me how eager I am to be inside of her. With another swat and then another, my breath quickens with eagerness.

She squirms slightly, and muffles her cries as I spank her ass again and again.

At the end of thirteen, her ass is red and there are tears on her cheeks. I press my fingers against her and then slip them inside of her, stroking her front wall. Her moan is fucking heaven. It's then I see a tear fall.

"You did so well," I praise her and remove my fingers only to rub a hand over her glowing skin. "Are you hurt?"

She shakes her head and then tells me no.

"These are good tears then?" I question, leaning down to kiss her cheek. "Yes," she answers and I soothe her ass again before telling her, "Now it's time to stand up."

I help her to her feet, and Ella wobbles a bit as she finds her balance. She pulls herself upright and looks me in the eyes without wiping the tears from her face. So I do it for her.

"Ask me something," I say. "Ask me while the camera's watching."

"I'm not sure what to ask," she says. "I just want to touch you."

"Keep your hands at your sides," I say and to ease the immediate disappointment, I add, "You can touch me later."

"What's your favorite thing about me?" Ella asks after a moment.

"How red your ass is right now," I joke but then I tell her, "How I feel like this was meant to be. Like there isn't another person in this world that could want me and need me exactly how I want and need you."

Ella thinks for a minute. "Do you ever wish you could go back?"

No.

There's a chill that spreads over every inch of my skin. I know the answer right away, but I don't want her to think I'm telling her what she wants to hear.

If I had the chance, would I go back? Would I try to change things?

The answer is still the same.

"No, jailbird. I wouldn't. How could you even think that?"

Her head shakes softly and she swallows audibly. Her bottom lip quivers and before she can say anything, I pick her up and toss her on the bed onto her knees. Lowering my lips to the shell of her ear, I tell her, "I'm going to fuck that thought out of your pretty little head and you're never allowed to think it again."

As I slam inside of her to the hilt and she struggles to stay upright, I remind her, "You are mine and I'm exactly who you're meant to belong to."

I almost add "right now" but the words stop short. She is mine and she will stay mine. That is all that matters.

chapter 8

Ella

EVERY TIME HE LOOKS AT ME LIKE THAT, NOTHING ELSE EXISTS. It seems to get more intense as the nights go on. Four nights in a row now, we've spent our evenings in the playroom. Tonight we're in my bedroom, but with that look, we might as well be in the playroom.

"Kiss me," he says. The command is roughly ordered and I obey immediately.

Every small touch seems longer as time seems to slow. Heat and want dance along every inch of my skin. His fingers barely graze my curves as he breaks the kiss. I shiver from the touch and then bite down on my lower lip, peeking up at him and waiting.

He doesn't make me wait long.

"Strip." The singular word is deadly on his lips.

His hungry gaze watches me and I take my time, making my motions as seductive as possible. Slowly tugging the fabric off and watching as his gaze roams down my body in longing. My bra unclasps easily enough and he licks his lower lip watching my nipples harden as wisps of cool air caress my skin.

As the last piece falls into the puddle of fabric, he groans, his right hand flexing and his gaze finally coming back to mine.

He murmurs in contemplation, "What toy do I want to use on you tonight?"

With one step forward, I dare to take a bit of control.

"Do we need toys?" I question, reaching down and gripping his already hardened length through his slacks. "I just need you inside of me."

"My greedy girl," he says and I swear it's the sexiest thing I've ever heard. With lust reflecting in his eyes, all I want is more. More of his praise. More of his touch. Anything that involves more of *him.*

"Your good girl too, aren't I?" I whisper, maintaining eye contact all the while, and drop to my knees in front of him. The carpet is rough against my knees and I don't care. My breathing is heavy and I'm careful not to fumble as I unbutton his slacks, then tug the zipper down.

With a heavy groaned exhale coated in desire, Zander spears his fingers through my hair while his other hand helps me pull down his pants and boxers all at once.

The instant I'm able, the head of his cock is in my mouth. I moan around him, sucking the bit of salty precum from the tip and then massaging my tongue against the underside of his cock.

His hand wraps around the back of my neck as I take more of him into my mouth, all the way to the back of my throat.

"Fuck, Ella," he hisses and warmth flows through me. I hollow my cheeks, giving him pleasure. My nipples pebble from the chill of the room and I love it. I love this. I love him.

His cock presses against the back of my throat and I nearly gag on him, but I don't stop. I'm far too eager to please him.

He permits this for only a moment before surprising me by yanking me up and tossing me onto the bed. It seems so effortless for him as I bounce slightly and then sink into the luxurious sheets.

My chest rises and falls as he climbs onto the bed after me. His broad shoulders are carved from pure muscle and the sight of him staring at me as if he wants nothing more in his entire life leaves me breathless.

He breaks my gaze only to grab the pillow behind me.

"Spread your legs for me," he orders while placing the pillow under the small of my back. I do as I'm told, allowing him to position me however he wants while every nerve ending lights with fire in anticipation of what he's going to do to me.

Of course I obey him, spreading my legs for his hips to fit exactly where I need them, but he grips my upper thighs and pushes them back further, pinning me in an angled position so he can see my pussy easily. As my heated skin tingles in anticipation, he lowers himself, groaning as he takes a languid lick of my slit. His hungry eyes reach mine after sucking on my clit. They're dark and foreboding.

"When you come, you're going to thank me. Do you understand?"

Nodding, I eagerly agree. "I'll thank you."

"Good girl," he tells me before lowering his face back to my clit. He's unforgiving as he massages his tongue against my hardened nub. The vibrations of his groans of desire spread goosebumps up my skin as the pleasure hits me like waves crashing against the shore. More and more intense until I'm desperate for my release.

"Zander, please," I beg him and he lets go of my thigh to press two fingers inside of me, curving them and ruthlessly stroking my G-spot. I come recklessly under him. My climax is violent and arrives faster than I could have expected.

Even still, I thank him like he told me to do.

I spread my legs for him but he pushes my thighs up higher and pins them back. Fuck. He angles me and thrusts in deep. Deeper than he's been before and heat engulfs me. "Z," I say. There's a plea in my voice I can't help.

He leans forward, his hard body against mine and groans, "So fucking tight but I'll loosen you up." As he rocks, the pleasure builds and his pubes rubbing against my clit only heighten everything. Lighting every nerve ending aflame.

My heart pounds in my chest as the intensity climbs.

Every thrust pushes me higher and higher.

Every glance up his hazel eyes are on mine.

Every kiss silences desperate cries of pleasures. And all the while my heart races, my blood heats and the words "I love you" threaten to spill from my lips.

I resist which makes it all the more surprising and emotional when he whispers at the shell of my ear as I drift off to sleep in his arms, sated and spent, "Thank you for loving me."

There's a *tick, tick,* in my chest as I pretend to be sleeping. I'm falling, I know I'm falling and I'm fucking terrified of what that means and mostly, of ever losing him.

chapter 9

THE COMPARISON OF ELLA'S HOME TO MINE IS NIGHT AND DAY. That's all I can think as I fill her fridge with groceries that are meant for both of us. Sports drinks all in a row line the bottom shelf of the fridge and they're for me, not her. I've practically moved in and there's a piece of me that's unsettled in doing so. There are so many loose ends that need to be tied up. The sound of someone coming through the back door steals my attention.

It's Kamden. His expression appears wary, almost angry.

"Hey," he says, shutting the door behind him. "Are you busy?"

"Just putting these away." I hold up a gallon of milk and then turn my back to him, opening up the door and asking, "Something you wanted to talk about?"

My hackles bristle whenever he's around. I'm not sure if it's possessiveness or if it's because he knows more about Ella than I do. Or because there are secrets between us, but I know he loves Ella. I know he'd do anything for her. The possessiveness rises again. I don't know if that makes him an ally or an enemy.

"Yes. There's something we need to discuss." He hovers around the table in the breakfast nook, seeming unable to make up his mind about whether he should sit or stand for this conversation.

I don't like it. Kam is a bit of a wild card in this situation, and I'm still not sure what to think about him.

"Whatever you need to talk to me about, just say it. Ella's upstairs resting." I finish putting the groceries in the fridge and face him.

Kamden's eyes darken. "It's about the cameras."

"I don't work for The Firm anymore," I say and then gesture. "This place doesn't need to be full of cameras."

"Yeah. So I saw." Kam pulls up his phone and taps the screen. There's a video of me removing the cameras. Well, fuck.

"What is it? Did you want to see us fucking?"

He rolls his eyes and drops his arm. "I want to see her safe. That's what I want."

He's not as angry as I expected he'd be. Not even with me being kind of a prick. There's an uneasiness about him, but that's not necessarily a sign he's working against us.

"Look, I just … I need to know she's safe. All right. You could have at least given me a heads-up before you made that change."

"Sorry." I can understand what that's like. It makes me soften toward him. Maybe he does want what's best for her. "I'll keep her safe," I add, and I sure as hell mean that. It's a promise.

Kam nods like he believes me. He finally sits down at the kitchen table, but he's restless like he hasn't said all he wanted to say yet. His foot taps. He opens his mouth, then he shuts it again. I keep my eyes on him and wait. People who want to talk will always open up if you stay quiet and give them the space they need.

Kam lets out a rough breath and narrows his eyes at me, a thoughtful expression on his face. "At first I thought you were into her because of the money."

My eyebrows quirk up but I stay silent.

"I looked into your finances," he explains. "Found something interesting."

"You found out about the insurance," I guess.

"Yes. I found out," Kam continues, "that you're wealthy in your own right … from Quincy's death, but you don't seem to have touched any of it."

I swallow hard at the mention of her name. I've never touched it for a reason. Even now, I'm technically unemployed but I haven't had to dip into it yet, and I don't know that I want to. I'm immediately uncomfortable at having Kam say it out loud, but I sit with the emotion rather than letting it turn to anger. I do have enough money to last a lifetime if it's managed correctly. The fact that Kam knows about it doesn't change anything.

"No," I tell him. "I haven't touched a dime."

He studies me for a few seconds. "I don't know what to think of you, Zander."

"And I don't know what to think of you."

"Yes, you do." Now he's exasperated. The anger reappears in his eyes. Or is it just frustration? It could go either way. "I'm someone who will do anything to protect her. Anything."

"And?"

"And I'm willing to let in others who will do the same." He looks at me intently, willing me to respond.

"Or," I counter, "you're someone who won't mind pushing people out if you think they've gotten too close."

Kam smirks at me. "You're more like James than I realized. More bitter, I think. James didn't hold on to things like you do."

He's genuinely angry by the time he's done speaking. His face is turning a little red. He opens his jacket and pulls out a bottle of alcohol.

"Ella's not allowed to have that here," I tell him, my voice hard.

"She's not an alcoholic," he says and then adds, "This is for me, though." After a swig, he eyes me. "I'm not an alcoholic. Do I cope with it? Do I misuse it at times? … I'm working on it. Spare me your judgment."

"Drink all you'd like. I just don't want Ella to have it."

"Yeah." Surprisingly he agrees and Kam motions with the bottle. "I know there's an association between misuse and …" He hesitates and the color drains from his face.

"Suicidal thoughts." I complete the sentence for him.

Kam nods and then says, "I don't know if you know, but when she gets like this, it fucks me up a bit."

I watch him. Carefully this time.

Kam unscrews the top and tips back the bottle. After taking a pull he offers it to me, but I decline with a gesture.

"When she gets like this?" I question. "You say that like it happens often."

Kam lets out a sarcastic huff. "I thought we were bonding here."

I give him a humorless laugh in return. There's a moment of silence. Kam has another swig as I look out the back window. He didn't drive here, because there's no car outside. He walked.

That must mean he was fucked up before he came. He wasn't planning to drive. That's one point in his favor. If he'd driven here, drunk behind the wheel—

"Nobody drunk should ever be behind the wheel, especially not if they're fucked up," Kam says, as if he can read my mind. He stares into the distance and I watch the memories go through his eyes as he takes another sip from his bottle.

Nerves have me on edge. "You all right?" I ask him.

"I've just been thinking," he answers.

"About what?"

"Just what she's been through." Kam was the one to witness it all firsthand.

"It wasn't just after James died," he says after a while, abruptly, like he snapped back to bonding with me. Or like this is too heavy for him to keep inside anymore. "She had a difficult life."

I think about all the information Cade gave me. All those files.

Slowly, I pull out a chair at the table and take a seat with him.

I take a moment to study him. He came here with alcohol in his jacket pocket, and he's been talking openly about her rough childhood. I don't know what has him so upset, but maybe if I just listen, he'll feel like elaborating.

"Her childhood wasn't her fault," he says and then finishes the bottle.

But what if Kam thinks he has some responsibility for that? If he blames himself for things that happened to her, then it would explain how he's behaving right now. If he was involved in how things played out for her, even more so.

I'm not sure how to press him for details. I haven't worked with Kam like that. Taking a deep breath, I settle on acknowledging the obvious.

"From what I've heard, it was pretty rough."

"'Pretty rough' is putting it mildly," he comments. I wonder if he's only telling me this because he knows that I'm looking into it.

"You know what happened to her mom?" he asks.

"Yes," I say, searching his gaze. "Is there something else you want to tell me about that? Maybe something I don't know?"

Kam looks at me for a long, long time. Too long of a moment passes and then he runs a hand down his face. "No," he says finally. "I just wanted to talk. I just wanted to ask you about the cameras."

It already seems like a year ago that he asked me about those cameras. That was his pretense for showing up. It barely lasted five minutes.

"You sure?" I question.

He hesitates for a beat. "Yeah. Will you give me a heads-up first next time you plan to change something major? Just so I know?"

Nodding, I tell him, "I can do that."

"I think I shouldn't have had that last drink," he mutters while rubbing the back of his head.

"You want a ride back home?" I offer and he stares at me for a long moment once again.

Kam stands up from his seat at the table, answering "no" and tucks the empty bottle back into his jacket pocket. He glances toward the staircase. "I'm going to head out. Tell Ella I said hi."

chapter 10

Ella

THE HUM OF THE ENGINE AND THE BRISK WIND ARE MORE relaxing than I could have imagined. I've been down on this road so many times, but I've never just driven. With the window rolled down, the wind rushes between my fingers and the hint of a smile graces my lips. We round another corner of the long, winding road of the mountain. Nothing but gorgeous foliage and mountainscapes to see.

"You were right. It is a nice drive."

"I like the sound of you telling me I'm right," Z comments, twisting his strong hands on the leather steering wheel.

He glances at me with a wicked look in his eyes and a cocky grin.

We're both dressed casually. In jeans and T-shirts, like a normal couple on a normal day. Even still, he's devilishly handsome with that perfect smile and rough stubble.

For a moment I'm lost in him and then I glance back, a streak of black catching my eye and I see the car behind us. The Firm is still monitoring every move we make.

I don't feel the sinking dread that I used to knowing that I wasn't allowed to be alone. There's a bit of peace to it now, but sometimes I do just want to be alone with Zander.

It's been two solid weeks of us acting like a normal couple. Maybe acting isn't the right word, but I know we're pretending that the therapy sessions, meetings and constant PR calls are normal. There was an emergency hearing from the judge as well, given that our relationship is now public. That gave Kam and Cade a few gray hairs each.

More articles have come out and Kam suggested a PR move. This drive is potentially one of them. He said paparazzi got a heads-up that we'll be out on a twilight drive along the mountainside. Kam said the magazines catching images of me and Zander doing "normal things" would be good for public peace of mind and ease any worries or concerns that I'm unwell or that our relationship is problematic.

One article suggested Z was taking advantage of me. They sensationalized the forbidden aspect of our relationship, intentionally leaving out that his position in The Firm was withdrawn and that he isn't in charge of my care … at least not legally. That particular article prompted this drive. I didn't expect to love it so much. The peace and quiet. The normalcy of it all.

"What was your life like before me?"

Z glances at me for a moment, then looks back to the road. The trees whip by as we round the corner, making our way up the side of the mountain. "Hectic, always changing." He clears his throat and readjusts his hands on the wheel. "We had jobs back-to-back. I was constantly on one side of the country and then the other. Nothing was ever settled."

I cock a brow and joke, "So you feel like you're settling?"

His first glance carries concern until he sees my smile. "I feel myself wanting to maybe settle down … for the first time," he clarifies and glances my way. Gauging my expression.

"Shocked to hear that?" he questions with a smirk. My brow is raised, I know that much but I didn't think I was giving so much away.

"Just … hearing you talk about settling down is new. That's something we haven't really talked about."

"Do you want to?" he asks.

I want him to tell me how it will happen and then make it my reality. I want it to just be. I want us to just be. That's not what I say, though.

"I'm not sure how that can happen with a tail," I comment and gesture behind us.

He groans, relaxing into his seat. "I could gun it," he jokes and at that very moment, I perk up instantly.

"What?" Z notices and I ease the worry in his tone.

"That spot. Go up and to the right," I direct him, patting his arm and doing what I can to contain my excitement.

I recognize everything about this place. The row of trees, the way they disappear and the sharp drop-off that is just on the other side through the rocky climb.

Nostalgia wraps around me and, in a rarity these days, it makes me smile to remember these times.

"Back in my late teens we'd come up here. Park the car," I tell him and the moment his hand is on the gearshift I unbuckle my seat belt and climb out. The brisk air of the mountains is colder than I expected. We're at a higher elevation than back at the house.

"Where are you going?" Z calls out, his door closing with a thud and then he jogs around the front of his car, chasing after me.

I head toward a small bit of brush by the edge of the cliff and it's almost exactly how I remember. My gait is measured but I can't contain this excitement. As Z stops by my side, I'm vaguely aware that Silas parks behind our car.

"What are you up to?" Z questions with a knitted brow but a barely contained smile that must match mine. As I pull my jacket tighter, Z rests an arm around my shoulders and I lean into him.

"Can't you hear it?" I ask him as the rushing water gets louder and louder. Even the fresh smell is memorable. Everything about this place is just the same as I remember.

"A waterfall?" he says, keeping pace with me as I lead him toward the summit of the cliff.

"They would never catch us here." I slip out of his grip to get closer to the edge, the footpath becoming more rock than brush.

"Who are they?" he questions as the trees become sparse and more of the waterfall can be seen. At the top, looking over, it's breathtaking. I remember the feeling of being here, but my memory could never do justice to the actual sight, which is stunning.

I turn to face him but keep walking and say, "Anyone and everyone.

It's our safe place." Almost comically, I nearly trip on the last statement, and catch myself before tumbling forward.

With a firm grasp, Z pulls me closer to him. There's still a good ten feet of nearly flat rock till the edge, but he acts like I could have fallen over.

"Ella," he says, practically reprimanding me and I laugh in response.

"It's fine. I'm fine." I try to shake him off but he's adamant.

"It's dangerous," Zander tells me in a low tone and I know not to push him much.

"Not with you here," I say and take another step forward, but he holds my elbow just enough to keep me from going toward the edge of the waterfall.

The water is gorgeous. The rushing waves reflect the sunlight and everything about this place is peaceful. The white noise, the fresh atmosphere, and the clean yet woodsy smells in the cool air.

Closing my eyes, I imagine this may be what heaven feels like.

"It's dangerous, Ella," he repeats with emphasis and I have to laugh.

"We used to jump," I tell him, the youthful memory bringing a smile to my lips.

"From here?" he says and the shock in his tone is comical to me. I keep my distance, though, so as not to worry him.

Nodding, I keep the smile in place and tell him, "Yeah, from here."

"Why the fuck would you do that?"

I shrug and give him a rueful grin. "Because we were young and dumb and it was here."

"Who's we?"

"Me. Trish. My girlfriends." I shrug again and he wraps an arm around my waist.

"Don't worry. I'm a good listener and I heard you tell me not to jump," I joke, taking his hand in mine.

He roughly chuckles and squeezes my hand back.

"Besides," I say and peek behind Z to where Silas is watching from a short distance away, "I wouldn't want to give your backup a heart attack."

I'm rewarded with another short, rough chuckle.

"What about Kam?" His tone is more serious now although he tries to play it off.

"What about him?"

"Did he ever jump with you?"

"He knows but he's never jumped." I confide in him without thinking twice. Which is dangerous and yet there isn't an ounce of worry in the confession. Although I know I'm on the edge of unraveling something that's been kept tightly wound and should remain that way. "He's picked me up a time or two before, late at night, soaking wet even."

"You trust Kam," he says almost like it's a question. His gaze stays pinned on me, no longer interested in the fall in the least.

"I don't just trust him, I love him and if you knew—" I stop myself before finishing my statement but Zander picks up where I left off. I swear he knows what I'm thinking before I do sometimes.

"If I knew all your secrets ..." he starts.

"If you knew all my family's secrets and those of his too ..." I say and trail off, then huff humorlessly and look away but not for long.

With his thumb on my chin and his forefinger beneath it, he tilts my head up so I look him in the eye. His gaze is intense and he pauses a moment, searching my eyes for something before confessing, "I'd still love you."

The intensity is all too much. Like something breaking and crumbling apart in a way where it will never be repaired. Something I don't want to be fixed. Something I don't want to think about ever again.

He leans down, his warm breath meeting mine and he nips my bottom lip before capturing my mouth with his, silencing the sudden gasp from the hint of pain.

He's good at that. My Z ... my Dom. He excels at silencing the pain.

"That's my girl," he whispers against my lips and I smile.

A warm feeling in the pit of my stomach flutters like butterfly wings as he kisses me once again. Deeply, with longing, then hungrily. I meet his want with my need and deepen the kiss that much more.

chapter 11

It's tense as Cade and I sit facing one another on the opposite ends of the meeting table in The Firm's temporary office. Damon's here too. Along with the rest of the guys.

Anxiousness creeps up the back of my neck, but I do everything I can to shake it off. It didn't hit me in the moment, but looking back on it, I'm sure I lost the respect from the members of The Firm. What happened … I'd do it all over again. There's no way I could ever not be with her. She's mine and she's meant to be mine. But that doesn't mean I'm proud of how it happened. Or that I can't acknowledge I made mistakes that put The Firm and even Ella, at risk.

With a steady inhale, I keep my composure and wait for the mandatory meeting to begin. No doubt it was ordered by Judge Martel.

Scanning the room, it's obvious no one is comfortable. We're all a little restless. I can tell by the way Damon taps his foot and keeps checking the large clock on the wall. He's not usually one to get antsy about meetings, but he's right now, he's impatient.

"So." Cade taps a stack of papers against the desk, straightening them. "We have our update on the conservatorship to submit to the judge. Here's what we're handing in, Zander."

Shock lifts my eyes to his and then back down to the report.

He pushes the papers toward me. It's a slim file. There is no legal reason I should see this right now. That anxiousness increases tenfold thinking there must be something damaging, something my brother is letting me see ahead of time to save our personal relationship.

I'm silent as I page through it carefully. When it came to Ella, I let my emotions get the better of me. I acted recklessly, but I'm not going to do it now.

I read the cover sheet, the second page, the third and so forth. Then I flip back to the beginning and read it again. All the while the men watch silently. The clock ticks incessantly.

Then I look into Cade's eyes. "This report leaves out a few things."

It's an intense statement to make. At The Firm, we pride ourselves on our integrity. Clients can trust us not to misrepresent the situation. This report Cade handed me might not contain outright lies about her progress, but it does tell a different story from the full truth of the last few weeks.

"I didn't think some details were necessary to include." Cade's talking about the night they caught me with Ella. My expulsion is also not included in the update.

It doesn't say that I've been disciplined in any way.

The report doesn't capture my brother's disappointment in me or how shaken Damon was when he realized what I'd been doing. There's nothing about the two of us other than that there is now a personal relationship that is deemed appropriate by The Firm. *Appropriate.*

"What does this mean?" I question.

My brother takes in a steadying breath, his thumb tapping lightly. There's a seriousness about him but something else is there in his gaze. "You are no longer removed. That was a temporary status. You are back as a member of The Firm."

Once again, shock hits me. He pulls something out from under the table. It's my gun in its holster.

I look at him, then stare at the gun. It's only now that I'm able to admit to myself how much I wanted this. I didn't want to be kicked out of The Firm. I was willing to live the rest of my life with the loss of it if that's what I had to do to keep Ella. But I never wanted to be separated from my brother this way. From all my brothers. I never wanted to be on the outside like this.

I'm afraid it's too good to be true. I'm afraid to even reach for the gun. "Are you sure?"

He nods, but then I look at the other guys one by one. "I don't want this to be a split decision," I tell them all. It's possible there was a vote and some people didn't agree.

"It was unanimous," Damon says, cracking a smile. "We had a long-ass meeting about it." His smile widens and he adds, "We all want you back."

I haven't been this relieved since I brought Ella back from the brink after her breakdown. I feel like I'm taking a real breath for the first time in days.

"Go ahead," Cade says.

This moment feels as important as the first day I signed on with The Firm.

I lift the gun carefully from the table, stand up, and put my holster back in its place. When I sit down, Cade is pushing something else across the table to me.

My ID.

Those are the only two things I needed.

"How's it feel?" Cade asks and for the first time all day, he grins at me, everything feeling lighter.

"It feels damn good," I answer him and the guys laugh. Each of them stands and claps me on my shoulder in turn.

"It's good to have you back," Silas says and then adds, "Not that we could have got rid of your ass anyway." That gets the room filled with laughter again.

The shock still hasn't left me as I sit there, the reality sinking in. I never dared to hope that it would turn out this way. In fact, I planned on the opposite happening. I was ready to spend the rest of my life missing this job and all that comes with it.

I slip my wallet into my back pocket, and I can't help feeling like this is a sign. Like this was meant to be. Ella's meant to be with me, and I'm meant to be with her. I'm also meant to work at The Firm. If the universe had a problem with that, there's no way I'd be back in.

Thank God I'm back in.

"Now, let's get down to business," Cade says and the atmosphere turns more serious. The guys retake their seats and I already know where this is going.

Cade drums his fingertips on the table, returning to his usual brisk personality. "We've seen some things with these … elite circles." He looks around at all of us. "Any disagreement with my read on that?"

Damon shakes his head. "No." Silas leans back, his arms crossed and shakes his head too.

Cade returns his gaze to mine. "Ella was into some of it. Somebody is blackmailing her."

My blood turns cold. "Does Kamden know?"

My brother nods once and says, "I filled him in last night. He said he's almost certain he knows who it is and will trace it back."

"Does Ella?"

"No."

"Is he going to tell her?"

My brother stills. "We have asked that he doesn't say anything to her at this time."

I nod in agreement. "She's doing well. Very well. She's happy. There's no reason to alarm her if we can take care of this."

"That's what we suggested to Kamden. He agreed to give us a deadline before he takes things into his own hands."

I swallow the ball of anger in my throat. "What do they have on her?"

"Video," Cade answers, his tone solemn.

Shit. Video's the worst kind of evidence. It can be faked or manipulated, but most people don't have the necessary skills or technology. Video is usually trustworthy, and that's what makes it so dangerous. Even if it's fake, you can still be fucked over. People believe what they see more so than any other kind of evidence.

"Is it credible?" I ask.

"From what I can tell, yes," my brother confirms. "Kamden agrees. That's why he believes he knows who may have sent it."

"How much?"

"Two million."

"The hell's in it?" I ask.

Cleaning up messes like this is a specialty of The Firm's. We help people get out of impossible situations. I'm so glad they let me back in. If I hadn't known about this, Ella would have been at even more risk.

I wouldn't have been able to protect her from the various threats in her life.

If my brother had kept me in the dark …

It would have torn apart our relationship. These are things I need to know. I remind myself again that it's all right. I *am* back in The Firm, and Cade did tell me. I have what I need to keep Ella safe.

Cade watches me from across the table. I don't know what I was thinking before. Cade would have told me about this even if I wasn't working for The Firm.

"What's on the video?" I press and take a look around the room.

"It's a video of her parents." His tone is sober. "Family secrets. And some truly fucked-up abuse."

I sit back and take it in. "Is Ella in the videos?"

"No," he says. "Not as far as I know, but that could change as we find out more."

I have to take a minute to sit with that. Fucked-up abuse scars a person. Ella seems focused on James's death as the cause of her spiraling, but clearly her trauma began earlier. It wasn't a single moment that triggered her downfall. A chill runs down my spine as I'm reminded of what Kam said at the house. *That she had a difficult life.*

This must have been what he was talking about. That's why he was drunk last night.

"What exactly is in the video? Did Kam see it?"

"Yeah. And he recognized it. He said it's not the first time the video has been used as blackmail."

"Did they pay last time?"

"Kam said the problem dissolved itself."

"What the hell does that mean?" I ask even though I know. Cade shares a look with Silas and Damon looks down to the floor.

"The problem went away on its own and I believe it was buried ten feet under."

Fuck.

"So it can't be the same person?"

He shakes his head slowly.

My jailbird.

I want to be with her right now. I fight off a strong urge to get up and leave the table.

But as much as I want to hold her, I want to keep her safe even more. That starts here and now, at this table, with The Firm.

"Okay." I look Cade in the eyes. "Let's figure this out. Ella is depending on us."

chapter 12

Ella

THE PHONE IS CLUNKY AND OLD, BUT IT DOES THE TRICK.

I text Kam once I'm finished. You know I could open apps on the laptop too right?

Kam: Do I need to tell Zander to take it away?

I narrow my eyes at the old phone that's practically a brick.

Ella: No need. I don't have my passwords. I hope that eases his worries, but judging by what he says next, I'm not sure I accomplished that task.

Kam: No new accounts.

My eyes roll without my conscious consent.

Ella: I'm aware, Kam. I was just messing with you.

I debate on calling him to voice my discontent at not being able to send a GIF of a dog rolling his eyes, but I decide not to since he should be here soon and I can tell him face-to-face.

Life is slowly going back to what used to be normal.

Well, other than replacing what used to be and rearranging finances. Kam is taking care of that, though. In less than a week three homes have gone into escrow, all cash. I try not to think of it and instead I scroll, searching for new properties and wondering if we should sell this one.

The fall breeze blows in through the cracked windows of the downstairs office, bringing in with it the faint smells of the season. The crisp autumn has always felt like home in some ways.

The cool air wraps around my shoulders as I sink deeper into the corner of the sofa with my laptop balanced on a throw pillow. I have to readjust so I'm not sitting on my flannel button-down top. Paired with faded light blue jeans, the outfit is one of my favorites for fall.

Not quite chic or uptown, but Zander said he liked it this morning.

I peek up through the doorway, knowing he's in the sitting room with Cade going over details I don't want or need to be privy to. He looked cute today too. In just blue jeans and a worn black tee. It amazes me how expensive and authoritative he appears, even in the simplest blue-collar attire.

My focus returns to the screen in front of me as I scan a listing in Miami and then email the link to Kam. Smirking, I can already hear him joking about retiring in Florida.

We could retire if we wanted. We could start completely fresh, just me and Z. We could hide away and go off the grid if we wanted. We can do whatever we want.

Or we could continue maintaining the status quo. I would be content with that. Although part of me thinks it's all just a fantasy and that once The Firm is gone, Zander will leave too.

I click over my tab to the email with The Firm suggesting to the judge that another psych eval be done. One to determine my competency. And for another doctor to be brought in once their term has ended, someone who will take over with my care plan.

It's odd to read it, this plan and schedule for a potential release of conservatorship. There's a fear there too, wondering if everything will be okay once they're gone. At that thought, I know it will be, so long as I still have Z.

Instinctively, I click over to another tab and read the tabloids with a Cheshire cat grin. Biting down on my bottom lip to keep my giddiness contained, I read the article again.

There's the mention of a possible baby and rumors swirling in the comments. All because of a hand on my stomach in one picture snapped. There's nothing to that rumor but it brings up all the hopes I had with James.

We wanted a baby. Once we finally settled down, we both wanted a baby. And now that will never happen. When I was in my late teens and twenties, the idea of an infant gave me hives. How could I possibly be a mother when I can hardly care for myself?

Now, even knowing how lacking I am, I know I would love a baby. I would give that baby the world. When we bought this house, we'd planned to start a family here, knowing there'd be plenty of room to expand. That was what sealed the deal for us. Now everything has changed and it's so empty here.

Tormented emotions swirl deep in the pit of my stomach and I have to close the laptop, swallowing thickly and reminding myself that it's okay. The front door opens and closes, and the sound of it makes me pull myself together.

That was the past, and now I have the future to look forward to. Clearing my throat, I set the laptop to the side and do what I can to shake off the heavy feelings.

I have no idea if Zander even wants a child or what he would think of having a baby with me. Or whether I should. The last thing I want is for a child to be brought up in this world as fucked up as me.

"That's not what was agreed upon." Cade's voice is harsh and it echoes down the hall. The cracked door carries the heavy footsteps of him leaving and a remark from Kam that I can barely hear. I'm slow to move, and quiet as I can be, attempting to eavesdrop on what appears to be a tense conversation.

With the footsteps getting closer, I stay perfectly still by the door. Cade's shadow passes and I peek through to see his back as he goes out the back way.

The sliding door is faintly heard over my rapidly beating heart as I listen to Z and Kam argue.

Something about money. Something about a note.

A chill sends pricks down my arm and I move without thinking. Numbly I make my way to them in the sitting room. I only hesitate outside the door for a moment. It's the statement "I don't know if we should tell her" spoken from Zander that has me pushing the door open. The hinges creak, announcing my arrival in an eerie manner.

Both of them stand, Kam in a sharp suit and Zander just how I saw him last in laid-back attire.

"Ella." Kam greets me as warmly as he can, but his grim look is telling.

"What's going on?" My tone is even and I should be proud of that fact, but looking up at Zander I feel considerably less than proud. I'm an intruder in a conversation he obviously doesn't want me to hear.

"Nothing to worry about. Just give us a minute, please."

My cheeks heat with embarrassment and there's a dull thud in my chest.

"I thought I heard my name," I comment weakly.

"Zander is learning some things," Kam comments condescendingly, his gaze fixed on Zander although he's talking to me.

"What things?" I question and Z responds to Kam rather than me, "She doesn't need to know." His voice is calm, much more so than before, and sympathetic.

With a half step forward, I refuse to leave and let them discuss me without being able to speak for myself.

"She knows more than you ever will," Kam says. His eyes flash to mine and there's a pain there I wish I hadn't seen. He swallows thickly before picking up his jacket and slipping it on. "I'll let you decide what you'd like to do."

With that he leaves. Barely squeezing my shoulder, quickly kissing my cheek and heading out without stopping when I ask him not to leave.

So many memories return. All of the times James and Kam got into it. There were a number of tense conversations and all for good reason.

But this?

"What happened?" I question Z the moment I can and pinching the bridge of his nose, he asks me to stop. To let it be so he can figure it out.

It's hardly placating and I'm quick to open my phone.

"Who are you calling?" he questions and I answer "no one," turning my back to him and telling him he can have his minute. I'm quick to make my way back to the office and text Kam.

Ella: Talk to me.

There's the sound of a muffled bang from the sitting room and I'm vaguely aware of Cade coming back inside. Frustration echoes down the corridor and I can't ignore it.

Betrayal and anxiousness run thick in my blood.

I text Kam again.

Ella: What happened?

When he doesn't reply right away, I text him for a third time.

Ella: I'm begging, Kam. Please, what happened?

Kam finally answers and it doesn't ease a damn thing.

Kam: You should probably talk to Zander before me.

Ella: Are you sure?

My heart races, not knowing if Z will even tell me. I look down the hall and I can barely hear him talking to his brother, but their voices are far too hushed to hear a thing. Cade won't tell me what's going on, I'm certain of that.

The phone pings.

Kam: I'm sure. Ask him to tell you.

As the conversation continues, my worries intensify.

My first question is the one most obvious to ask.

Ella: Is it something like ... like that would have made James mad?

His answer makes my blood run cold.

Kam: Yes.

Ella: Something Z did?

Kam: No. Z didn't do this.

Ella: Can't you just tell me?

Kam: Is that the way you want it to go? Or do you want to ask him to tell you?

chapter 13

Zander

ELLA FACES OFF AGAINST ME, HER PHONE IN HER HANDS, HER cheeks pink with emotion. I fucked up. I know that. We shouldn't have spoken about Ella when there was any chance she could hear. I can feel her slipping and it's a first for us since her breakdown.

It won't be the last.

Ella taps out one more message on her phone, then lets out a frustrated sigh. "You could tell me what it's about at least," she murmurs, peeking up at me, her head down, but her shoulders squared.

"Boundaries, jailbird."

"You need to tell me what you were talking about. It's not okay for you two to decide that you're going to keep things from me. How is that fair?" The leather chair in the office groans under her weight as she sits down, only to immediately stand back up. She paces as she types out another message.

Kam better not fucking tell her. "That's not what's happening," I say, attempting to reassure her.

"Isn't it?" She holds up her phone so I can see the text from Kamden on the screen.

Kam: Is that the way you want it to go? Or do you want to ask him to tell you?

"He won't tell me. Kam apparently thinks I should ask you, so that's what I'm doing. What were you talking about?" she asks.

Good. Knowing that Kam isn't going to put this knowledge on her is a relief, but I keep my expression neutral.

"We will take care of it." This is as much a test for her as it is for me. She gives me the burden, and I bury it for her. A chill runs down my spine, knowing that's exactly how Kam handled it last time. Or at least that's what he implied.

"I don't want you two to take care of all my problems and not even tell me about them." Ella shakes her head, her long hair swishing around her shoulders. Swallowing thickly, she says, "I should know."

"Ella," I say and her name is a warning.

"You just have to tell me," she says, her tone pleading.

Defiant. All I can think right now is that she's being defiant and this will play out one of two ways. I give her nothing but silence.

With a frustrated sigh, Ella pushes past me. I follow quietly behind her, deciding how exactly to handle this. To handle her. She moves quickly through the house and to the kitchen, where she opens one cupboard, then the next. A box of tea appears in her hand and she puts it down hard on the countertop.

"Ella, stop."

"I'm having tea," she says, her voice high and strained. "That's all I'm doing. If you won't talk to me, then I'm going to sit down and have a cup of tea." The water rushes down as she fills the kettle. Once it's filled, she turns it off with pent-up anger and adds, "Is there a problem with that?"

I cross to her in two steps and take her chin in my hand. The kettle lands hard on the counter and her shocked eyes look up at me.

Her chest rises and falls quickly. She's going to break down in a few minutes if I don't stop this, and I *will* stop this. Ella doesn't need to be swept up in fear.

It's just that now isn't the time to tell her.

"Jailbird, I'm sorry you overheard our conversation. We should have had it elsewhere."

She lets out a shaky breath. "No, you should include me," she pleads.

"No." My voice is firm. "I'm not going to tell you at this moment."

"Is it bad?" she whispers and I tell her it's nothing I can't handle.

With her lips pressed in a thin line, she stares past me, not at all happy.

"I apologize for causing you fear and distress, but now's not the time for you and me to discuss the topic. You need to be reminded of the rules." I keep my voice quiet. "The way you're acting right now makes me think you're being purposely disobedient."

Those last two words do exactly what I'd like them to do.

A new flush comes to her cheeks. Telling Ella she's acting out deliberately is the same as telling her I'm going to punish her, and she loves to be punished. It reinforces our connection to one another and it's a healthy release for her. It would probably do her good.

She takes a deep breath and lets it out slowly. "I'm not disobeying, Z."

"Look at me." Her dark eyes move to mine and stay locked on me. "Good girl." I tuck her hair behind her ear and her eyelids go heavy at the simple touch. "We will discuss this in our next session. All right?"

"I would appreciate it if you didn't keep things from me," she says, her voice shaking. "I think you should put an end to all this and just tell me what I need to know."

No.

Instinctively I understand that speaking to her about it now would only make the situation more fraught. I don't have a plan for what to say, and talking about this with Ella requires serious consideration, not spontaneity. There is far too much on the line to leave things to chance. I will tell her when I know exactly how it will be handled and ended. That way she'll have nothing to concern herself with.

"I'm taking you to dinner." There. That's a decision. Move our venue. Give us both some time to reset and calm down.

Ella's expression falters. "I know that's not what you were talking to Kam about."

"No, jailbird, it wasn't. But I'm not ready to talk about it with you. And you're not ready to hear it."

"Z …"

"Do you trust me?"

She bites her lip. "Yes."

"I know it's hard, jailbird, but you need to keep trusting me now."

"Well, it feels like you don't trust me. It feels like you're hiding something because you think I'm too fragile."

"That isn't the case." She tries to look down and away. "Ella. You are not weak. You're my submissive and I provide for you. This is what I want from you. Control in all things. I crave your burdens. Give them to me."

There's a shift. It's slight, but it's there. "But …"

"Trust me."

I know what I'm asking from her, and it's not easy to give it. But if we're going to get through this, and we are going to get through this, we need to be able to sit in these uncomfortable spaces."

Ella gives a shallow nod.

I lean down and kiss her.

When our lips touch, it doesn't erase the tension. I can still feel it in her body. But on a physical level, there's no misunderstanding between us. It's her lips against mine and then her tongue against mine, both of us seeking the other. It makes me hot for her. Too hot.

I pull away slowly from the kiss. "Come on. Get your shoes."

Her brow furrows. "I'm not dressed to go out."

I smirk down at her. She looks beautiful even if only in a flannel button-down and a faded pair of jeans. "Then I'll wait. You can change and we'll go wherever you'd like, jailbird."

"You make me feel like a jailbird more now than I have in a very long time."

Tension fills the room again. All I want is to put all of this behind us. The tumultuous and terrible things she's experienced. The growing threat that I'll handle along with the rest of the team. I want her to have a life like any other person who isn't a client of The Firm. As close as a socialite like her can get, anyway.

I can almost see it. A life beyond secretive conversations and conservatorships. I can practically envision her, happy at my side for whatever life throws at us.

The silence goes on for a beat too long, as if Ella is going to argue with me. The expression on her face looks like she's on the verge of spiraling. Of getting caught up in the meaning of us and The Firm and why I call her *jailbird*.

"Are you mine, Ella?" There is no negotiation in my tone.

She seems to return to me. "Yes," she says.

I lean in close to her mouth and nip her bottom lip. "Yes, what?"

"Yes, sir."

No matter what's happening between us, there's always a dark twinkle in her eyes when she responds to me that way.

"You're always my fucking jailbird. Now go get changed."

chapter 14

Ella

T HE TIP OF MY BLACK STILETTO HEEL TAPS AGAINST THE BASE of the table. The anxiousness is not quite leaving me. We've never been like this. At odds. Given the power dynamic between us, there isn't a damn thing in my favor.

I've never felt this kind of vulnerable with Z. An unsteady exhale leaves me as he places our drink orders and the waiter leaves us in the private back room to ourselves.

Three of the four walls are furnished with hundreds of bottles of wine. It's as if we're in the middle of a beautifully lit cellar, ready for a romantic dinner below a black iron chandelier designed to look like a classic candelabra.

The room itself is intimate and the smells of savory seasoning and sweet wines stir my appetite, even with the nervousness of knowing Z is keeping something from me.

His strong hand settles on my thigh, his thumb running back and forth where the emerald silk velvet of my dress meets my bare skin. It's a simple designer dress with a deep V-neck and long sleeves, yet it ends midthigh. I haven't worn something that hugs my curves like this in a very long time, let alone something so decadently expensive. His black suit is custom tailored and high end.

To anyone peeking in, I'm certain we would appear to be a power couple. Especially given how he's acting as if there isn't a damn thing wrong.

It was a long and quiet drive, but that hand of his has barely left me. It's as if he thinks he can contain me so long as he has physical possession of me.

Truth be told, it is comforting and he's not entirely wrong. But my mind won't let go of it. The wheels in my head turn and every possible horrid scenario fills my mind.

"Settle, Ella," he murmurs. I'm half surprised Z ordered me wine, but that only adds to the racing thoughts. Is it because he intends on telling me something that he thinks I'll need alcohol to absorb?

No, no, that's the opposite. Damon made it clear as did Zander, when my spirits are low, I should avoid alcohol. It can no longer be a coping mechanism. Not in any way.

I swallow thickly, turning my attention to the candles lit on the table. That means then, that he's not going to tell me whatever it is that's happened.

"Do you think I'm weak and that's why you can't tell me?" I ask him again. I know that must be why. He could still carry my burdens, even if he told me what they were.

"You are not weak. I will tell you once I've decided it will benefit you."

I nearly ask who he thinks he is to decide what is and isn't good for me and the audacity of that thought has me reaching for the prosecco. The sweet drink is chilled perfectly; the bubbles crisp and refreshing.

Thankfully, we're interrupted by a young waiter presenting the chef's specials and a list with the fish of the day.

My appetite comes and goes as I ruminate on the possibilities. With a gentle squeeze, Z comforts me and orders for me as well, but it's not enough.

Just as the waiter leaves us, one hand on his skinny dark red tie and the other holding the menus, I prepare to lay it all out for Z. To tell him with finality that I can't be left in the dark on issues that pertain to me.

My lips part and my shoulders square to face him, but not a word slips out. I'm caught in his heated gaze. Fire crackles there and my body is paralyzed from the look he gives me.

"I require your obedience," he tells me, his gaze dropping from mine to my lips. "You are struggling with that tonight," he adds and his hand is released from my thigh. Leaving a chill to settle where the contact has been every moment he's been able to rest it there since we left.

As he sips his drink, an Arnold Palmer, I watch him.

"I am struggling," I admit and gather my strength to make my demands, but again I'm cut off.

"You have no reason to," he tells me and unbuttons his jacket, slipping the expensive fabric off of his broad shoulders and turning his full attention to me. His scent, masculine and woodsy greets me as I stare back at him.

"I don't know that."

"I'm telling you that. You should not worry. Not about anything. I have it handled." He's firm in his resolve. The control in his tone grants me a sense of security but still, I hesitate.

As he clears his throat, the cords in his neck tighten, and his presence seems to command the air to bend to his will. The strength and authority I know this man to be capable of come back full force. Like a switch flipping. A deadly one that demands obedience.

"You will not ask any more questions. Is that understood?" he tells me and I want to agree. I know I need to; I desperately need to let it go.

My bottom lip wobbles and my gaze flicks from Z to the candlelight.

"You are better than this," he murmurs and it cuts me, deep and unforgivingly. "You need to listen to me." It's not meant to. His tone is gentle and coaxing, yet the weight of it is too heavy for me to carry.

"I listen," I object.

"I need you to trust me." He grips my chin, giving me the physical contact I long for, more so than I realized until he's staring deep in my eyes. "Trust me."

"I trust you," I confess and his hold on me drops.

"Do you?" he asks and his voice is testing. His tone is low and his dark eyes narrowed at me. There's a shift between us and it steals my breath along with every bit of my strength.

"I don't mean to—"

"Stop," he orders. He signals for silence and I'm quick to obey. He is my Dom. *My everything.* Swallowing thickly, I nod. It feels as though I'm a child in trouble. Worse than that, I feel like I'm on the verge of losing anything and everything that matters to me. All because of his disappointment. How does he have such a hold on me?

Insecurity runs rampant through me as I twist the napkin in my lap. The chill across my skin is quickly heated when Z reaches out, his thumb resting on my bottom lip and a heat sparking in his eyes. "You are my good girl, Ella. You're going to listen to me now, aren't you?"

Nodding eagerly, I'm desperate to just go back to a few moments ago. I don't want to push him. I don't want to lose him.

As if reading my mind, he leans forward, kissing the crook of my neck and then whispers at the shell of my ear, "I am here for you, Ella. My very existence is for you. You have me, you will lean on me tonight and in every way I tell you to." His words send a warmth through me, a comforting security I desperately need. "Won't you, my little bird? You'll let me take care of you in every way, even if it pushes your boundary … you haven't said your safe word. Have you even thought of it?"

No. His statement resonates deep within me. The safe word never entered my mind.

My heart races at the sound of the private door opening and Z pulls back, appearing completely unaffected. As if he didn't just have my entire world in his hand to do with as he pleased.

"And for you, miss," the waiter says, setting down the plate of perfectly seared scallops. "To start," he adds and asks if I'd like fresh ground pepper. He holds the pepper mill in offering and I answer "No, thank you" as politely as I can, attempting to contain myself and hold back the intensity that's been building since I took my seat in the burgundy leather dining chair.

Before the waiter leaves, I notice Zander pass him something that appears to be cash.

"What was that?" I question as soon as we're alone.

"A note to stay the fuck out for the next twenty minutes," Z answers as he pushes back the chair, towering over me as he unbuttons his shirt.

"Z," I protest breathlessly as he lays his shirt over the back of his chair and then pulls mine out, turning it with a commanding force and dropping to his knees in front of me. A thrilling shock takes hold of me. "What are you doing?" I barely manage to whisper as my blood heats.

"I don't want to dirty the shirt." He stares into my eyes. "I've decided I'll start my meal with your cunt," he tells me and my cheeks flare with heat that starts at my chest before bringing a warm flush all the way to my temples.

With his hands on the inside of my thighs, he spreads my legs, forcing the green velvet fabric to rise up.

A gasp leaves me as he grips my hips and pulls me to the edge of the chair. To keep my balance, I grip his shoulders, his bare skin hot under my touch.

"These need to come off," he says and slips the lace down my thighs, leaving openmouthed kisses as he goes. His name escapes my lips amid heavy breaths of disbelief.

"You'll be quiet," he tells me in between kisses and when I agree, he licks my entrance all the way up to my clit. My back bows from the sudden touch and pleasure races through me.

My head falls back as he sucks and licks, toying with me and my sharp nails dig into his shoulders. I can't help but moan and the moment I do, he stops to grab the cloth napkin and brings it to my lips.

"Do I need to gag you?"

"No," I'm quick to answer and eager for him to continue.

"If you can't be quiet, I'll be forced to stop. Is that what you want?"

"No, I'm sorry."

"I know you are, but more than that, you're mine. Are you?"

"Yes." The single word is desperate.

"And you know I'll take care of you and that you should listen to me. You should trust me."

"Yes." My heart pounds desperately as he stares back at me, waiting for my submission. I've never wanted to give it to him more.

I reach out to him, my body moving of its own accord. I can barely push the words out when I say, "I trust you, Z. I can't—" I have to pause to swallow. Closing my eyes as I do and when I open them, Z stares back at me with a raw intensity that seems to see through me. Through everything surface level and deep down.

"I can't feel like we're not okay … I'm sorry and it's—"

"We are better than okay, Ella. You will always be mine. Even if you push me and fight. Even if you're disobedient. Even if you want more than I can give you for the moment." He kisses my wrist, keeping his eyes on me. "I will satisfy you another way and you will forget all about whatever it is that made you feel like we weren't okay."

A moment passes that crackles between us before he asks, "Understood?"

"Yes."

"Who do you belong to, Ella?"

"You, sir," I answer in a whisper.

I love you is on the tip of my tongue, but the words are silenced by his next command.

"Put your legs over my shoulders and enjoy what I do to you."

I nod in obedience and Z doesn't just eat me out, sucking and licking every inch of my heat until I come hard on his tongue. Once he's had his fill of that, he bends me over the table and fucks me so hard, I swear the table will break. It turns out, he did need to gag me.

THE FIRM'S OFFICES HAVE A COMPLETELY DIFFERENT ENERGY now that we're in prep mode for the event this weekend. Cade sits at the head of the table, file folders and a tablet in front of him. He scrolls through the information on the screen, his expression serious.

"Did Kam confirm his suspicions?" he asks, looking at me.

"On the sender of the letter?"

Cade nods. Damon slides a piece of paper over to him, and Cade glances at it before flipping it onto another stack within reach.

"Yeah. It's him. The same conclusion we came to." I can't even speak about these latest developments without anger churning in my gut. We matched a thumbprint but it's Kam who knew immediately. He knew who would have access and motive. There's no way I'm ever telling Ella a damn thing about any of this. No one should go through what she went through. "And the event Ella's friend is throwing is where he expects the drop-off."

Cade cracks open a dossier acquired on the suspect Kam has led us to. I've read it a hundred times over. It's him. The vile fuck has a name and it's at the top of my hit list. It takes everything in me to remain calm.

"Ah." Cade nods. "So that's why you're so inclined to go to a fashion show opening?" There's a hint of a joke in his tone that somewhat lightens the mood.

Hell yes it is. "That's right. Kam agrees it would be good to place her there as well. For PR, for us and also to address the situation person-to-person."

The humor fades from Cade's expression. "He's not going to see her, correct?"

"There are two hundred people expected to be at the event, including the press. We'll keep her away," Dane answers for me. Thank God he did. Just the thought that he would be near her makes my skin crawl.

I have to remind myself that he isn't the one who did those things. But to threaten her with that information … it's incomprehensible.

"So he will be at the event and we will confront him as we've done in the past." Cade switches off the screen of the tablet and looks first to Dane and Silas, then to me. "Are we prepared with ammunition of our own?"

Blackmail the blackmailer. "What we have on him is far worse and with one click, the police will be informed of everything. The blackmail and his other misdealings." Again, Dane answers. This isn't the first time we've handled these issues delicately. The police are never informed and the individual goes away quietly, not willing to risk us destroying their lives. I, however, wouldn't mind simply pulling the trigger.

"Has Ella been informed?" Cade asks.

Now the anger is replaced by worry. "No. She has no idea."

Cade exchanges a look with Damon. Heat coats the back of my neck at the thought of her finding out what happened. "How has she been in your sessions?"

Damon answers easily, "She's working through some things. Much more stable than she was when we took the case. Ella has shown a lot of progress when it comes to processing her feelings instead of letting them turn harmful. There is no question of her mental capacity. I feel confident signing off for the judge and ending her conservatorship."

"So long as the event goes accordingly. She needs to show stability there, not just in counseling sessions," my brother comments and the thin skin around my knuckles turns white as I ball a fist.

"She'll be fine," I add, talking over Damon who then agrees with me.

My brother picks up a pen and jots down a note on a sheet of paper. Once again he glances at me. "Are you sure *you* can handle this?"

"I have no doubt."

I'm absolutely confident that with me by her side, Ella will make it successfully through the event without it throwing her into a spiral. I'm even confident that she can do it by herself. Damon has observed her work as far as her mental health, but I know that her inner strength is far deeper than he can imagine.

It's me I'm more worried about.

I'm not just pissed. I'm furious. A threat against Ella feels like a threat against my heart. I want to kill this bastard. How dare he threaten her? And with that of all things?

The video he sent makes me sick to think about. I watched it because, as a member of The Firm, I need to have all the information available to me. I wish it hadn't been necessary.

The video was of her father, along with a group of men. All of them were with a much younger Ella. There was a side-by-side comparison of what they'd done years before with her mother.

Rage heats every inch of me and I have to readjust in my seat, unable to keep still.

If there was any doubt that he was abusive, the tape was evidence enough. It wasn't a very long video, but it was long enough to know exactly what was going on.

"Any word from Kam?" Cade questions.

I take a deep breath and push the memories of that tape, along with my anger, down to a level where they won't damage my professionalism. "Kam said that this isn't the first time he's pulled this kind of behavior."

"So it's not the first time Ella has dealt with blackmail," Damon adds thoughtfully.

She's fragile, though. Strong. So damn strong. But fragile. I know Ella could get through this alone if she had to, but she shouldn't have to. "Kam's pretty adamant that he should handle the situation himself but I assured him we've done this before."

"You don't think he'll push back? Like he and Ella did last time there was a disagreement?"

My muscles stiffen, knowing he's referring to Kam's threats to destroy The Firm's reputation … because of me.

"No. He won't."

"What changed?" Cade looks me in the eye. "You had some doubts the last time we dealt with a situation involving Ella and Kam."

"I was unsure of where we stood as a couple last time. Now I know. And Kam is aware of that too."

The other guys shuffle in their seats. It's like they can sense my confidence about this. I'm not sure whether they're having doubts now or if it's something else.

"And where is that?" Cade asks, voice calm.

"She's still figuring a lot of things out, like Damon said." He was truthful in his assessment. And I trust his opinion on Ella's status too. There's a reason we're close friends. We wouldn't be if I didn't trust him. "As long as she'll have me, I want her. In all ways."

Cade glances at Damon, who gives him a subtle nod.

"You think it's going to last?" my brother questions.

"I know it is. She needs me, and I need her."

A frown briefly crosses his face. "Zander, she might not always need—"

I put my hand on the desk, cutting off his words. "Yes, she will. She needs someone like me and wants someone like me. Even if I wasn't brought up in the same circles as she was. I'll manage, and I'll fit in. Enough to get the job done. Enough to be … enough for her."

Damon gives me an asymmetric smile from his side of the table.

Cade leans back in his seat, putting both hands ahead of him. "All right, all right. You can get off your soapbox. I hear you."

"*We* hear you," Damon says, leaning forward and glancing around at all the other guys. "And it's about damn time. Next question. Should we tell Ella what's going on?"

"She doesn't need the stress." Nobody should have that kind of pressure hanging over their head from some sick prick, but especially not Ella. It's not her responsibility to protect herself from the guy, anyway. It's ours. *It's mine.* And that includes the planning.

"Are you sure?" Cade looks skeptical. "It might be triggering for her.

But isn't it better to prepare her in case something happens? Damon, what do you think?"

My best friend looks at me, as if he's weighing what I'll think as well. He might take me into consideration, but I know he won't change his opinion to placate me. He'll say what he thinks, even if I disagree.

"I think transparency is always best."

Cade drums his fingers on the tabletop. "Kam said to let him handle it. Maybe we should listen to him."

It's a struggle. I want to have control over everything I can when it comes to the event. Yet I also understand that some things will be out of control no matter what I do.

"What are you thinking, Zander?" Cade asks.

"Yeah. You've clearly got some issues. Tell us what it is," Silas says.

The problem, I realize, is that I started hiding things when I got involved with Ella. I felt secretive about it, and that extended to my own feelings about things with The Firm.

I can't operate like that anymore. Part of being back on staff is being open with them. We can't protect Ella effectively unless we're honest with each other. We can't protect any client effectively unless we're truthful.

"I'm frustrated," I admit. "My emotions shouldn't control how we proceed with the next steps, but if this guy was dead ..." My fists clench on the table. "If he was dead, there wouldn't be an issue."

"I agree with that," Damon says. "It's the son of one of the men in the video. Everything would be a lot less complicated if none of those guys had ever existed."

Cade muses out loud, "Are we certain she should attend? I understand it's best for the alibi and a public confrontation. But she doesn't have to be there."

All eyes are on me.

I sit in silence for a few more beats, thinking. "She's going and I'll tell her about the party. That will make her happy," I tell the guys. "It will add more substance to our report for the judge and I'm sure Damon would feel more confident in his assessment if she does as well as he thinks she will in a public setting with press and social pressure."

"It's not about making her happy," Cade says. "But—"

I cut him off. "It's about protecting her. I'm very fucking aware of that."

What Cade might not be able to understand, is that keeping Ella happy is part of protecting her. Of course her physical safety is always going to be a top priority for me.

But physical safety isn't the be-all and end-all. Her heart needs happiness, too, and letting her know about this party will give her a spark of joy. After all she's been through, she deserves it.

A life without happiness isn't a life at all.

"We're all going to go to that event and put an end to this." It's the beginning of the end for so many things for Ella.

chapter 16

"I GIVE UP" IS MEANT AS A STATEMENT OF WEAKNESS OR exasperation. Or at least I always thought that's what it meant and that you were less than if you "gave up."

But releasing control and worries, giving them to Z … giving up has never felt so freeing. With James, he let me lean on him, he didn't take control. He didn't consume the burden and leave me free to just … be. I loved him so very much for being my partner.

Zander is more than just my partner, though. So very much more.

I've decided to let him handle anything and everything he wishes. The moment that switch was made, everything fell into place far too easily. It's almost too good to be true. Between Zander and Kam there isn't a worry in the world other than pleasing Z. Which is exactly what he commands.

My cheeks are sore and my lips are slightly swollen as my knees rub against the carpet.

"Do you think you've pleased me?" he asks in a husky whisper. Zander's voice alone sends shivers along my naked skin. I love the timbre of it, the deep need laced in between his masculine and controlling tone. He needs me just as much as I need him. He needs to take care of me as much as I need it. It's all simply too good to be true.

I murmur around his cock, humming that I have pleased him before peeking up at him through my thick lashes. He's naked, every inch of him. Dim light that peeks through the curtains from the moon outside slips across his hard muscle and deep grooves. He's a sex god, a greedy Adonis who's left me sore and satisfied and eager to do anything and everything he wishes.

I've *pleased* him for three days straight since the restaurant incident. Which I would very much like to do again.

I lean back to rest on my legs which are folded underneath me, the heels of my feet digging into my bare and reddened ass to catch my breath. I keep my balance, gripping his muscular thigh with my left hand and stroke him with my right.

His hand spears through the hair at the back of my head and he tightens a fist around it, forcing me to look up at him.

He stares down at me with longing, and all I can hear is my racing heart. I don't deserve him, but I'll do whatever I can to keep him.

"How do you want me?" I question coyly and in an instant, his lips crash against mine with a hunger that I thought long ago would have waned.

If anything, the closer we get, the closer I want to be to him and it seems the same for him. *Please never leave me.*

"Just like that," he murmurs in a tone drenched with lust and tells me to put my hands on my thighs. "Tongue out and open wider," he tells me, nearly breathless with want. I do as commanded and watch him stroke himself, finding his release with a deep groan as he stares into my eyes.

His cum is warm and salty. "Swallow it," he commands and I do. Every bit of it.

As I shift from where I am, I can still feel him inside of me and the tender skin on my backside adds a hint of pain that only intensifies the pleasure.

He spanked me for mouthing off, fucked me until I came, and now this: finding his release in my mouth. It's the perfect fucking punishment, if I do say so myself. I watch as he gets dressed, putting on his dark gray pajama pants from earlier.

A smile plays at my lips as he lifts me gently and I cling to him until he carefully places me in bed with my tender backside up. I knew it was coming. It's routine now.

Even without the covers, without his touch on me, my entire body is lit with a warmth that stays with me all day and night.

It's a comfort and satisfaction that I desperately wish to hold on to.

He hums as his hand grips my ass and I respond immediately. My back arching, my bottom lip dropping. The sudden pleasure and pain were unexpected.

"You'll be quiet when I tell you to be next time won't you, little bird?"

"Yes," I answer immediately and he releases his grip, giving me a soothing rub instead. The cool gel I know all too well now soothes the heat the moment he rubs it in.

"I do love that mouth of yours," he growls as he rubs across my ass and upper thighs. I can't help the heat and the blush that comes over me. His praise is my drug.

I don't even remember what I said that led to a punishment. Probably something snarky and he bit back, so I bit harder. All I know is that he's far too aware, I was pushing just to push. Topping from the bottom is what he calls it.

"If tomorrow goes well, The Firm will issue a statement to the judge and all should go through easily enough."

"Kam told me the wheels were loosened," I confess to him, although I'm sure he already knows. He just may not know that Kam told me. I slip my arms beneath the pillow and peek back at him.

His shoulders rise and fall with a steadying breath. I realize he and Kam have differing opinions on what I should be privy to, but the two of them seem to have hashed things out from what I know.

Z's grunt, rough but barely heard, is telling. He doesn't like the manner in which Kam gets things done. Bribes and such. "The wheels are loosened, yes." His reluctance brings a smile to my lips that I try to hide in the crook of my arm.

The cool gel offers immediate relief and once he's done, he puts the cap back on and tucks it away back into the bedside drawer before climbing in bed with me. The mattress dips and groans with his weight as he climbs over me and then brings the comforter up around both of us.

I snuggle close to him as he wraps his arm around me. It's hard to believe this is real. That I could have another happily ever after, but that's exactly what it feels like.

"So you'll behave tomorrow in every way at your friend's opening. You won't push me, not even to play," he warns even though he doesn't have to. I'm acutely aware of everything that's at risk.

"I know," I tell him simply and then plant a kiss on his chest.

"Good girl." With his fingers under my chin, he tilts my head up to kiss me chastely. With his hand still there, his eyes searching mine, he tells me, "I got you something."

Surprised, I still, searching his eyes for what it could be. There's a mischievousness there and I love it.

He smirks. "You love gifts, don't you?"

"I do," I admit in a whisper and then sit upright on the bed, cross-legged with the blanket settled in my lap and not quite covering my breasts. My ass is still sore, but as he reaches into the bedside drawer, I can hardly pay the pain any mind. It's a good sting, one that adds to the residual pleasure.

A slim rectangular black box wrapped with a ribbon is revealed as he turns around. At first, I thought it was a ring maybe. I'm surprised by the disappointment that lingers for only a second.

"I thought you could wear it tomorrow," he tells me.

As I lean forward, he offers me the jewelry box. I pull at the red satin ribbon, letting it fall to the bed and open the gift.

A delicate rose gold chain lays in the box and hanging from it, a woven diamond ring. The sparkling layers are entwined with rose gold shaped like flower petals.

"Z?"

"It's a promise ring and a collar," he tells me calmly but with something else there.

"A promise?"

"That I'm yours and you are mine, and I will take care of you, Ella. For as long as you will have me."

"That will be forever then," I answer quickly, teasingly almost but I can't hide the emotion that chokes me up. I'm quick to remove the chain and brush my hair back to put it on. It's long enough that the ring hangs low and rests between my breasts. I imagine the dress will cover it and I kind of like it that way. It's a promise the world won't see. Not unless I want them to.

"I'd like to get you one too, maybe?" I offer him as I slip the necklace around my neck. Z helps me when I struggle with the clasp.

He doesn't respond at first and my heart runs wild, wondering if he wouldn't want that. We've never talked about rings or marriage or children or any of that. And just as the insecurity sweeps in, he kisses the crook of my neck and his touch alleviates any and every doubt.

"I would like that very much," he murmurs at the shell of my ear and then pulls back just enough for me to be able to stare into his gorgeous hazel eyes. I want to ask him if tomorrow could be our first and last public outing. If we show the world our love and that I'm fine, and then we vanish. We give them just enough to leave us alone.

I want to say so much and make plans, but all of them jumble and I don't know how to say it right. I want him to myself. I want to be left alone with him. It doesn't sound right in my head, though, so I settle on a single truth instead.

"I love you," I confess. Unable to move or do anything else out of fear that this will all go away if I do.

"I love you, Ella. More than you know."

chapter 17

"HOW ARE THE NERVES?" DAMON ASKS AS HE ADJUSTS HIS jacket.

"Still fucked," I admit to him under my breath.

"It's all going to go down as it's meant to," he assures me.

"I'll be calm once this is over."

Damon nods in agreement and then looks me up and down from where he stands in the threshold of the living room. "Well, at least you look like you've got your shit together."

I let out a huff of a laugh and gesture to my friend's cobalt blue suit that complements his dark brown skin. "You shape up nicely too. Trying to find a date tonight?" I question with a smirk.

He smiles wide and broad, then says, "I think these women may be a little too high maintenance for me." He pats my shoulder and gives it a squeeze. "Tonight is going to be just fine. Everything is going to go according to plan."

I'm still nodding in agreement as he leaves me alone in the living room. The Firm is going first, scouting out the place and conducting reconnaissance. Silas stayed behind to drive us to the event once we've gotten the green light. I glance in the mirror again, making sure I look like the man who should be on Ella's arm tonight. I'm more dressed up than I have been in years. Tux. Tie. Everything. A spritz of cologne Ella picked out as well.

I've worn suits for The Firm just about every week for years, but this is another level. She's a socialite, or at least used to be. I could never imagine living with this constant pressure that comes with being in the spotlight twenty-four seven. If this is what she requires, I will be the man on her arm, the one leading her and standing by her side. Glancing toward the hall, I attempt to listen for her and hear nothing, so I check my watch one more time.

Whenever she happens to arrive, that is, I'll be the "man candy" on her arm, as Kam referred to my duty tonight. Releasing tension in my shoulders, I check the message from Kam, the one from Cade and as I do, my phone pings to let me know they're ready whenever we are.

Ella's been locked in her bedroom and the bathroom with a stylist for the last few hours, so I can't imagine how much longer she could possibly need. I spent as much time as I could getting myself ready, but there's just not that much for a man to do.

My clothes are on and I'm left with time to think.

I text them that I will inform them once we leave. As I hit send, the nerves amp up again.

Tonight is when everything changes. I hope, given all The Firm's planning, that we put an end to the blackmail threat quietly so we can provide everything Judge Martel requires without any hiccups. I want it all to be over by the time the sun rises. The conservatorship, the judge ruling in her favor, any and every threat. I'm ready to start our forever tonight. She's ready. I know she is.

Disastrous scenarios are possible, but I don't want to entertain them.

All of the unfortunate business will be behind us by morning.

I pace the living room of her house, trying to imagine a limit to the things I'd do for her. There really isn't one. I'd give her the entire world if I could. She accepted my collar, my ring.

She's mine. In every way and yet there's this lingering warning. Tonight will end it all. I will end it all so she is only mine and there is no question about that fact. Not from her, not from a single soul.

Tomorrow she is mine, only mine and we start our forever.

Muffled voices get a little louder upstairs, distracting me. A woman laughs. One of the stylists, I think.

"Are you sure?" Ella asks after a door is opened, the sounds carrying down the staircase. I make my way toward the foyer to gather her for tonight.

"Yes," the woman answers. "Head on down. Do you need me to walk you?"

"Oh, no. I've got it. Thank you." As I make my way to her, the steady rhythm of her heels brings her closer to me.

Her stilettos click softly on each step and I go toward the sound. I'm drawn to her that way. I couldn't make myself stay away if I wanted to.

Before I've fully faced her, I'm paralyzed by the sight of her.

She takes my breath away. My bottom lip drops open slightly as I'm stunned by her beauty. Ella is gorgeous in a burgundy gown that skims the floor, carrying it with a grace that proves she was born to be dressed in silk. Her dark hair falls in soft curls. Her makeup is subtle and natural apart from deep red lips that match her dress. The color brings out her beauty in a way I didn't know was possible.

She's so strikingly beautiful that my first thought is: I don't deserve her and I could never be the man worthy of being beside her. Until she speaks. "Z …" Her gaze drifts down my body as she pauses on the bottom step and my heart races. "You look perfect. I love you in a tux, my God."

It's only then I can breathe. I lick my lower lip as I stare back at her and she blushes deeply. "You're breathtaking, my jailbird."

Her soft smile makes her that much more beautiful. I'm never going to see a more gorgeous woman. No one will ever be able to argue with me on that truth.

Ella finishes descending the staircase and meets me at the bottom where I'm quick to wrap my arm around her waist.

"I don't want to mess up your makeup," I say, "but I really need to kiss you."

"You won't mess it up." She lets out a quiet laugh. "They're professionals. It'll last no matter what happens tonight."

That comment makes my chest tighten with nerves that I'd forgotten about. "Nothing's going to happen tonight."

"No, of course it won't." Ella's eyes shine as she looks me over once again. "I can't get over how good you look in a tux," she says softly.

"I'm nothing compared to you." With that I lean down and plant a kiss on her lips.

"Are we ready?" she asks.

I let myself look at her for one more long moment. This is the calm before the storm. Even if nothing goes wrong tonight, it'll be busy. Cameras and socializing and press. It's going to be the opposite of Ella's quiet house and the calm routines we've built up over her time with the Firm.

"Yes. Let's get you in the car."

Ella

Lights, camera, action.

There's a familiar buzz and thrill that lights through me, but also a tinge of fear. I remember my first appearance on a red carpet. I was fourteen and I had nothing to fear. Cameras flashed, I posed, I granted interviews to anyone who asked.

The first time I was labeled a socialite was two years later. At the party celebrating my sweet sixteen I arrived covered from head to toe in Chanel's new line that was released the week after. I was the "it" girl. Access to wealth beyond imagination and friends with anyone who was anyone … because of who my father was and how many dollar signs were attached to my name.

Then at eighteen, after a sex tape scandal, all the hottest designers begged me to wear them. All I got was attention. Good and bad both. Kam took me under his wing when things got too heavy. "Any press is good press" is a lie when mental health is added to the mix.

The number of people who told me to kill myself after I was photographed with a director who was married was in the thousands. Rumors spread like wildfire. I posed because he asked. The man wasn't even my type but I was a homewrecker nonetheless.

And yet, with the onslaught of negativity, the lights never stopped flashing. The comments poured in and Kam made sure to fix it all. Putting out one fire after the next.

As Silas drives the car away and Z gives my hand a squeeze, I stand tall off to the right, knowing they're waiting. There's a banner and bright lights set up for the private fashion line reveal.

Martinis served on silver platters right after. I recognize half of the photographers and a reporter at the entrance. At least thirty people stand out front of the massive estate. The guests are waiting on the right side of the red velvet rope; photographers and press crowd the other side.

Trish told me the only reporter I'll be speaking with tonight has been paid off. Kam gave him a list of softball questions to ask so I won't be surprised or caught off guard. It's rigged, so to speak.

"You all right?" Z questions, soft and low. In the shadows beside the grand foyer, only feet from where the night will begin, I feel nothing but doubt.

I don't know if I can go through it all again. The highs are the best highs, but the lows … the lows have almost killed me so many times and I don't know how many lives I have left, but I want this one. I want my happily ever after without this.

"We can go back to the house," he offers.

"No, no, just preparing myself," I tell him. Moving to my tiptoes in my heels, I plant a kiss on his lips.

The perfectly manicured lawn is split with a paved path that will lead us to the start of the event. A photo, a sound bite, a martini and then I can hide inside.

"Are Kam and Trish inside? Do you know?" I ask Z as a cool breeze comes by, much colder than I expected. Warmth is just around the corner.

"They are. Everyone is." Z then asks, "Do you want my jacket?" He's already removing his tux jacket and I have to stop him, grabbing the expensive fabric, pulling it back into position and tapping his chest.

"I'll just move quick so we're inside fast," I tell him and then take his hand. "Let's do this." I tug, but he doesn't move. Looking back, I find his gaze searching mine.

"We don't have to if you don't want to."

"I think tonight …" I trail off, then clear my throat and tell him what

I've been thinking all last night and today. "I think tonight, I will show them that I'm all right and I prove that people can have second chances. And then I can walk away if I want, knowing I at least said goodbye in a way that makes me feel like I did what I needed to."

His brow furrows when he asks, "Is that what you want?"

Nodding repeatedly, I swallow the lump in my throat. This is the goodbye I want to leave them with. A pretty dress. A pretty smile. And telling the world how happy I am to be here. Even after everything that's happened, I want to tell them what a wonderful night it is to be alive.

"It is. I really have to do this." Another kiss and Z wraps a strong arm around my waist, kissing my bare shoulder and whispering, "Then let's get on with it, my little bird."

He leads the way and my heart rampages, the rapid thumps growing louder and louder in my ears as we get closer to the event.

"Ella!"

"Eleanor!"

The photographers call out my name and I face each of them with Z behind me and then at my side. The first snaps are posed. Then I grab Z by the tie, surprising him and kissing his cheek and then his lips while the bright lights flood the area.

"I wasn't expecting that," Z says and smirks, both of us very aware the cameras are still flashing.

All I offer him is a simper. They could photograph me kissing this man all night long if they wanted.

The calls of my name, the laughter and white noise—I've been here before, but it feels different now. It's broken, part of it like heaven and the other side hell.

"Eleanor, my love!" Charlie, the reporter Kam handpicked, motions for me and I escape to him, knowing there's a drink and sanctuary after this moment.

"Charlie." I greet him by reaching out and holding on to his left arm, the one not holding the mic. I give a half hug with a wide smile and there's a flash and then another as a paparazzo captures the moment. "I've missed you," I say, keeping my tone playful and my voice loud enough to be heard over the gaggle of people around us.

"Oh, not as much as I've missed you." We air-kiss on each cheek as we've done since I was only a teenager before I release him and take a step back where Z gathers my arm around his.

"And this is your …" Charlie questions immediately, getting right to the point and eyeing Zander.

"My knight in shining armor," I answer with a simper and then add, "Well, in Armani, but you know my tastes are little more grown up than fairy-tale stories."

Charlie laughs at my joke and I peek up to see Z smirking, handsome as hell and for a moment it all fades into the background. When I was a little girl, I dreamed of this. This very moment and yet all I want to do is steal away with him now.

"Do you have any exclusive details you could offer me?" Charlie questions with a raised brow, holding the microphone out for me. "Maybe?" He pushes forward and I debate for only a second.

"I think I may be in love," I tell him and then look back at Z to find him smiling down at me. I don't know if he's playing his part perfectly or if he just happens to be perfect.

"Oh my!" Charlie's eyes go wide and I laugh.

"Got to go, my love," I tell him and turn slightly to leave.

"Anything you can tell us about the launch tonight before you go?"

"It's going to be thrilling," I answer him and then add, "This designer is to die for."

"Have a drink for me, Ella," Charlie calls out as I take two side steps toward the house.

I'm quick to reply with my normal response, "I'll have two!"

As Z leads me away, toward the front foyer where warmth is already pouring into the night, he whispers comically at the shell of my ear, "The hell you will," and I let out a genuine laugh.

The chandeliers are breathtaking in the dimly lit expansive space. Kelly's open floor plan has been rearranged and redesigned just for tonight. With a raised runway running through her living room, the floor-to-ceiling glass doors are all open, allowing the runway to end in her perfectly manicured backyard. Every piece of furniture is white, blending into the marble floors. The black runway provides a stark contrast that's truly stunning and half the guests are already seated, the other half chatting and drinking and laughing. Everyone is dressed in creams, golds and black.

Kelly shakes her hands out before accepting two martinis, garnished with olives, from a silver platter. The theme of tonight is *Sex and the City* chic and I am here for it. And somehow dressed appropriately.

"It's a great turnout," I tell her as I sneak up behind her, kissing her cheek.

"Ella, baby!" she squeals, passing the drinks back to the waiter dressed in a simple black suit and tie. He's young and handsome, more than likely a model hired for the evening.

"I should have had you model tonight," Kelly says with a pout. She looks me up and down, adding, "You look stunning."

"Well, thank you but that's a bit of the pot calling the kettle black," I reply with a knowing smile. She does a little twirl in her gold gown adorned with crystals.

"It's reminiscent of Marilyn," I comment and she lets out a girlish squeal with her lips pressed in a broad smile before telling me, "I know, right?"

"It's one of the designers?" Zander asks from beside me and it's only then that Trish sees him.

"Uh, yes, but also, damn Zander," she says, then pats his arm with a shocked but overwhelmingly impressed expression. "You clean up nice, Playboy."

He gives her an asymmetric grin and replies, "Thank you." His arm finds its way around my waist again and I lean into him just slightly.

Friends, fashion, drinks and celebration. I do love this part.

"Hold on," Kelly says, holding up a finger before pulling out her phone. She snaps a quick picture and as she does I see a few other guests, who I'm not familiar with, doing the same. "I have to send this to the hubby. He's on a business trip that I will never forgive him for."

She types away with a smirk, no doubt bragging about the party but also telling him how much she misses him. She's a romantic at heart.

"And this," she says, handing a drink to me, "is for you."

"Oh, I uh—" My hand raises slightly and Kelly moves forward before I can reject it completely. "Virgin, my dear," she whispers. Peeking up at Z, he nods.

"I can listen to orders too," Kelly comments and then laughs at her own joke.

I accept the martini glass and sip. All the while, Z watches.

"Good?" he questions and I nod.

It's refreshing and goes down easy. I don't know exactly what it is, but there isn't a hint of alcohol in it.

With a hand on either side of my waist Zander asks in a murmur if I like it and I tell him it's delicious.

"Good." He kisses me and then asks if I'll be all right for a moment here.

"Yes, but where are you going?" I question.

"I'll be back in just a moment. Stay where you are and don't leave," he commands.

"Z, is everything okay?" I ask although I keep my voice down. Kelly is keeping a watchful eye on me although she's currently handing out drinks to a pair of women passing behind us. Knowing she's occupied with them for a moment, I part my lips to question him further, but he stops me.

"There's nothing you need to worry about. I'm just meeting with the team for a moment. You'll be fine here. Or would you rather I stay?"

A moment passes and Kelly returns to my side.

"I'll be fine," I tell him. "Go." My heart does a pitter-patter watching him leave me after he kisses the back of my hand.

Kelly is unaware of the shift and claps against her martini glass, letting out an *aww*.

"He really is a knight in shining armor, isn't he?" she comments.

"That he is," I answer with a half-smile and sip the virgin drink once again.

"Ask for Ella's Snowball at the bar and you'll get one of these," Kelly informs me before looking past me and squealing with delight.

Her throat is going to be sore and her voice gone by the morning.

I half turn with the drink to my lips only to have the glass nearly taken away.

"Hold on now," Trish says and sips the drink, lifting her off-the-shoulder black chiffon gown with her left hand and holding the martini glass with the right. "Z told me no alcohol for you tonight and to help be your keeper."

I would laugh like Kelly does but instead I hush Trish. "Don't call him Z here—that's just for us. I don't want anyone to overhear."

There's a moment of contemplation in Trish's eyes, followed by a soft smile. "What?" I question.

"Nothing, just … just déjà vu. You know when you get that it's supposed to be a sign that you're in the exact place you're supposed to be."

The quiet reflective moment is over with the DJ requesting guests be seated in the next ten minutes for the show to start.

"Cheers, my loves," Kelly says as she hands Trish a drink and Trish hands mine back.

Our glasses clink and the lights dim further.

"We're needed up front," a man in a gray suit with a silver striped tie says over Kelly's shoulder. Kelly finishes her sip, and quickly introduces him to us before running off with him.

I vaguely recognize his name from some event a while back and I'm fairly sure the two of them had a fling back then. It's practically ancient history, though, since it was before Kelly got married.

"Good luck tonight," Trish says.

"You got this," I add and off Kelly goes, hand in hand, dressed to the nines with a French designer and the spotlights shifting to be on them.

Applause fills the room and I join in looking to my right and then my left, waiting for Zander to emerge.

"Do you want to take our seats?" Trish questions, already tugging on my arm.

"I want to wait here I think," I reply and again I look over my shoulder for Z. "He said he'd be right back."

"He might be a little bit," Trish comments and I stare back at her with my blood running cold.

"What do you mean by that?" My voice is deathly low as the designer takes the floor, announcing the new line and partnership with Kelly.

Trish searches my face seemingly confused before asking, "Did neither of them tell you?"

"Tell me what?"

She only gets a few hushed comments out before Zander is back at my side. Shivers climb up the back of my neck as I stand there, absorbing it all as quickly as possible so as not to show that I now know what he wanted kept from me. There's a pounding in my chest as he kisses my cheek like nothing's wrong and asks the two of us, "Could I walk you to your seats, ladies?"

A moment passes before a smile graces my lips and I let him take my hand.

All the while, turmoil and fear rage inside.

Still, it's: Lights. Camera. Action.

chapter 18

Zander

WITH ADRENALINE POUNDING THROUGH MY VEINS, THE last thing I want to do is leave Ella, even for a minute. I loosen the tie at my throat and make sure my presence won't be missed.

There's a round of applause as Kelly passes the microphone back to the MC and the lights dim even lower so the spotlight is only on the runway. Ella's hand hasn't left mine since we sat down. We're strategically placed in a private corner. It's easy to come and go.

Kamden thought of everything.

As I prepare to leave, Ella squeezes my hand and her dark eyes peer up at me.

I don't want to walk away from her side. Unfortunately, it's necessary. This is part of the job. And it's my responsibility, as Ella's Dom and the man she loves, to ensure her safety. There's a flicker in my chest as she stares at me, as if she knows I'm leaving again.

I'm the man who loves her. Anything less than what I'm going to do tonight wouldn't live up to our relationship.

I lean closer to her, breathing her in before telling her, "You stay with Trish." I keep my voice low so that only she can hear, but I make sure she knows it's a command. "You'll stay right here, or accompany her if she needs. You will not drink alcohol, and you're going to keep your phone on."

My pulse hammers as I prepare to leave her. She will be fine and I won't be gone long.

A moment passes of silence as she stares back at me and then swallows, looking down before looking back at me. "You'll be fine, my jailbird. You'll be perfect even," I tell her, reassuring her and kissing her temple. "I'll only be gone for a moment and I'll be back before the show is over."

Ella looks deeply into my eyes. I can tell she's responding to my tone. Her face flushes, and a hint of worry comes to her expression, but she gives in, trusting me as she should.

"Yes, sir," she finally says. She leans in and kisses me. Her lips brush against mine and I almost find myself lost in the moment.

This is the start of our forever and I'm going to destroy everything and anything that stands in the way of that. With one last squeeze of her hand, I leave her and give Trish a nod. As I pass through the back, Silas is there, hands clasped in front of him. He nods my way and I return it as we share a glance.

She is safe, I remind myself and quicken my pace.

As I make my way through the event space, I keep in mind that whatever happens tonight has to be done quietly. We cannot afford for the police to get involved. If they are, any chance of a judgment in her favor regarding her conservatorship is fucked.

No kinks, no hindrance. With the show starting, there's only a single waiter in the hall, and he doesn't see me as he heads to the kitchen. Apart from him, the hall is vacant. I turn the corner, knowing the meet is to take place by the garage. As I glance at my watch, movement ahead catches my attention.

Heat dances along the back of my neck as I spot Kam, slipping out of a side exit and into the side yard of the estate. He's not a member of The Firm and with the secrets he's kept, I don't know if I can trust him.

Moving quickly, I catch up with Kam. I track him to a staircase that winds up the corner of the event space. He's just moving out of view when I begin to take the stairs behind him, keeping my footsteps as quiet as possible. I'm not sure how he'll react when he realizes I'm following him.

He's not supposed to be at the meet so I don't know what the fuck he's doing. Glancing at my watch again, it's nearly 9:30, the time of the drop. My heart hammers as another door opens and then closes with a creak. I rush to catch the heavy door before it shuts completely. If he hears it, he'll know someone's behind him.

Then again, it doesn't really matter. Kam's reaction isn't as important as what he knows.

He exits the stairs at the third floor and moves down the hall with long, confident strides. He knows exactly where he's going. This estate is a winding maze, but I'm certain he's been here a hundred times before or more. After all, Ella said the group of them have always been close and it's Kelly's home. Kam doesn't even look back as he approaches a door near the end of the hall, opens it, and goes inside.

Immediately, voices rise. I can't tell what they're saying but they aren't friendly tones.

Swallowing thickly, I steel myself and move slowly toward the door taking each step carefully, my hand on the butt of my gun. The door stands open and I position myself so that I can see inside.

I peer in through the threshold. It's a large office, one with an anteroom containing a silver bar cart holding bottles of wine and whiskey. The dark liquids are illuminated by the single light from a standing lamp. The small chamber leads to a bigger room with a heavy wooden desk and behind it, shelving with books and antiques. Judging by the stacks of boxes and rolled-up rug in the corner, I can't imagine anyone uses this office for any purpose other than storage. Shadows move about the room as the voice tells Kam he shouldn't have interfered.

Fuck. A dull click can be heard and it's then that I pull out my gun. *Fuck, fuck, fuck.* We need the team here.

What the hell is Kam thinking? Adrenaline races as I text Cade 911 and the intense situation escalates further with a round going off and the voice not belonging to Kam yelling out, "Fuck, man." The click is heard again and all I can gather is that Kam gave a warning shot before speaking clearly enough that there's no doubt when he says, "I told you that you would regret it if you didn't leave her alone."

"I'm sorry. Kam. It was a mistake. I take it back."

"You can't take back threats like that," Kam says although the words are muffled.

I ease in through the doorway, preparing for chaos. This wasn't the plan and all I know is that I have to get back to Ella. This needs to end now.

It happens fast, the second I turn the corner.

Kam raises a pistol with a silencer attached. I can't see his face, but I can tell from his posture that he's not unfamiliar with firing a gun or upset at all about doing it.

I glance at his target as my pulse races, a man I recognize from the dossier. He shakes his head, hands up, staring at Kam. He's dressed to impress as well in an expensive tux, and not much older than me. Kam says, "Once you're a threat, you're always a threat," and fires.

The bang is nearly inaudible but the gut-wrenching heave from the suspect is telling. The man looks down to what was once a perfectly pressed white button-down, quickly soaking up blood right in the center of his chest.

The man looks up at Kam, wordlessly dropping to his knees, then down flat.

A moment passes and then another as I stand there in shock. Ella's closest friend peers down at the body and waits a few beats before stalking to the body, checking to see if the man is alive.

Kam turns his head and looks right at me. "He's dead. You need to find the safe. The video's going to be in there and it needs to be destroyed." He holsters his gun. "The backup safety net's already been secured."

Backup safety net. I barely hear him. The shock of what I just witnessed is still sinking in.

For the first time all evening, and maybe in months, I'm uncertain about my assumptions. Not so much at Kam's words, but his demeanor.

"You just killed a man in cold blood."

"It was him." Kam glances between the man and me. "We already confirmed it. You know that. His fingerprints were on the envelope. When I asked him how he wanted the money, he had the balls to smile and say, 'The security firm is taking care of it.'"

The body cooling on the floor is evidence that I underestimated Kam. No signs of life come from the corpse.

"You've done this before," I say to Kam, and the statement comes out flat.

"I didn't do this. You did this." It takes me a moment to register what he's said as he comes closer, passing me the gun he used. "Give me your gun," he demands and I only second-guess switching our weapons for a moment. My prints will be on a gun just used to kill a man, but as I look down between the one he's holding and the one I have in my possession, I know he used my gun. One registered to me.

"Fuck," I mutter.

I'd been holding this gun, one that's slightly different but not enough that I questioned it, down at my side, aimed at the floor. For a single moment I hesitate, but it passes. I'm already in this with him. We're in this together now.

With a chill settling down my spine, I swallow thickly before flipping over the gun and handing it to him.

"Don't worry," Kam says easily. "Your secret is safe with me."

I give a humorless laugh. "You set me up?"

He shakes his head and with that small motion plus the look he gives me, I feel a sense of ease. "I didn't. I brought you in. That's what I did. I brought you in on one condition."

"Brought me in?"

"In the circle with us. Like I said, on one condition."

"What the hell's that?"

A grin spreads across Kam's face. "You marry her. A whirlwind romance. Legal only, if you want. The marriage can exist only on paper if that's all you want it to be. I don't care. But you're going to marry her to protect you both."

I stare back at him, searching his expression for some clues on what the hell his reasoning is.

Kam gives me a sad smile. "If you don't want to marry her, you can leave. You're in or you're out, and either way, you're not going down for this." He gestures to the gun in my hand and adds, "That was just for insurance purposes, if you know what I mean."

"If I leave her, you tip off the cops?" I ask for clarification.

"No," he corrects me. "If you *hurt* her, I destroy your fucking life."

We share a look of understanding before I nod, slipping the gun into the holster and telling him flatly, "We don't have any problems then, other than how we're going to cover this up and keep it from Ella so she doesn't get hurt."

"She knows it all, Zander."

A soft rustle in the hall draws my attention a second before Trish comes into the room. She crosses the anteroom with measured steps and glances down at the dead body. Then she looks at Kam. "Is everything okay now?" She's not at all afraid, only cautious.

"We still need the safe," Kam tells her. "The tape, specifically."

"I know where it is," Trish answers and then says, "I can take care of that."

It dawns on me, that murder isn't something that's unfamiliar to … as he called it, the circle.

Heels click behind me, and Ella enters the room at the same time my phone buzzes and then buzzes again. I glance down to see my text never sent to Cade. He's sent me two messages in the meantime, though.

Cade: Where are you?

Cade: The exchange hasn't happened yet. We're still waiting for him to arrive.

Dread washes over me, knowing this isn't over yet. "Z?" Ella whispers and Kam ignores her, unrolling the old carpet in the corner of the room. Trish has already left.

"Ella, don't—" I attempt to shield her, but what's done is done and there isn't much I can hide from her as she walks in.

I brace myself for her emotions to overwhelm her, but she only glances at the body and then back up to me.

"You could have told me. But it's okay you didn't."

"Kam," I start, not withholding my anger that he would go behind my back.

"Not me—" Kam answers from where he's crouched on the floor, hands in the air at the same time Ella tells me.

"Trish didn't know that I didn't know," she comments softly, again looking behind me. "She wouldn't tell me what he had"—she pales staring down at the lifeless man before looking back up at me—"but I know who he is so I'm pretty sure I know what you saw."

I swear I can feel her heart break at this moment. Tears prick her eyes as she stares up at me.

"You don't need to worry about that, my jailbird," I murmur, vaguely aware that Kam is listening. Gripping her chin between my fingers, I force her to look up at me.

"You still love me?" she asks, her hand reaching up to the center of her chest and it dawns on me that the ring I gave her last night is there. Just beneath the deep red silk.

"Of course I still love you …" I trail off and take in a steadying breath, hating that there's any doubt at all from my Ella. "I don't want you involved in this and you should worry that you disobeyed me."

"I didn't," she says and perks up. "You said I could accompany Trish."

I'm speechless for a moment, staring down at her knowing she is once again topping from the bottom. "We'll discuss this later," I tell her and then kiss her gently. Then another kink in the chain dawns on me. "How did you get away from your security detail?"

"Silas?" she says and I nod, swallowing down the disappointment that she outsmarted the fuck out of me. "I left Silas by the powder room in the east wing on the first floor."

"Go now, back to him. And you will text me once you are back with him. You will say nothing at all about what happened and you will go back to your seat and wait for me, is that understood? No … going around my rules or loopholes."

My cunning, beautiful girl has the nerve to smirk at the last line. "Your ass will pay for that, Ella."

She bites down on her bottom lip and it slips out easily as she murmurs, "Yes, sir."

"Kiss me," I command her and she does. As if there isn't a worry in the world.

"Now go." I send her off and she waves at Kam, telling him goodbye as well.

It's only when she's gone that I breathe out deeply, staring down at the unanswered messages from my brother and then to my left, to the dead body Kam has dragged onto the rug.

"Since I seem to be playing your game by your rules … How do we cover this up?" I ask.

Kam's on his knees at the edge of the rug and I join him on the other side. "He lost a hell of a lot of money," Kam explains with a grunt as he rolls the body up in the rug while I help. "As of two hours ago, his wife left him because she discovered the mistress he's had on the side, along with the bank accounts being emptied. I'm guessing the cops are going to think he either ran off with the money to a remote island or killed himself."

He says it so nonchalantly.

I look down at the body, his lower half now wrapped in a rug. There's no way this guy could have killed himself like that.

"His body will be cremated by tomorrow." Kam stretches with his arms above his head, then cracks his neck. "You probably don't know how this works, Zander. We decide what goes on paper. The coroner has already determined that he shot himself after receiving phone calls from both his wife and mistress. They both left him over the loss of millions of dollars in a single week. It's not uncommon."

I'm speechless. The ease with which the explanation leaves Kam's mouth is unfathomable.

The coroner hasn't decided anything. The coroner hasn't even seen the body. Yet Kam speaks like he knows it's a done deal. He watches me with tired eyes. This man isn't a ruthless killer, just a realist about the world Ella comes from. He said he would do whatever it took to protect her, and he meant it.

He doesn't do this for the adrenaline rush. There's a limit, and Kam has reached it, appearing far more battered than I've ever seen him.

"We're going to take care of one another," he tells me. "You understand?"

"I think so," I say.

"You need to know so. There's no going back. I don't enjoy this, Zander. I don't want this. But we do what we have to. You can understand that, can't you?"

"I can."

"Good, then marry her," he says. "Legally, at the very least. There needs to be that level of protection."

"What about my brother? What about The Firm? They're waiting for me and for … him."

"Your brother and The Firm can never know the details. They can learn of his disappearance when it's reported in the papers."

That one hits differently. A chill runs through me as I glance down at the body, the rug now wrapped around it twice and firmly secured.

"I don't like lying to my brother."

"You have to," Kam says easily. As if he already knows I will go ahead with it.

I don't want to lie to Cade. I did it once before, and it ended up with me nearly getting kicked out of the goddamn group. And I don't like lying to the rest of the team.

But if this is what it takes, I'll do it. Anything for Ella.

I make the deal with Kam, finalizing tonight. "I'll keep this secret, so long as after tonight I can take her away from all this. Somewhere safe."

"Somewhere warm," he adds, seemingly agreeing with me. "I'd like to retire from this bullshit as well. You have a deal. Take her away, protect her. Provide for her. She'll always have a home here and that doesn't mean we're going away. But a bit of quiet will be good for her I think."

"So that's a deal."

"It's a deal," he says with finality.

Kam said he brought me in because we understood each other, and it turns out he's right. I'll do anything when it comes to her.

Even keep this secret.

The uncertainty still plagues me. Kam must see it in my expression as we stand together, a dead body at our feet. "I can tell you don't like this, keeping it from The Firm, but if they know, they're a threat. That means other people might come for them."

"I don't want to involve them," I admit.

"Good. Neither do I. Keep them safe. All men like us protect the ones we love. We keep the people around us safe, whether that means keeping a secret or ending a life. That's what we do."

There are certain circles where the rules are different. Where your mother can blackmail your father into marriage. Where he can then abuse her and their child when she's at the age of his friends' liking.

Where relationships are used as bargaining chips and money is more important than truth. Where lies can be spread and believed. Where palms can be greased and problems go away.

Those are the circles where murder is a way of life for those nasty moments that threaten to destroy you.

Kam was my savior when he helped get rid of my father, but he couldn't ease the pain that lingers from a life brought up like that. He would know.

I thought James was my escape and I was his. He was my happily ever after in a fucked-up fairy tale written with a diamond-crusted pen and passed around in dark corners of coke-fueled parties.

He took me away and showed me life could be different. And then fate caught up with me, that cruel bitch.

"He asked you to marry him?" Kelly asks, glancing down when I look back at her in confusion. I clear my throat and do everything I can to shake off the sudden emotion that's overwhelmed me.

"You keep fiddling with it," she comments.

Peering down, the rose gold ring still on its chain sits between my fingers.

"If you don't want people to know, you better slip that back in," Kelly warns and then takes a sip of her champagne.

The after-party is in full swing, the music so loud, the bass vibrates my chest. "Do you think anyone saw me—"

I don't have to finish. Kelly reassures me just like I've done for her a hundred times before. "No one, babe," she whispers and tells me she loves me. "You okay, though?"

"Just … a lot," I answer her, not knowing if she's aware yet. I don't want to be the one to tell her.

She gives me a sad smile and takes a curl of mine in her hand before setting it back into place. "If it means anything at all," Kelly tells me, "I think James would have liked him. Even if he's quiet and brooding, he's protective of you. You can tell and James would have liked that."

"Thanks," I murmur and return her smile.

When James died, I swore someone did it. An enemy saw to it.

But the evidence was on camera. It was only a tragedy.

He suffered my karma. All the reckless bad I'd done in my life … and he was the one who suffered the consequences.

I thought I was okay seeing that man upstairs … but the sight of him lying so still … "I need Zander, I think."

"I'll cover for you, babe," Kelly tells me and kisses my cheek before striding back to her party.

I'm halfway across the room to my security detail dressed in a sharp black suit, when Trish grabs my elbow. The sudden touch makes me gasp and pull back until I see it's her. "It's just you," I say with my hand on my chest, catching my breath.

"Shit, sorry. I didn't mean to scare you," she tells me before looking left and right.

"Are you okay?" she asks me.

"I'm scared."

"Don't be. It's taken care of. Kam tied up the loose ends."

Shaking my head, I close my eyes and remind myself we're standing in the middle of a crowded room. "But he knows. Zander …"

"My brother trusts him. I trust him. You do too, right?"

My head shakes again as I try to explain, "I love him … I'm worried that he … he knows what I've done now."

"Oh," she says and breathes out, my concern finally getting through to her.

"He knows I'm … that I've done things." I speak just lower than a murmur, just barely enough for her to hear, "Enough things that the sight of a dead body doesn't faze me."

Her lips turn down slightly before she decides to say, "Go find him. I bet the moment you two are alone, everything will be all right and you'll stop worrying."

She nods as she speaks, as if she's convinced herself as well.

"Thanks, I'll go do that."

"Let me know how it goes, all right?" she questions and I give her a quiet nod before continuing my way to the detail watching me.

"Silas, where's Zander?" I ask him.

"He'll be back in just a moment. How are you doing? Is there anything I can get you?" he asks.

"I'm just fine, and looking for a dance partner," I joke with Silas who somehow manages to look even more straitlaced than usual.

"I'm going to have to pass on that one," he answers with his hands raised. I let out a small laugh and leave Silas be in search for Zander. Plenty of time has passed and Kam knows he'll need to be seen soon. Or else everyone will know he was missing.

He stands with his hands clasped beside the hired security and no one would know he's only here for me.

Well … it's possible someone could find out, but Kam would squash that from being released in a heartbeat. As far as social media is concerned, I'm back, in love and doing so much better.

Thanks to Charlie's exclusive and the snapshots taken only hours ago, the hashtags #SecondChanceInLove and #KnightInShiningArmor are trending all over the internet now.

No one is the wiser and they don't have to be.

The thing is, I don't know how to not be crazy.

For a moment I was with James because we ignored it all. Kam kept us safe in our little bubble. Well, it's more like *they* kept me safe in my little bubble.

Kam's killed for me. James killed for me. I don't want Zander to kill for me, but I think he would. No. I *know* he would. That doesn't matter, though, not right now. What matters is that I know I'd kill for him.

I think he might want to prove he can protect me here, but we have lived different lives and this world … this world that reigns over me is manipulative and abusive. Its mercilessness is never ending.

And that is one thing Zander is not. He's too good for me. We both know it.

My only hope is that he takes me away. Somewhere off the grid where no one can reach us.

As I'm rounding the corner towards the bar for another snow … whatever Trish called it, I spot him, like a beacon, standing tall and laughing at something said to him at the bar. A man in a suit stands next to him, laughing as well.

It seems casual. Small talk at the bar while waiting on drinks. He blends in so well. So easily and yet he's nothing like any of the men here. I'm caught in a trance when he turns, facing me, a drink in each hand and his gaze meets mine as if he knew I was watching all along.

As he smirks, heading toward me, I can't help but blush. Even if it's all an act.

There's a side of me that would stay just like this and deal with the hell that comes with this life, if he would pretend like nothing's changed.

But I know tonight has changed everything.

With that somber thought, he reaches me and hands me my drink. With one sip, I know it's the same one as before.

"Are we okay?" I ask him and to my surprise he tells me, "I don't know how I'll be able to fool my brother. I think he'll suspect and I'm just hoping he doesn't ask."

It's all spoken under his breath and then he takes a swig of his drink.

I hesitate to clarify. "I mean us. Are we okay?" I gesture between us, feeling the nightlife fade to nothing as he stares back at me.

"We need to stay for at least another hour and when we get home, I'm going to punish you for doubting us." He leans forward as the heat rises between us and whispers in the crook of my neck, "From here on out, any question if we're all right will be met with my palm to your ass."

chapter 20

Zander

I've lost track of time in the shower in Ella's house. The steam has surrounded me for what feels like forever. My thoughts keep distracting me.

There's a lot to process from the evening. A hell of a lot. I have some uncertainty about whether I'll be able to keep it a secret from Cade.

But no. Of course I will. That was the price, and it's worth every penny. I don't think he suspects anything just yet but when the reports come out that he's missing, I know he'll ask me. After all, I admitted I wanted that prick dead. Fuck. I brace my palms against the tiled wall and let the water come down on me.

He's my brother, they're my team. If they ask or push for information, I'll ask them to look the other way. God knows I've done the same for each of them before. They owe me. They damn well know they do.

The bathroom door opens and Ella steps inside, bringing me from the menacing thoughts back to the present.

"Jailbird," I murmur so low I don't know if she even heard me. I can see her through the glass, though it's pretty well fogged up. I want this night washed off my skin.

"Can I come in with you?" she asks as the water beats down around me.

"Of course you can." I open the door for her and tell her, "Always."

She strips off her dress, letting the expensive silk pool around her feet and then her lace bra and panties come next. Her necklace stays on as she steps into the shower. That eases something in me. Something that feared this moment. The quiet car ride with Silas driving was difficult enough. Then I had to leave her to debrief. Now that the two of us are alone, it feels right again.

Her dark hair is wet almost immediately as she leans her head back, letting the spray hit her face. Her body trembles slightly and I hold her, pulling her back into my chest. With an arm around her waist, she clings to me. Her eyes are still closed. Ella seemed a lot more put together at the party, but now everything seems to be hitting her. That's to be expected.

"You did so well," I compliment her and kiss her temple. It's only a small sad smile that she gives me in return, her eyes still closed.

"Could you hold me for a while?" she asks.

"Yes." I pull her in tighter and love that she holds me back. "You held yourself together perfectly," I tell her.

"Did I?" she says with a little laugh. "I don't feel held together."

"Tell me how you're feeling," I say.

"I want to forget tonight."

"Is there anything I should be worried about?" I ask her.

She shakes her head against my chest. The water feels warm and cleansing. This transition is going to be difficult as hell, but the shower seems to be making it easier. "After this, we're leaving everything that happened tonight behind us."

"I hope so," she murmurs and that's not the answer I want to hear.

"Talk to me," I say and rock her slightly, giving her time to adjust and decompress.

"I'm scared," Ella admits and it's only then that her dark eyes open and stare ahead.

I almost tell her that we're going to be fine. That Kam has a strategy, and I'm going to follow it. That this is the life I'm choosing. I'm choosing her.

I have to think every sentence over before I can speak.

"We're going to be okay," I tell her, and I mean it. Fully. I'll sacrifice anything for her, which means we'll both be good.

"We are?" Ella looks up at me through her lashes.

"Yes, little bird. We are free of all of this shit after tomorrow."

Her gaze turns hopeful and then I tell her, "For the rest of our lives, we will be together and I will take care of you in every way possible."

She pulls me down to kiss her right there in the hot water. I feel all the tension go out of my muscles and then the rest of my body. I just want to feel surrounded by her. I'm taller than Ella but the heat of the shower helps. She kisses me slow from over her shoulder and then deeper until finally she moans into my mouth.

I want this with her always.

"I still need to spank your ass," I murmur against her lips as my hand slips to her front, down between her legs so I can rub her clit. "But I want you now and I'm going to fuck you so hard tonight you forget everything else other than what I do to you right now in this shower."

Her moan of approval is all I need to massage her breast, tugging her nipple and kissing her savagely. Every passing second getting hotter and heavier. I take her roughly, and her legs nearly give out as she comes.

I pick her up into my arms, spread her legs around my hips, and thrust inside her. Ella gasps. She grinds down onto my cock, her head pressed against the wall of the shower, her back braced in my arms, but then she slows the pace.

"I just want to look at you." She wraps her arms around my shoulders and holds on tight. The water splashes against my back as I kiss her once and then again.

"I don't know how long I can let you do that." I honestly don't. She feels so good wrapped around my cock. Leaning forward to kiss her again, I almost call her jailbird. But after tonight, I don't think I could ever call her that again. She's only my little bird now. Now and forevermore.

I peer down at her in my arms. Ella's hair is beautiful like this, with wet strands in her face. Her cheeks are rosy from the heat of the shower, and her body ... Well, I'll never want for anything with her.

"Tell me it's going to be okay?" she asks although it's spoken like a demand.

"There's nothing to worry about," I tell her, not because I'm trying to convince her. Because I believe it so strongly. We have nothing to worry about.

"I feel safe with you," she says and then a smile slips onto those gorgeous lips. "I guess that's always been true. Did you feel it too, even all the way back in that courtroom? That first day?"

It's true. "Yes," I say, then kiss her. "And that feeling is going to last until the end of our lives." I thrust up once and kiss the crook of her neck.

Ella grinds down onto me again arching her back, tipping her head back, and I let out a groan. "I'm going to come if you keep doing that."

My balls draw up and my toes curl from the pleasure that brings me right to the edge. I push her back against the shower and fuck her mercilessly.

Ella tips her head forward and looks into my eyes as she moans. There's no deeper connection than this. Her breathing quickens and she pleads my name in a way that makes me pause, buried deep inside of her.

"Are you okay?" I murmur, barely keeping my voice in check. My body shakes with the need to come but I won't do it until Ella comes too. "Is something wrong?"

"No," she gasps. "I'm just … I love you, Z."

"I love you too." I kiss her deeply as I fuck her with a primitive need.

She comes with a gasp and a cry that turns into a moan. It's the most beautiful thing I've ever seen.

chapter 21

Ella

A HANDFUL OF MONTHS CAN MAKE QUITE THE DIFFERENCE. Crossing my ankles as I sit on the sofa in my blue room, I'm feeling especially thankful for the lit gas fireplace with its blue flames. Outside, snow is just starting to fall.

I remember the first time these men came into this room and took hold of my life. It feels like a lifetime ago. Here we are in nearly the same positions, but everything has changed.

"There we are," Kam states firmly, clicking the end of the pen and handing the signed paper to Cade who checks it over and then signs himself.

"Is that the last of them?" Z asks from my right, an arm around my shoulders possessively. I lean into him and rest my head on his shoulder. I could hardly sleep last night and I know the moment the papers are scanned and filed and everyone leaves this room, I'm going to sleep soundly.

"It's the last of what he wanted to see, yes."

"There won't even be a hearing?" I question.

"Not in person," Kam tells me. "The judge said that with everyone in agreement it's as simple as dotting the I's and crossing the T's."

I don't dare smile, although one begs to appear as Z kisses my temple.

"I would say get a room, but we all know you two consider the entire house your room," Cade mutters as he stacks the papers and taps them on the coffee table to organize them neatly.

His comment forces me to smirk and the other men chuckle lightly. I bury my hands in my oversized cream sweater and bring my knees up to my chest. All the while, leaning against Z.

"If you're ever not okay, you know you can call me," Damon says from where he stands to the right of the fireplace.

"Me too," Cade says and I'm caught off guard. I look up at him, hoping there's never a reason we would need The Firm. "He can be an ass sometimes. You can call me, I'll kick his ass for you," he jokes.

A laugh bubbles up but it's muted. I appreciate the lightheartedness but it just hasn't hit home yet.

"You're tense, Ella. Loosen up, babe. You're free today. Now you could tell me to get out and I'd actually have to listen." Kam smiles a boyish grin. "Not that I'm going to listen, but you could do it."

At that Zander laughs a deep, rough chuckle that shakes me gently.

"I'll keep that in mind," I comment back.

"Let's give these two a moment," Kam suggests to the room.

Cade and Kam lead the men out to the kitchen and I watch them go. It won't be the last time they're here. As much as Zander is a part of my life, I'm a part of The Firm's life. Even if Z has decided to take a leave of absence for an indefinite amount of time.

He and his brother decided it would be best for him to take time off for this transition. Mostly because I asked him to. I am his greedy selfish girl, after all.

The moment the room is quiet and the men's conversation can barely be heard, Z turns me in his arms so I'm facing him. His black tee clings to his broad shoulders and his rough stubble is a bit more than a five o'clock shadow. His smile is easy and charming as if there's nothing to worry about any longer.

"He said I need to marry you," Z says far too calmly.

"What?" I can't hide the shock in my voice. "Kam said that?"

He only nods as I stare at him wide eyed.

"When I ask you to marry me, it will be because I want you to be my wife," he tells me with certainty as he slips down off the sofa.

My heart races as I stare into his hazel eyes flecked with gold. His necklace is still where it will always be. "You gave me a ring already," I whisper, my fingers fiddling with the rose gold ring through the sweater.

He smirks, pulling a ring from his back pocket and says, "I can give you more than one, can't I?"

My bottom lip drops at the sight of the oval diamond. It's surrounded by small black diamonds all the way around. My hand trembles as I reach out to take it.

"You have to say you'll marry me first," Z says, staring back at me with a devilish grin.

The moment I kiss him, a hand on each side of his face, a champagne bottle pops and applause fills the room.

With tears pricking the back of my eyes, I look to my left and see them all standing in the doorway, watching with genuine happiness for the two of us.

"Let her say yes first," Z manages to get out.

"Yes." I'm quick to answer. "Yes a million times, yes."

chapter 22

Two months later

OUTSIDE THE DOORS TO THE COURTROOM, I TAKE ELLA'S HAND in mine. These aren't the same doors I stood behind six months ago when I first laid eyes on her, but the dark grooved floor-to-ceiling doors are reminiscent of how we started.

She's dressed in a long white lace dress and I'm wearing a gray suit she picked out. The same suit I wear for court appearances. Funny, because this is one of sorts I suppose.

With a simper on her bloodred lips and a dark curl loose from her bun, she looks up at me. Nothing but happiness shines back in her chestnut eyes. My little bird looks stunning, actually. She had her stylist come over and do her makeup and her hair for the ceremony.

She planned every detail of today. It's amazing how quickly a girl can pull together a wedding.

It's nothing big like I thought she might want. There's no fancy ceremony in a tall cathedral. There's no press. And the reception is more like a laid-back after-party. No, this isn't the big deal I want to give Ella, but we can always do that later. Having a life together … that's the biggest deal of all.

"Are you ready?" I ask her, giving her hand a squeeze. She squeezes back and lets out a breath while giving me an uncontained, confident smile.

"Yes. I'm more than ready to be your wife, Mr. Thompson."

Cade claps his hand on my shoulder just then and I had nearly forgot he was there. "Let's head in?" he asks.

I smirk down at my soon-to-be wife and say, "Let's."

"We're next on the list," Cade tells me and I have to hold back my huff of impatience. It's not the sexiest part of a courthouse wedding. We had to wait for another couple in front of us, and then for the judge to rule on a traffic violation.

The man who got the ticket didn't have to pay his fine after all. The judge has been finishing up with him. He comes out the right door as my brother pulls open the left.

"Congratulations," he says, his face happy and bright. Our attire is the opposite of his jeans and leather jacket. Even without a veil or bouquet, I'm certain it's obvious what we're here for. I happily accept his good wishes.

"Thank you," Ella and I answer in unison and in this moment, I couldn't feel lighter or happier or like this moment was meant to be.

Our footsteps in sync with one another, we go into the courtroom together. Ella and I go down the aisle with my brother, Damon on my side and Trish and Kam on hers. My heart races as we take our places in front of the judge.

It's the exact opposite of how it was when things started. Ella was sitting up at that table with the lawyers. I was sitting in the back, wondering how a woman like her ever came to be in that position. I'd wanted to know everything about her.

Now I get to spend the rest of my life learning all the details I could ever hope to learn.

"Your paperwork?" The judge, an old man, smiles at us. I pass over the marriage license and he scans it as if it's the most important document of the day. "Witnesses?" he asks next.

My brother steps up. So does Trish.

The judge welcomes them, then comes down and takes his place in front of us. "Marriage is a civil union," he begins. "It's about two people coming together. And in spite of great odds."

Ella glances at me, uncontained joy on her face.

"We know that life can deal us some blows," the judge says. "Can put us through the wringer. But what I like best about weddings is that they're all about hope. All of them, every single one, is about hope. Take the bride's hands in yours," he tells me.

Without a second thought, I do what he says. I take Ella's hands in mine. I was already holding one of her hands. Now I have them both, clasped in mine. When she looks at me again her eyes are shining.

Hope. This wedding is about hope. That we're going to have our happily ever after together, an ending neither of us saw coming.

"Zander Thompson," the judge says. "Do you take this woman to be your lawfully wedded wife, in the eyes of God, in the state of Pennsylvania?"

"I do," I say.

"And Eleanor Bordeu," he says, "do you take this man to be your lawfully wedded husband, in the eyes of God, in the state of Pennsylvania?"

"I do," she whispers.

"The rings," the judge says. Cade steps forward with my ring for Ella. "Place the ring on her ring finger."

I do. Ella blinks down at it like it's worth more than all the money she had in her past. "This is a symbol of my love for you," I tell her. "I love you."

Ella repeats this process with my ring, only she's breathing harder. Tears escape from the corner of her eyes. "None of that, you'll ruin that dress with mascara," Kam jokingly whispers and Ella lets out a small laugh.

"This is a symbol of my love for you. I love you."

I miss a few sentences of the ceremony because I'm staring into her eyes.

"… vested in me by the state of Pennsylvania, you may kiss your bride," the judge announces.

I lean in and kiss Ella. My brother cheers. It's too loud for the courtroom, but it doesn't matter. Everybody's clapping. Our friends. Members of The Firm. It's a small wedding, a tiny wedding party, and the reception will be just as small, but I don't care.

We file out of the courtroom, our friends offering congratulations. A local photographer snaps photos of us outside the courthouse, all of us in different configurations. As the final photos are taken, my brother slaps me on the back.

"To the restaurant we go?" I question, not sure if she wants to take more photos or not. She said she wanted laid back, but with her, I'm not exactly sure she knows how to do "laid back."

Ella smiles up at me, a knowing look in her eyes. "I thought we could stop by the new place first. I … I have a second dress to change into."

Trish laughs beside us. "Color me surprised," she jokes and rubs her elbow against Ella's. "Small wedding, but big fashion."

Cade looks to her, then back at me. "So you two closed on the new place?"

"We signed on the dotted line more than once today," I tell him. We couldn't have done it without Kam.

Cade nods, smiling. "Were you happy with the ceremony, Ella?"

She nods eagerly. "I'm even more excited for the reception. We'll only be a few minutes behind you guys."

"I guess it's too late to tell you," Cade says, pretending to look worried.

"Tell me what?"

"That I'm not sure you've thought enough about marrying Zander. You might change your mind."

"Never," Ella says, laughing.

"We just need to pick up our new house keys. Then we'll meet you at the restaurant."

All of our friends agree with us. They're all so happy to be here. This is what it must feel like to start over.

"Don't take too long," Cade admonishes.

"You'd better not lose track of time," Trish says with a mock scowl. "Ella, I want to dance with you on your wedding day."

Kam comments dryly, "Don't let Zander keep you in that house all night."

"I won't. I promise," Ella tells them.

"Half an hour?" Trish says. "Forty-five minutes?"

"Half an hour," I tell her. Then I take Ella's hand in mine and lead her away from the people we love.

"Thirty minutes isn't a long time," she murmurs.

"All we have to do is pick up the keys."

"That's all?" Ella asks, her tone low and sensual.

"I can do a lot in thirty minutes, little bird. But we have a reception to get to. Then forever is waiting for us."

epilogue

Zander

One year later …

ELLA LEANS OVER THE BED, BEAUTIFUL AND VERY PREGNANT. This is just about the only way we can have sex now that she's in her third trimester. Her hands on pillows, me behind her.

Naked with her thick dark hair thrown over her shoulder, she peeks back behind me and lets out the sweetest, sexiest moan I've ever heard.

I sink into her again and again, slowly. It's past the point where we can have the rough, intense sex we used to have. She craves something different now. She still loves it when I pay extra attention to her clit, though. It's apparently more sensitive now.

But she's still mine in every way, so I put my hand around her throat just for the pressure and slow the pace even more. Her lips form a perfect *O*.

She feels like fucking heaven like this. Everything about her makes me crave more and more of her.

I want to feel her come around me, and she's hot and tight, even more so in her pregnancy. She pants as she gets close, then comes, throwing her head back in pure delight. It's a slow orgasm that seems to go on and on and on. The way her warmth strokes my cock nearly brings me to the edge with her. I linger in her new slickness.

I will never have enough of her.

I let my hands roam down her curves and I lose control, just a little, and pump into her harder. Ella braces against the bed and takes it. Her fingers curl over the covers, gripping them as she lets out a strangled groan. That sound is what does it for me, and I lose myself in her. She's so good for me. She always is.

Afterward, she turns just enough to kiss me. A quick peck before lying down and waiting for me to clean her up.

"Come," I command her and she protests with the smallest sound of resistance, snuggling into the sheets. "I want to shower with you," I bend down to tell her and nip her earlobe.

It only takes nudging her nose with mine for her to agree and the two of us make our way into the shower. It's all tiled in an antique blue, with top-of-the-line furnishings. Ella picked out every piece from the art on the wall, to the extra-large linen closets.

Even the shower is oversized so we could do just this.

Our house is the same way. A new build, out by the beach and as I turn the faucet on, the salty breeze blows in through the open window. We're not very close to the neighbors, which is how I like it. Ella too. We don't have to worry about photographers out here. There isn't a soul for a good half mile in any direction.

All I have to worry about is making sure she's rubbed down to her satisfaction under the hot water.

I marvel at her new shape. It's something else, seeing her grow so beautifully. Our baby will be born this year, almost two years after we first met. This last year has been nothing but calm, with me devoted to her and her devoted to me.

We'll bring that child here, to our house. I'll be able to take him or her on walks on warm mornings.

It'll be peaceful.

That's all I can ask for, really.

I take my time caring for her. Washing her body and kissing as I go.

She does this little hum I love all the while. Her eyes close and I know she's going to nap after this.

For me, I'll be monitoring what my brother emailed yesterday. A new case that he wants my opinion on.

"All done, you can leave me now and sleep," I say and tease her with a kiss on her shoulder.

"Mmm, you don't want to nap with me?" she offers and almost any other day I would at least lie down with her. "Not today, little bird."

Ella leans against me, warm and satisfied but with a pout that tells me she may push me, just to. That mouth of hers hasn't changed. It appears she's too tired for that. I help her out of the shower and she gathers a towel around her.

When we've finished with our shower and I've put the bathrobe over her shoulders, she tells me she wants to look over the nursery one more time today. I can only smirk and follow my wife to the room we've been in three times already today. It's directly next to the suite.

"I can't believe it's done," she remarks from the doorway.

"The baby's going to love it," I say.

"What about you?" she questions. "You'll probably spend a fair amount time in here too. I did choose the perfect glider."

"Of course you did, little bird. You choose all the perfect things."

"I love it here," Ella murmurs softly. It's a good thing. She's spent hours decorating the nursery, making sure each detail is perfect. And a small fortune. Kam is still in charge of the funds, though, and according to him, she is set for life and can spend multiple small fortunes. The two of them ganged up on me to let her have the nursery she wanted. After all, this baby will be our first and only.

Down below on the street, a car moves down the road. In front of our house, the driver brakes and pulls the car to the curb.

"Oh," Ella says. "I'm not dressed ... and that's Damon's car."

I almost disagree with her, saying it's just the same car as Damon's, not actually his. He doesn't have any reason to be here right now.

But then he steps out of the car, slams the door behind him, and jogs toward us. He barely glances around him, totally focused on getting to the house. The doorbell will ring any second.

"Get dressed." I press a kiss to Ella's forehead. "Looks like something's going on."

I don't tell her my brother said yesterday there may be trouble. I don't tell her he said something happened between a client and someone on the team. I barely skimmed his email; I haven't even opened the documents yet. But given that Damon's here … I'm guessing he did something he shouldn't have.

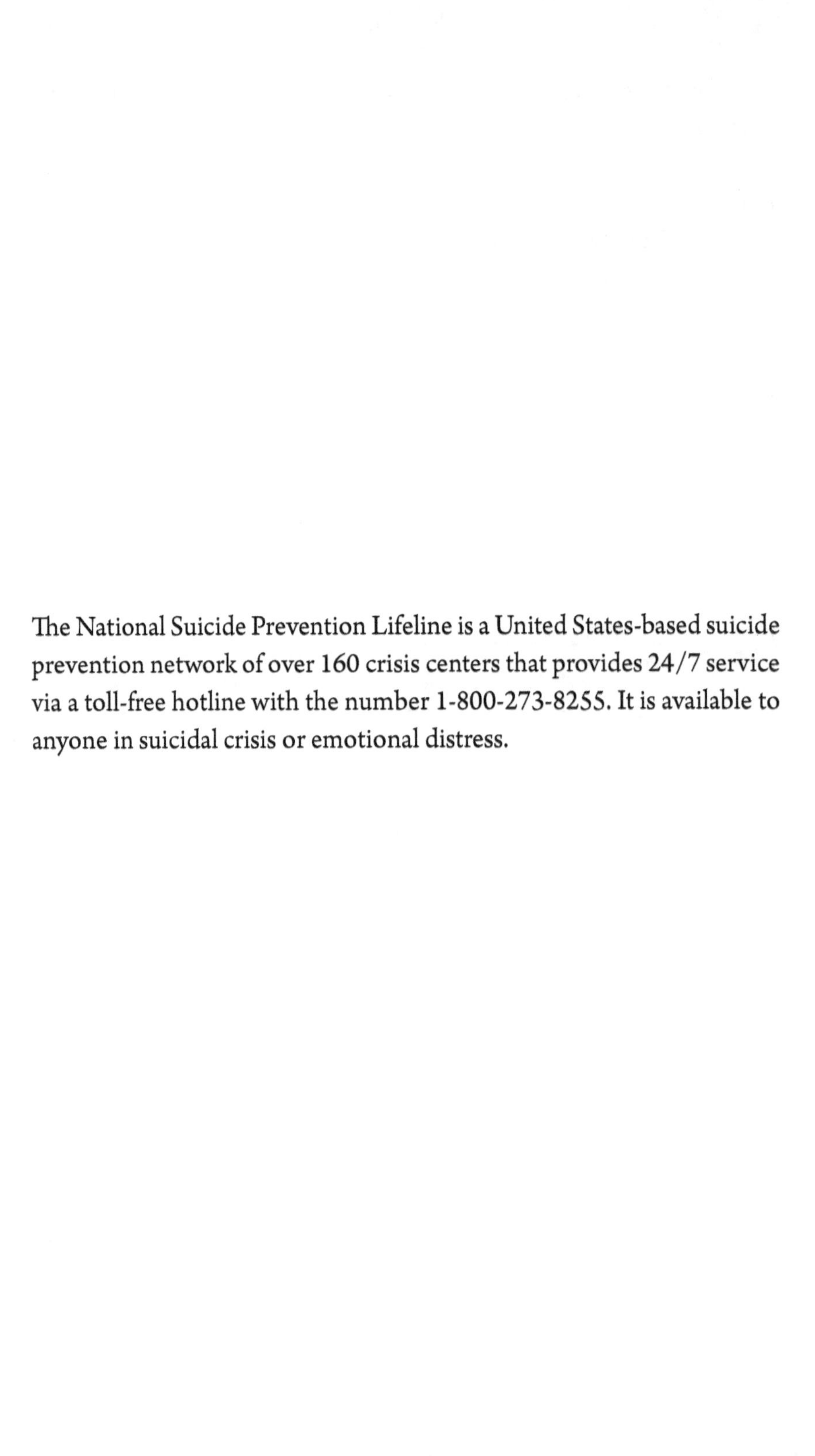

The National Suicide Prevention Lifeline is a United States-based suicide prevention network of over 160 crisis centers that provides 24/7 service via a toll-free hotline with the number 1-800-273-8255. It is available to anyone in suicidal crisis or emotional distress.

about w winters

Thank you so much for reading my romances. I'm just a stay at home mom and avid reader turned author and I couldn't be happier.

I hope you love my books as much as I do!

More by Willow Winters
www.WillowWintersWrites.com/books

connect with amelia

Amelia Wilde is a *USA TODAY* bestselling author of steamy contemporary romance and loves it a little *too* much. She lives in Michigan with her husband and daughters. She spends most of her time typing furiously on an iPad and appreciating the natural splendor of her home state from where she likes it best: inside.

For more books by Amelia Wilde, visit her online at

WWW.AWILDEROMANCE.COM